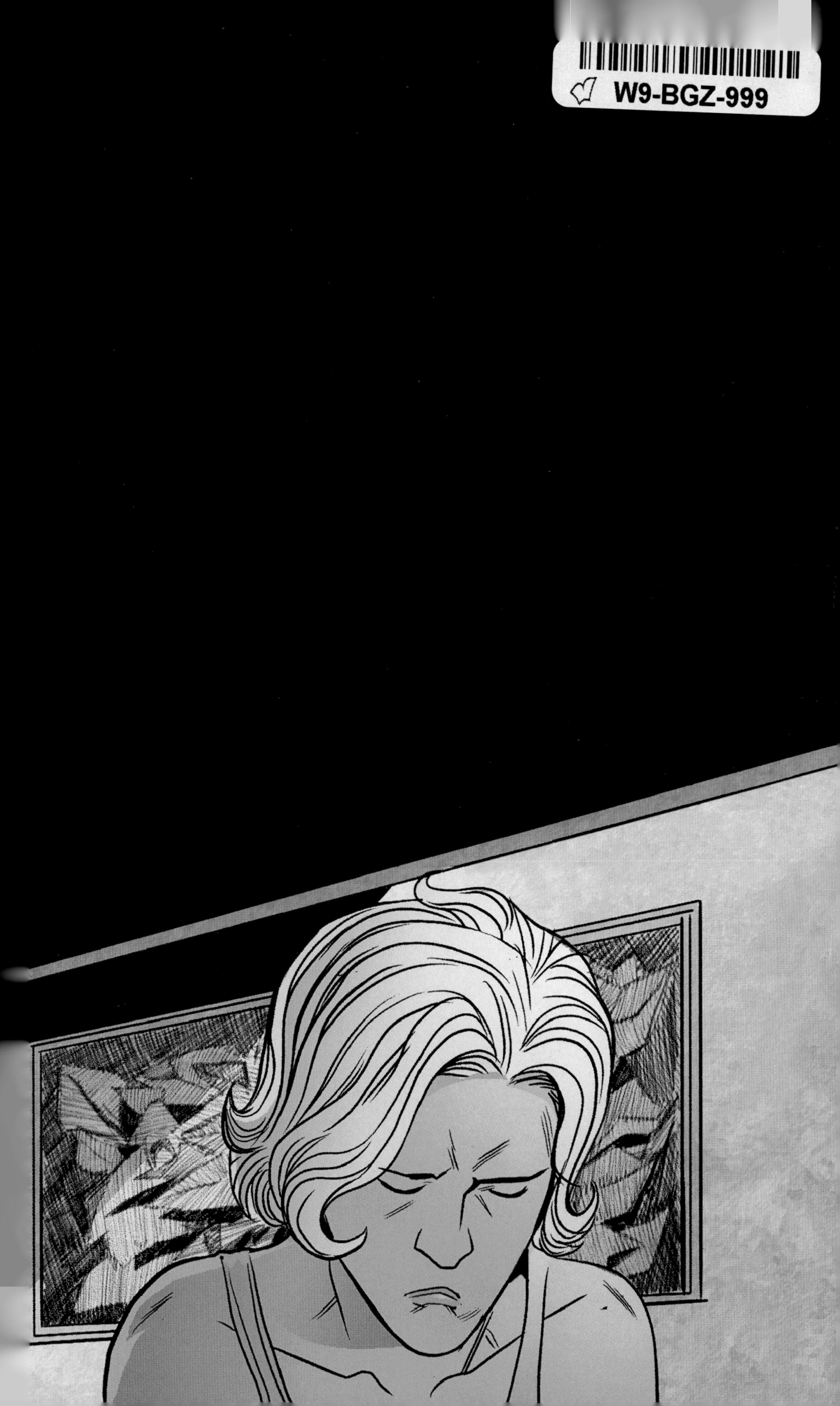

Image Comics, Inc.

Robert Kirkman — Chief Operating Officer
Erik Larsen — Chief Financial Officer
Todd McFarlane — President
Marc Silvestri — Chief Executive Officer
Jim Valentino — Vice President
Eric Stephenson — Publisher
Corey Murphy — Director of Sales
Jeff Boison — Director of Publishing Planning & Book Trade Sales
Chris Ross — Director of Digital Sales
Jeff Stang — Director of Specialty Sales
Kat Salazar — Director of PR & Marketing
Branwyn Bigglestone — Controller
Kali Dugan — Senior Accounting Manager
Sue Korpela — Accounting & HR Manager
Drew Gill — Art Director
Heather Doornink — Production Director
Leigh Thomas — Print Manager
Tricia Ramos — Traffic Manager
Briah Skelly — Publicist
Aly Hoffman — Events & Conventions Coordinator
Sasha Head — Sales & Marketing Production Designer

David Brothers — Branding Manager
Melissa Gifford — Content Manager
Drew Fitzgerald — Publicity Assistant
Vincent Kukua — Production Artist
Erika Schnatz — Production Artist
Ryan Brewer — Production Artist
Shanna Matuszak — Production Artist
Carey Hall — Production Artist
Esther Kim — Direct Market Sales Representative
Emilio Bautista — Digital Sales Representative
Leanna Caunter — Accounting Analyst
Chloe Ramos-Peterson — Library Market Sales Representative
Marla Eizik — Administrative Assistant

www.imagecomics.com

COPPERHEAD, VOL. 3
ISBN: 978-1-5343-0236-5
First Printing

COPPERHEAD

Volume 3

writer
JAY FAERBER
artist
DREW MOSS
colorist
RON RILEY
letterer & designer
THOMAS MAUER
cover artist
SCOTT GODLEWSKI

created by
JAY FAERBER & SCOTT GODLEWSKI

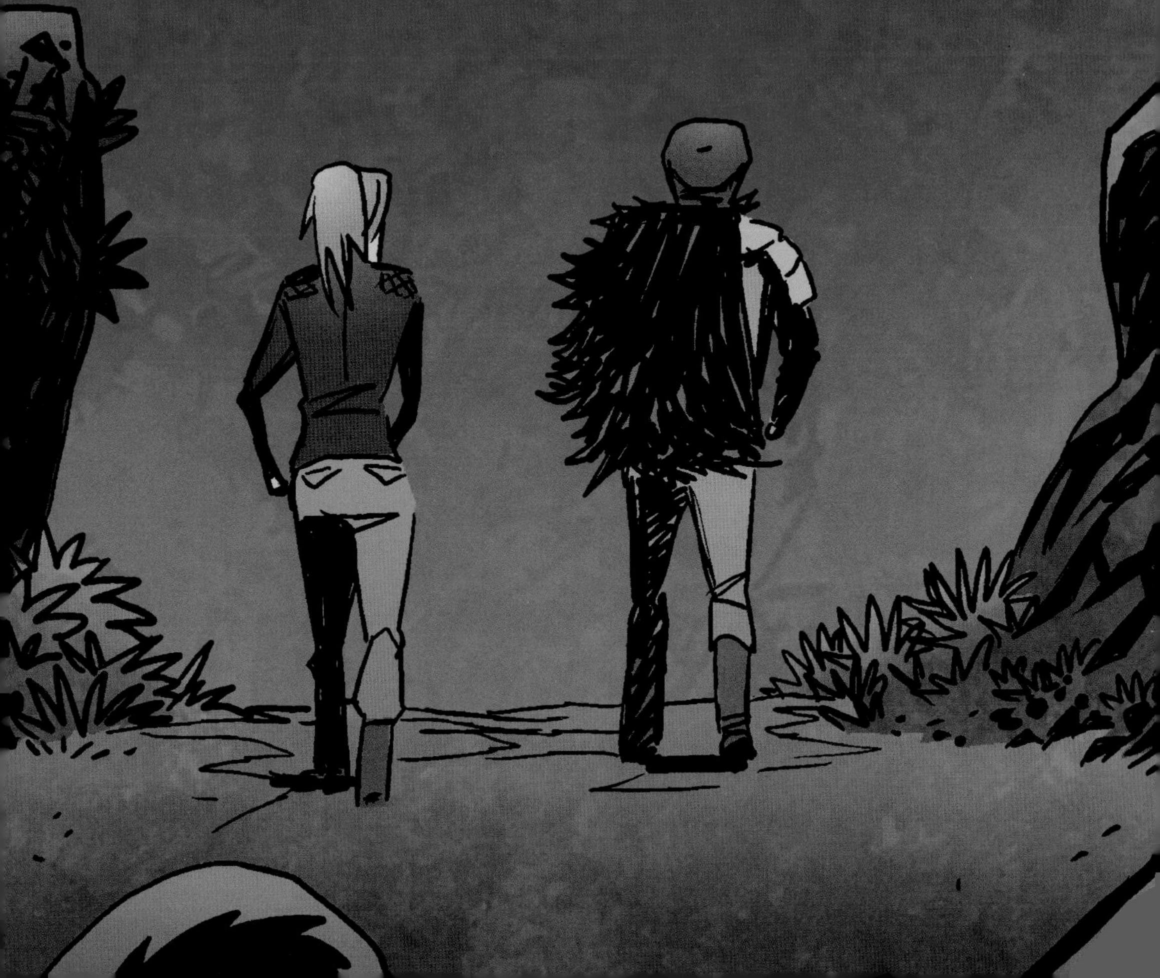

CHAPTER I

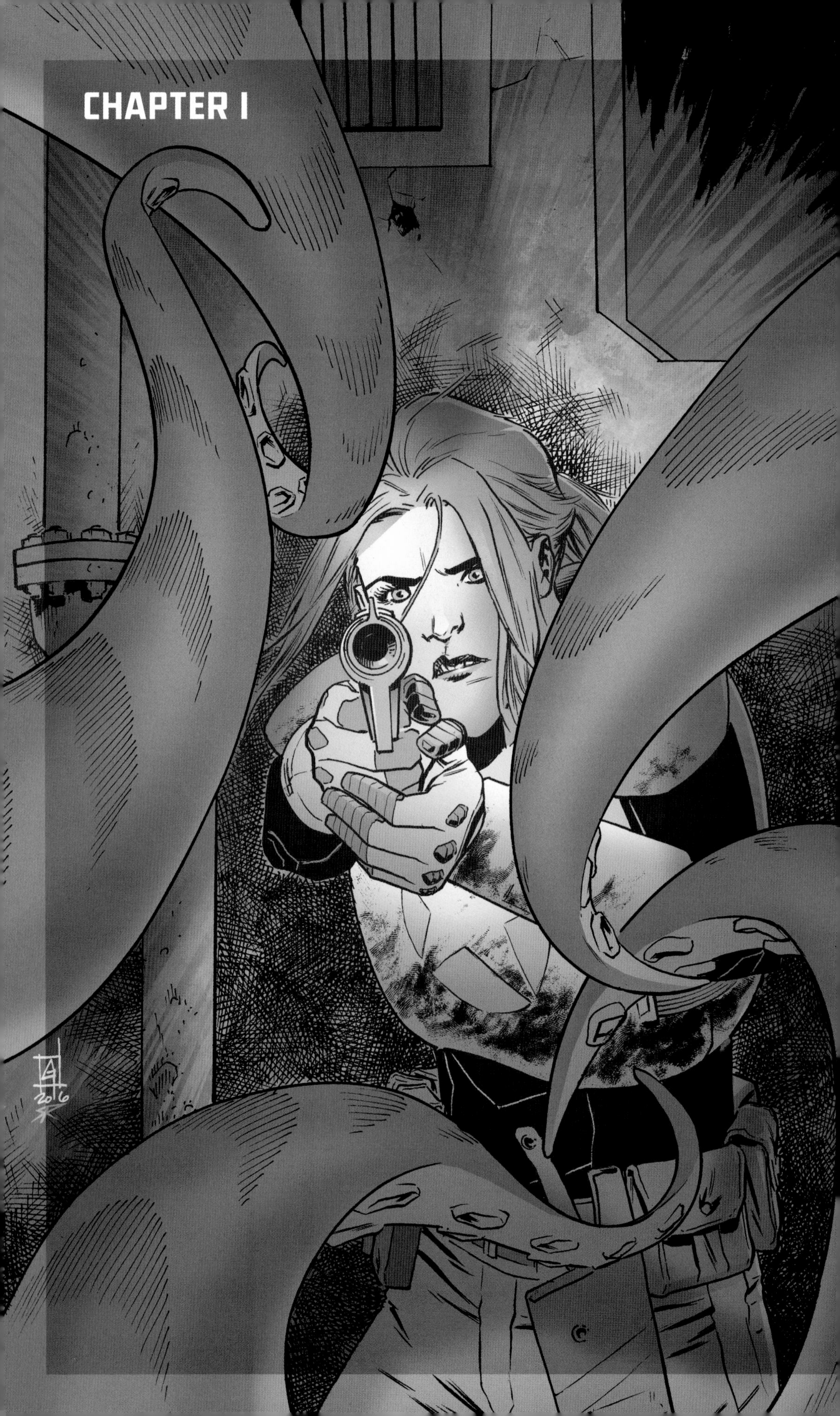

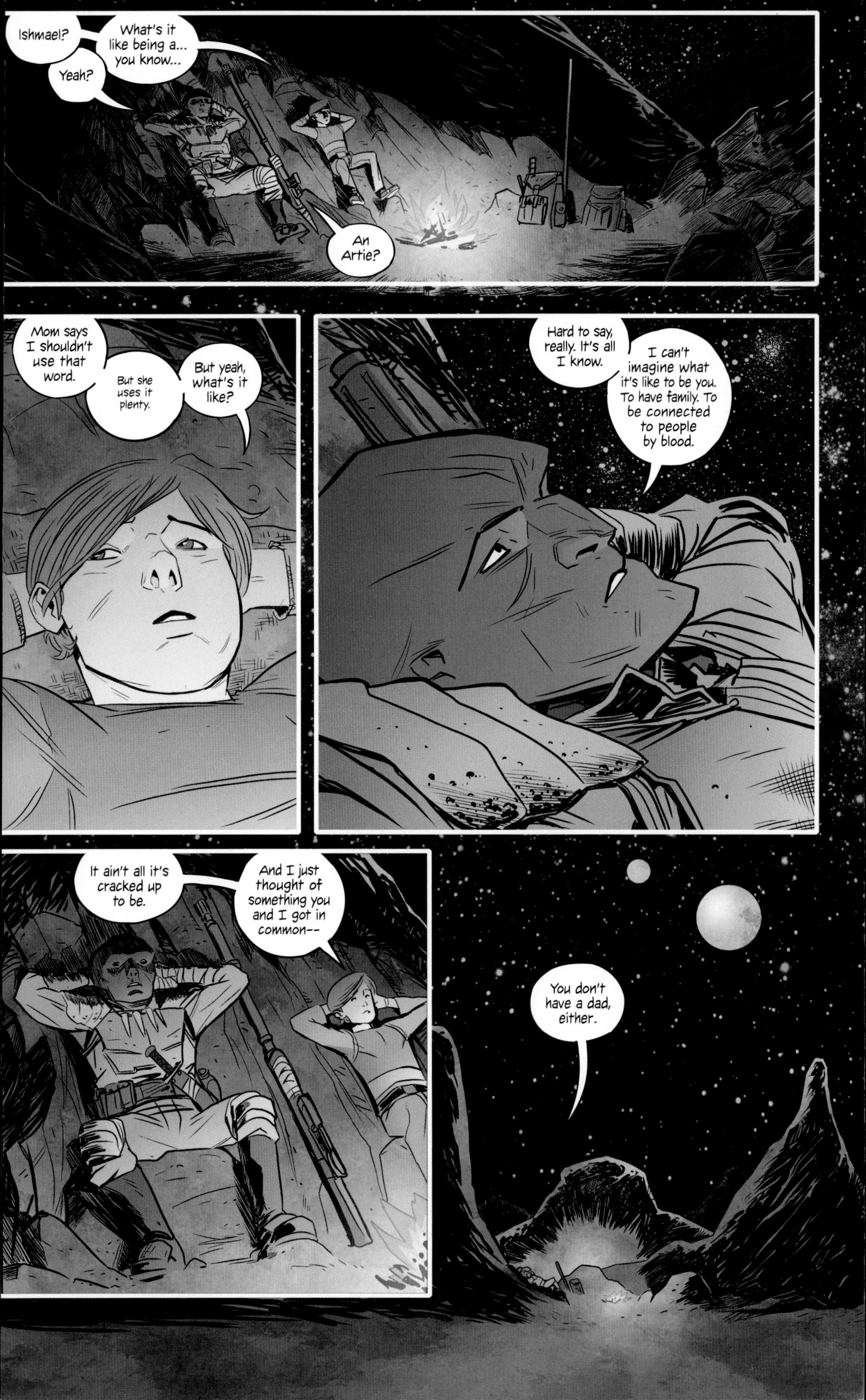
Ishmael?
Yeah?
What's it like being a... you know...
An Artie?
Mom says I shouldn't use that word.
But she uses it plenty.
But yeah, what's it like?
Hard to say, really. It's all I know.
I can't imagine what it's like to be you. To have family. To be connected to people by blood.
It ain't all it's cracked up to be.
And I just thought of something you and I got in common--
You don't have a dad, either.

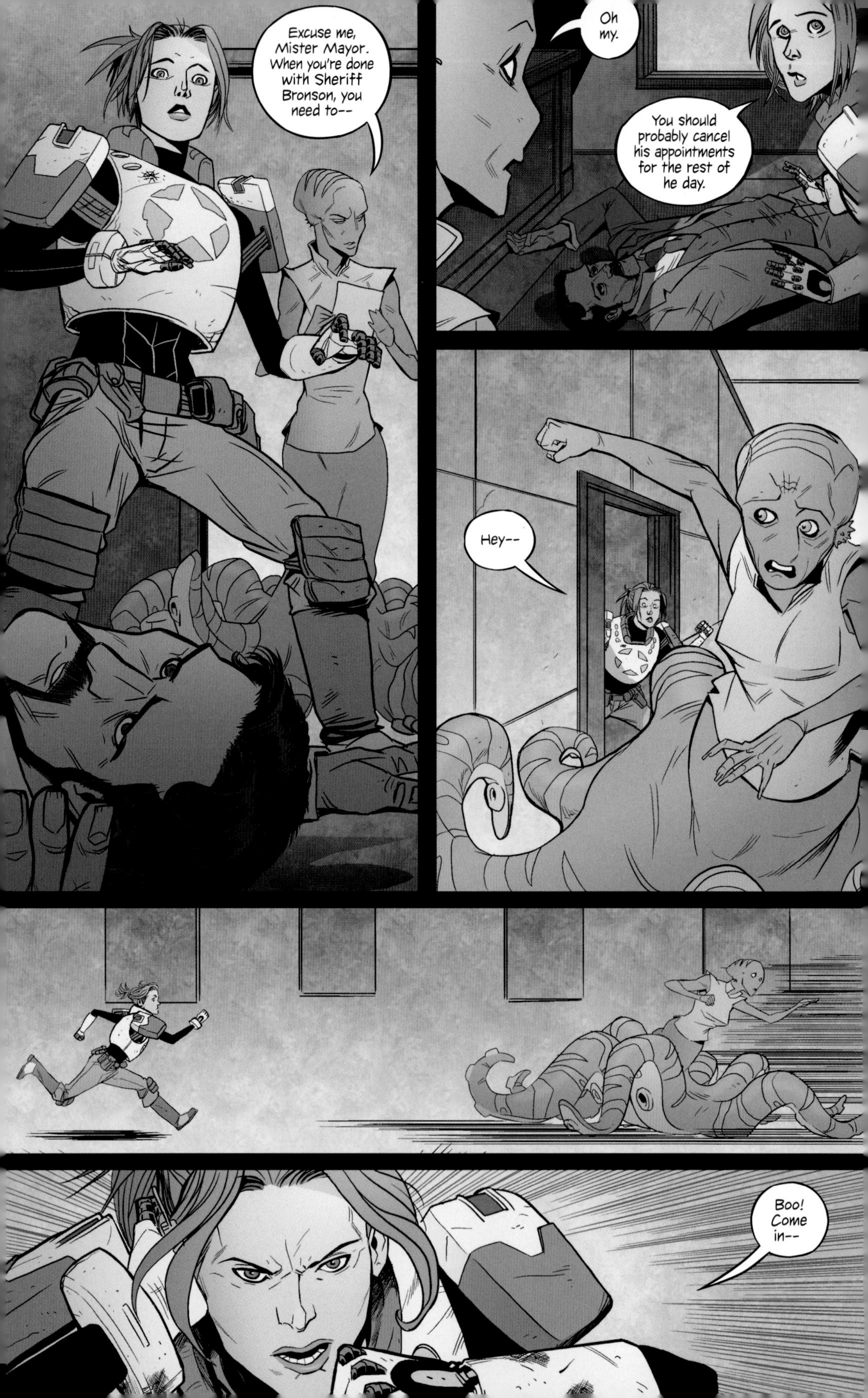
Excuse me, Mister Mayor. When you're done with Sheriff Bronson, you need to--
Oh my.
You should probably cancel his appointments for the rest of he day.
Hey--
Boo! Come in--

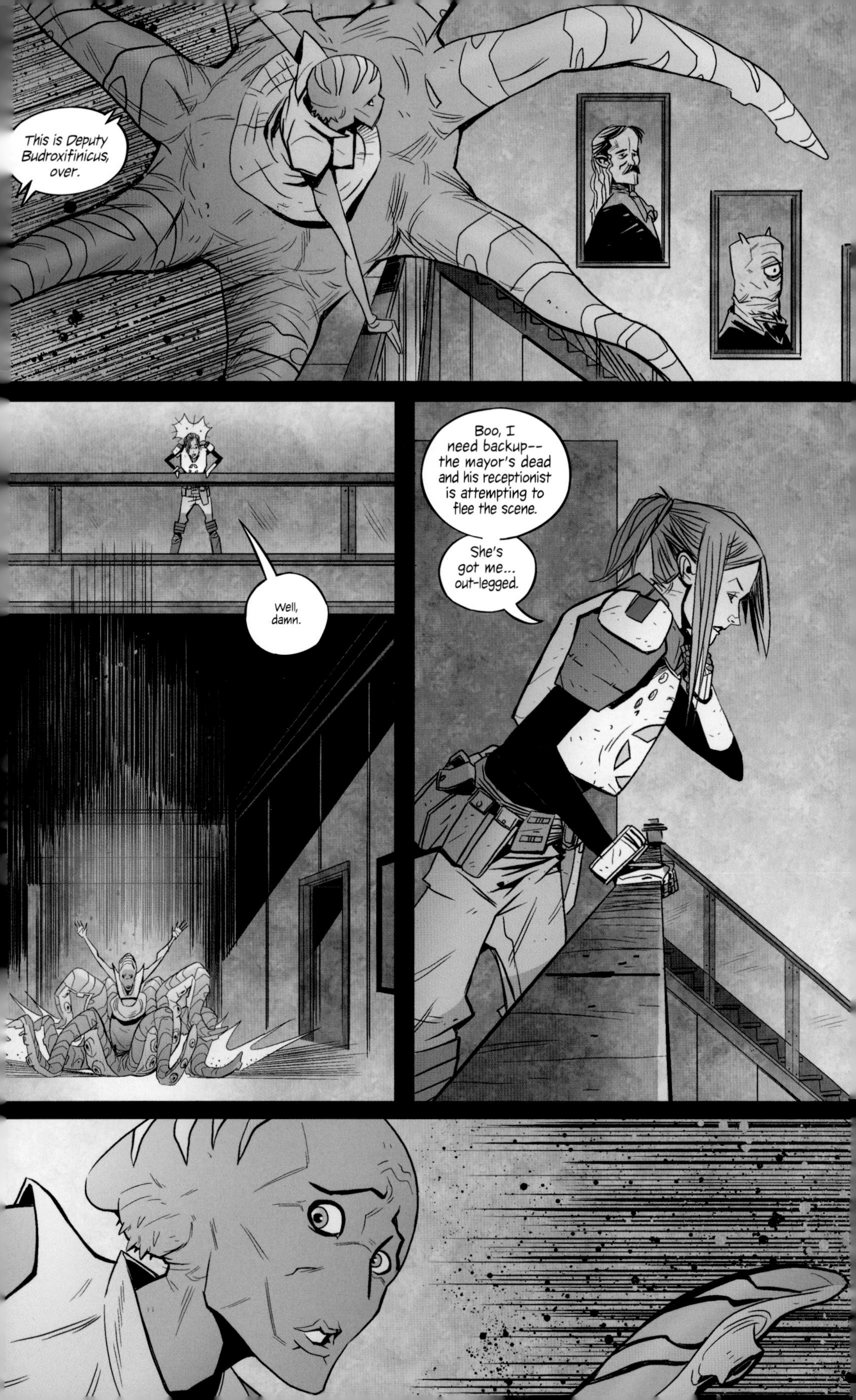
This is Deputy Budroxifinicus, over.
Well, damn.
Boo, I need backup--the mayor's dead and his receptionist is attempting to flee the scene.
She's got me... out-legged.

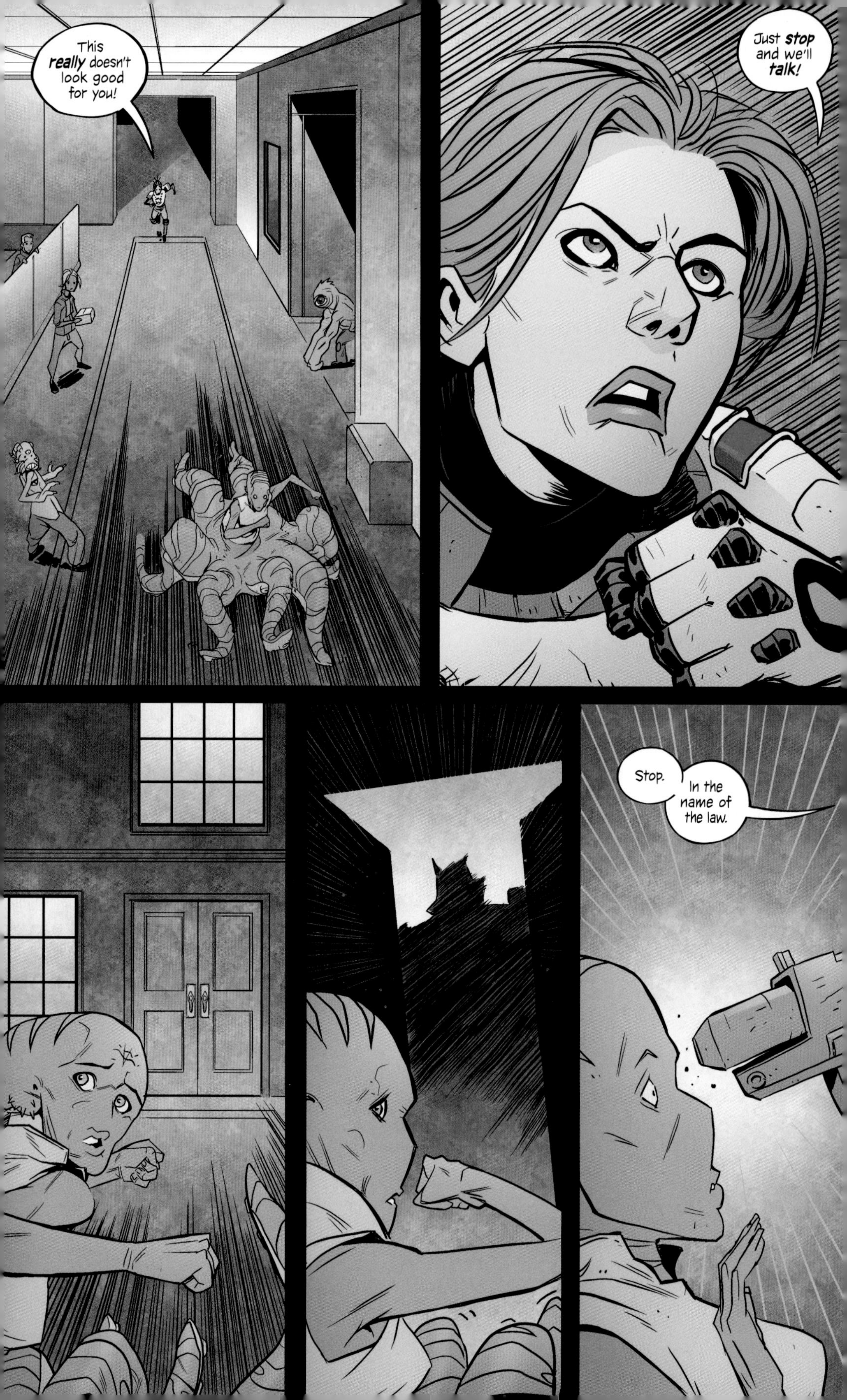
This really doesn't look good for you!
Just stop and we'll talk!
Stop.
In the name of the law.

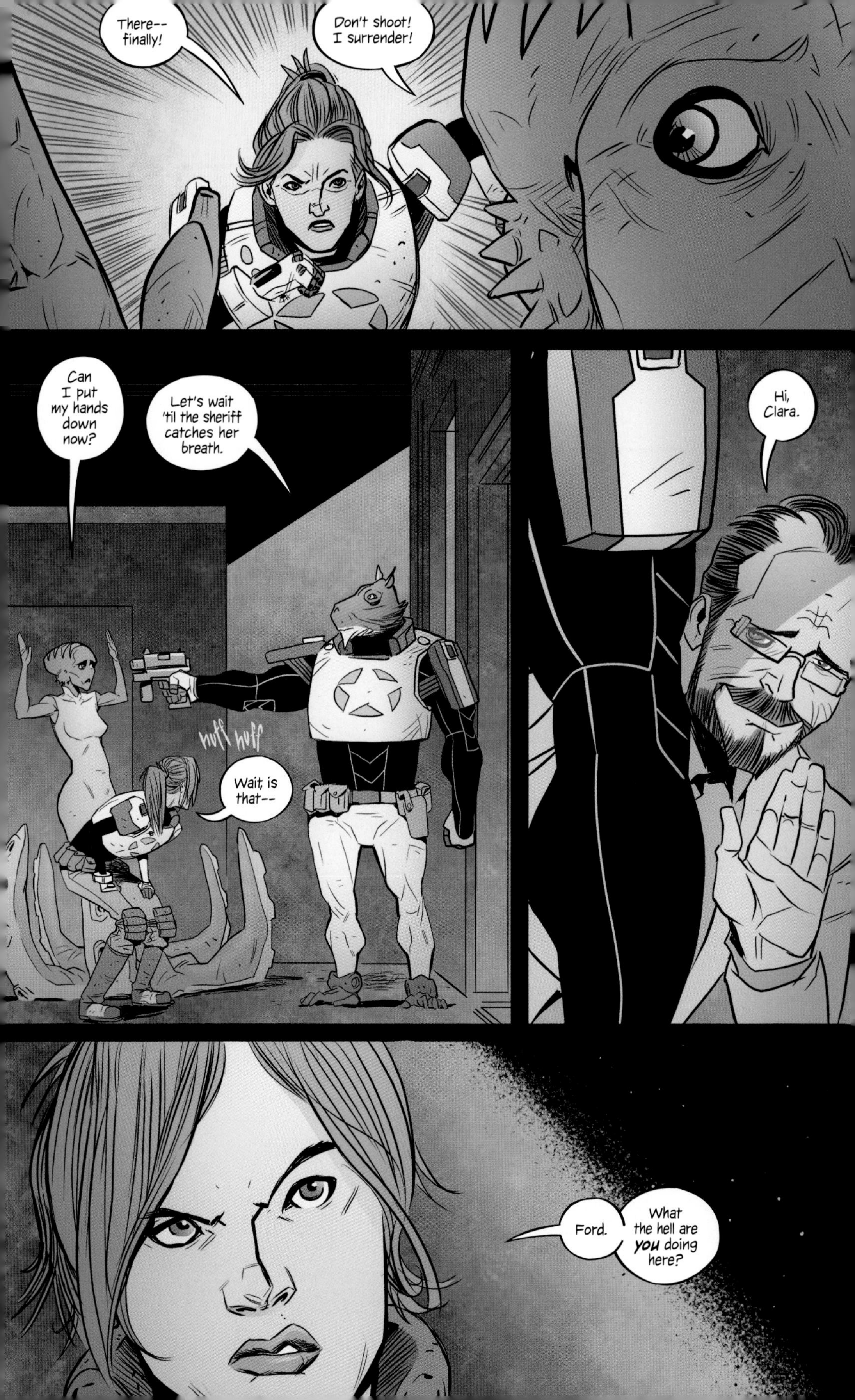
There-- finally!
Don't shoot! I surrender!
Can I put my hands down now?
Let's wait 'til the sheriff catches her breath.
huff huff
Wait, is that--
Hi, Clara.
Ford.
What the hell are *you* doing here?

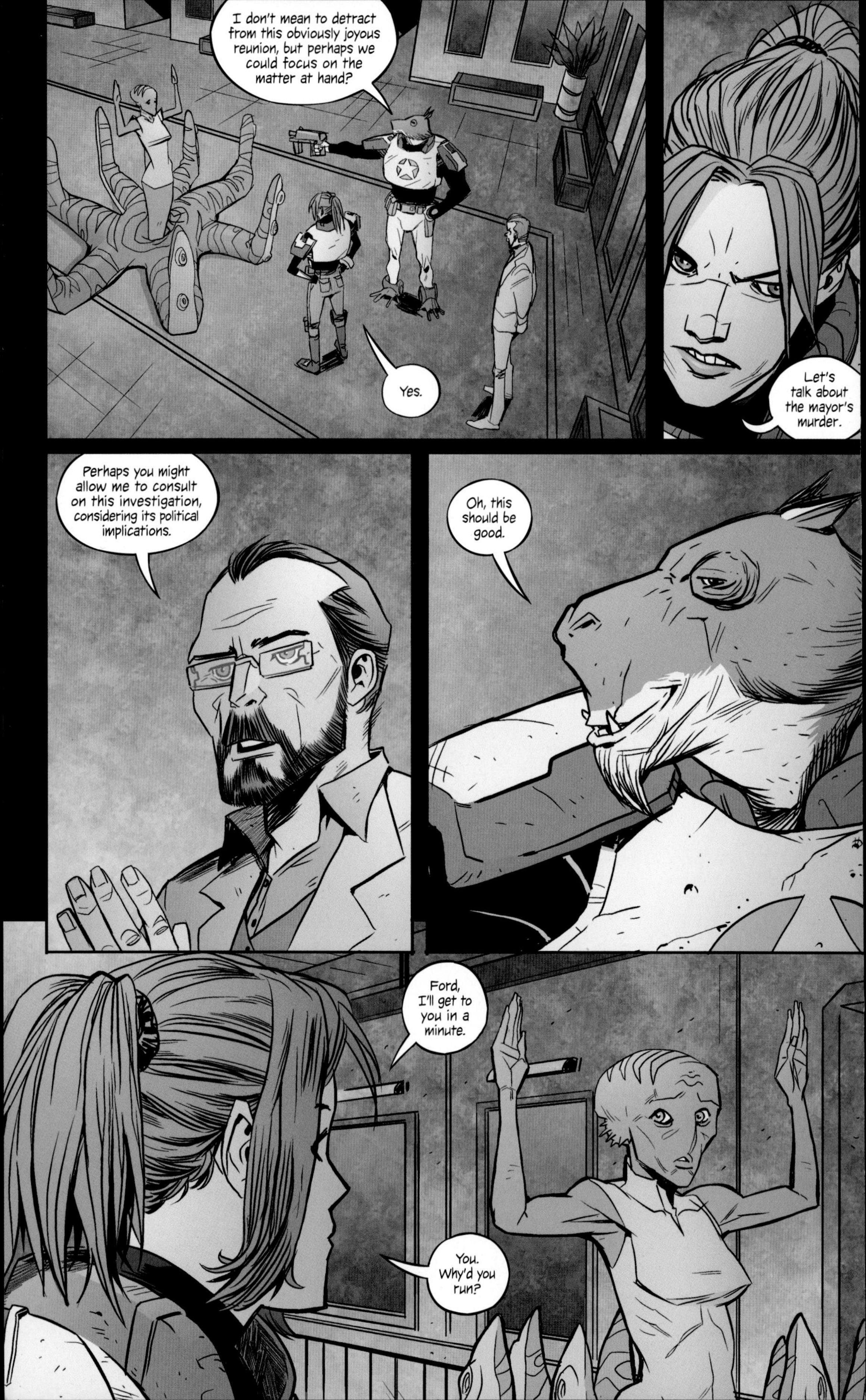
I don't mean to detract from this obviously joyous reunion, but perhaps we could focus on the matter at hand?
Yes.
Let's talk about the mayor's murder.
Perhaps you might allow me to consult on this investigation, considering its political implications.
Oh, this should be good.
Ford, I'll get to you in a minute.
You. Why'd you run?

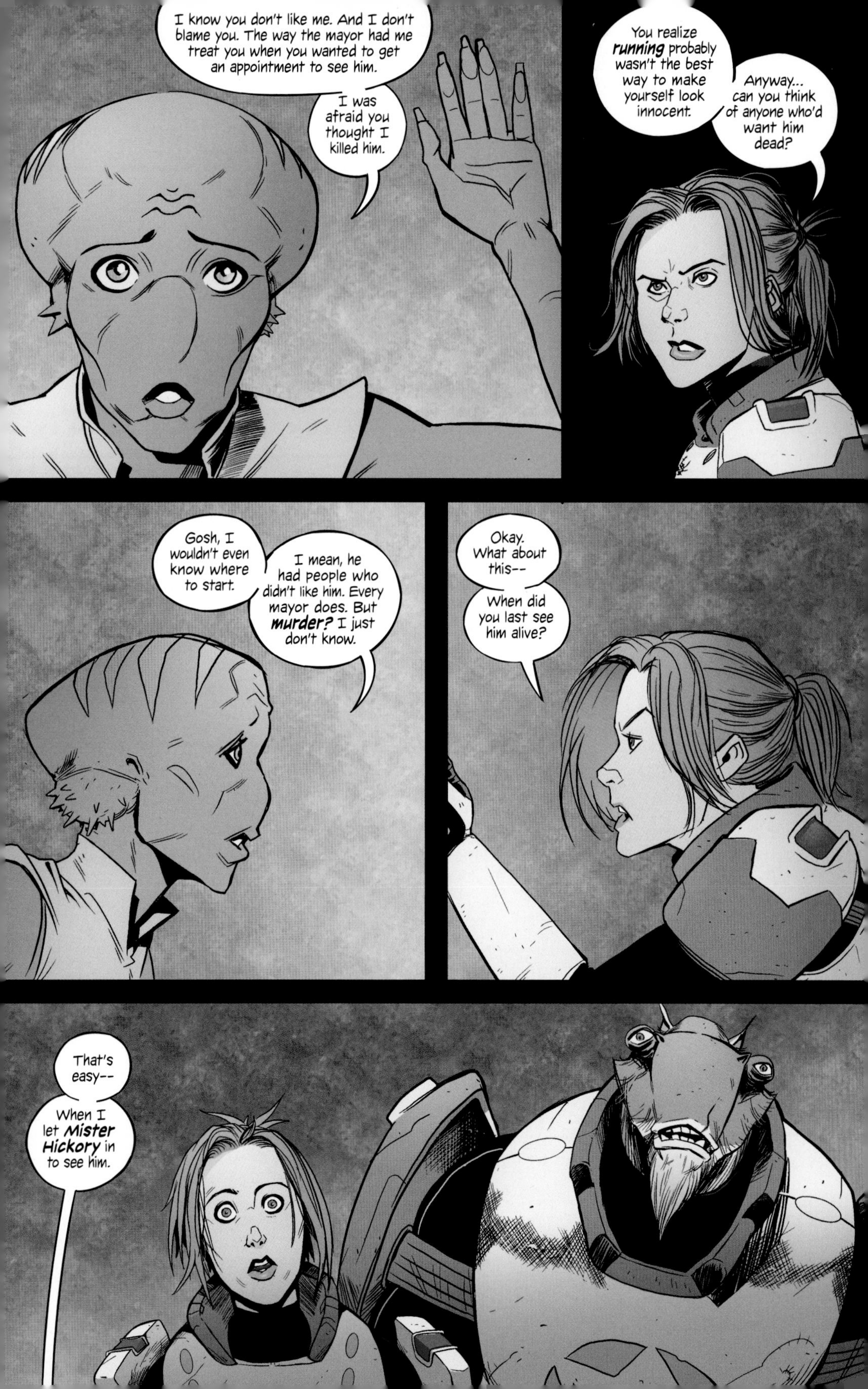
I know you don't like me. And I don't blame you. The way the mayor had me treat you when you wanted to get an appointment to see him.
I was afraid you thought I killed him.
You realize **running** probably wasn't the best way to make yourself look innocent.
Anyway... can you think of anyone who'd want him dead?
Gosh, I wouldn't even know where to start.
I mean, he had people who didn't like him. Every mayor does. But **murder?** I just don't know.
Okay. What about this--
When did you last see him alive?
That's easy--
When I let **Mister Hickory** in to see him.

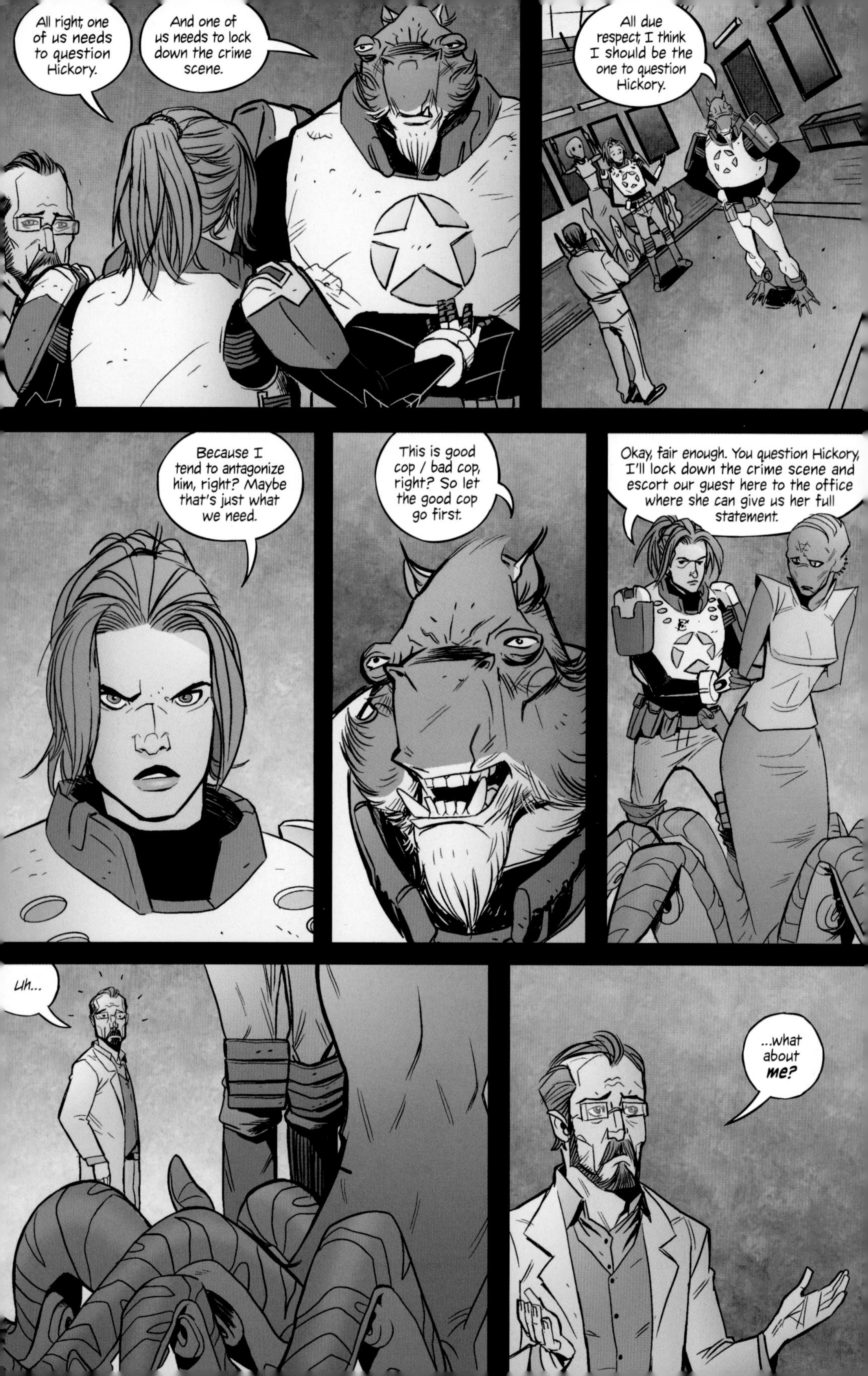
All right, one of us needs to question Hickory.
And one of us needs to lock down the crime scene.
All due respect, I think I should be the one to question Hickory.
Because I tend to antagonize him, right? Maybe that's just what we need.
This is good cop / bad cop, right? So let the good cop go first.
Okay, fair enough. You question Hickory, I'll lock down the crime scene and escort our guest here to the office where she can give us her full statement.
Uh...
...what about **me?**

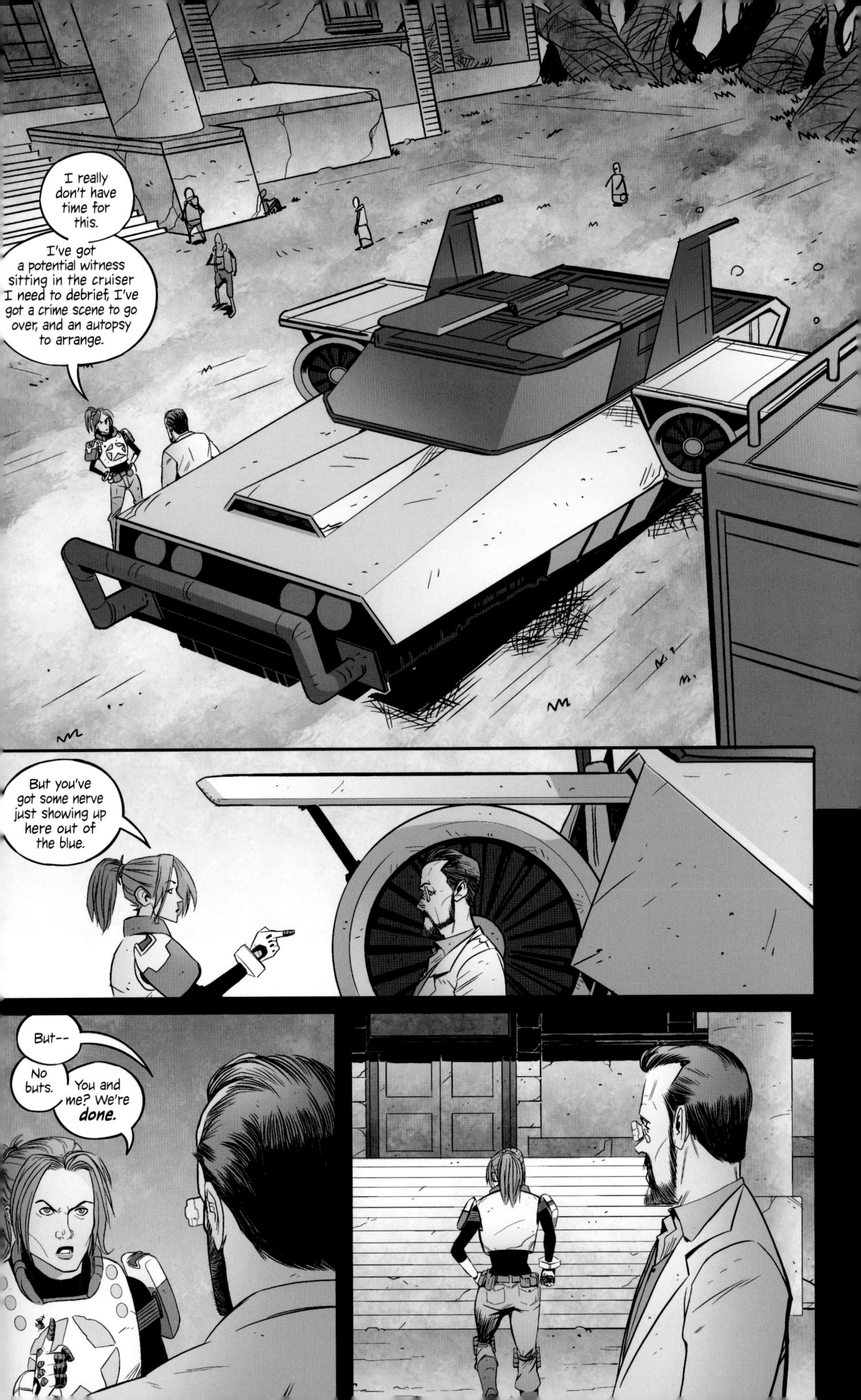
I really don't have time for this.
I've got a potential witness sitting in the cruiser I need to debrief, I've got a crime scene to go over, and an autopsy to arrange.
But you've got some nerve just showing up here out of the blue.
But--
No buts.
You and me? We're *done.*

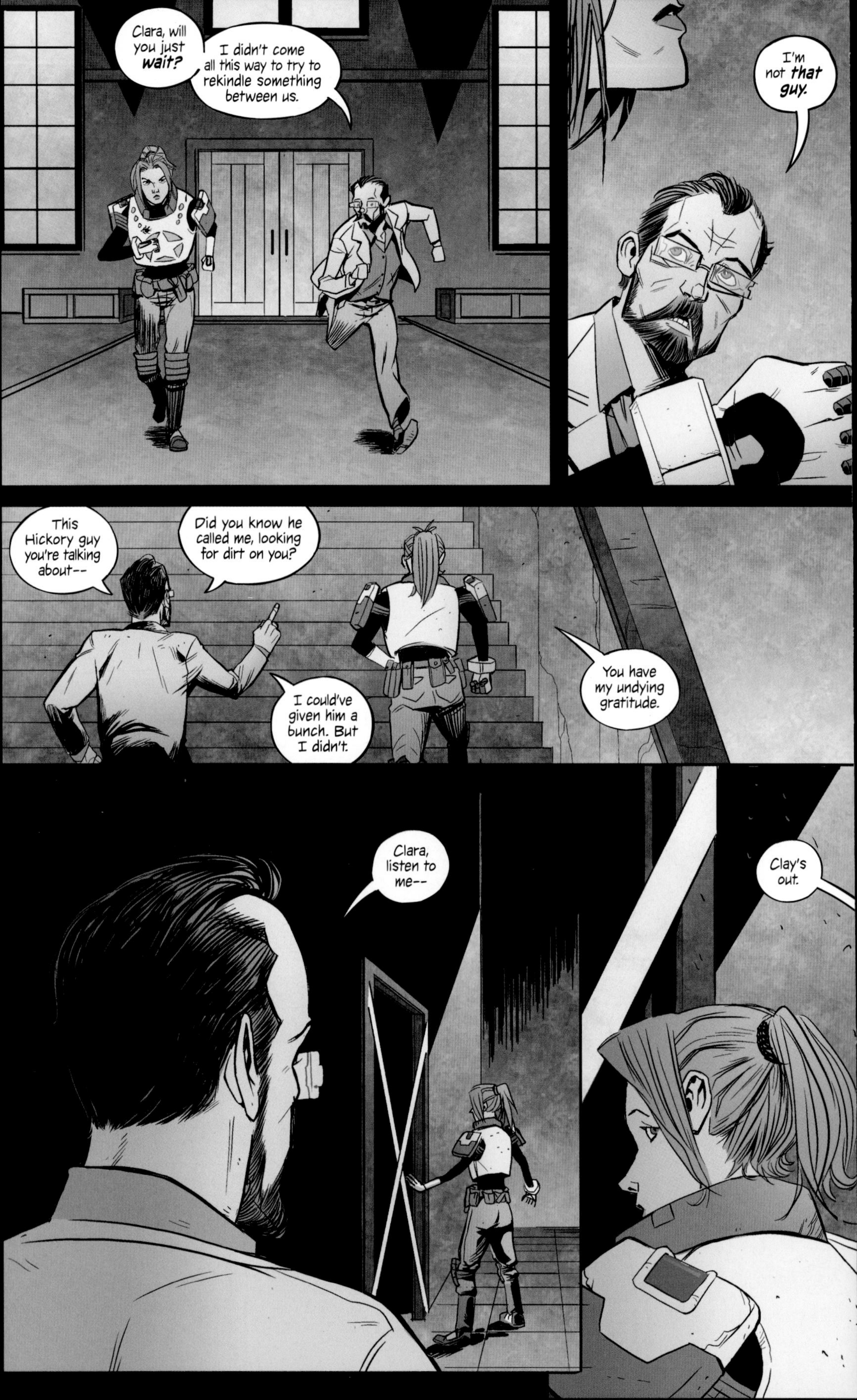
Clara, will you just wait?
I didn't come all this way to try to rekindle something between us.
I'm not that guy.
This Hickory guy you're talking about--
Did you know he called me, looking for dirt on you?
I could've given him a bunch. But I didn't.
You have my undying gratitude.
Clara, listen to me--
Clay's out.

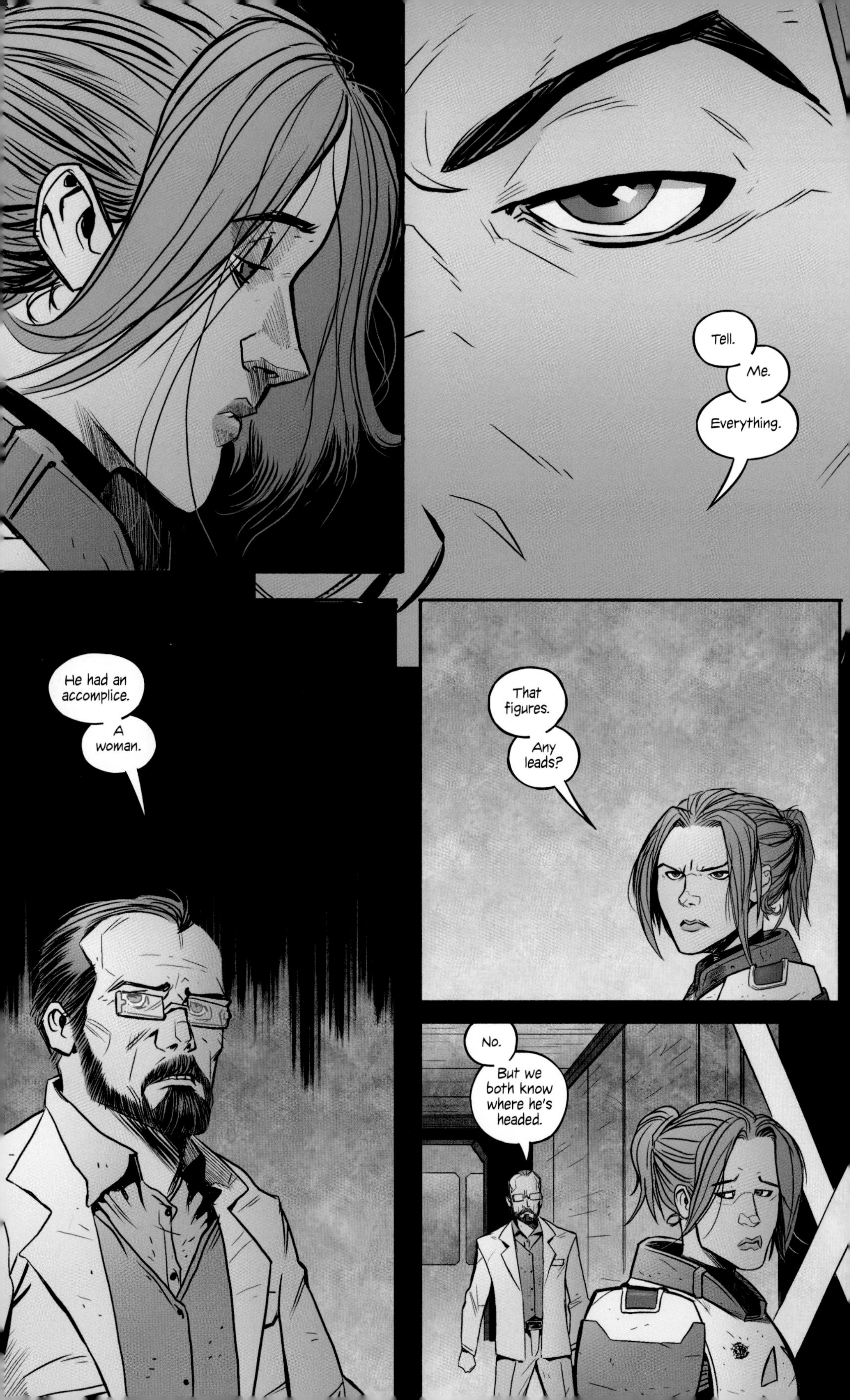
Tell.
Me.
Everything.
He had an accomplice.
A woman.
That figures.
Any leads?
No.
But we both know where he's headed.

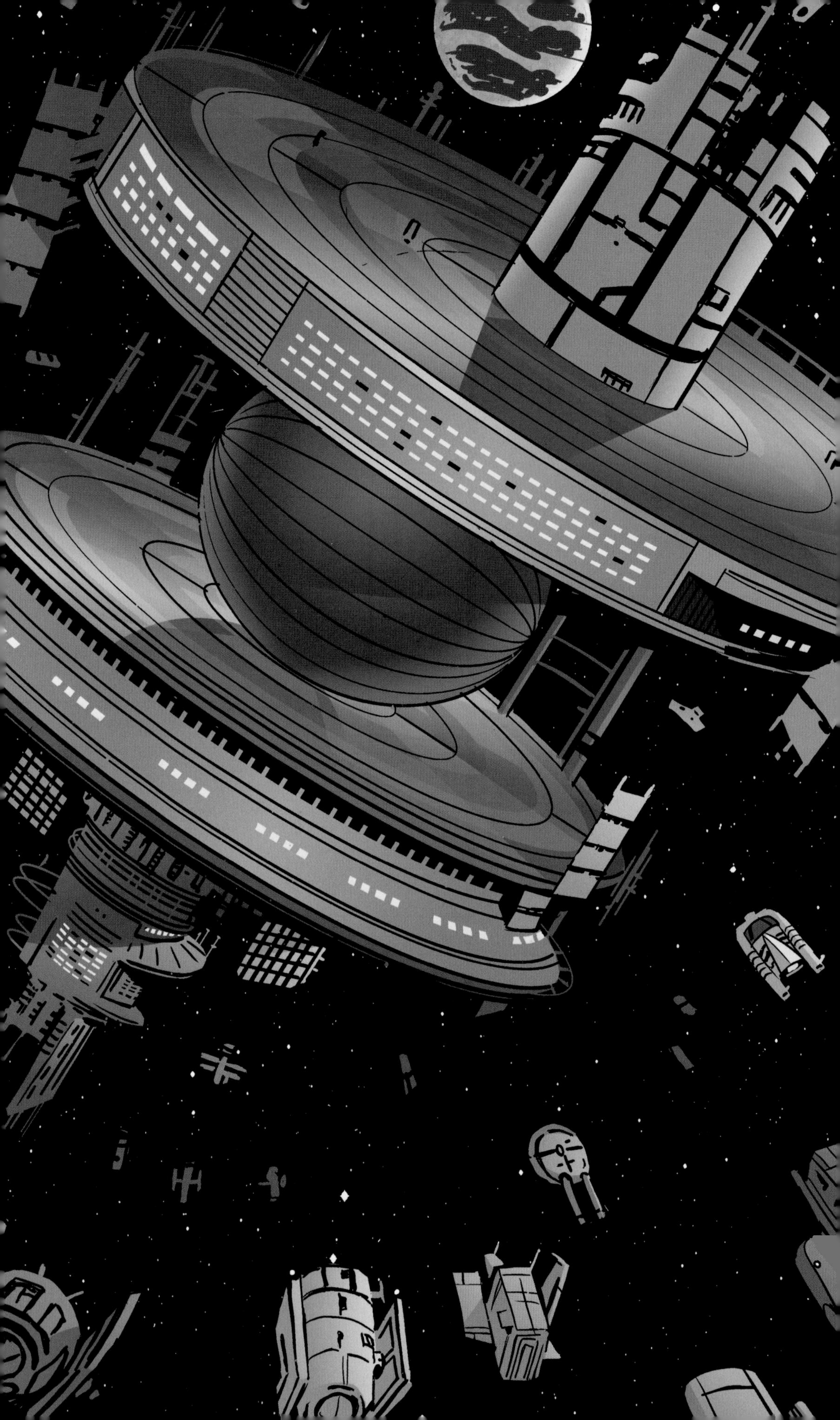

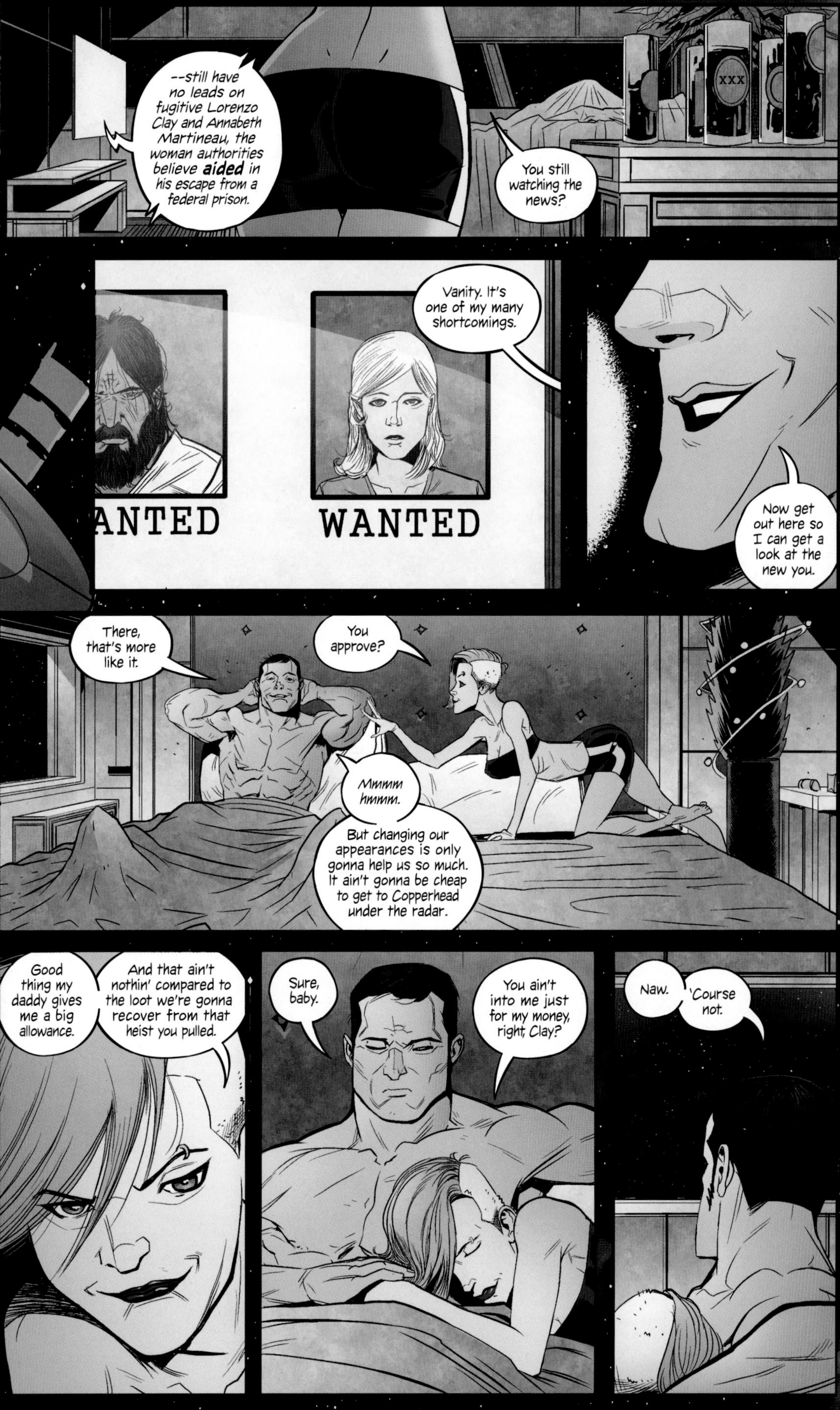
--still have no leads on fugitive Lorenzo Clay and Annabeth Martineau, the woman authorities believe **aided** in his escape from a federal prison.
You still watching the news?
XXX
Vanity. It's one of my many shortcomings.
ANTED
WANTED
Now get out here so I can get a look at the new you.
There, that's more like it.
You approve?
Mmmm hmmm.
But changing our appearances is only gonna help us so much. It ain't gonna be cheap to get to Copperhead under the radar.
Good thing my daddy gives me a big allowance.
And that ain't nothin' compared to the loot we're gonna recover from that heist you pulled.
Sure, baby.
You ain't into me just for my money, right, Clay?
Naw.
'Course not.

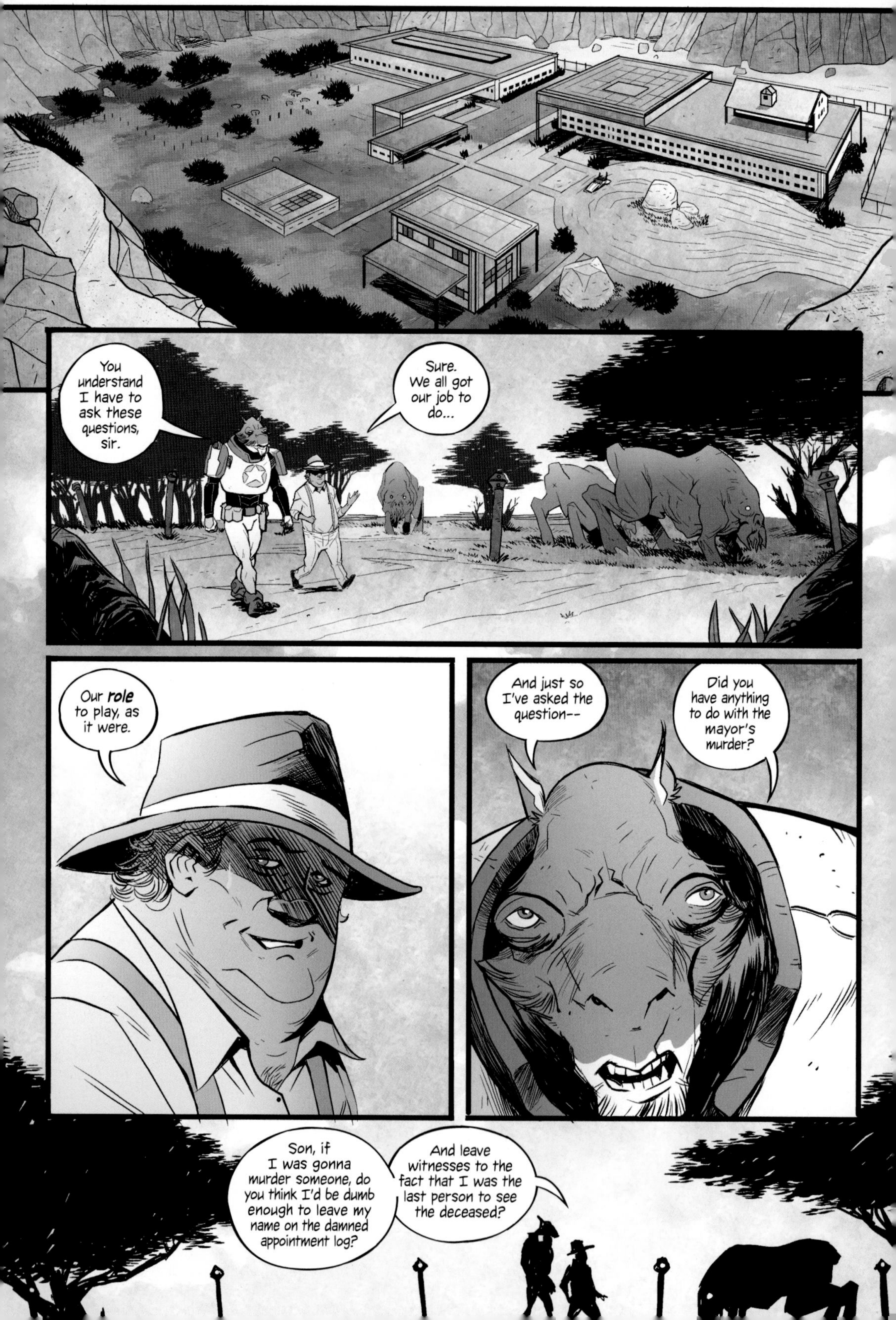
You understand I have to ask these questions, sir.
Sure. We all got our job to do...
Our role to play, as it were.
And just so I've asked the question--
Did you have anything to do with the mayor's murder?
Son, if I was gonna murder someone, do you think I'd be dumb enough to leave my name on the damned appointment log?
And leave witnesses to the fact that I was the last person to see the deceased?

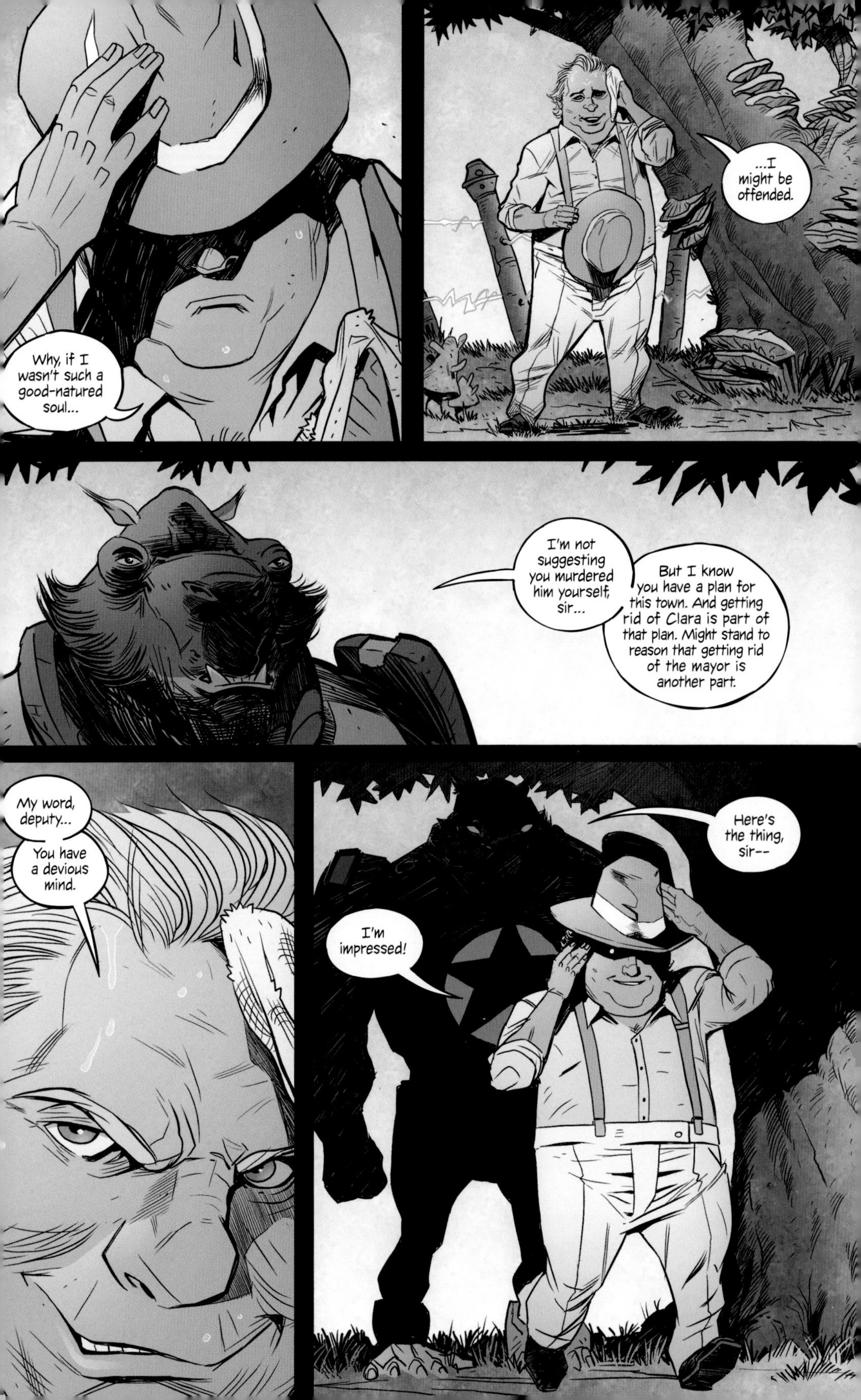
Why, if I wasn't such a good-natured soul...
...I might be offended.
I'm not suggesting you murdered him yourself, sir...
But I know you have a plan for this town. And getting rid of Clara is part of that plan. Might stand to reason that getting rid of the mayor is another part.
My word, deputy...
You have a devious mind.
I'm impressed!
Here's the thing, sir--

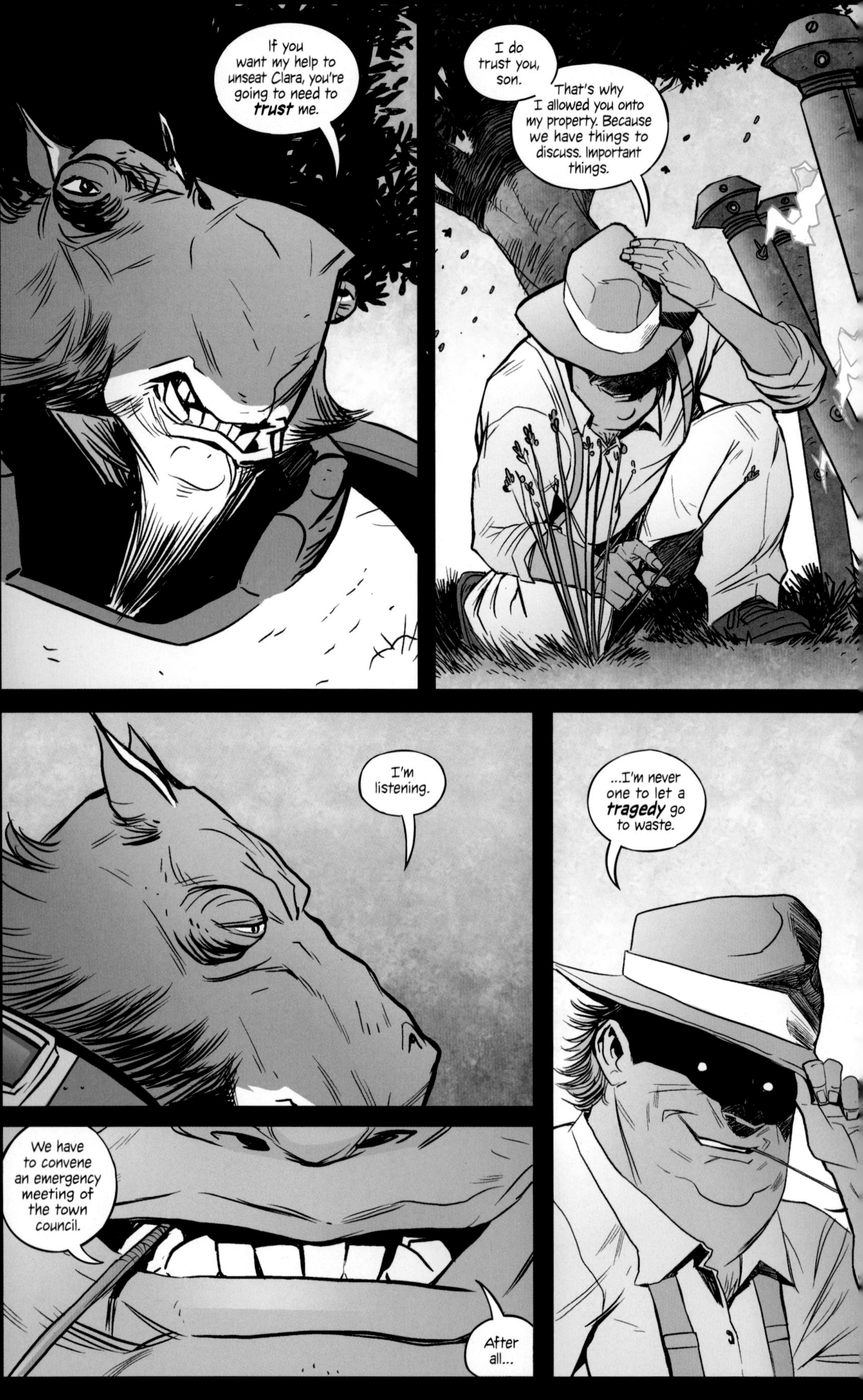
If you want my help to unseat Clara, you're going to need to ***trust*** me.
I do trust you, son.
That's why I allowed you onto my property. Because we have things to discuss. Important things.
I'm listening.
We have to convene an emergency meeting of the town council.
After all...
...I'm never one to let a ***tragedy*** go to waste.

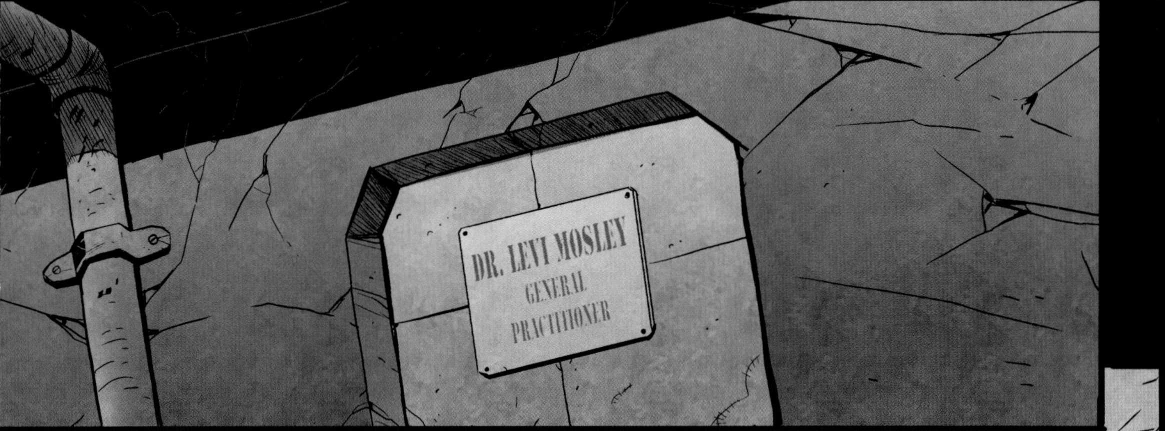
DR. LEVI MOSLEY
GENERAL
PRACTITIONER

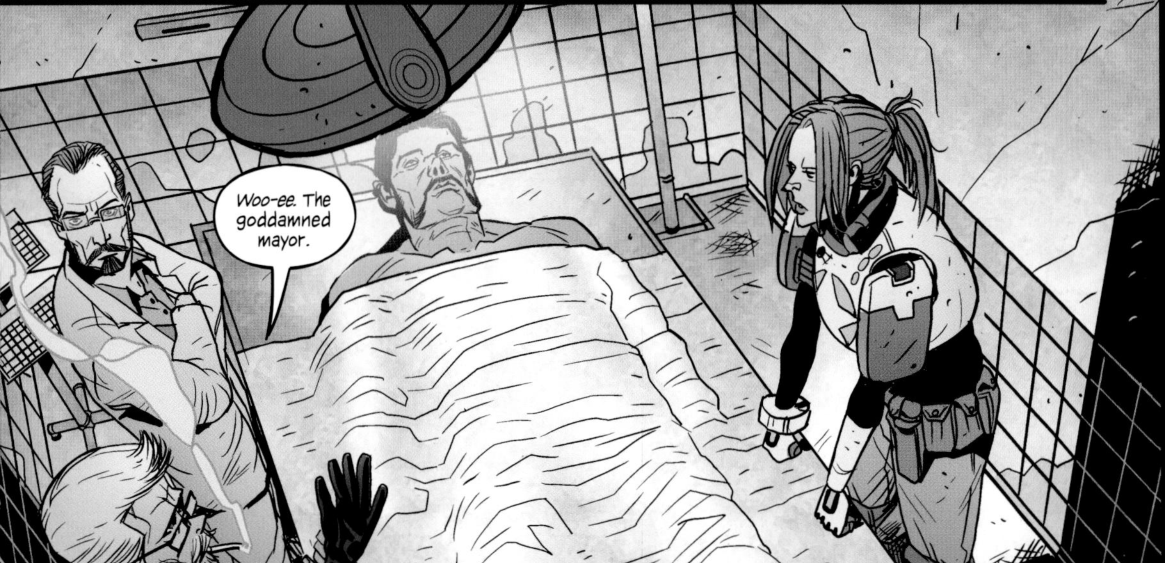
Woo-ee. The goddamned mayor.
Must be my lucky day. Some people in this town would pay good money to slice open his miserable guts.

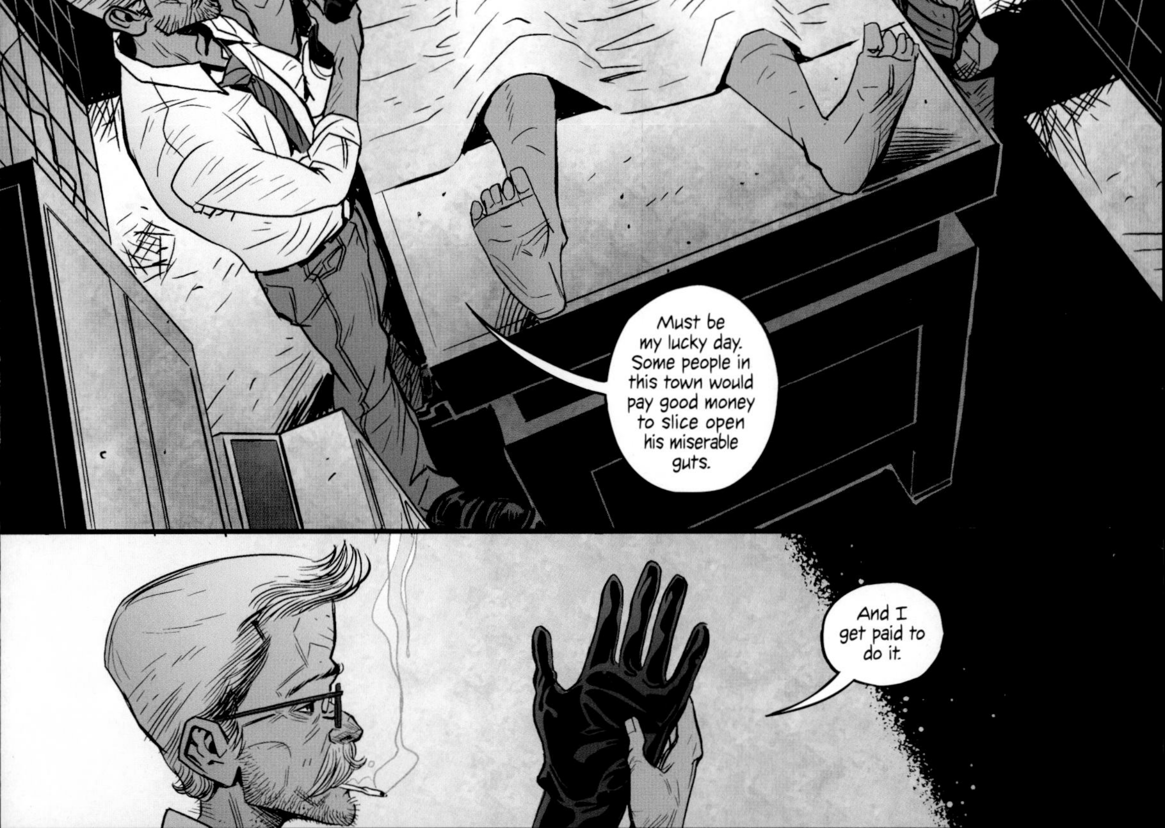
And I get paid to do it.

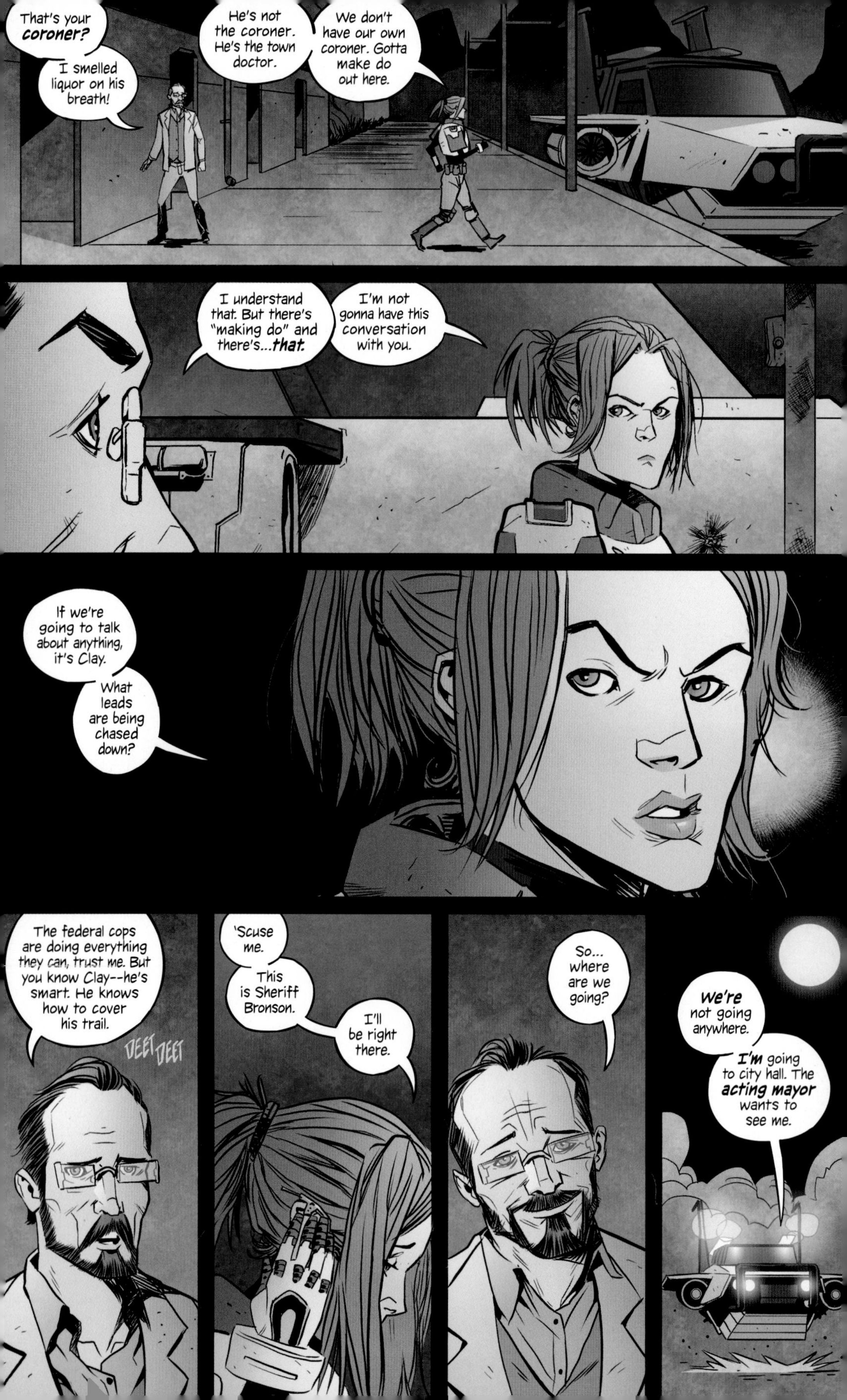
That's your **coroner?**
I smelled liquor on his breath!
He's not the coroner. He's the town doctor.
We don't have our own coroner. Gotta make do out here.
I understand that. But there's "making do" and there's...**that.**
I'm not gonna have this conversation with you.
If we're going to talk about anything, it's Clay.
What leads are being chased down?
The federal cops are doing everything they can, trust me. But you know Clay--he's smart. He knows how to cover his trail.
DEET DEET
'Scuse me.
This is Sheriff Bronson.
I'll be right there.
So... where are we going?
We're not going anywhere.
I'm going to city hall. The **acting mayor** wants to see me.

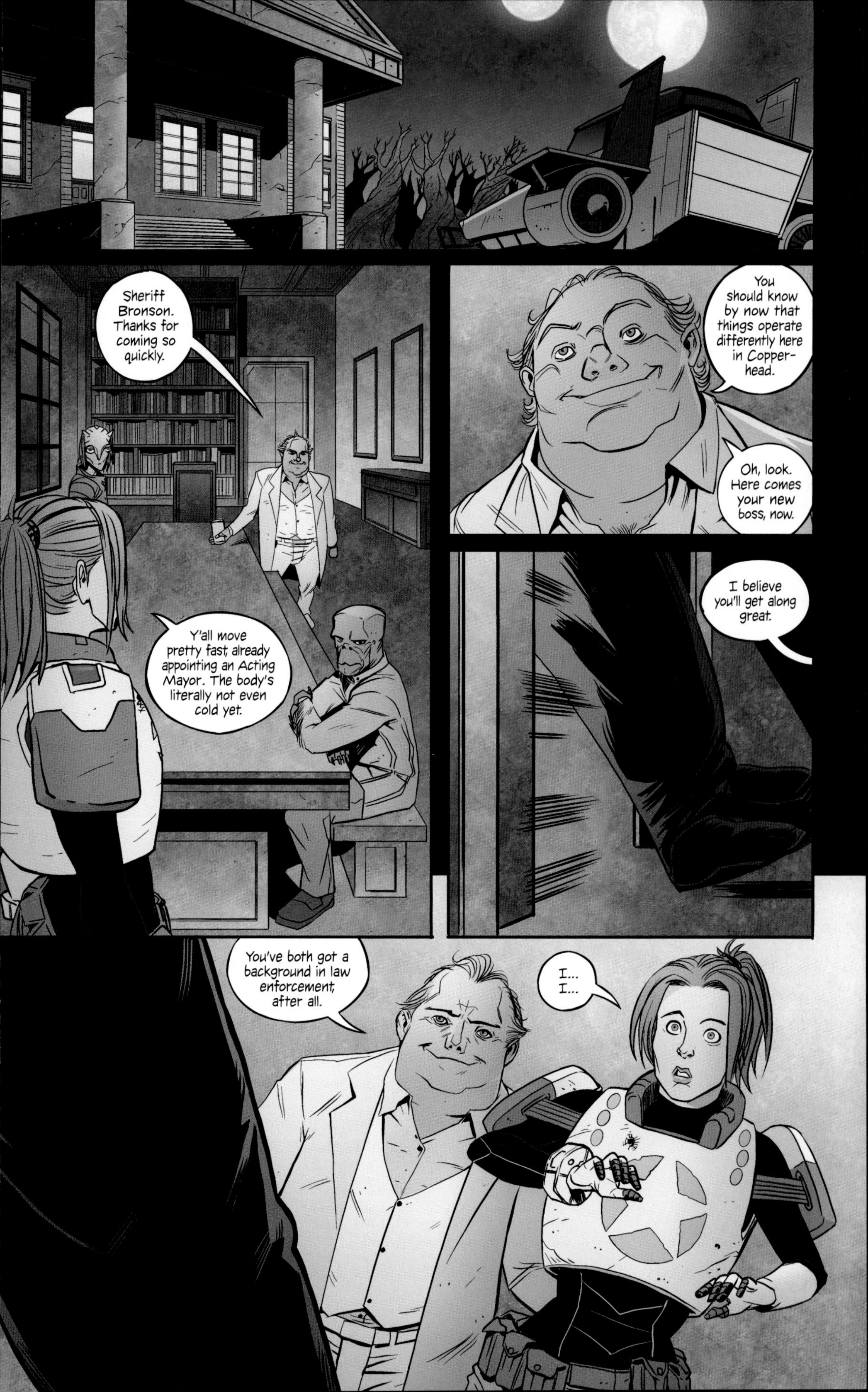
Sheriff Bronson. Thanks for coming so quickly.
Y'all move pretty fast, already appointing an Acting Mayor. The body's literally not even cold yet.
You should know by now that things operate differently here in Copper-head.
Oh, look. Here comes your new boss, now.
I believe you'll get along great.
You've both got a background in law enforcement, after all.
I... I...

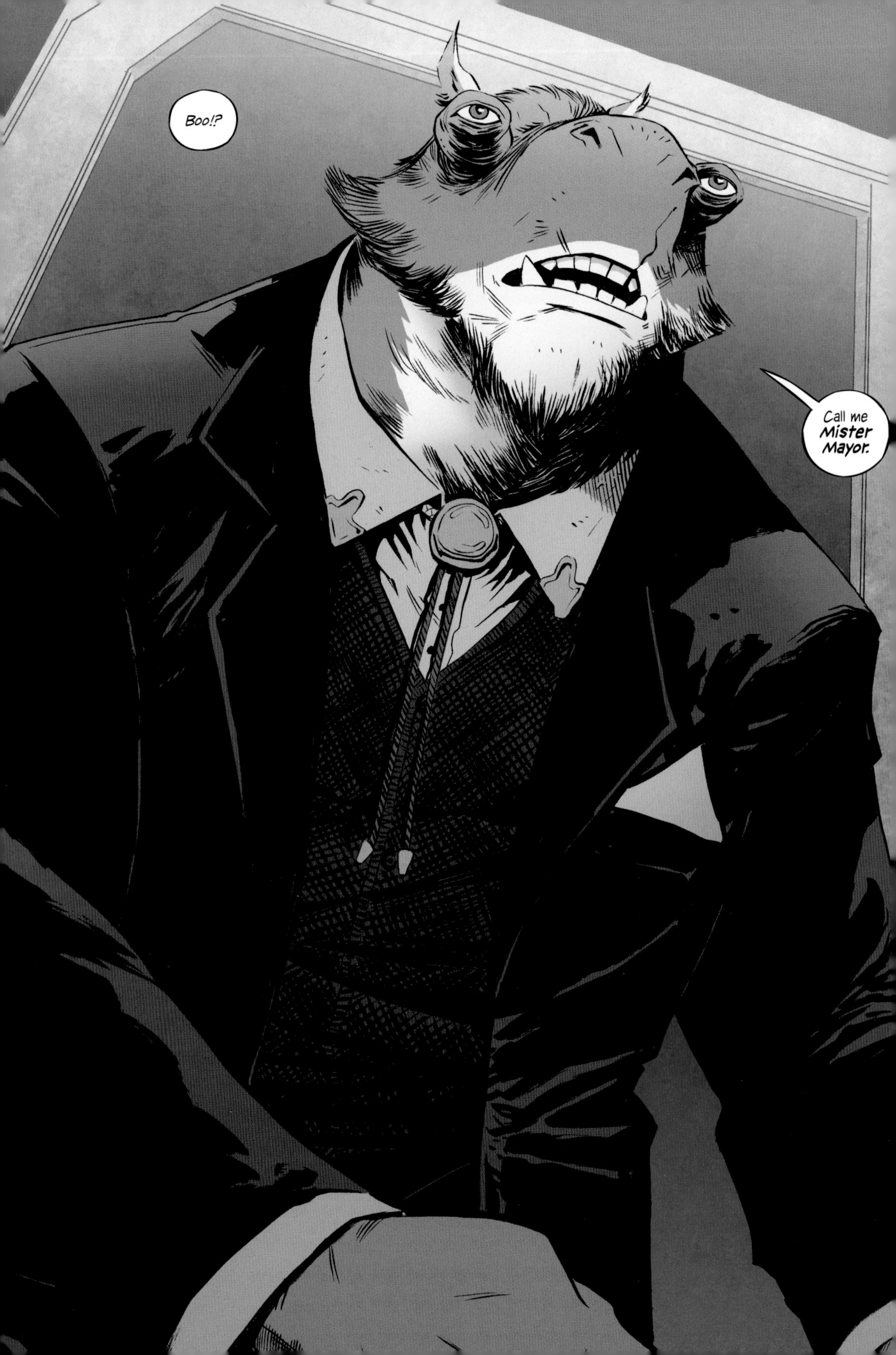
Boo!?
Call me Mister Mayor.

CHAPTER II

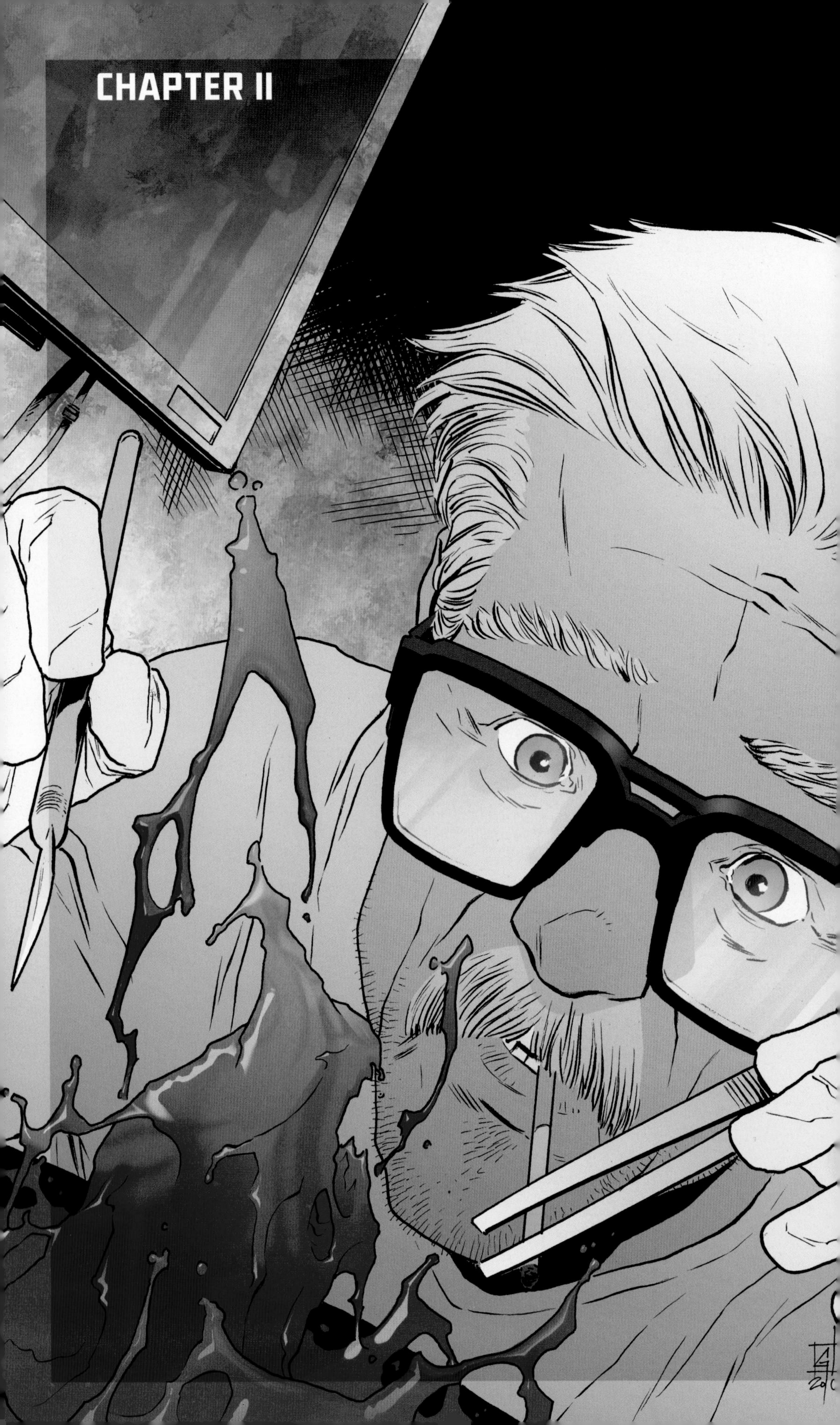

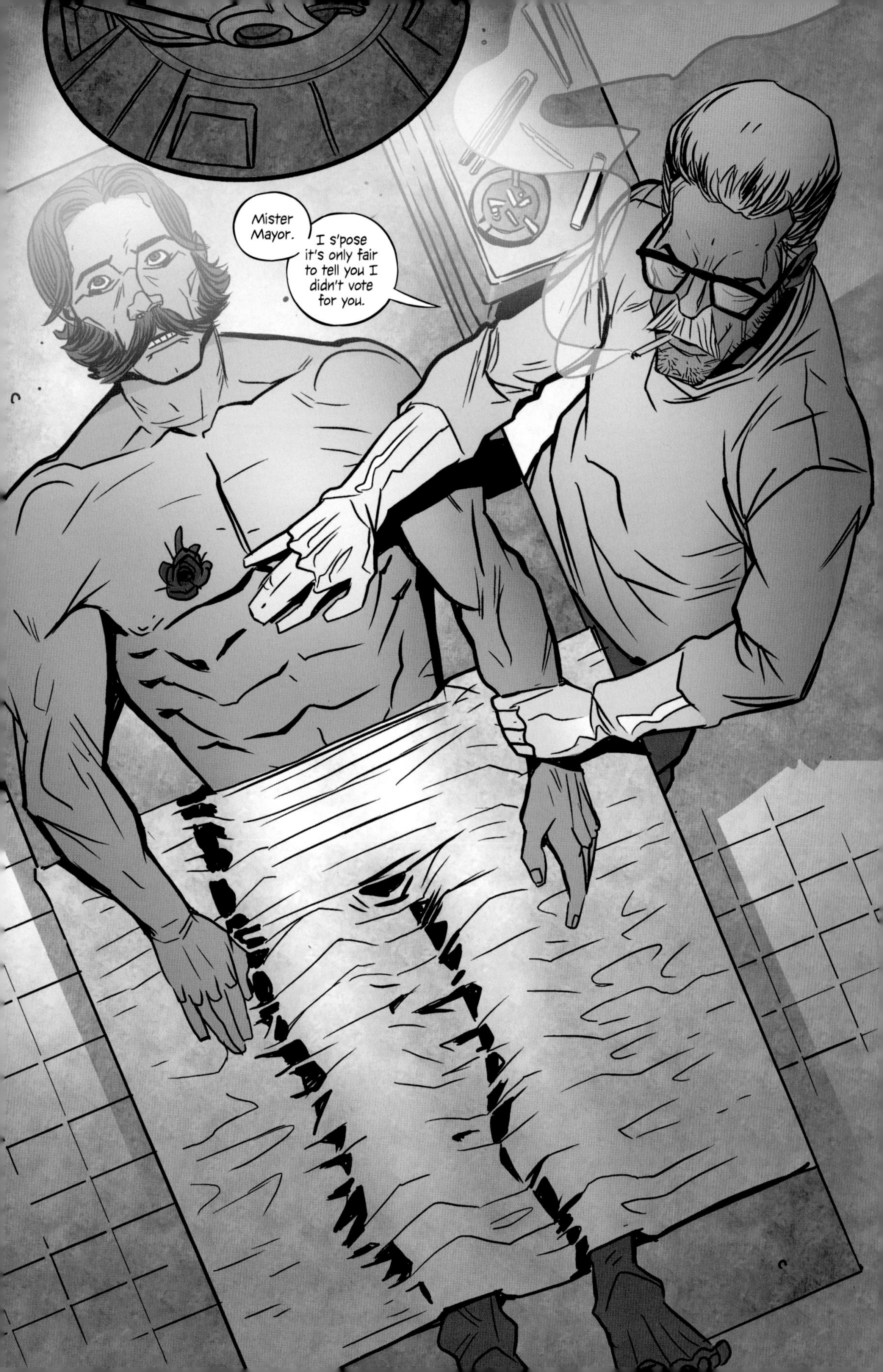
Mister Mayor.
I s'pose it's only fair to tell you I didn't vote for you.

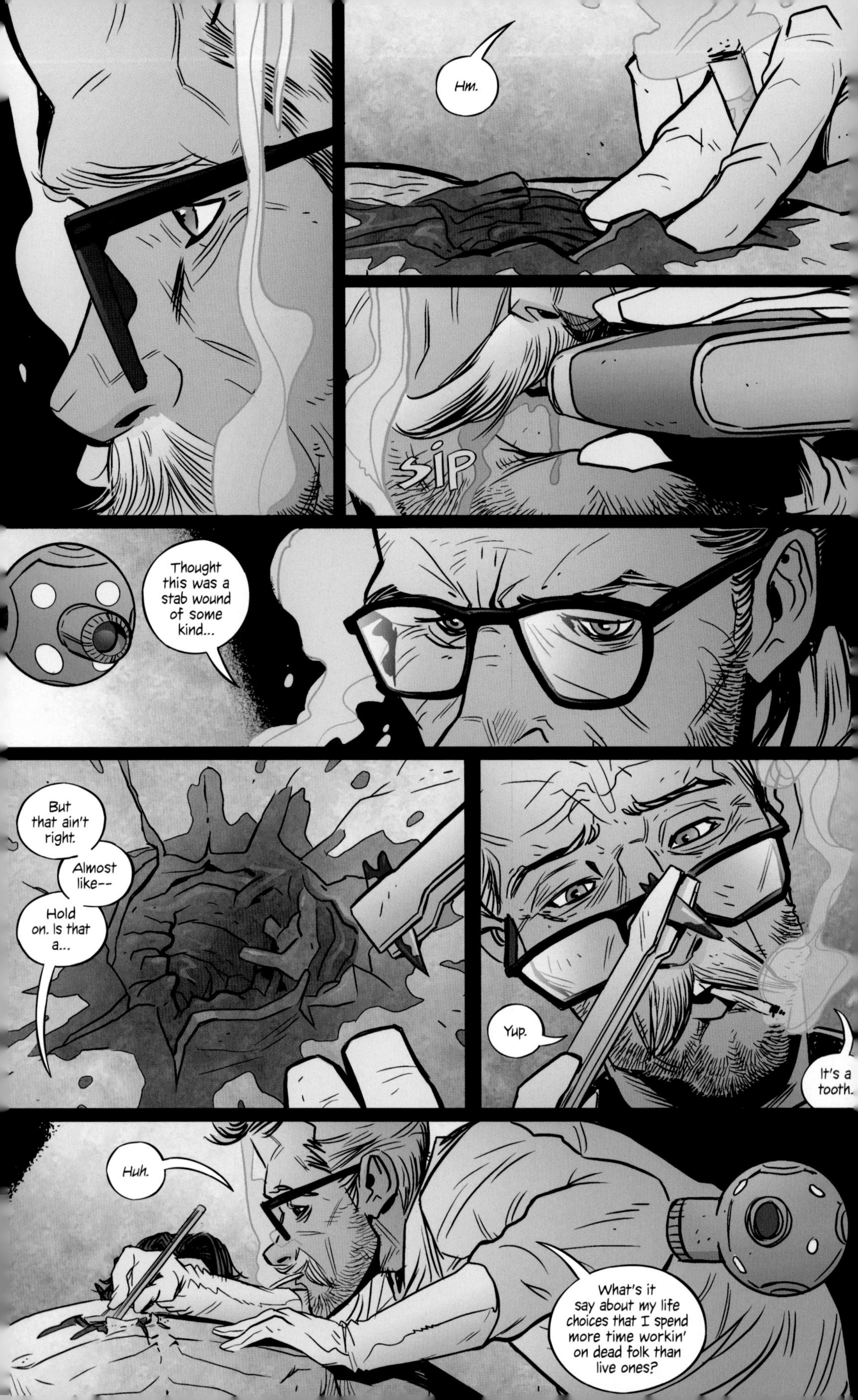
Hm.
SIP
Thought this was a stab wound of some kind...
But that ain't right.
Almost like--
Hold on. Is that a...
Yup.
It's a tooth.
Huh.
What's it say about my life choices that I spend more time workin' on dead folk than live ones?

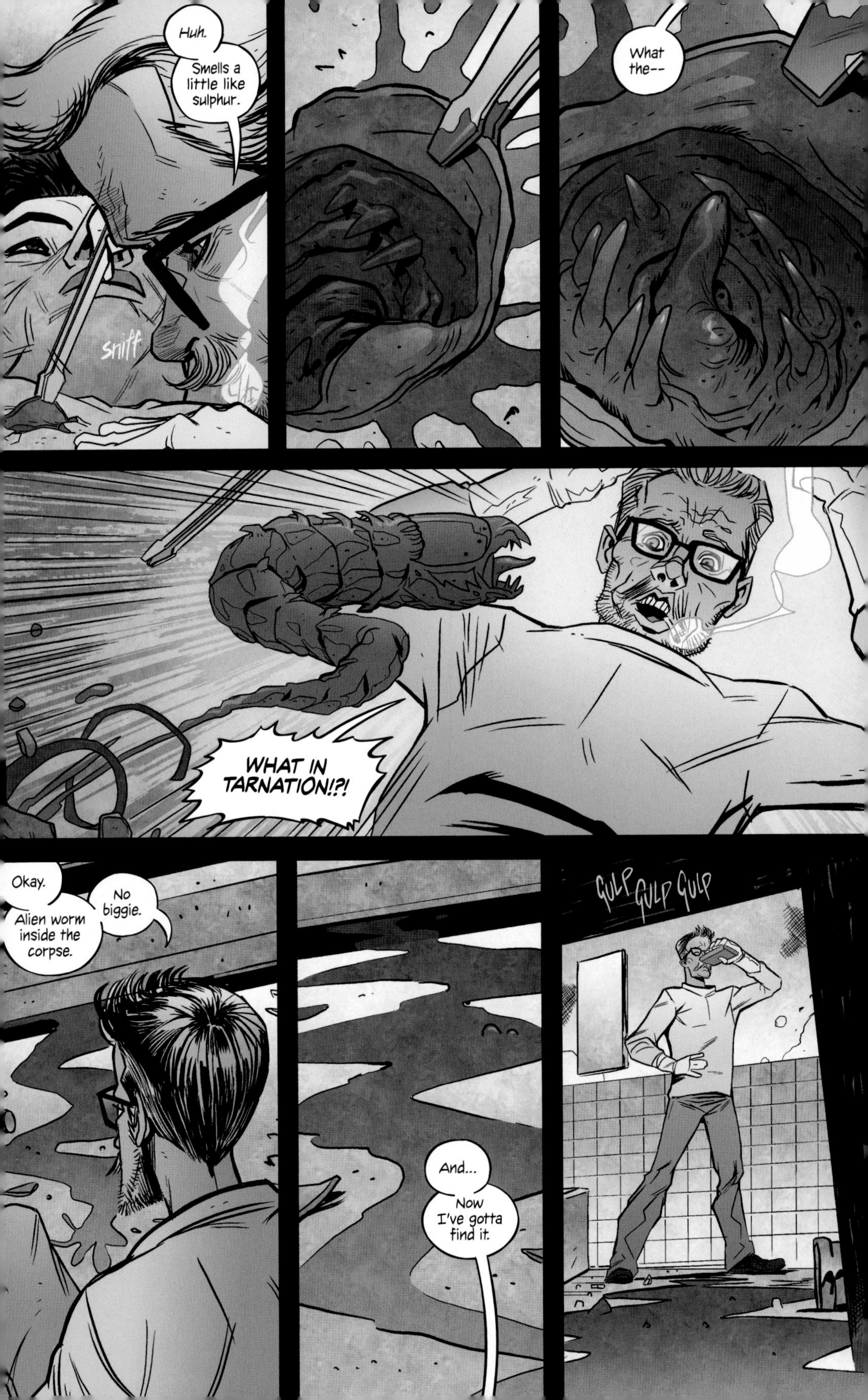
Huh.
Smells a little like sulphur.
sniff
What the--
WHAT IN TARNATION!?!
Okay.
Alien worm inside the corpse.
No biggie.
And...
Now I've gotta find it.
GULP GULP GULP

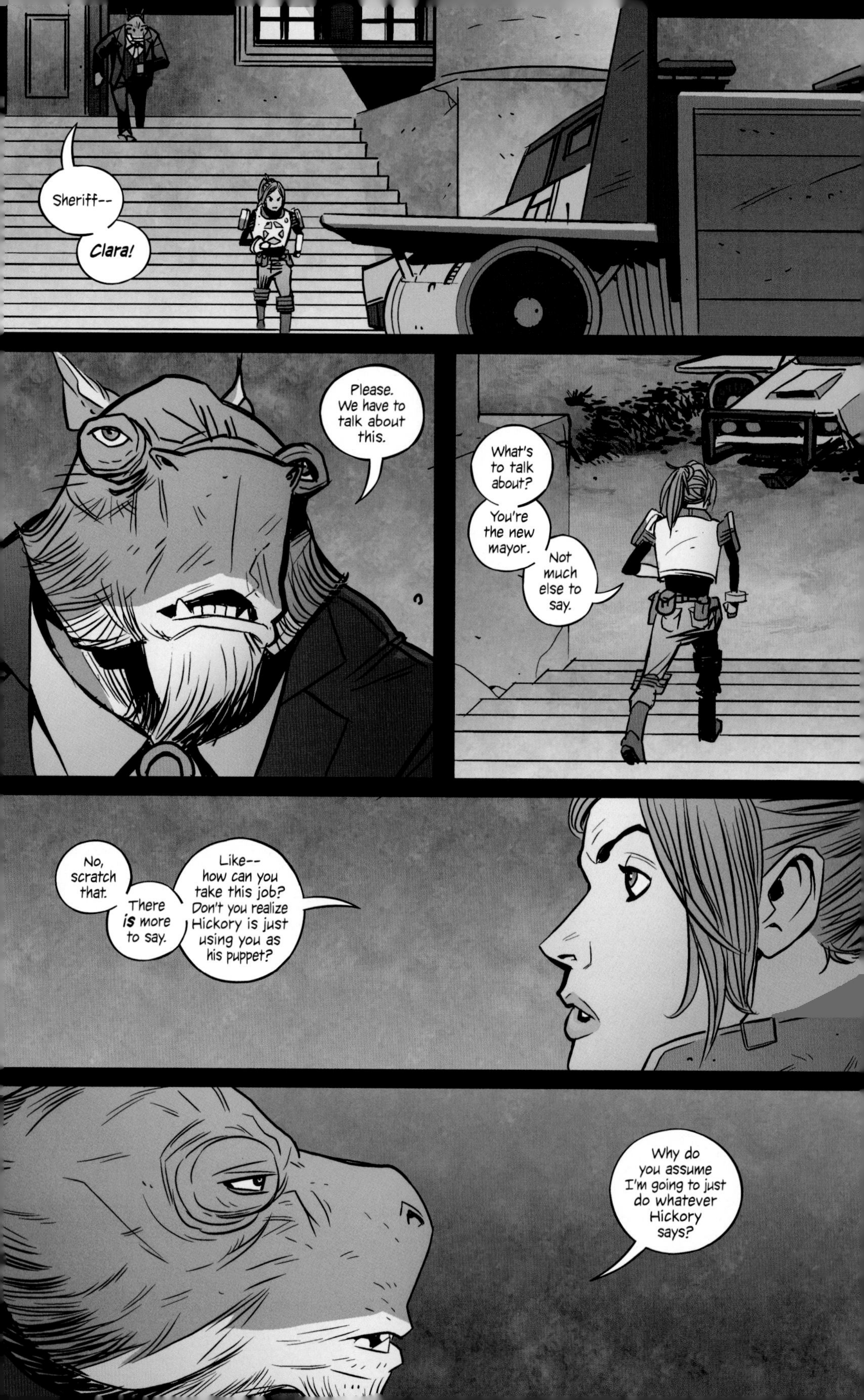
Sheriff--
Clara!
Please. We have to talk about this.
What's to talk about?
You're the new mayor.
Not much else to say.
No, scratch that.
There *is* more to say.
Like-- how can you take this job? Don't you realize Hickory is just using you as his puppet?
Why do you assume I'm going to just do whatever Hickory says?

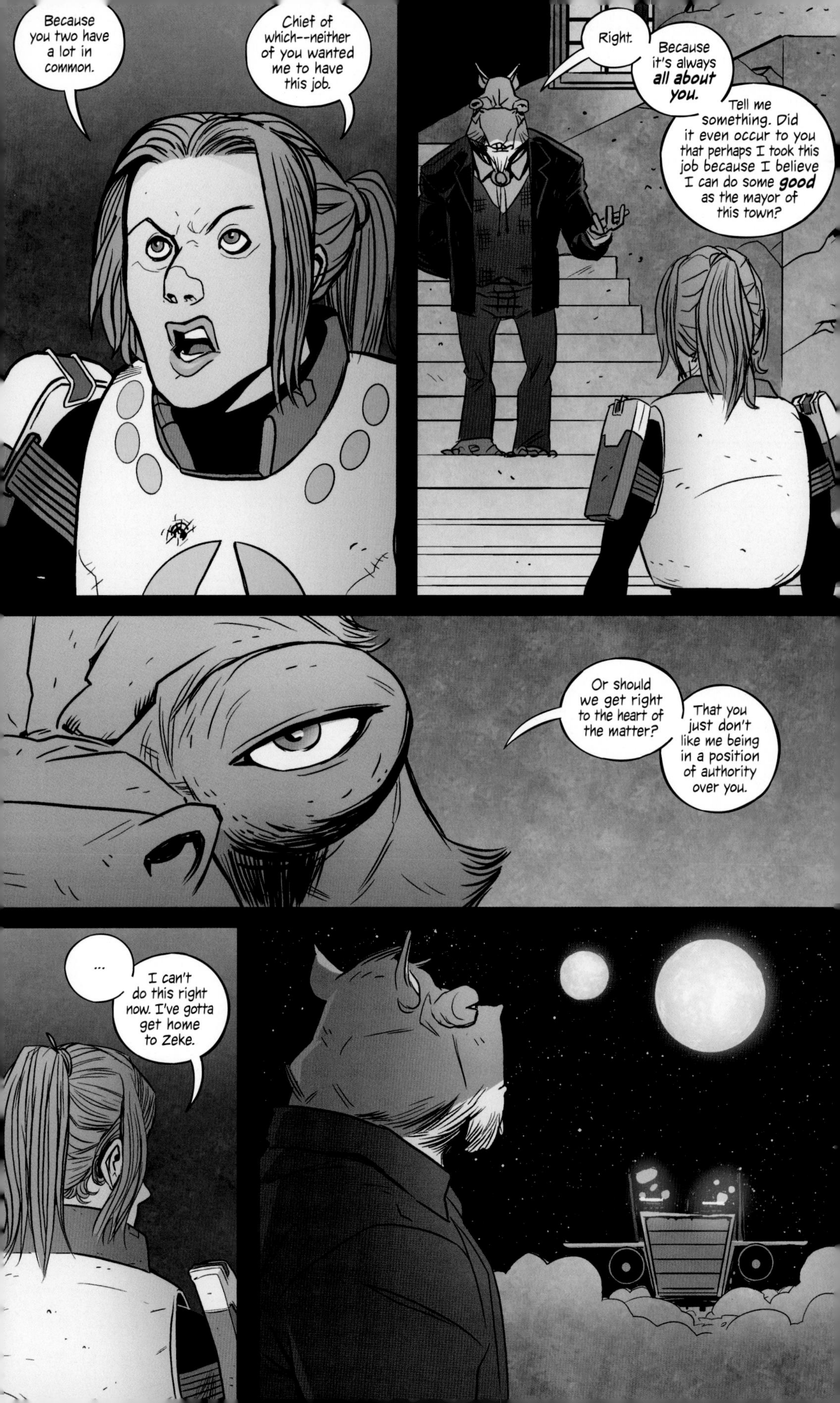
Because you two have a lot in common.
Chief of which--neither of you wanted me to have this job.
Right.
Because it's always **all about you.**
Tell me something. Did it even occur to you that perhaps I took this job because I believe I can do some **good** as the mayor of this town?
Or should we get right to the heart of the matter?
That you just don't like me being in a position of authority over you.
...
I can't do this right now. I've gotta get home to Zeke.

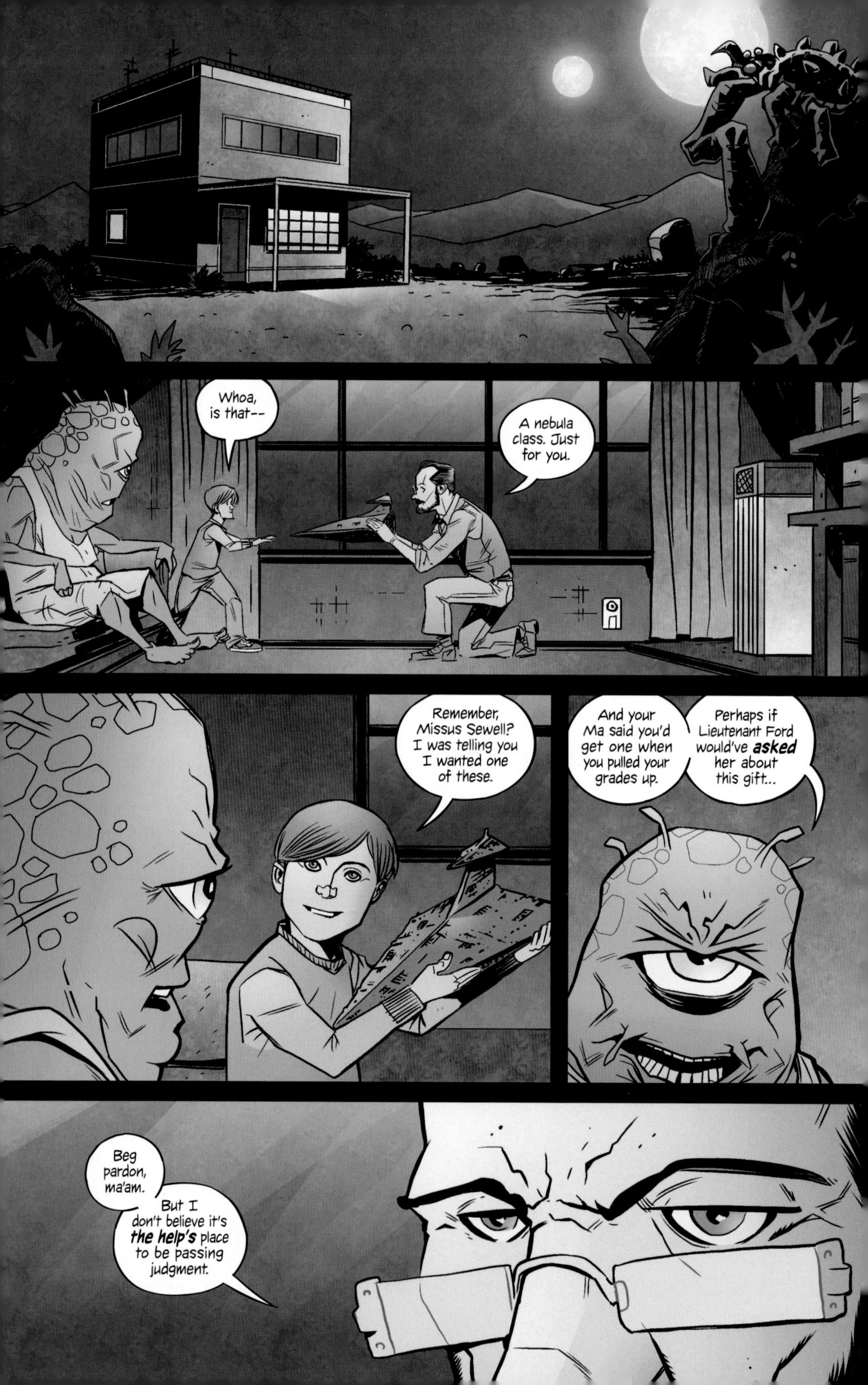
Whoa, is that--
A nebula class. Just for you.
Remember, Missus Sewell? I was telling you I wanted one of these.
And your Ma said you'd get one when you pulled your grades up.
Perhaps if Lieutenant Ford would've **asked** her about this gift...
Beg pardon, ma'am.
But I don't believe it's **the help's** place to be passing judgment.

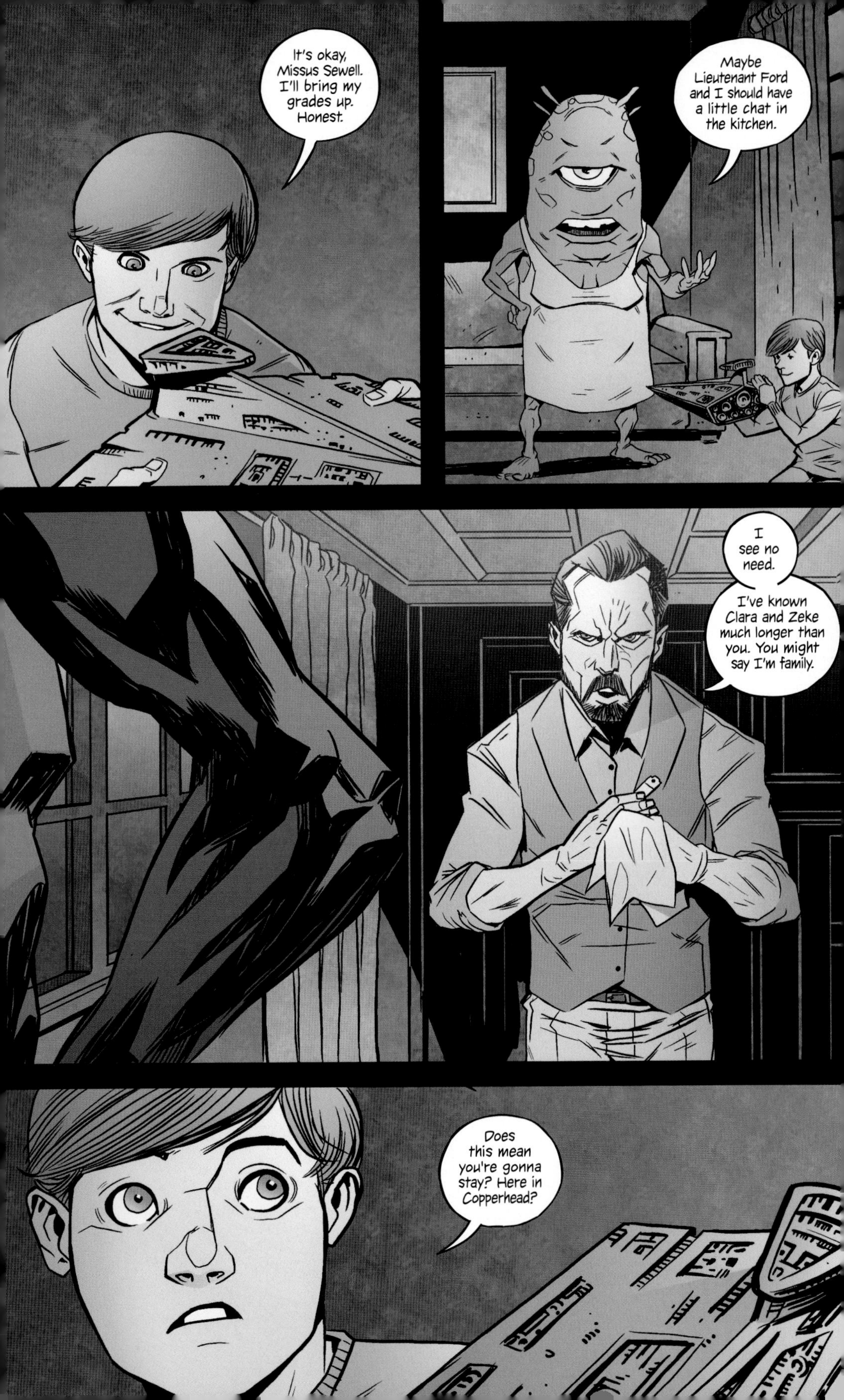
It's okay, Missus Sewell. I'll bring my grades up. Honest.
Maybe Lieutenant Ford and I should have a little chat in the kitchen.
I see no need.
I've known Clara and Zeke much longer than you. You might say I'm family.
Does this mean you're gonna stay? Here in Copperhead?

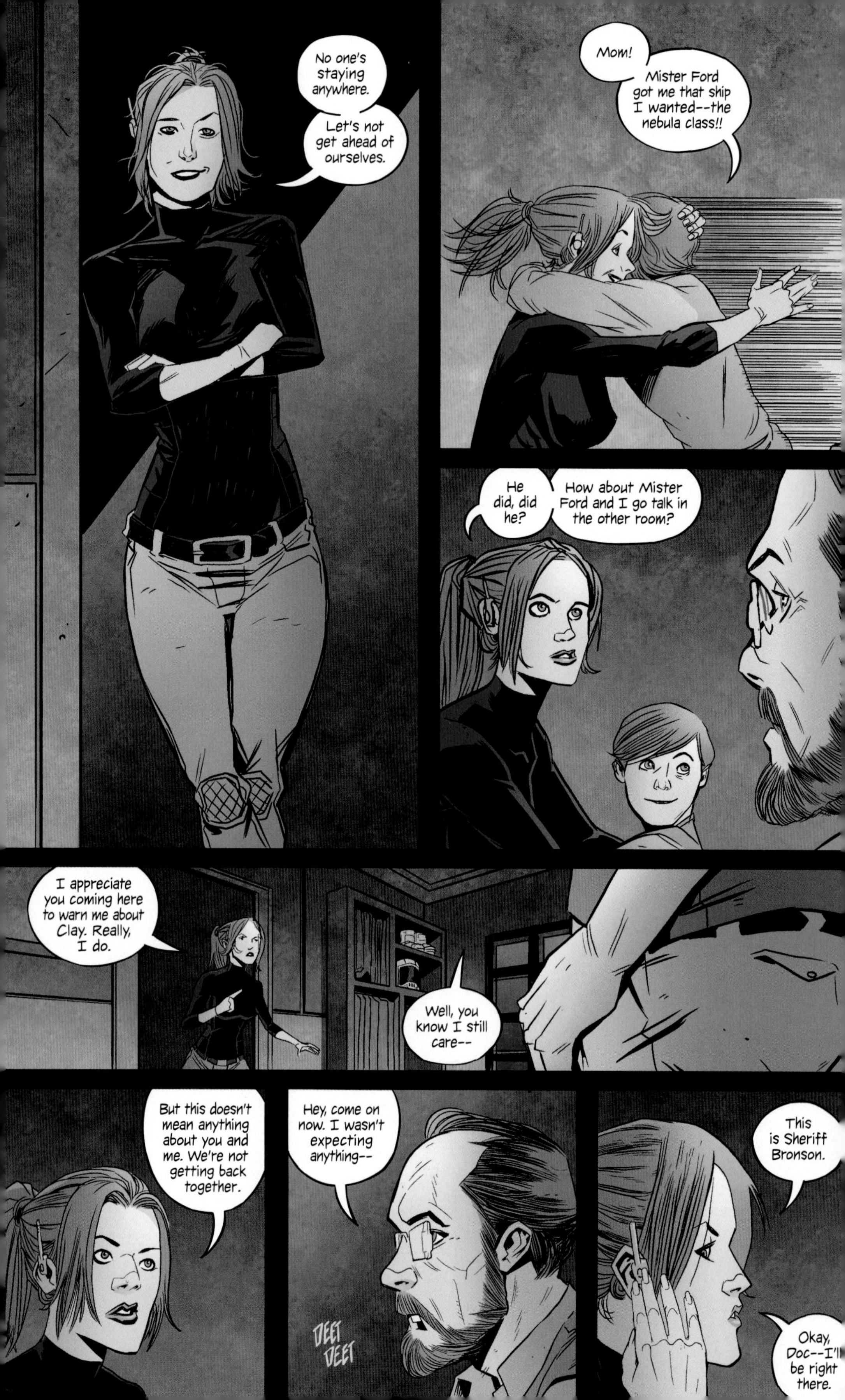

No one's staying anywhere.
Let's not get ahead of ourselves.
Mom!
Mister Ford got me that ship I wanted--the nebula class!!
He did, did he?
How about Mister Ford and I go talk in the other room?
I appreciate you coming here to warn me about Clay. Really, I do.
Well, you know I still care--
But this doesn't mean anything about you and me. We're not getting back together.
Hey, come on now. I wasn't expecting anything--
DEET DEET
This is Sheriff Bronson.
Okay, Doc--I'll be right there.

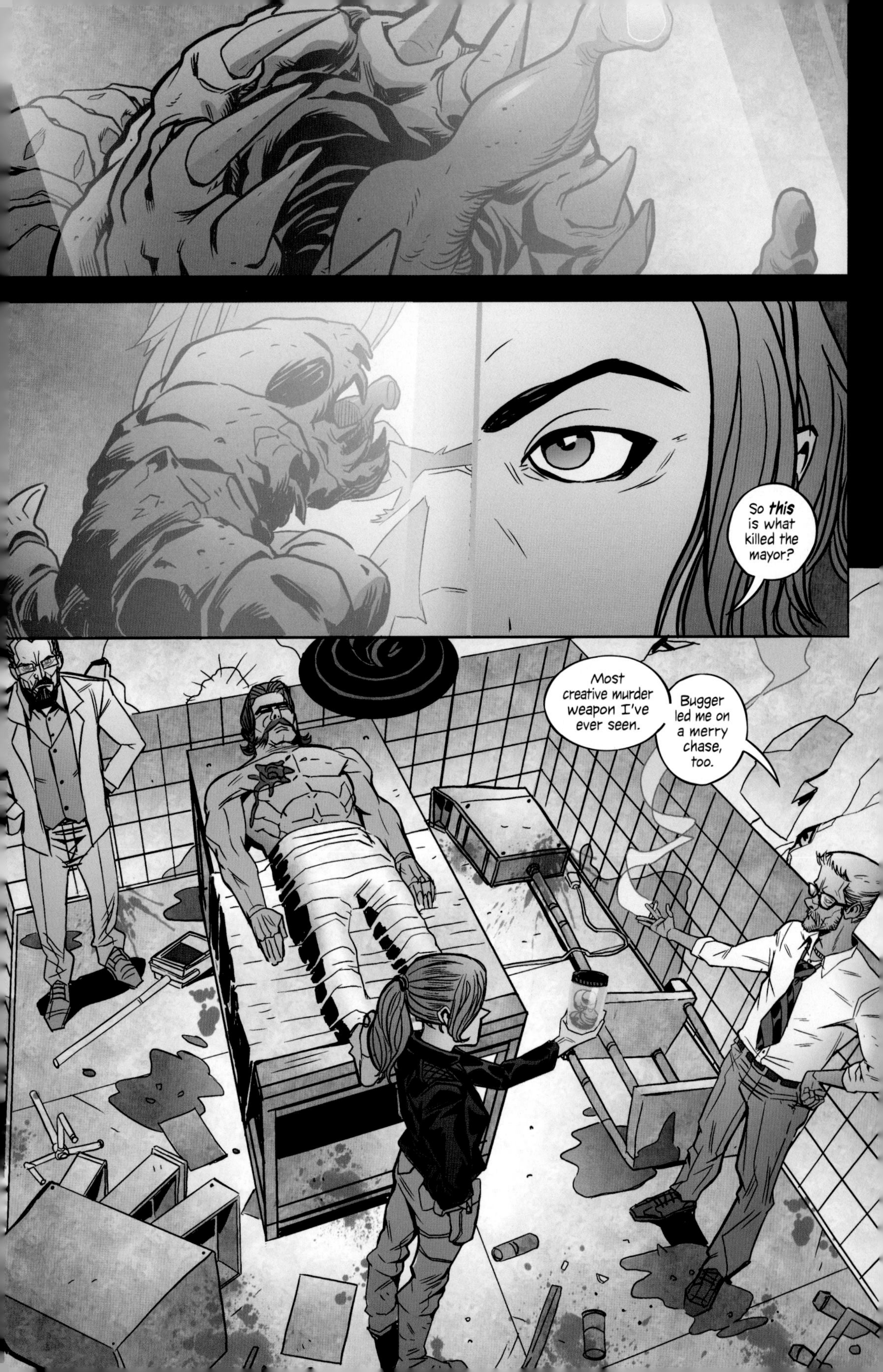
So this is what killed the mayor?
Most creative murder weapon I've ever seen.
Bugger led me on a merry chase, too.

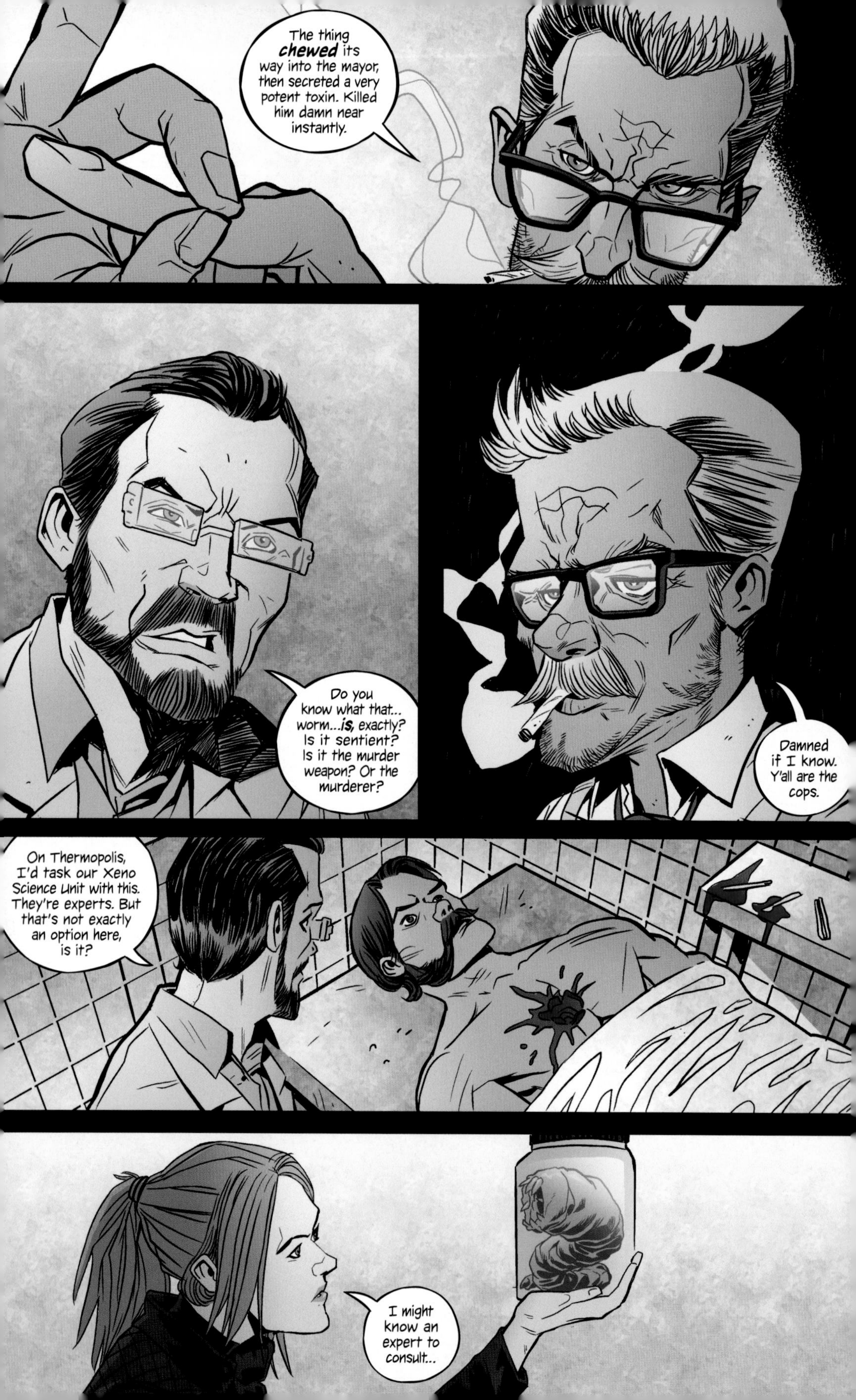
The thing **chewed** its way into the mayor, then secreted a very potent toxin. Killed him damn near instantly.
Do you know what that... worm...**is**, exactly? Is it sentient? Is it the murder weapon? Or the murderer?
Damned if I know. Y'all are the cops.
On Thermopolis, I'd task our Xeno Science Unit with this. They're experts. But that's not exactly an option here, is it?
I might know an expert to consult...

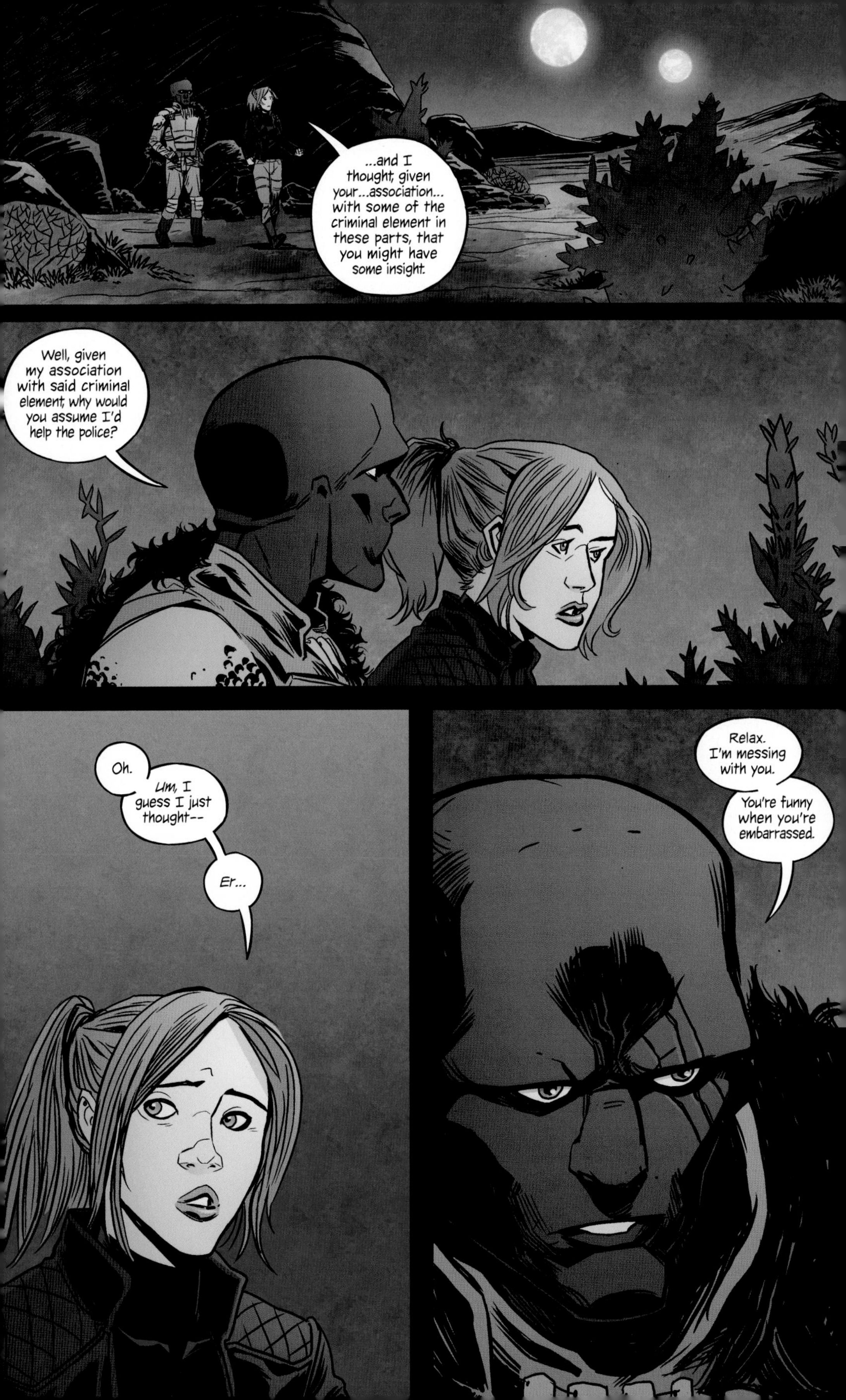
...and I thought, given your...association... with some of the criminal element in these parts, that you might have some insight.
Well, given my association with said criminal element, why would you assume I'd help the police?
Oh.
Um, I guess I just thought--
Er...
Relax. I'm messing with you.
You're funny when you're embarrassed.

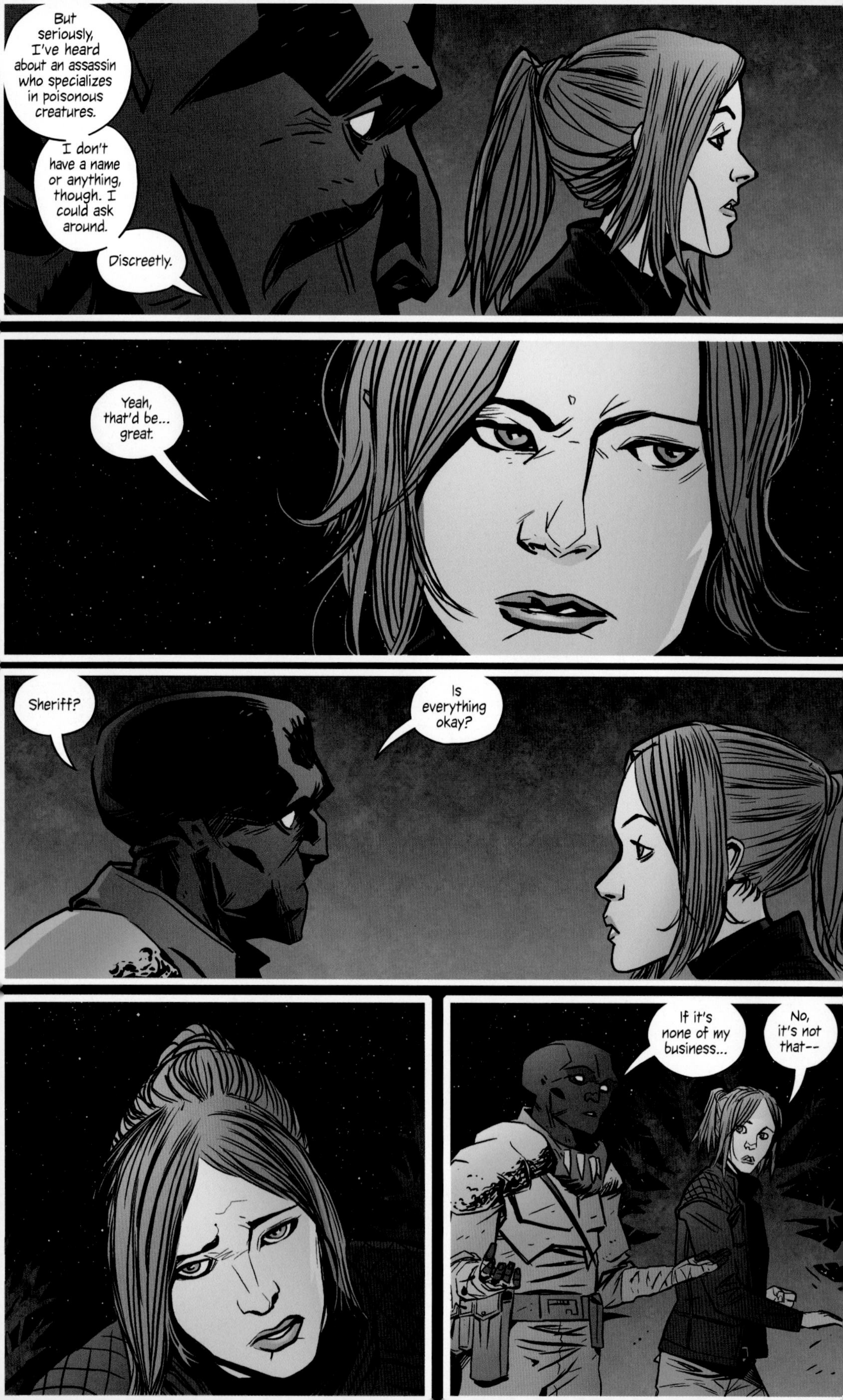
But seriously, I've heard about an assassin who specializes in poisonous creatures.
I don't have a name or anything, though. I could ask around.
Discreetly.
Yeah, that'd be... great.
Sheriff?
Is everything okay?
If it's none of my business...
No, it's not that--

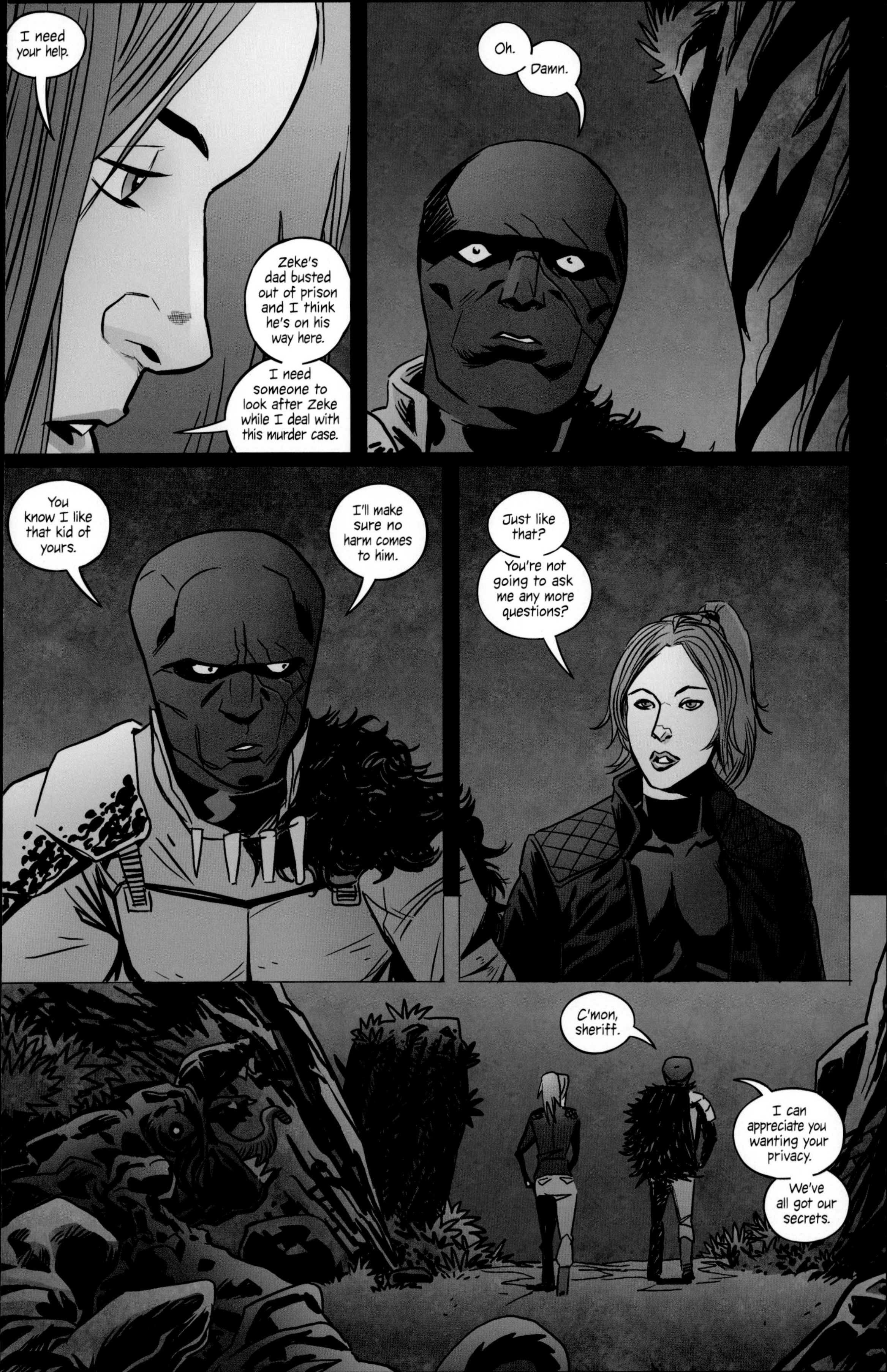
I need your help.
Zeke's dad busted out of prison and I think he's on his way here.
I need someone to look after Zeke while I deal with this murder case.
Oh.
Damn.
You know I like that kid of yours.
I'll make sure no harm comes to him.
Just like that?
You're not going to ask me any more questions?
C'mon, sheriff.
I can appreciate you wanting your privacy.
We've all got our secrets.

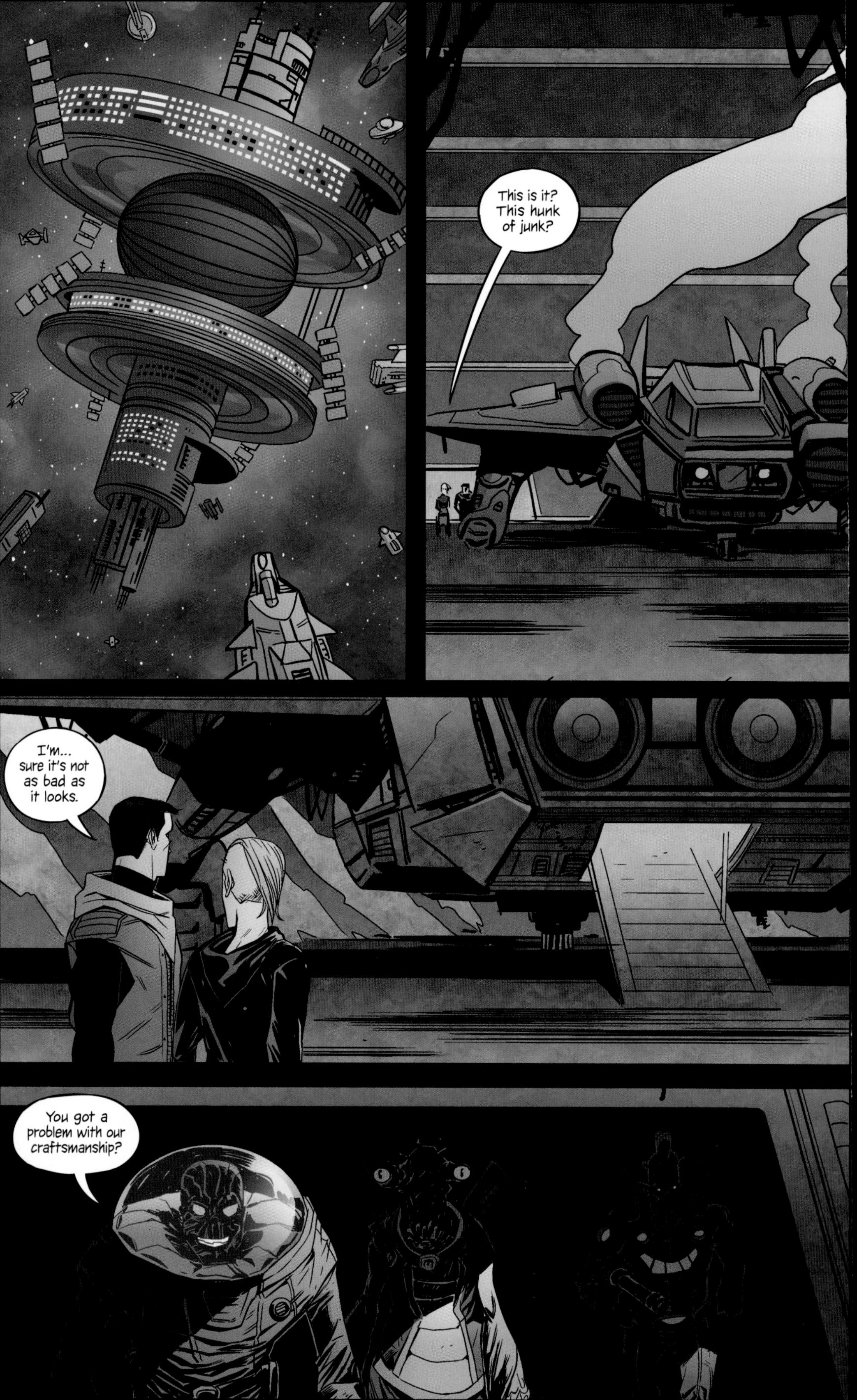
This is it? This hunk of junk?
I'm... sure it's not as bad as it looks.
You got a problem with our craftsmanship?

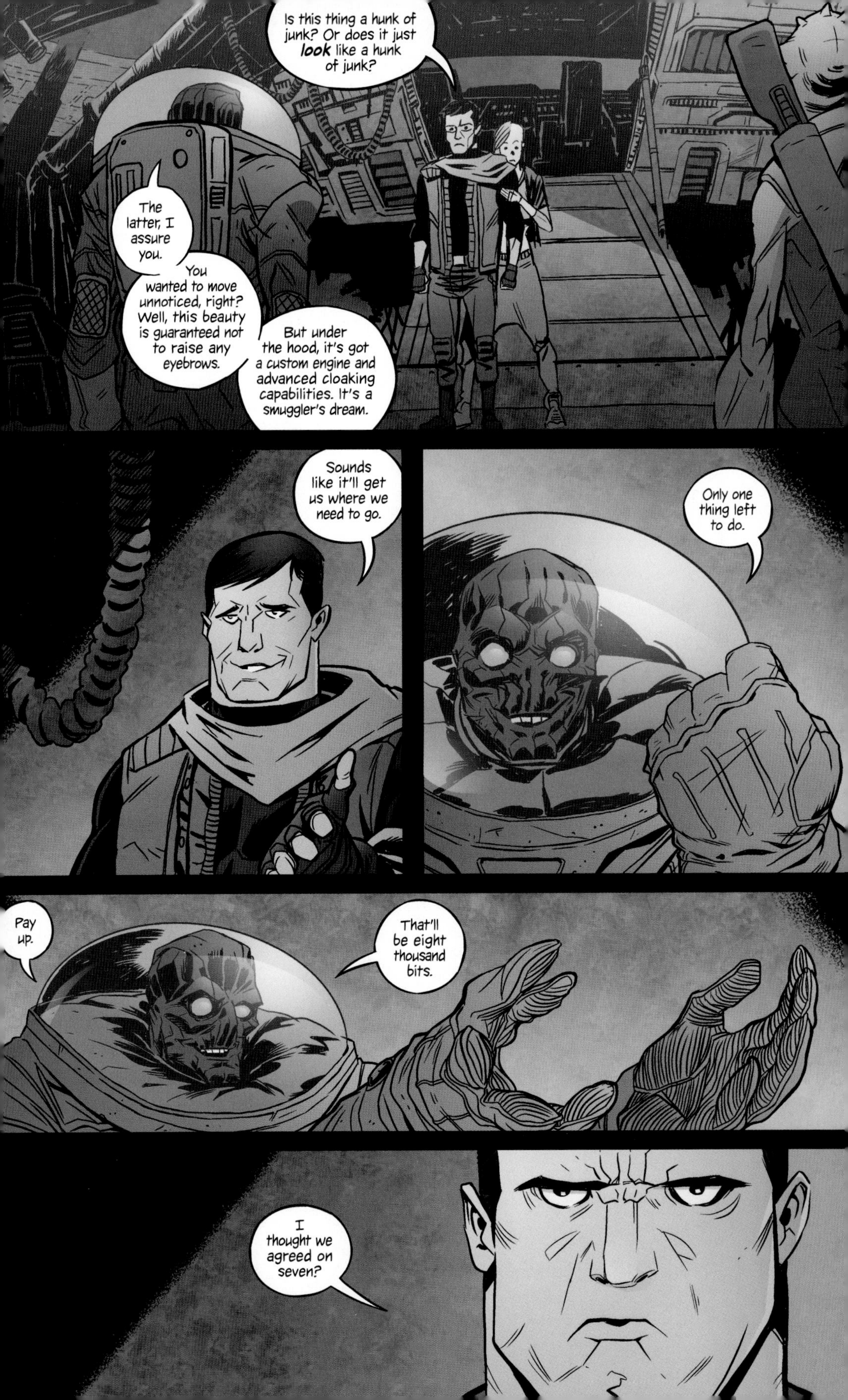
Is this thing a hunk of junk? Or does it just **look** like a hunk of junk?
The latter, I assure you.
You wanted to move unnoticed, right? Well, this beauty is guaranteed not to raise any eyebrows.
But under the hood, it's got a custom engine and advanced cloaking capabilities. It's a smuggler's dream.
Sounds like it'll get us where we need to go.
Only one thing left to do.
Pay up.
That'll be eight thousand bits.
I thought we agreed on seven?

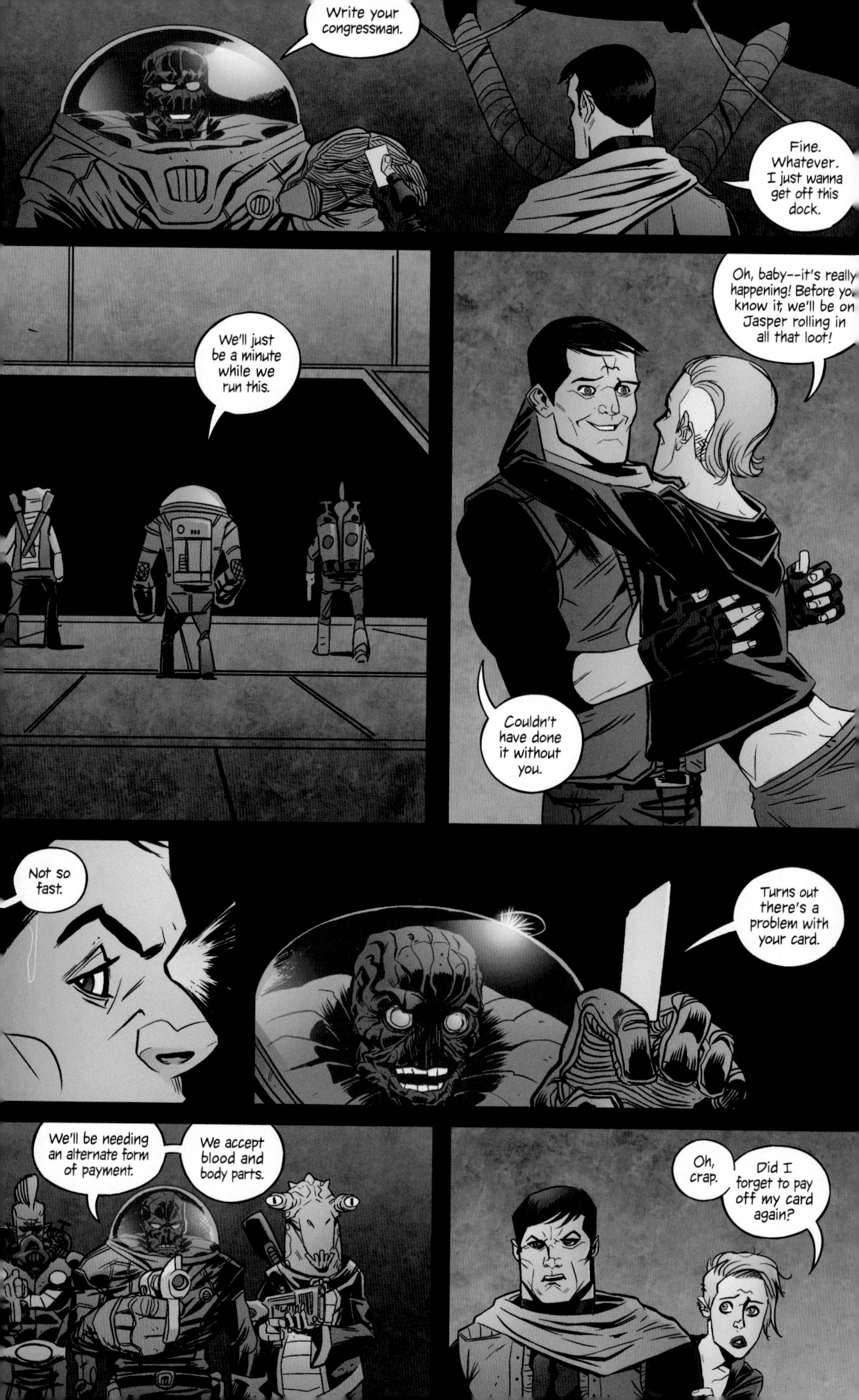
Write your congressman.
Fine. Whatever. I just wanna get off this dock.
We'll just be a minute while we run this.
Oh, baby--it's really happening! Before you know it, we'll be on Jasper rolling in all that loot!
Couldn't have done it without you.
Not so fast.
Turns out there's a problem with your card.
We'll be needing an alternate form of payment.
We accept blood and body parts.
Oh, crap.
Did I forget to pay off my card again?

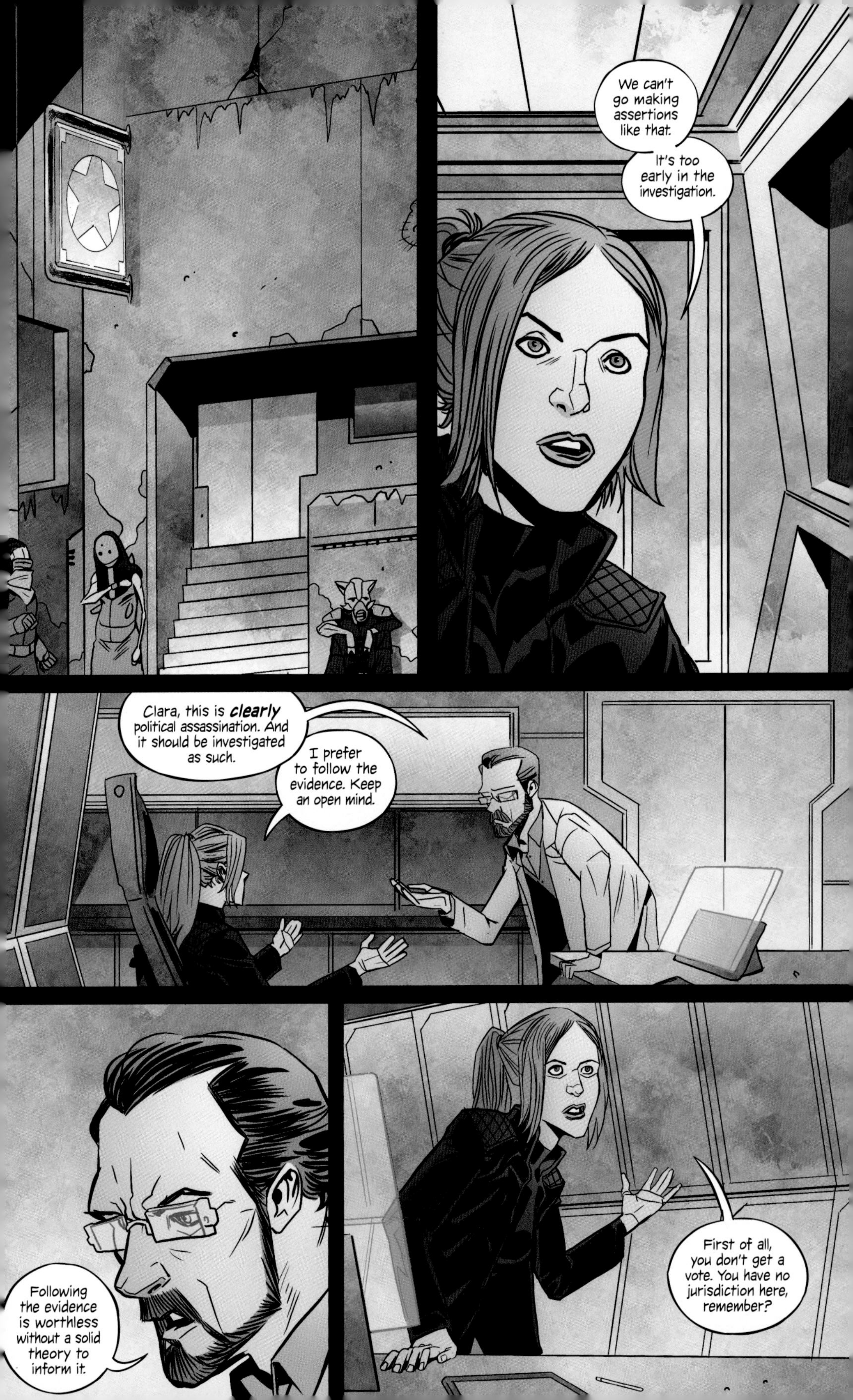
We can't go making assertions like that.
It's too early in the investigation.
Clara, this is *clearly* political assassination. And it should be investigated as such.
I prefer to follow the evidence. Keep an open mind.
Following the evidence is worthless without a solid theory to inform it.
First of all, you don't get a vote. You have no jurisdiction here, remember?

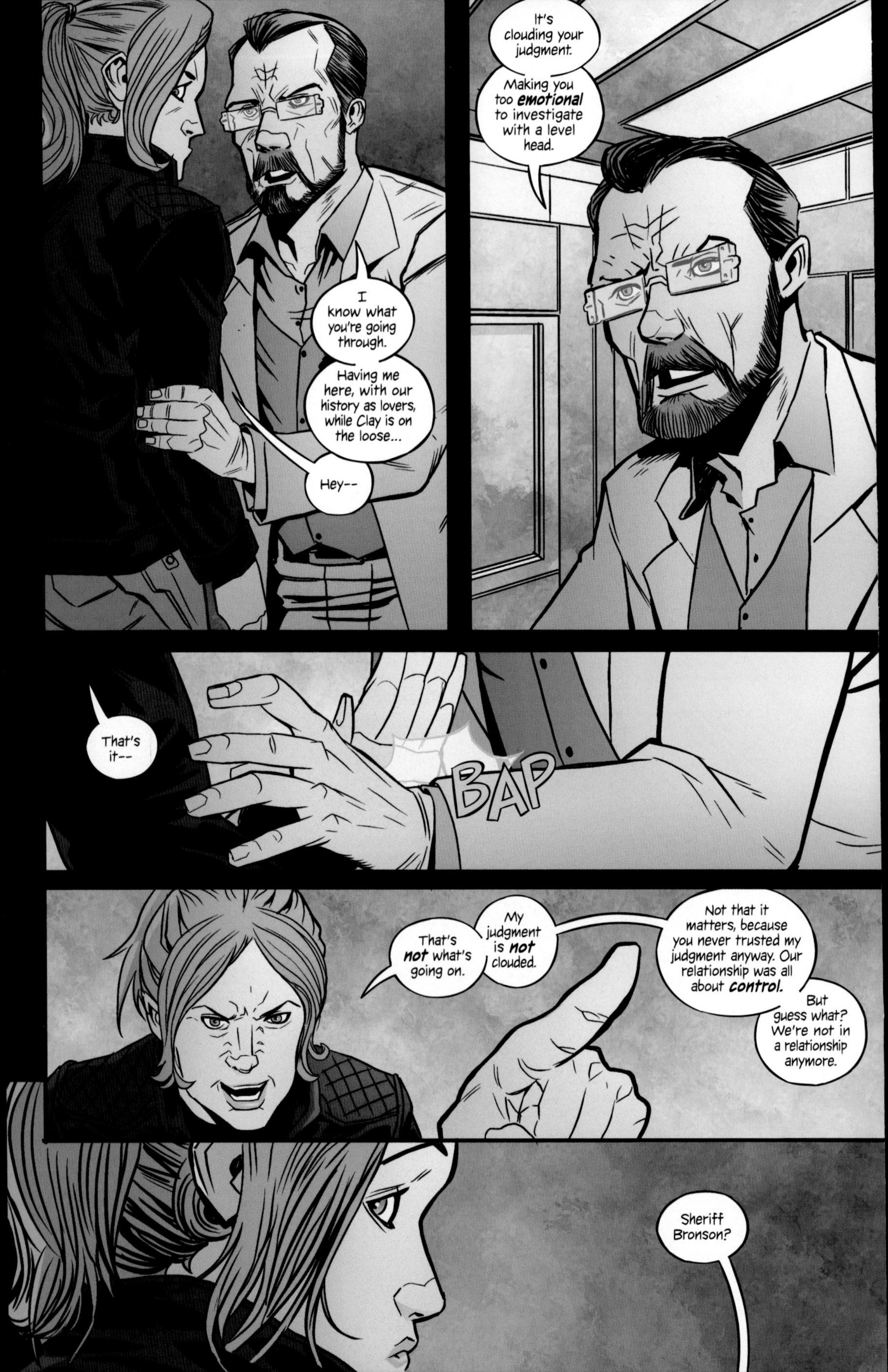
I know what you're going through.
Having me here, with our history as lovers, while Clay is on the loose...
Hey--
It's clouding your judgment.
Making you too **emotional** to investigate with a level head.
That's it--
BAP
That's **not** what's going on.
My judgment is **not** clouded.
Not that it matters, because you never trusted my judgment anyway. Our relationship was all about **control.**
But guess what? We're not in a relationship anymore.
Sheriff Bronson?

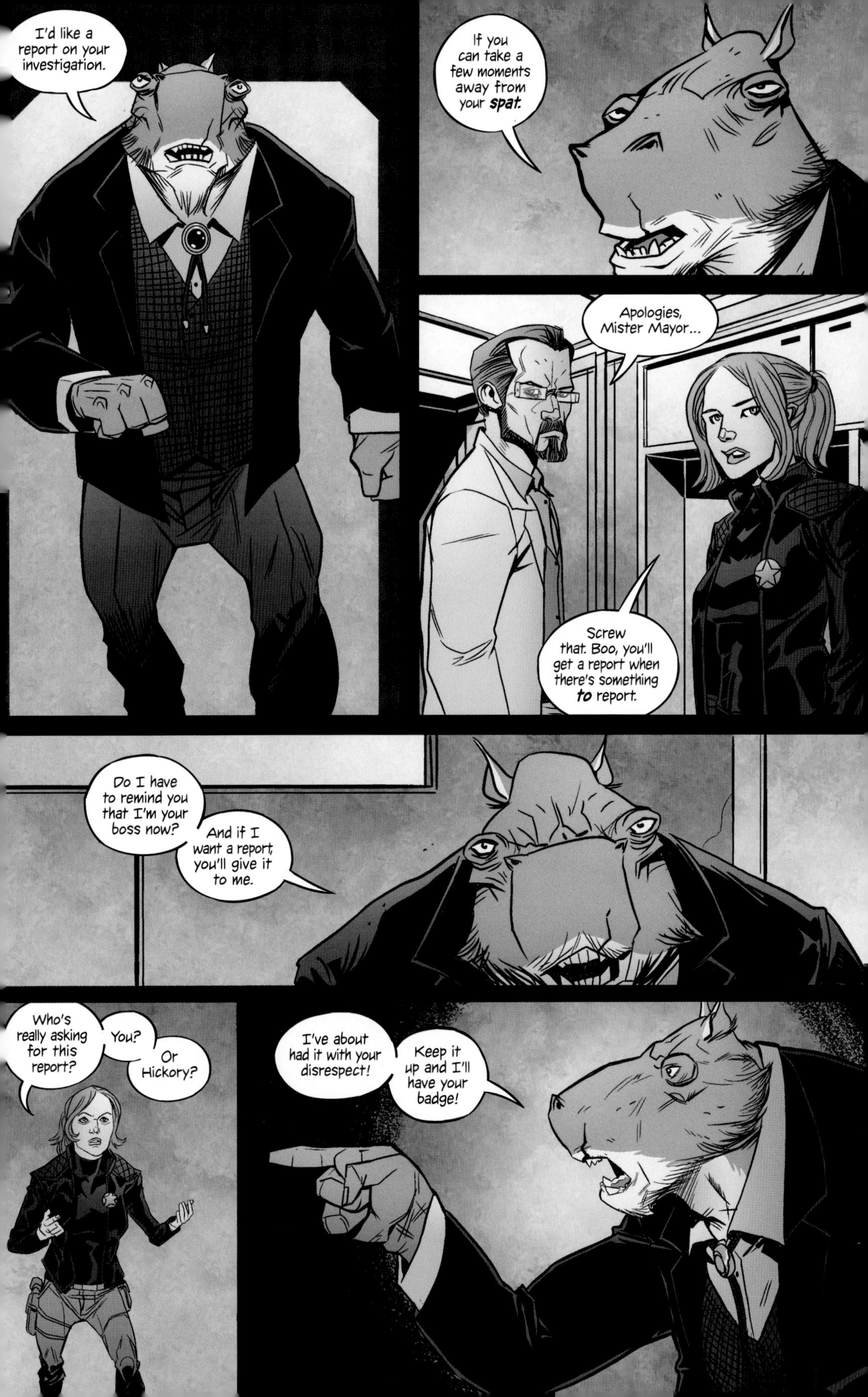
I'd like a report on your investigation.
If you can take a few moments away from your **spat.**
Apologies, Mister Mayor...
Screw that. Boo, you'll get a report when there's something ***to*** report.
Do I have to remind you that I'm your boss now?
And if I want a report, you'll give it to me.
Who's really asking for this report?
You?
Or Hickory?
I've about had it with your disrespect!
Keep it up and I'll have your badge!

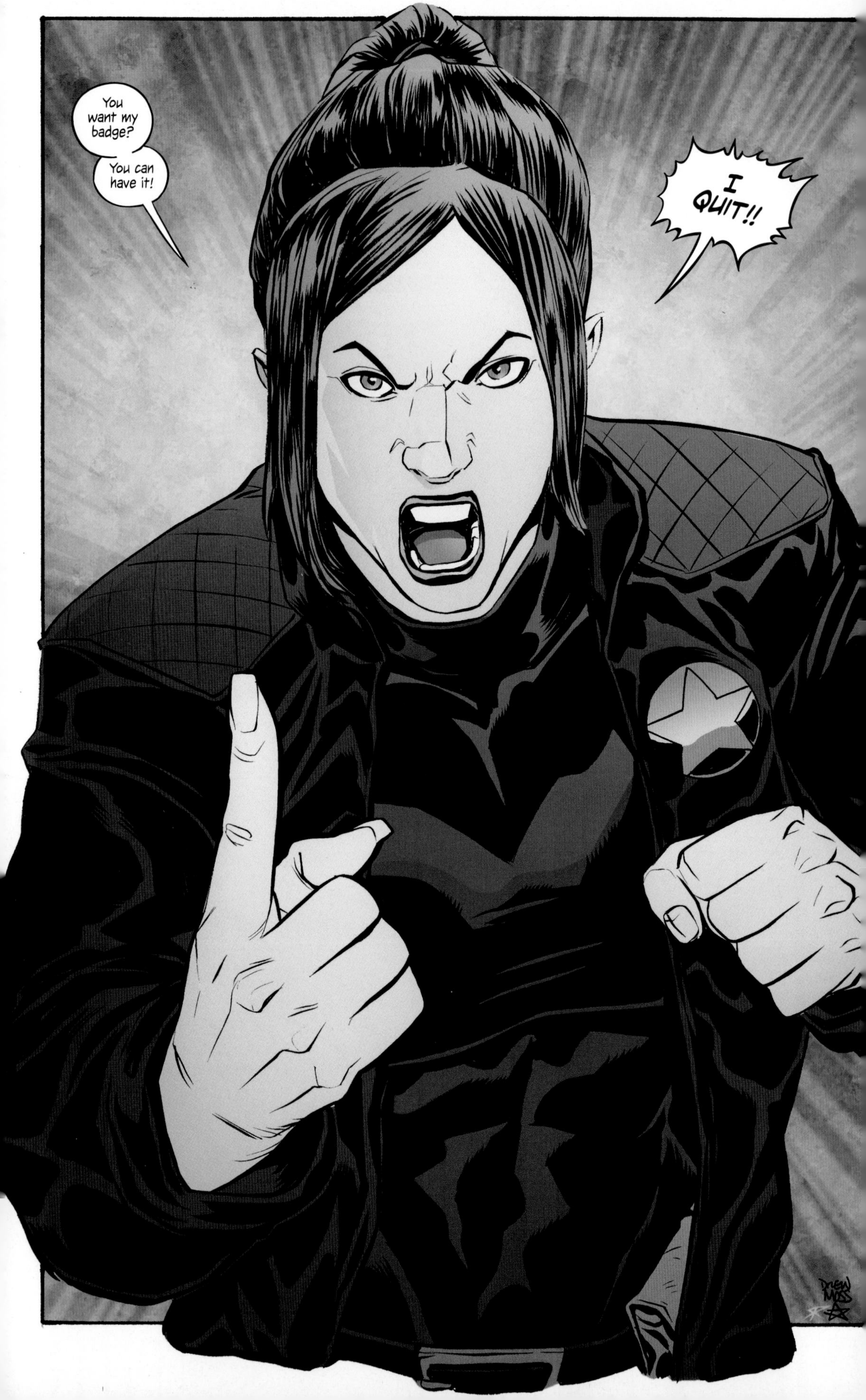
You want my badge?
You can have it!
I QUIT!!
DREW MOSS

CHAPTER III

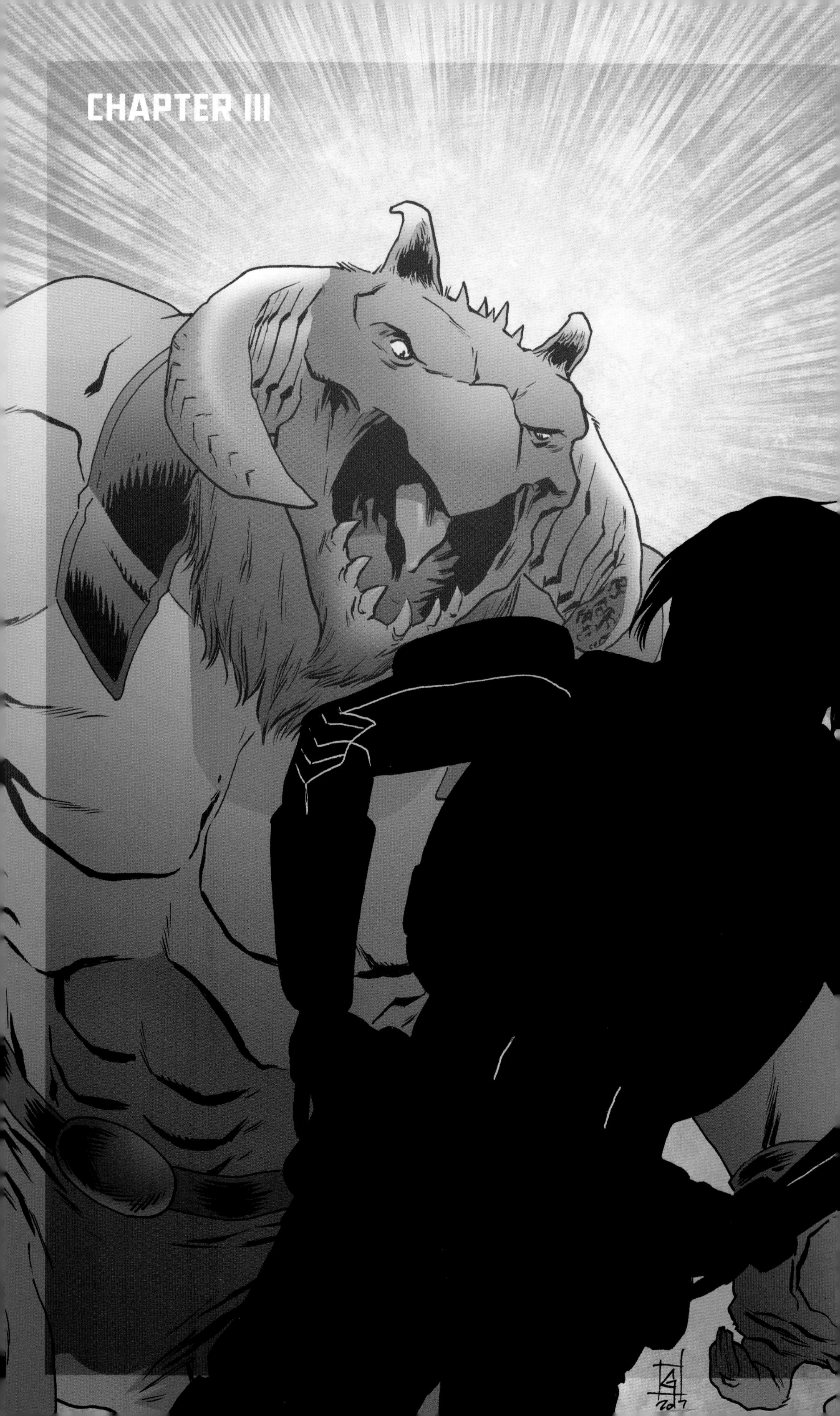

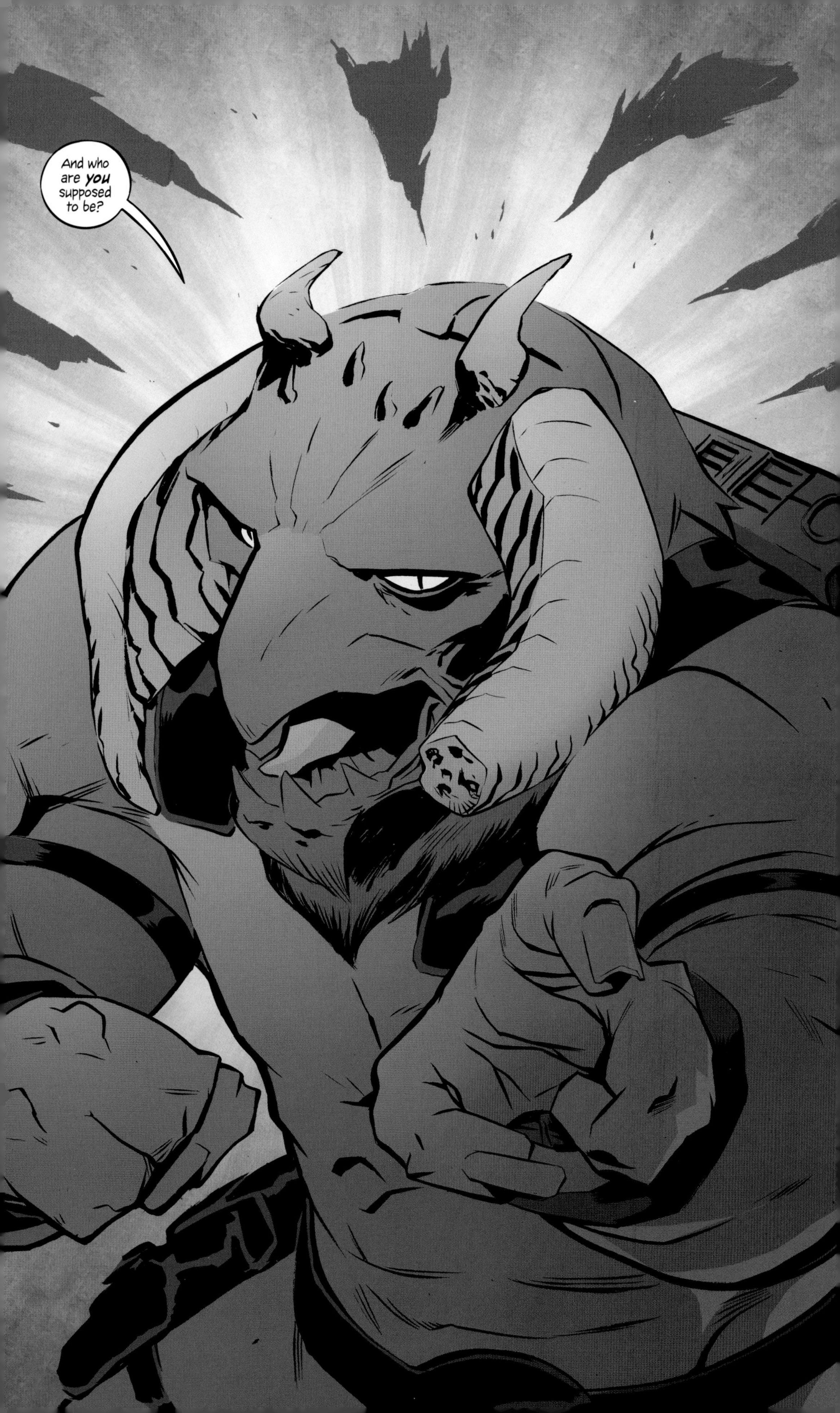
And who are ***YOU*** supposed to be?

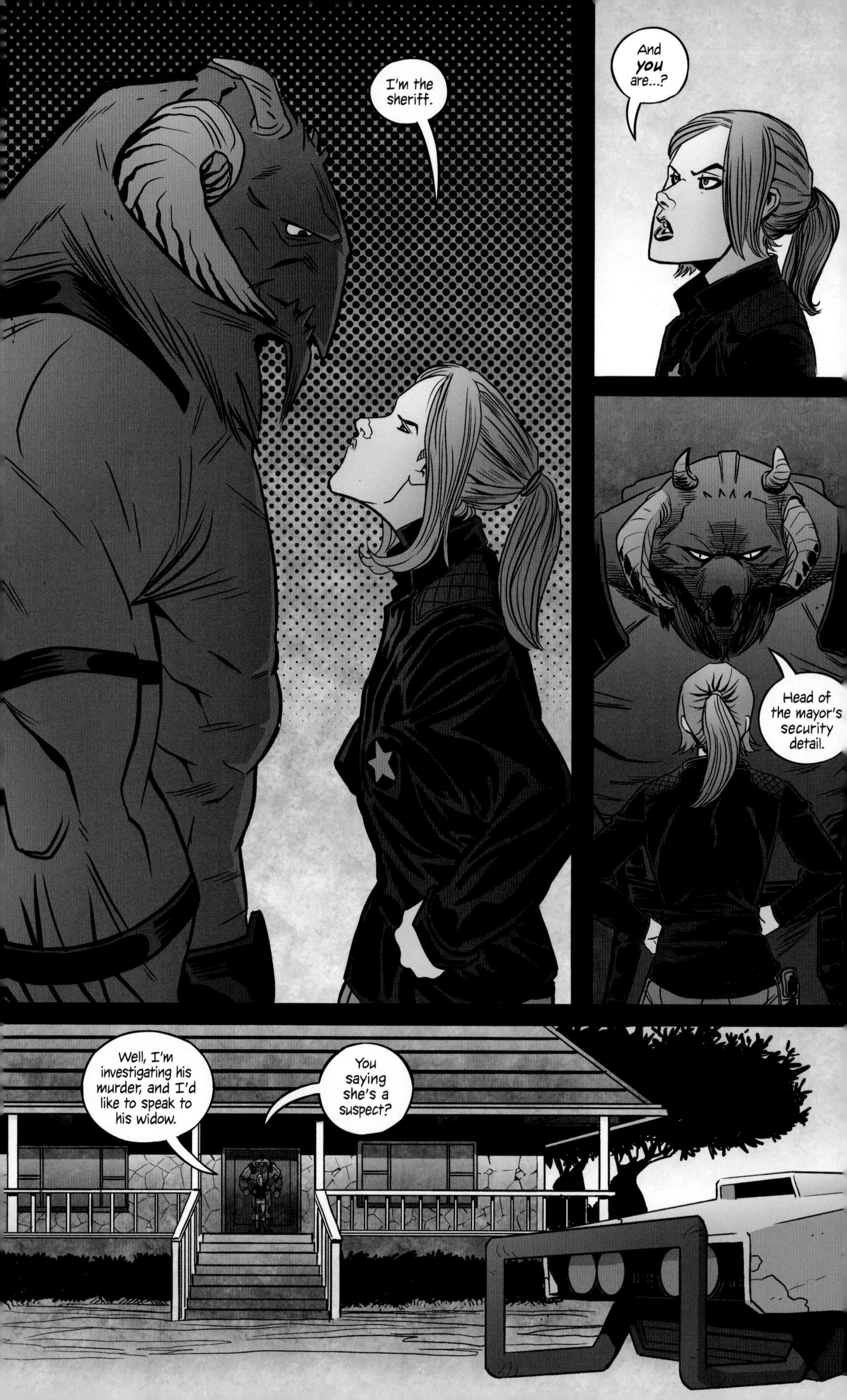
I'm the sheriff.
And you are...?
Head of the mayor's security detail.
Well, I'm investigating his murder, and I'd like to speak to his widow.
You saying she's a suspect?

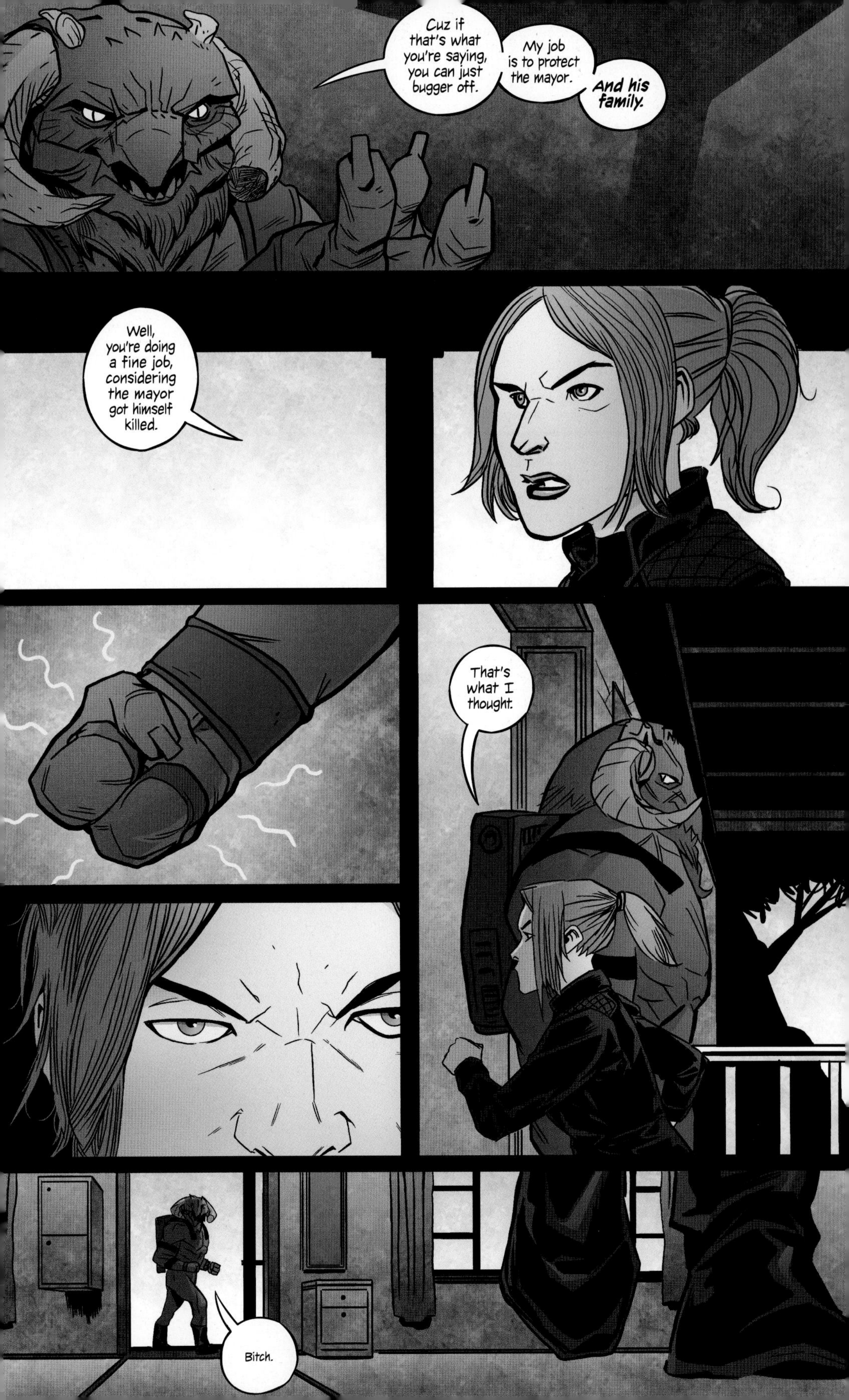
Cuz if that's what you're saying, you can just bugger off.
My job is to protect the mayor.
And his family.
Well, you're doing a fine job, considering the mayor got himself killed.
That's what I thought.
Bitch.

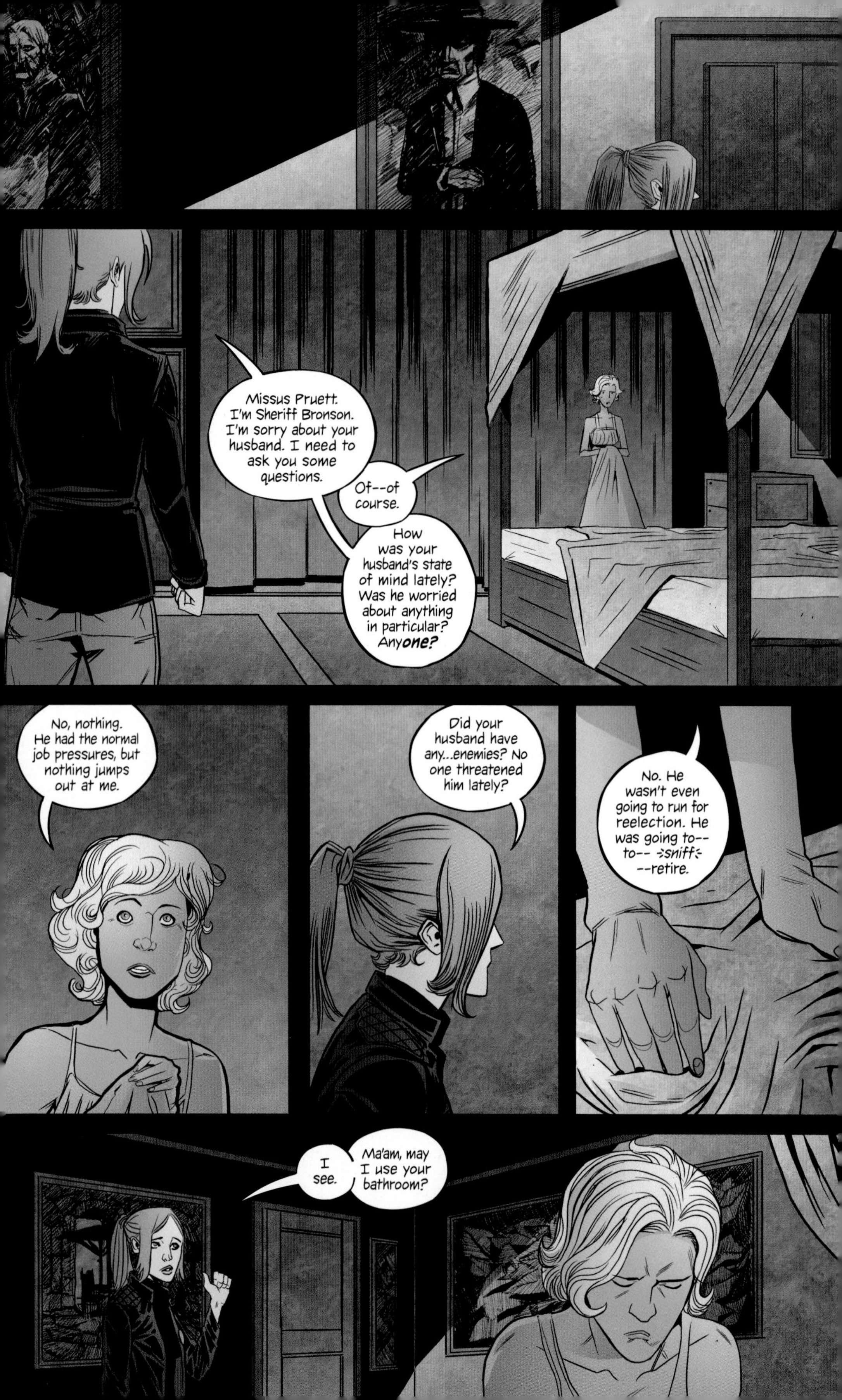
Missus Pruett. I'm Sheriff Bronson. I'm sorry about your husband. I need to ask you some questions.
Of--of course.
How was your husband's state of mind lately? Was he worried about anything in particular? Any**one?**
No, nothing. He had the normal job pressures, but nothing jumps out at me.
Did your husband have any...enemies? No one threatened him lately?
No. He wasn't even going to run for reelection. He was going to--to-- sniff --retire.
I see.
Ma'am, may I use your bathroom?

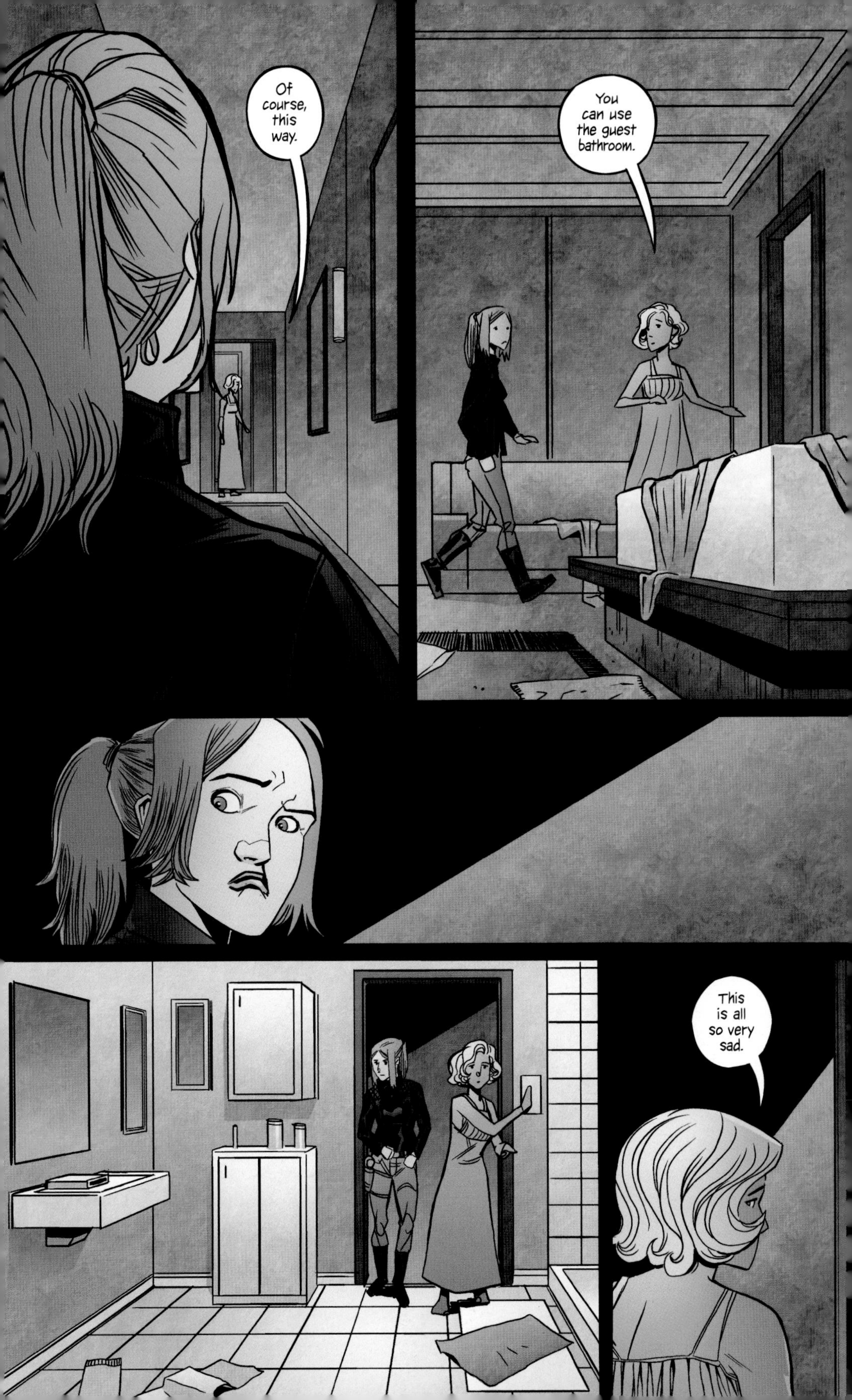
Of course, this way.
You can use the guest bathroom.
This is all so very sad.

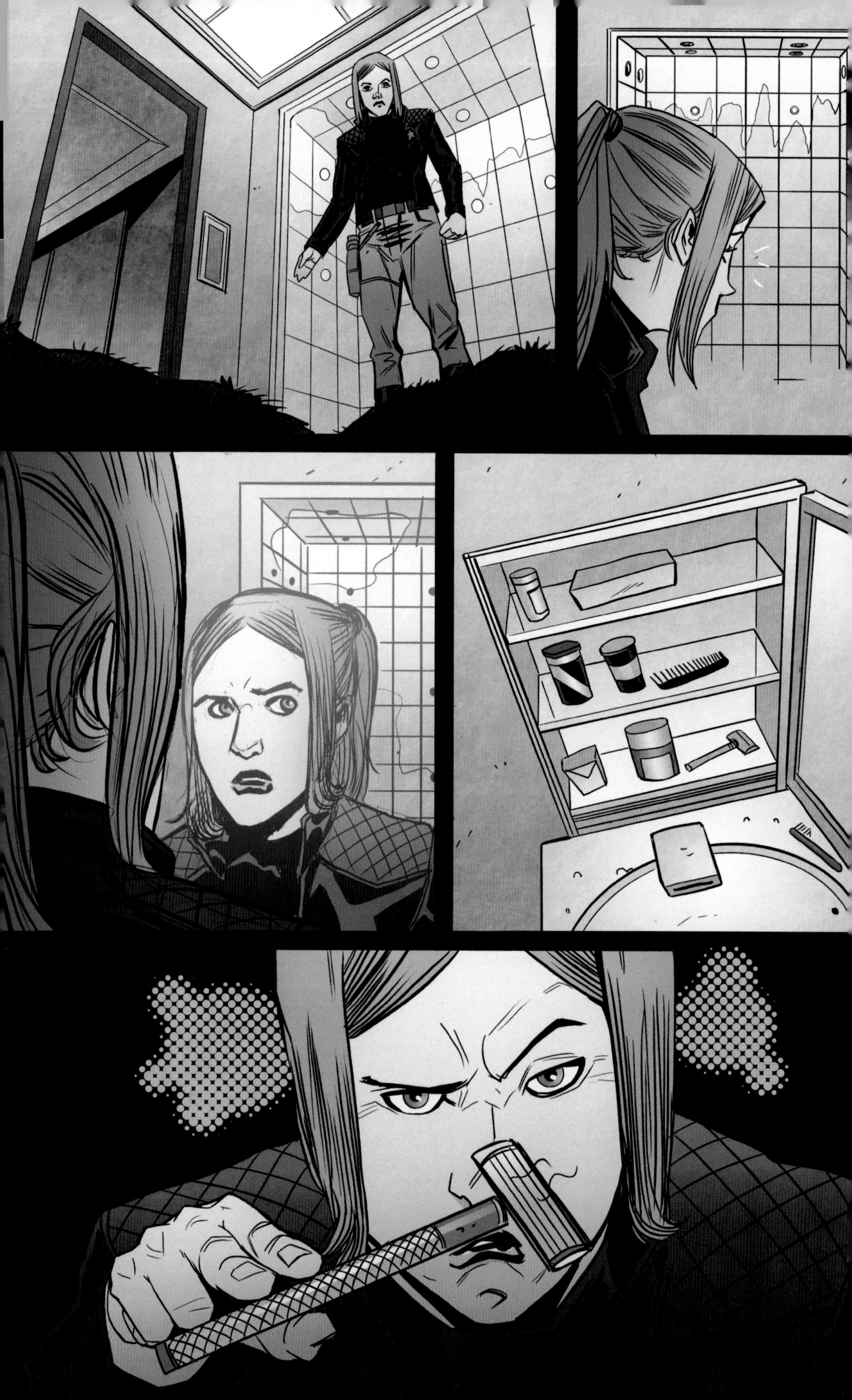

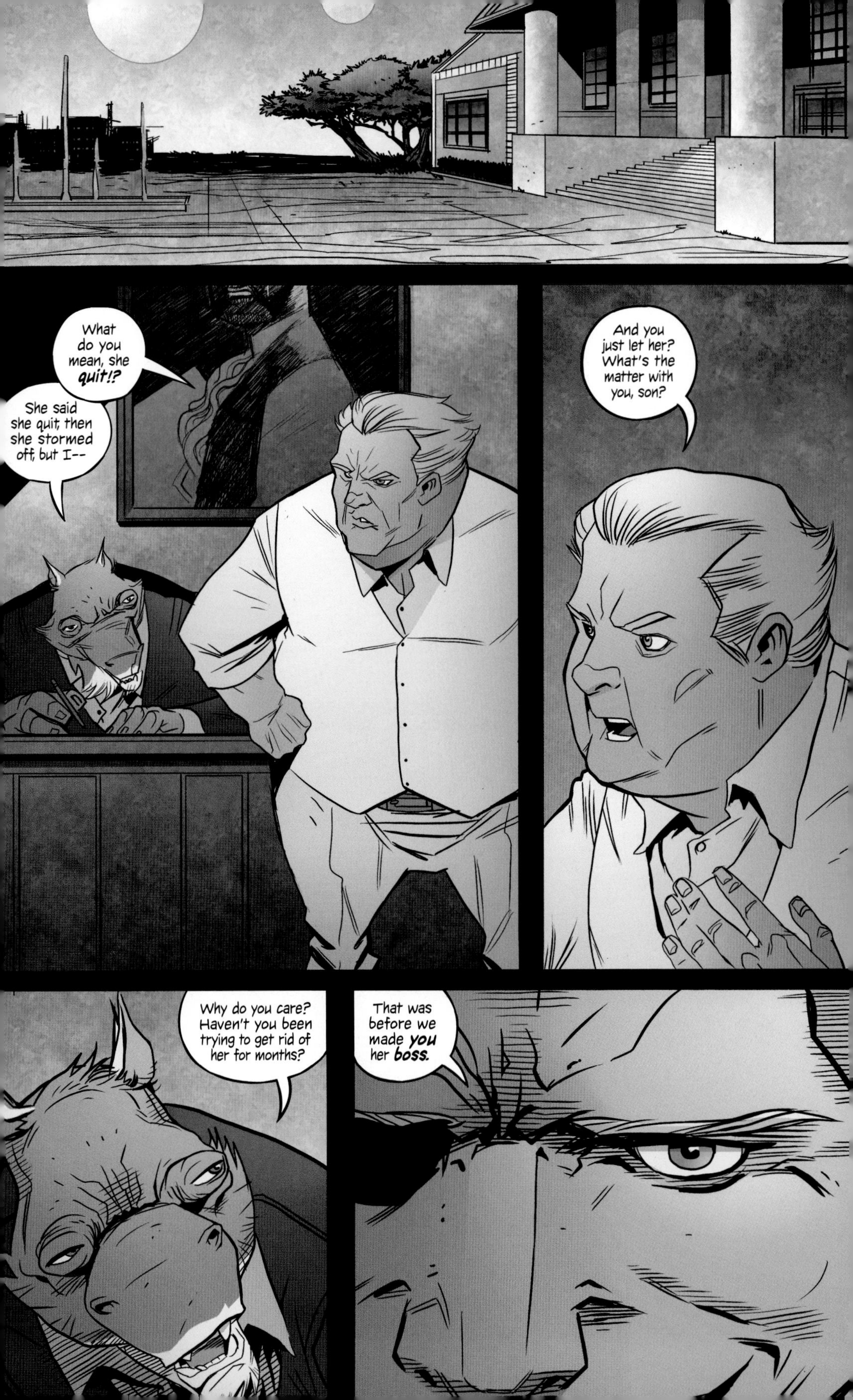
What do you mean, she **quit!?**
She said she quit, then she stormed off, but I--
And you just let her? What's the matter with you, son?
Why do you care? Haven't you been trying to get rid of her for months?
That was before we made ***you*** her ***boss.***

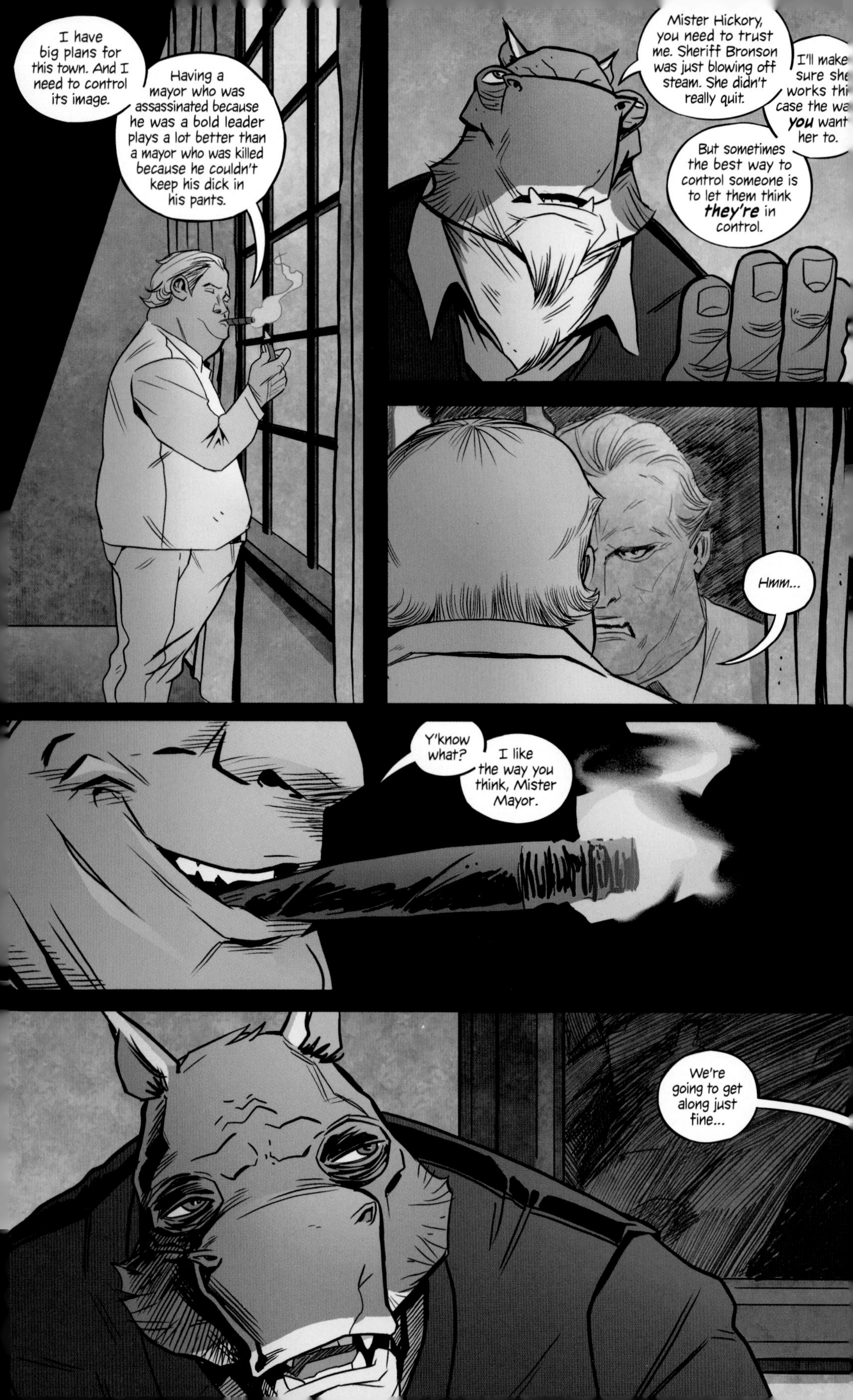

I have big plans for this town. And I need to control its image.
Having a mayor who was assassinated because he was a bold leader plays a lot better than a mayor who was killed because he couldn't keep his dick in his pants.
Mister Hickory, you need to trust me. Sheriff Bronson was just blowing off steam. She didn't really quit.
But sometimes the best way to control someone is to let them think **they're** in control.
Hmm...
Y'know what?
I like the way you think, Mister Mayor.
We're going to get along just fine...

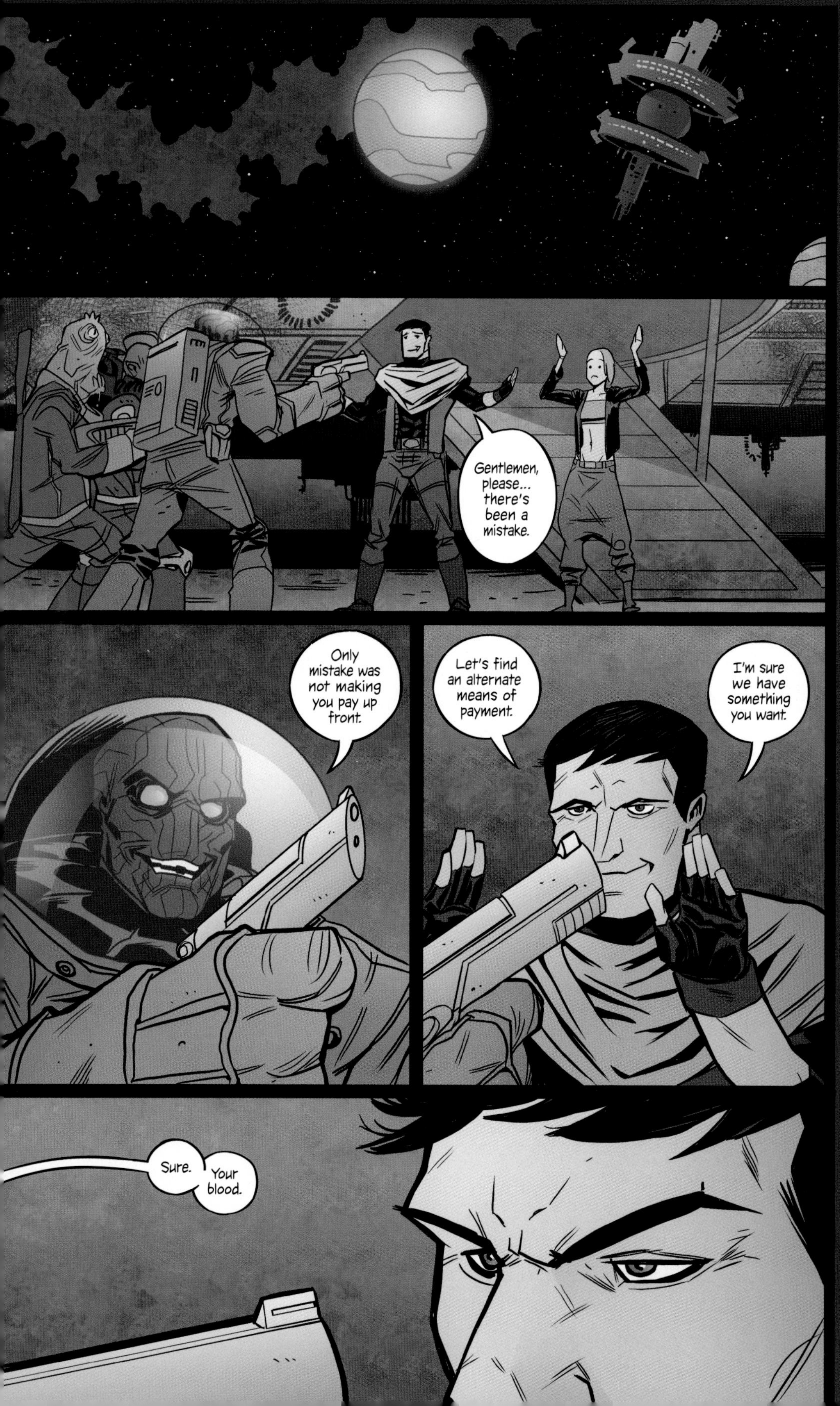
Gentlemen, please... there's been a mistake.
Only mistake was not making you pay up front.
Let's find an alternate means of payment.
I'm sure we have something you want.
Sure.
Your blood.

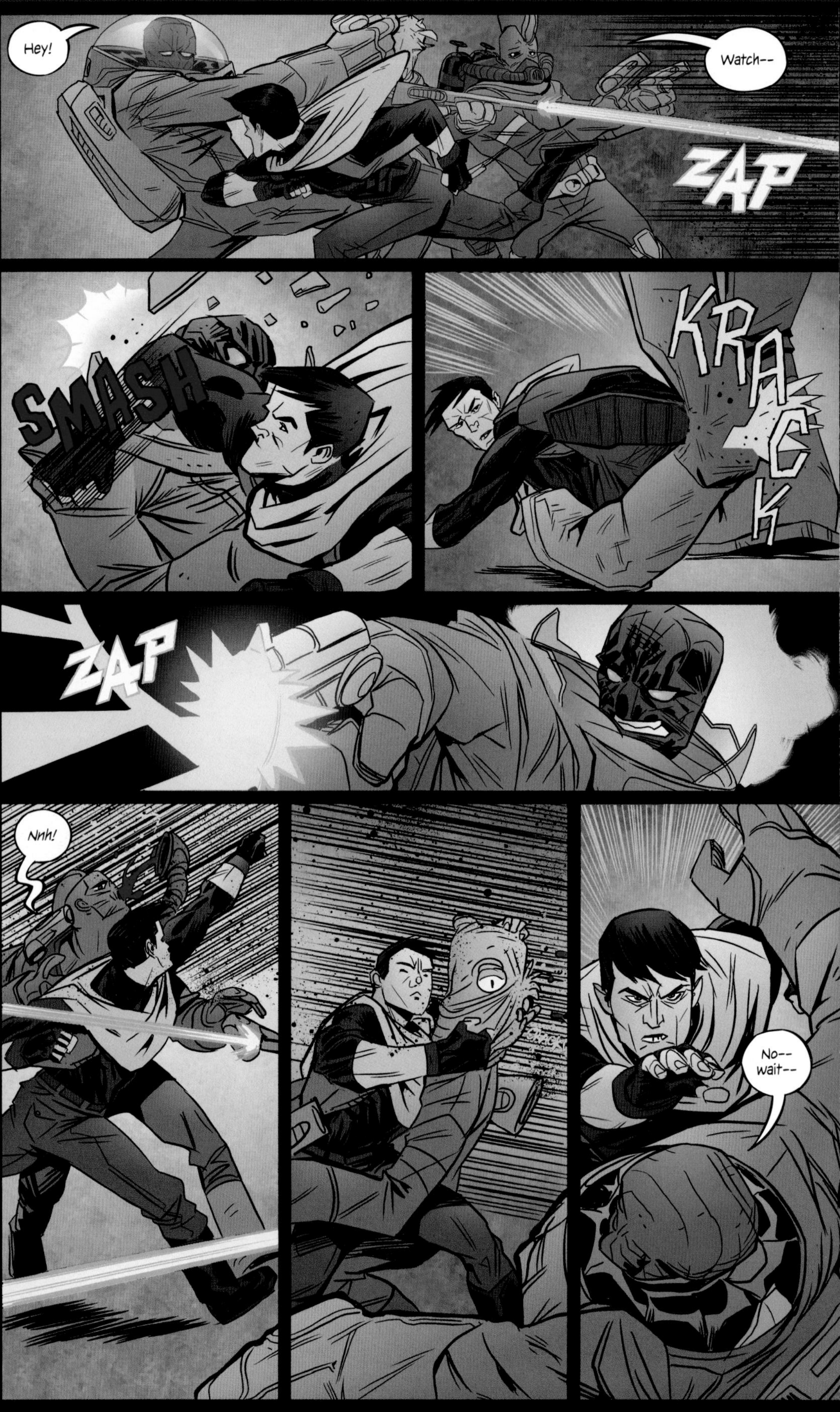

Hey!
Watch--
ZAP
SMASH
KRACK
ZAP
Nnh!
CRACK
No--
wait--

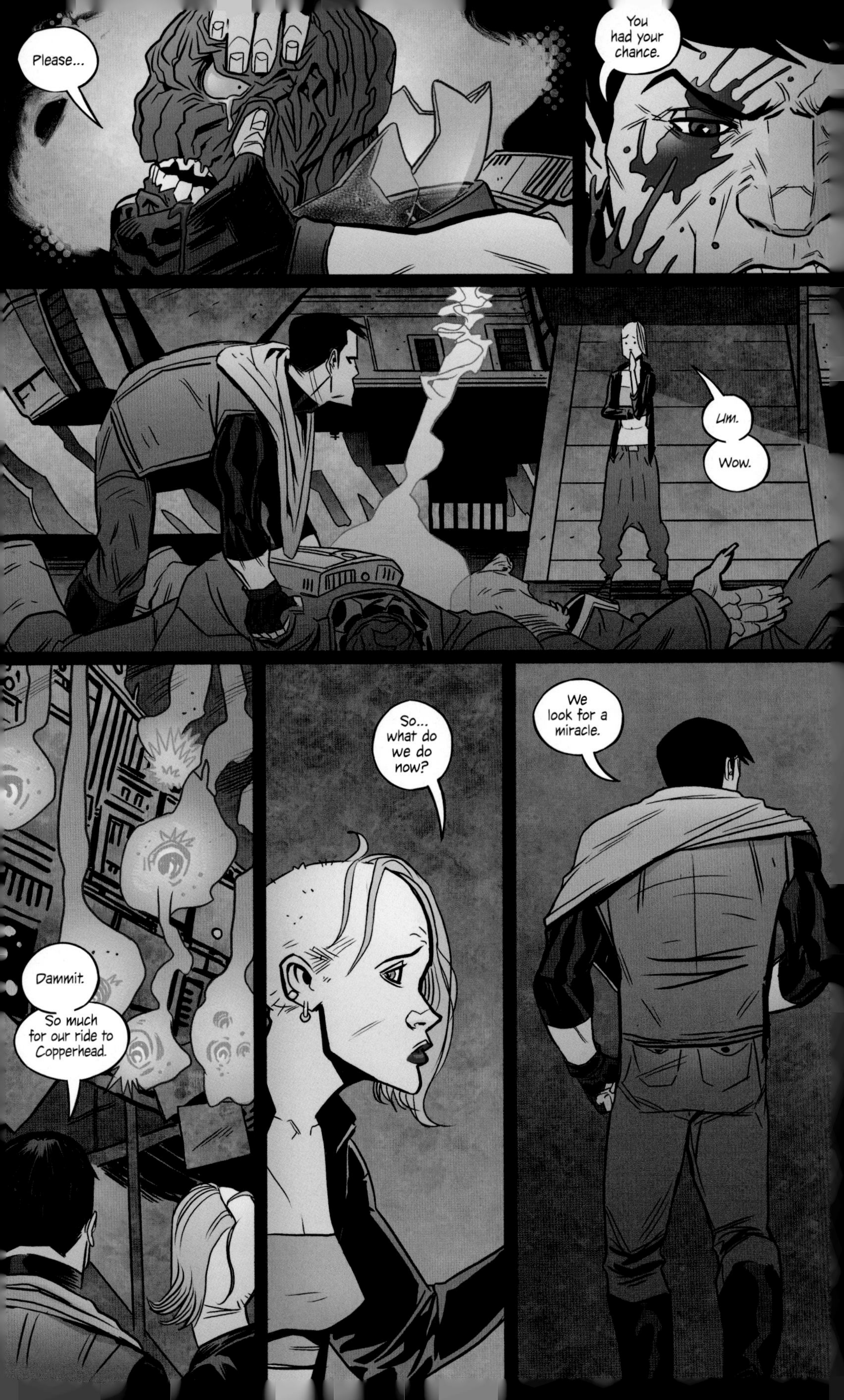
Please...
You had your chance.
Um.
Wow.
Dammit.
So much for our ride to Copperhead.
So... what do we do now?
We look for a miracle.

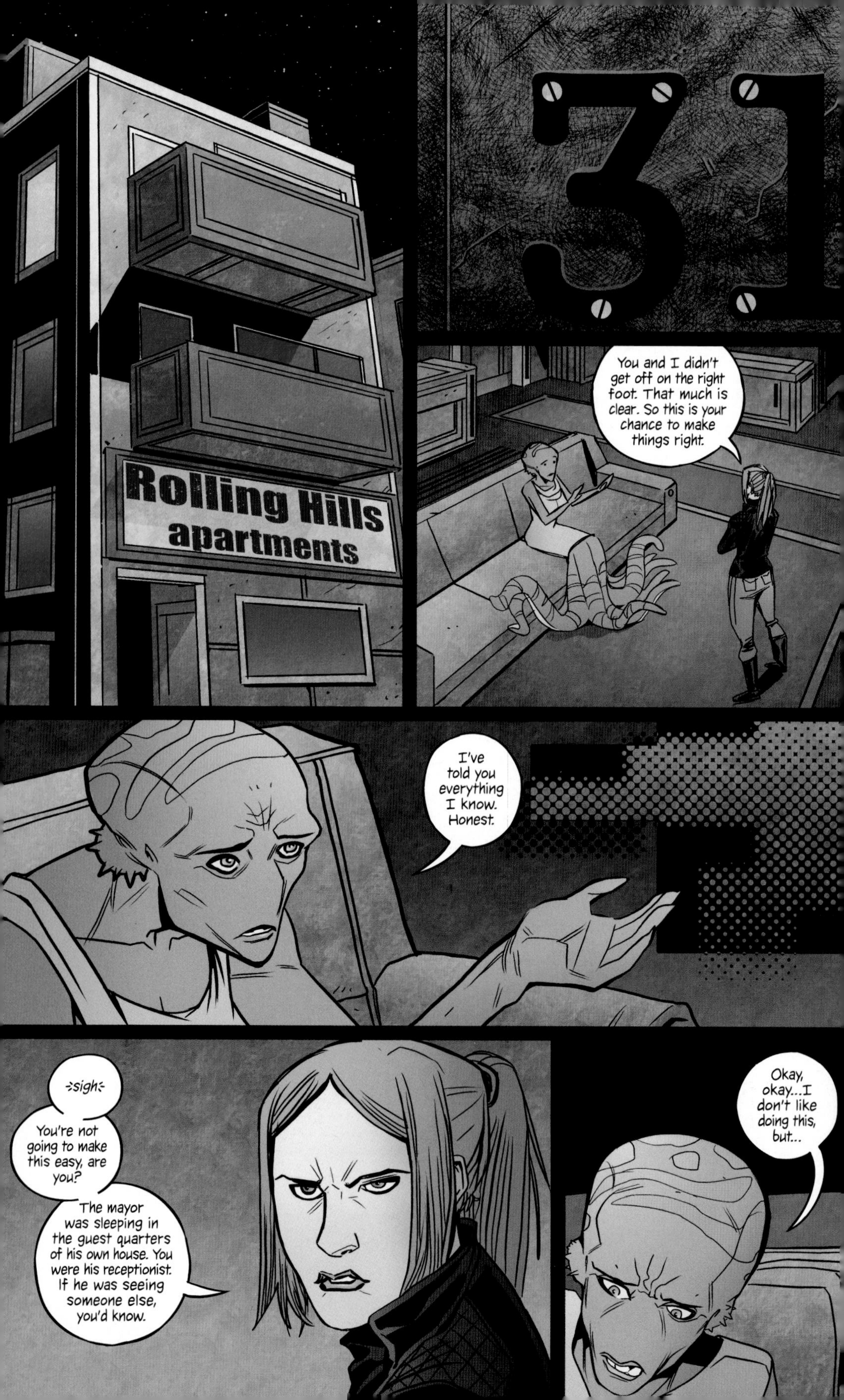
Rolling Hills apartments
31
You and I didn't get off on the right foot. That much is clear. So this is your chance to make things right.
I've told you everything I know. Honest.
-sigh-
You're not going to make this easy, are you?
The mayor was sleeping in the guest quarters of his own house. You were his receptionist. If he was seeing someone else, you'd know.
Okay, okay...I don't like doing this, but...

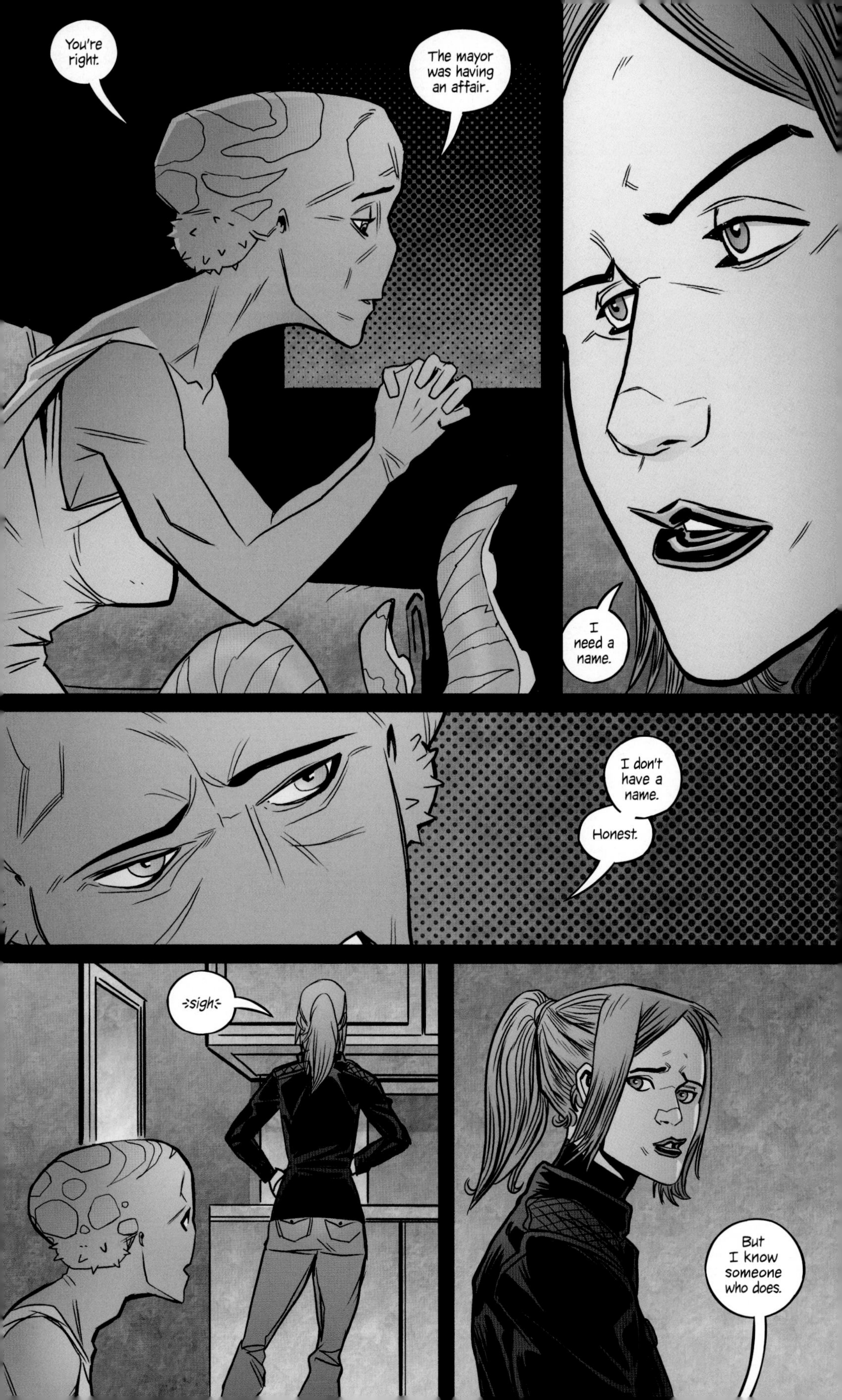

You're right.
The mayor was having an affair.
I need a name.
I don't have a name.
Honest.
sigh
But I know someone who does.

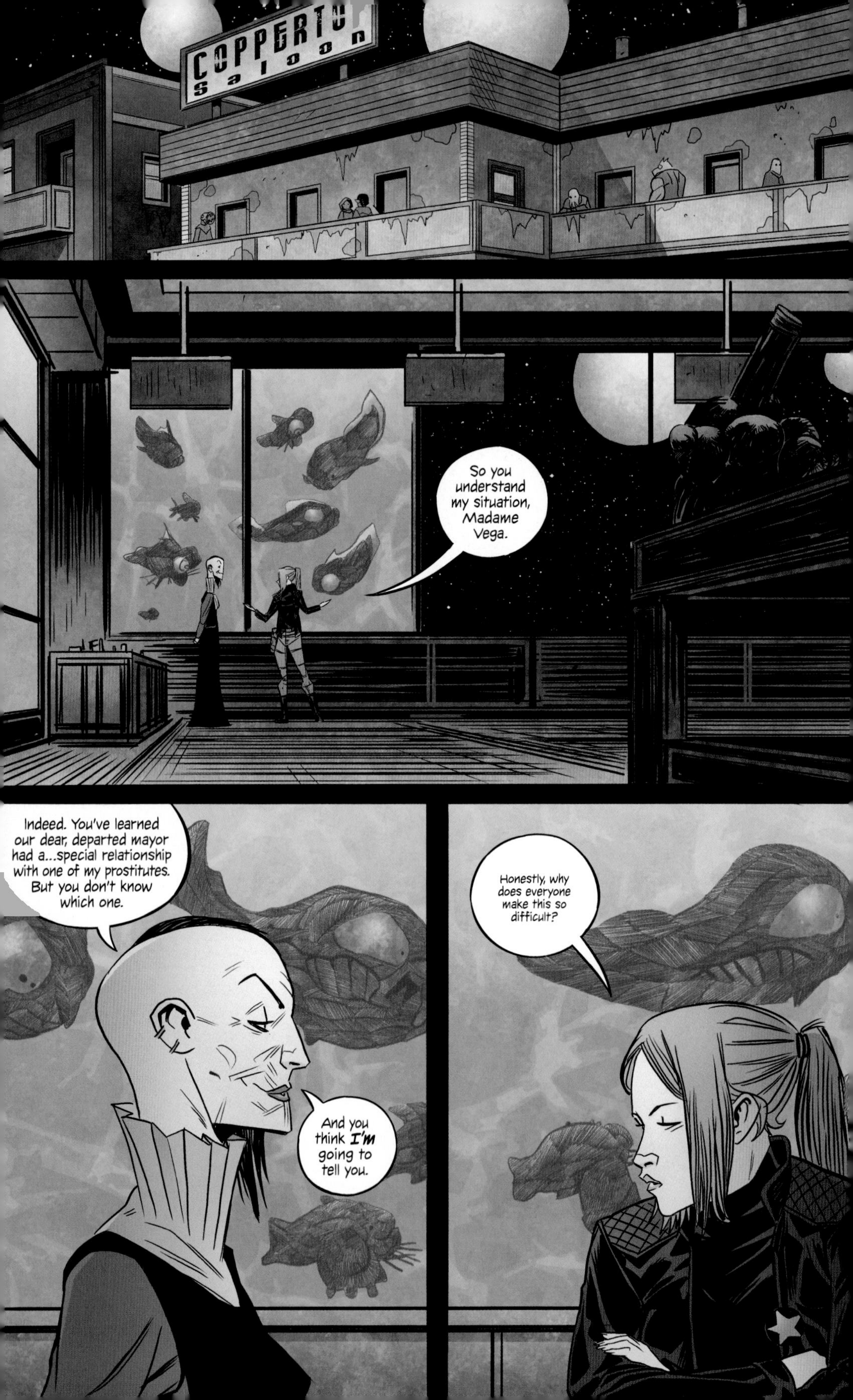
COPPERTO
Saloon
So you understand my situation, Madame Vega.
Indeed. You've learned our dear, departed mayor had a...special relationship with one of my prostitutes. But you don't know which one.
And you think *I'm* going to tell you.
Honestly, why does everyone make this so difficult?

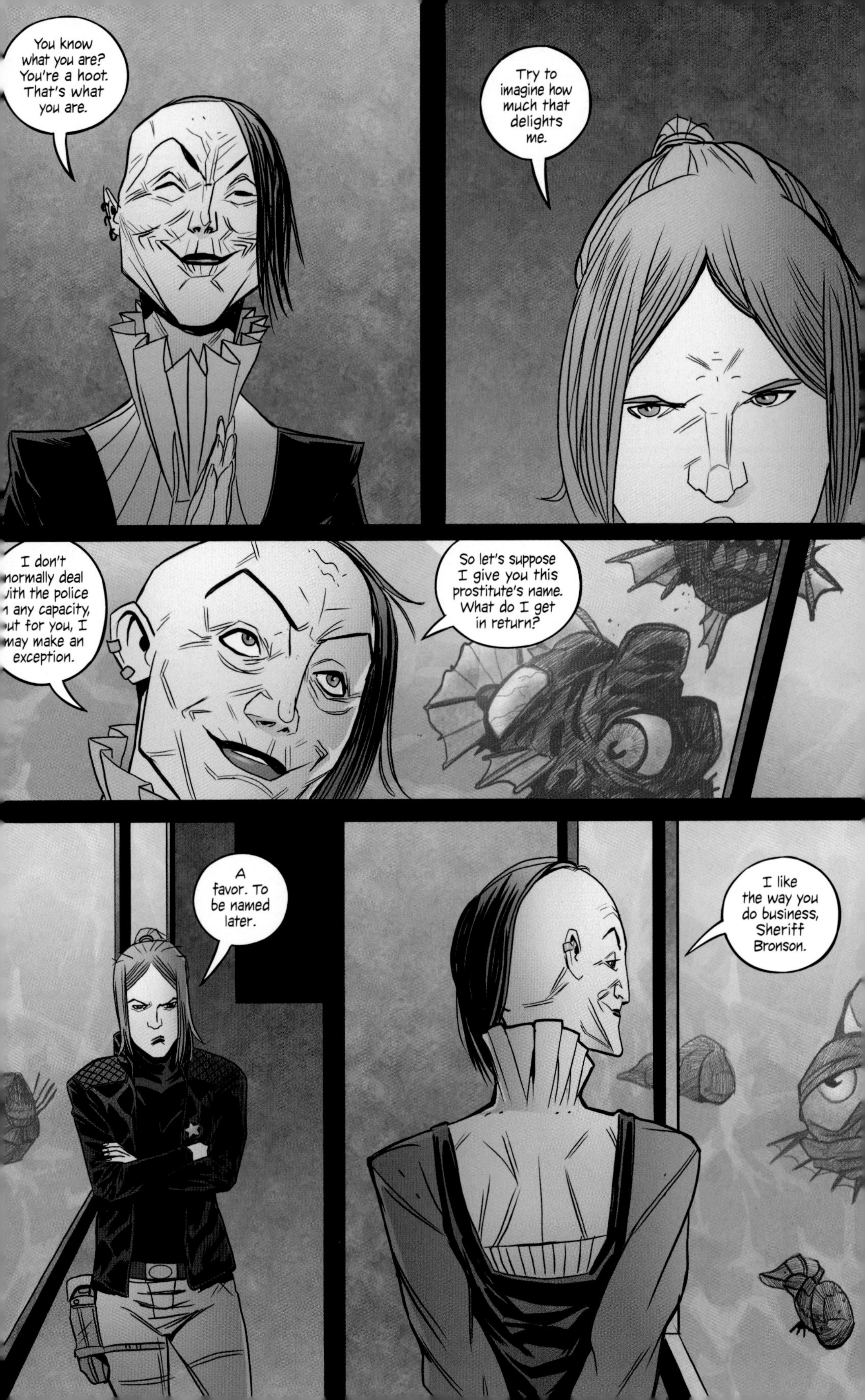
You know what you are? You're a hoot. That's what you are.
Try to imagine how much that delights me.
I don't normally deal with the police in any capacity, but for you, I may make an exception.
So let's suppose I give you this prostitute's name. What do I get in return?
A favor. To be named later.
I like the way you do business, Sheriff Bronson.

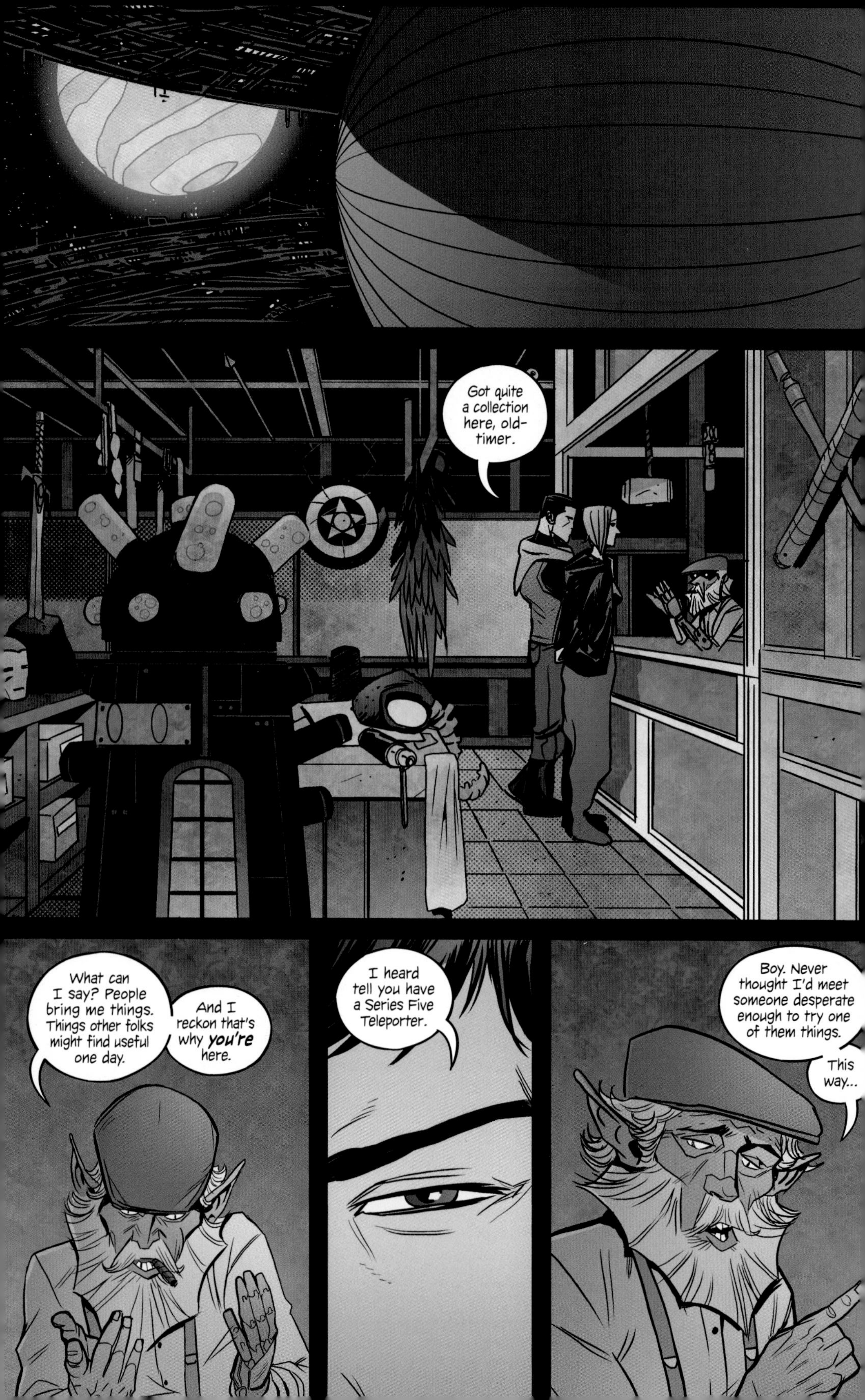
Got quite a collection here, old-timer.
What can I say? People bring me things. Things other folks might find useful one day.
And I reckon that's why *you're* here.
I heard tell you have a Series Five Teleporter.
Boy. Never thought I'd meet someone desperate enough to try one of them things.
This way...

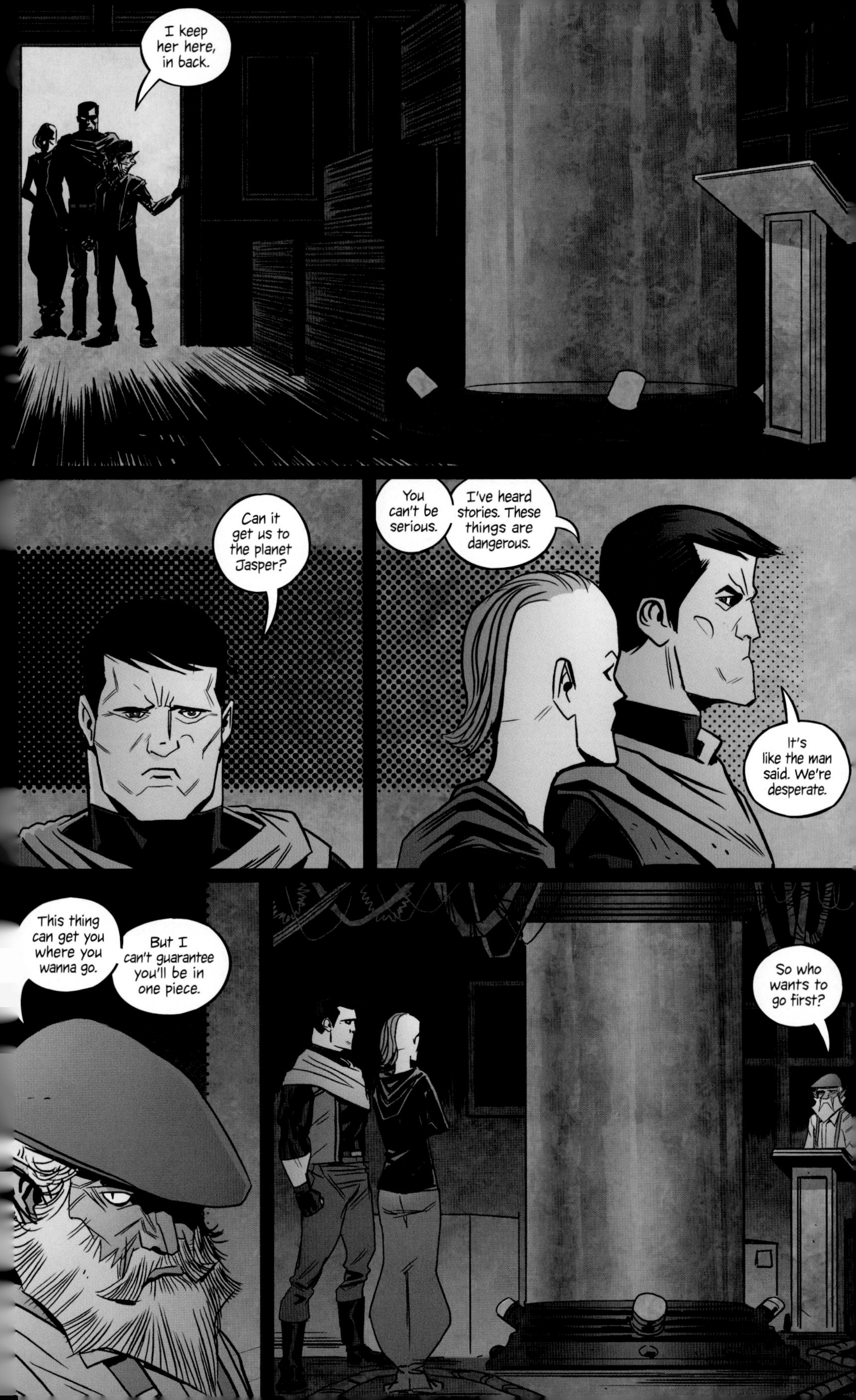
I keep her here, in back.
Can it get us to the planet Jasper?
You can't be serious.
I've heard stories. These things are dangerous.
It's like the man said. We're desperate.
This thing can get you where you wanna go.
But I can't guarantee you'll be in one piece.
So who wants to go first?

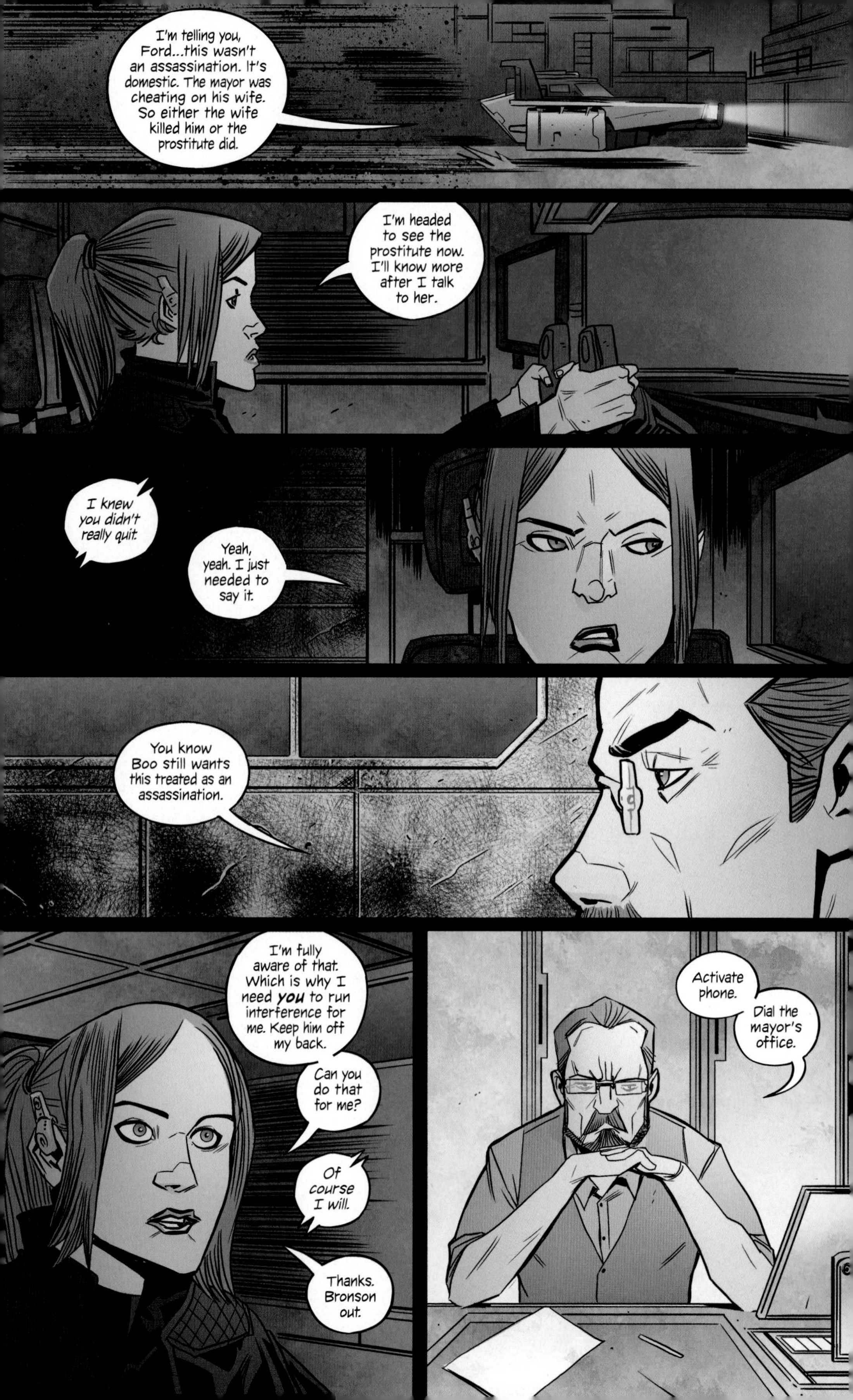
I'm telling you, Ford...this wasn't an assassination. It's domestic. The mayor was cheating on his wife. So either the wife killed him or the prostitute did.
I'm headed to see the prostitute now. I'll know more after I talk to her.
I knew you didn't really quit.
Yeah, yeah. I just needed to say it.
You know Boo still wants this treated as an assassination.
I'm fully aware of that. Which is why I need *you* to run interference for me. Keep him off my back.
Can you do that for me?
Of course I will.
Thanks. Bronson out.
Activate phone.
Dial the mayor's office.

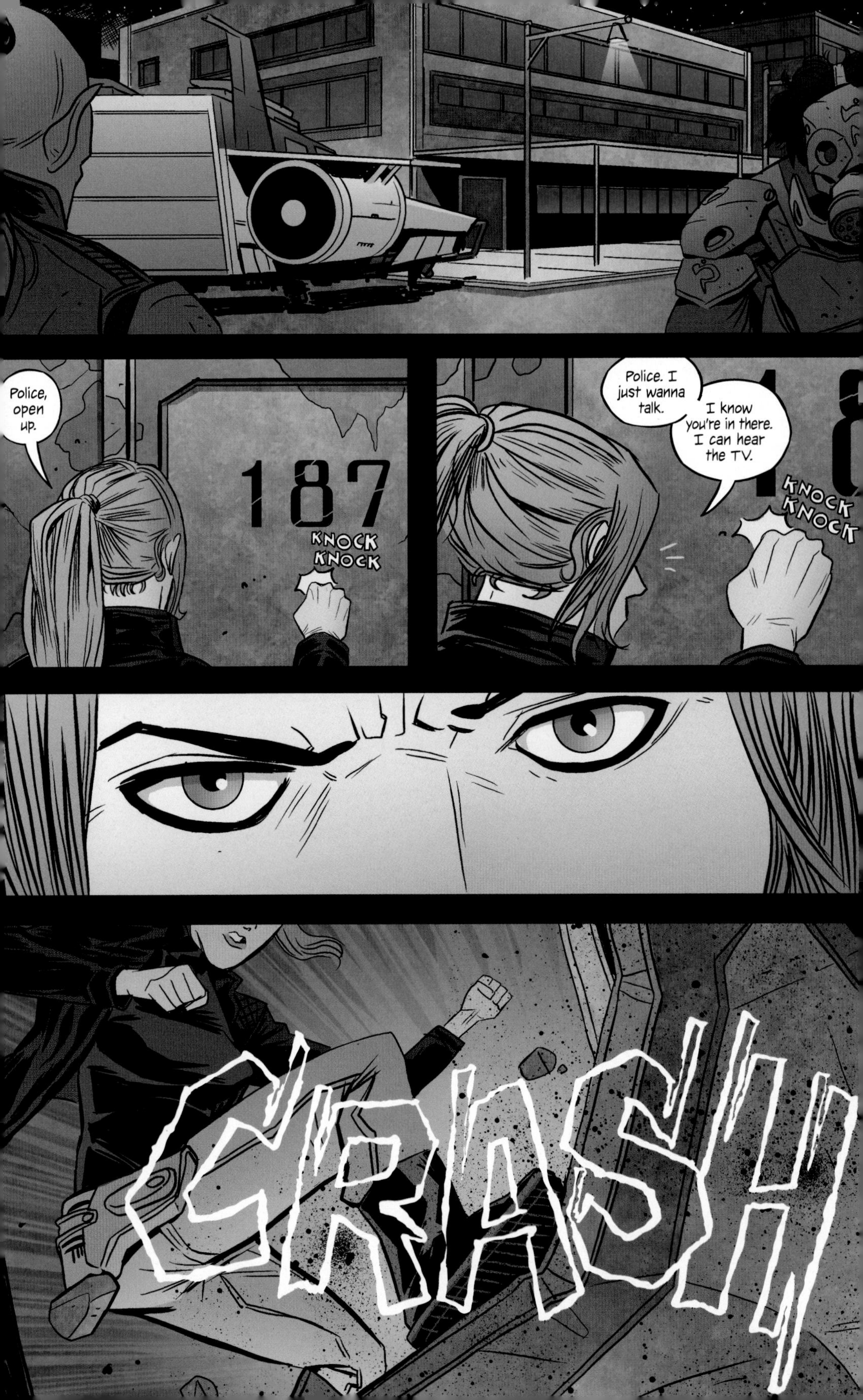
Police, open up.
187
KNOCK KNOCK
Police. I just wanna talk.
I know you're in there. I can hear the TV.
KNOCK KNOCK
CRASH

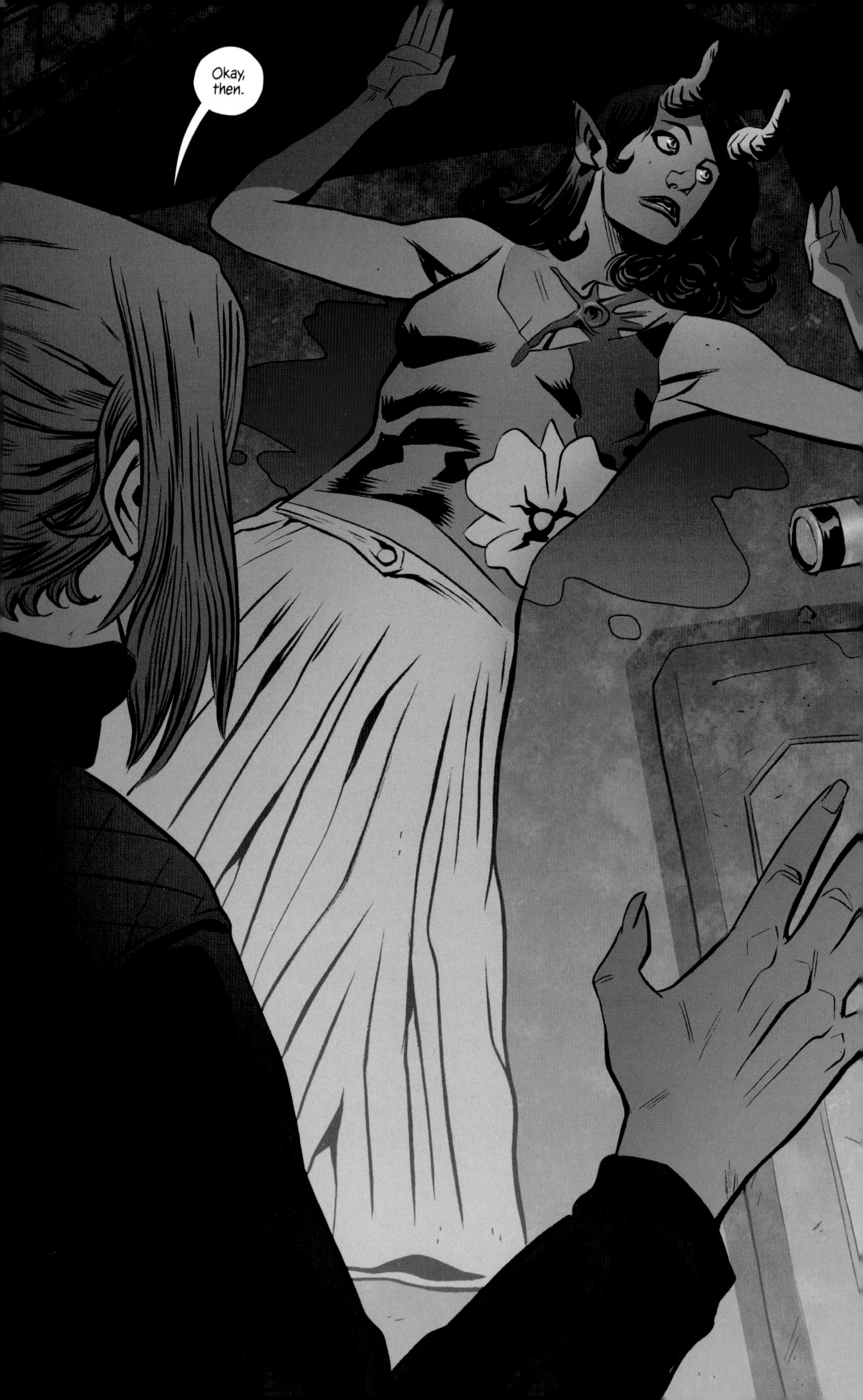
Okay, then.

CHAPTER IV

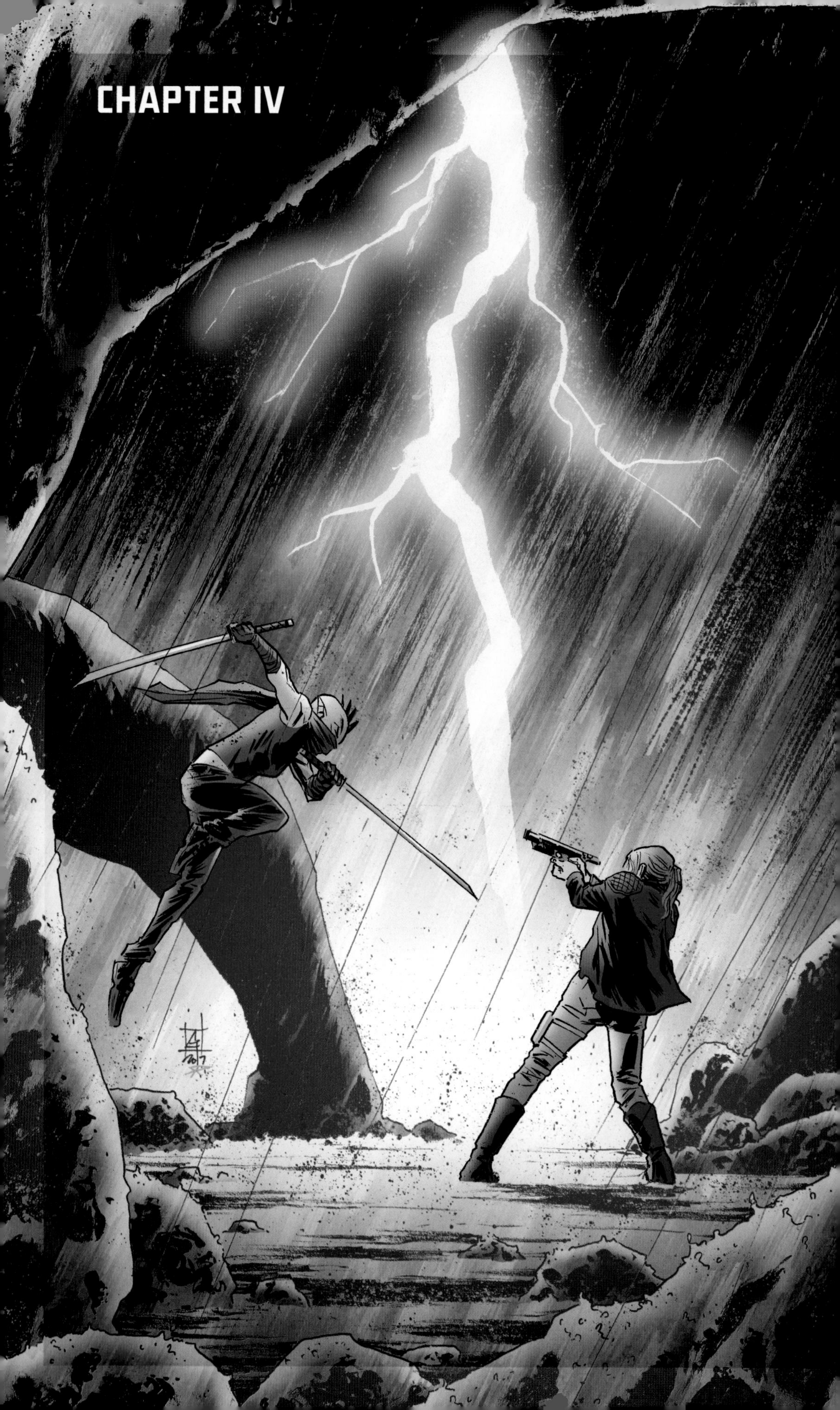

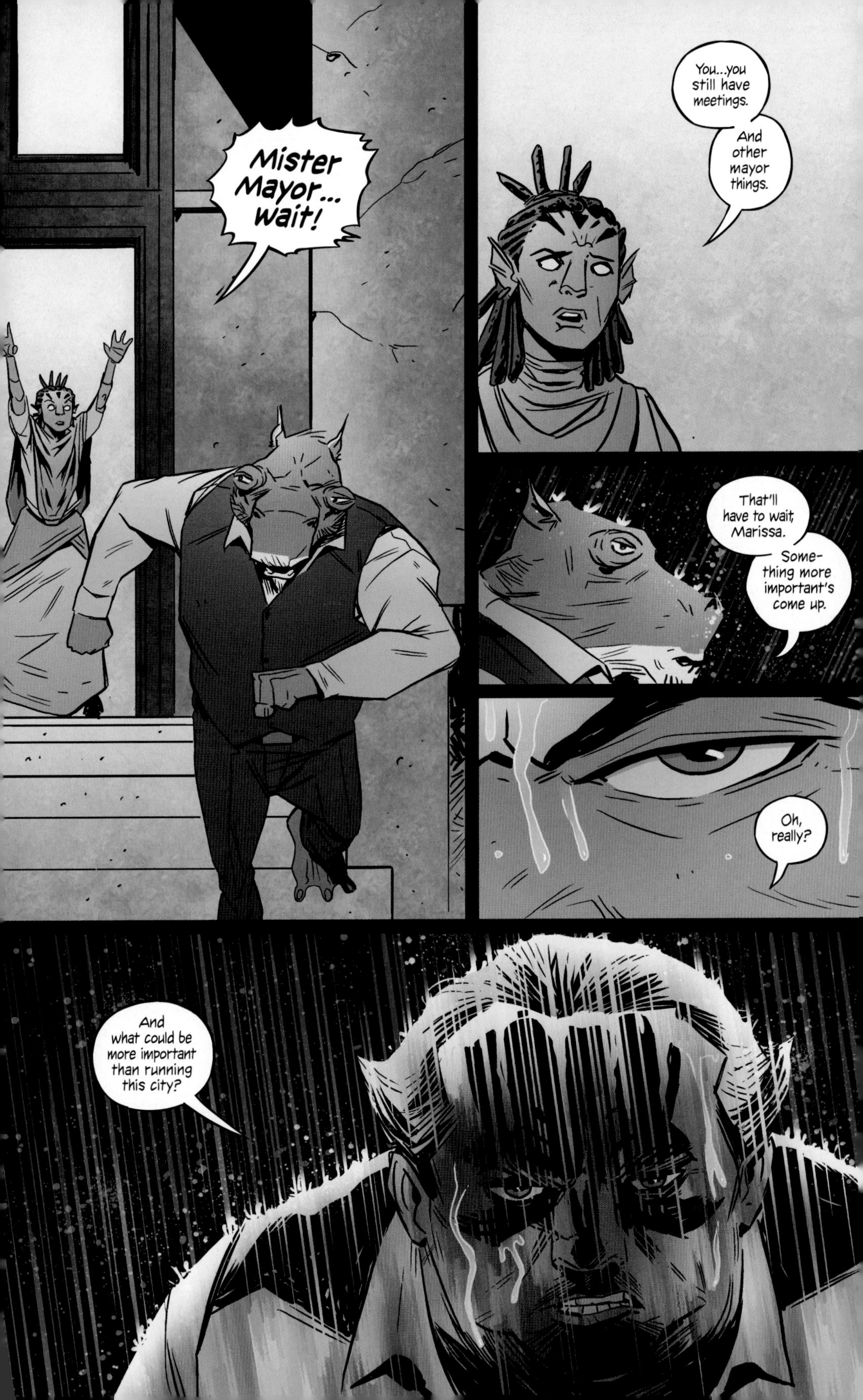
Mister Mayor... wait!
You...you still have meetings.
And other mayor things.
That'll have to wait, Marissa.
Something more important's come up.
Oh, really?
And what could be more important than running this city?

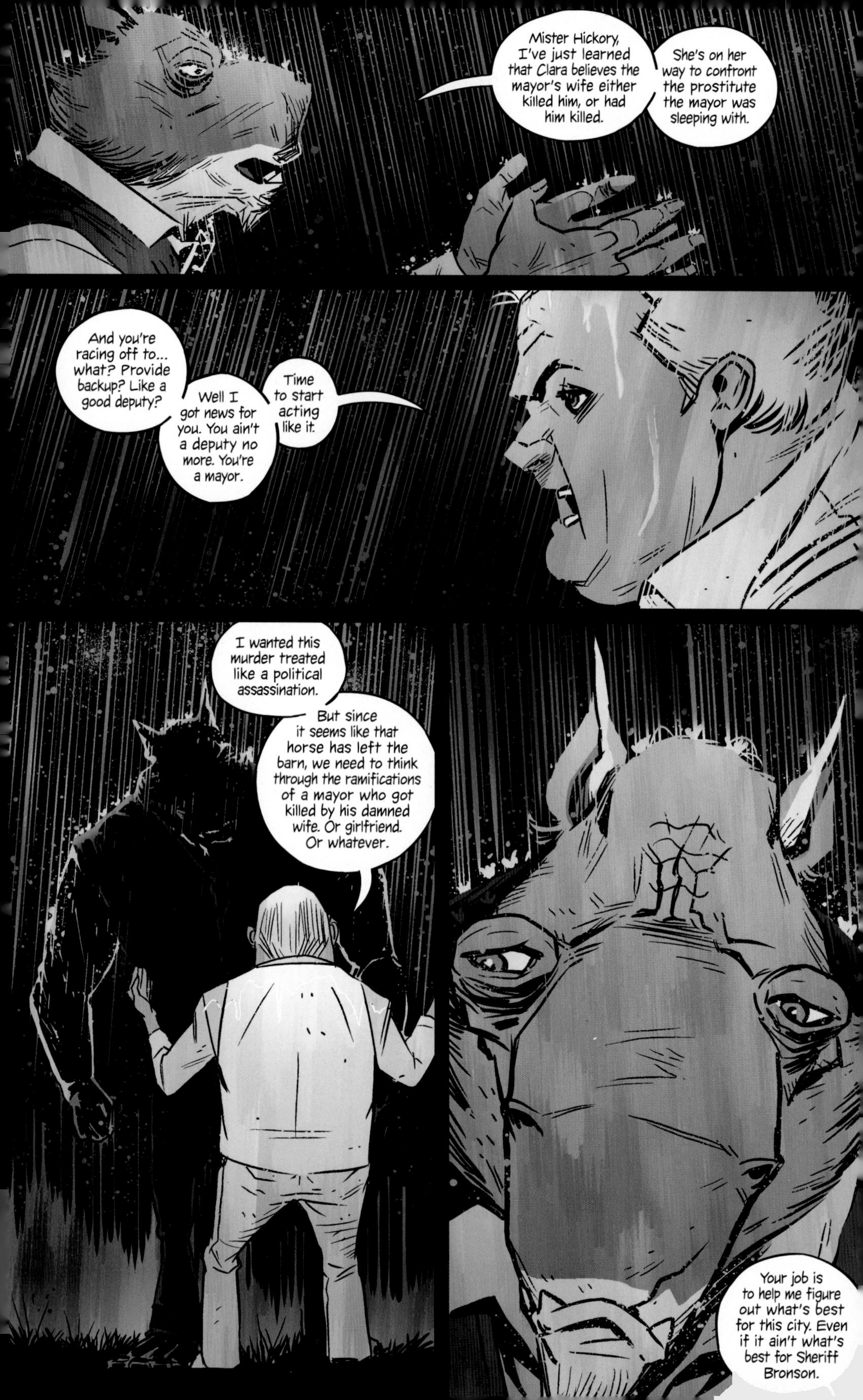
Mister Hickory, I've just learned that Clara believes the mayor's wife either killed him, or had him killed.
She's on her way to confront the prostitute the mayor was sleeping with.
And you're racing off to... what? Provide backup? Like a good deputy?
Well I got news for you. You ain't a deputy no more. You're a mayor.
Time to start acting like it.
I wanted this murder treated like a political assassination.
But since it seems like that horse has left the barn, we need to think through the ramifications of a mayor who got killed by his damned wife. Or girlfriend. Or whatever.
Your job is to help me figure out what's best for this city. Even if it ain't what's best for Sheriff Bronson.

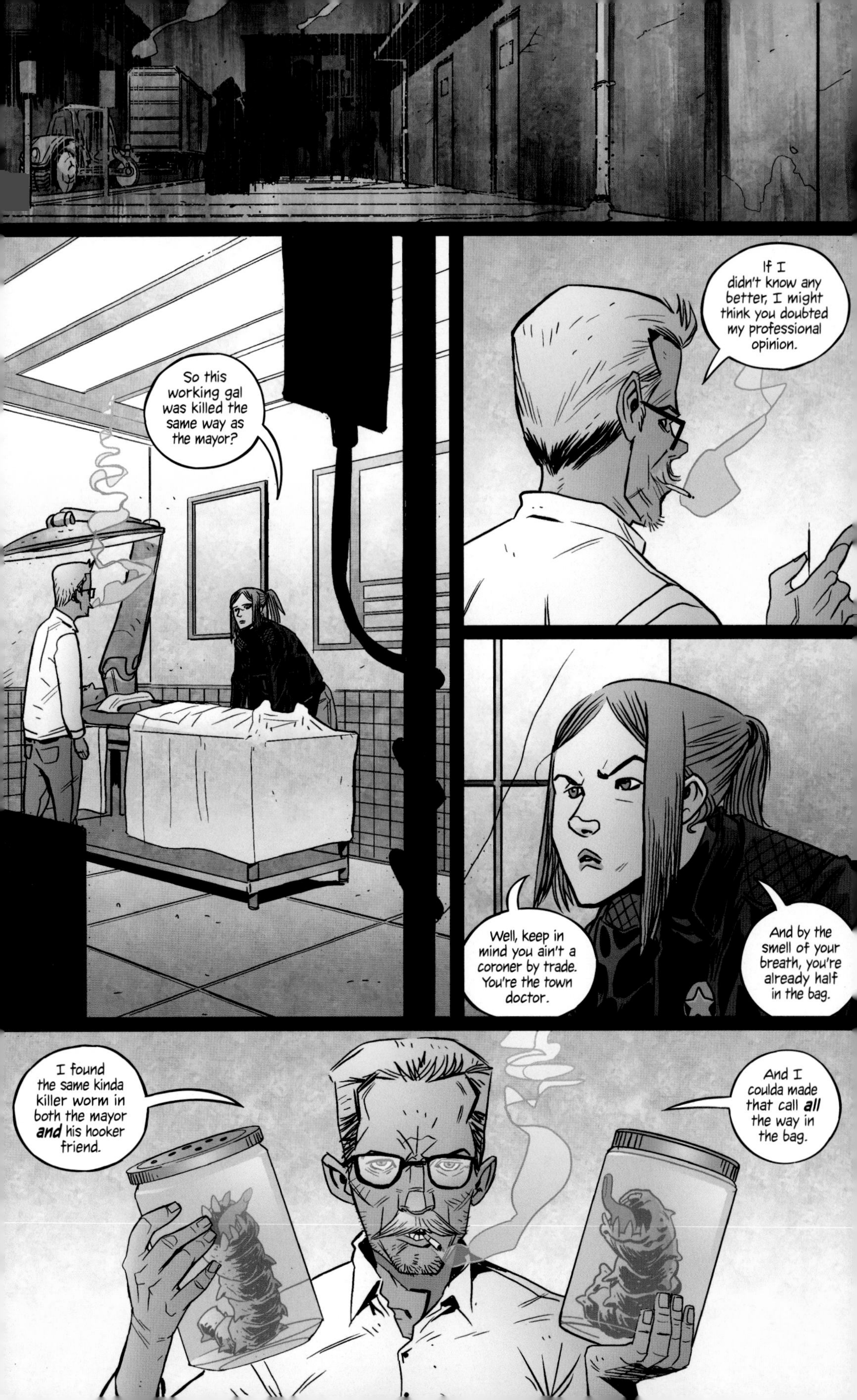
So this working gal was killed the same way as the mayor?
If I didn't know any better, I might think you doubted my professional opinion.
Well, keep in mind you ain't a coroner by trade. You're the town doctor.
And by the smell of your breath, you're already half in the bag.
I found the same kinda killer worm in both the mayor **and** his hooker friend.
And I coulda made that call **all** the way in the bag.

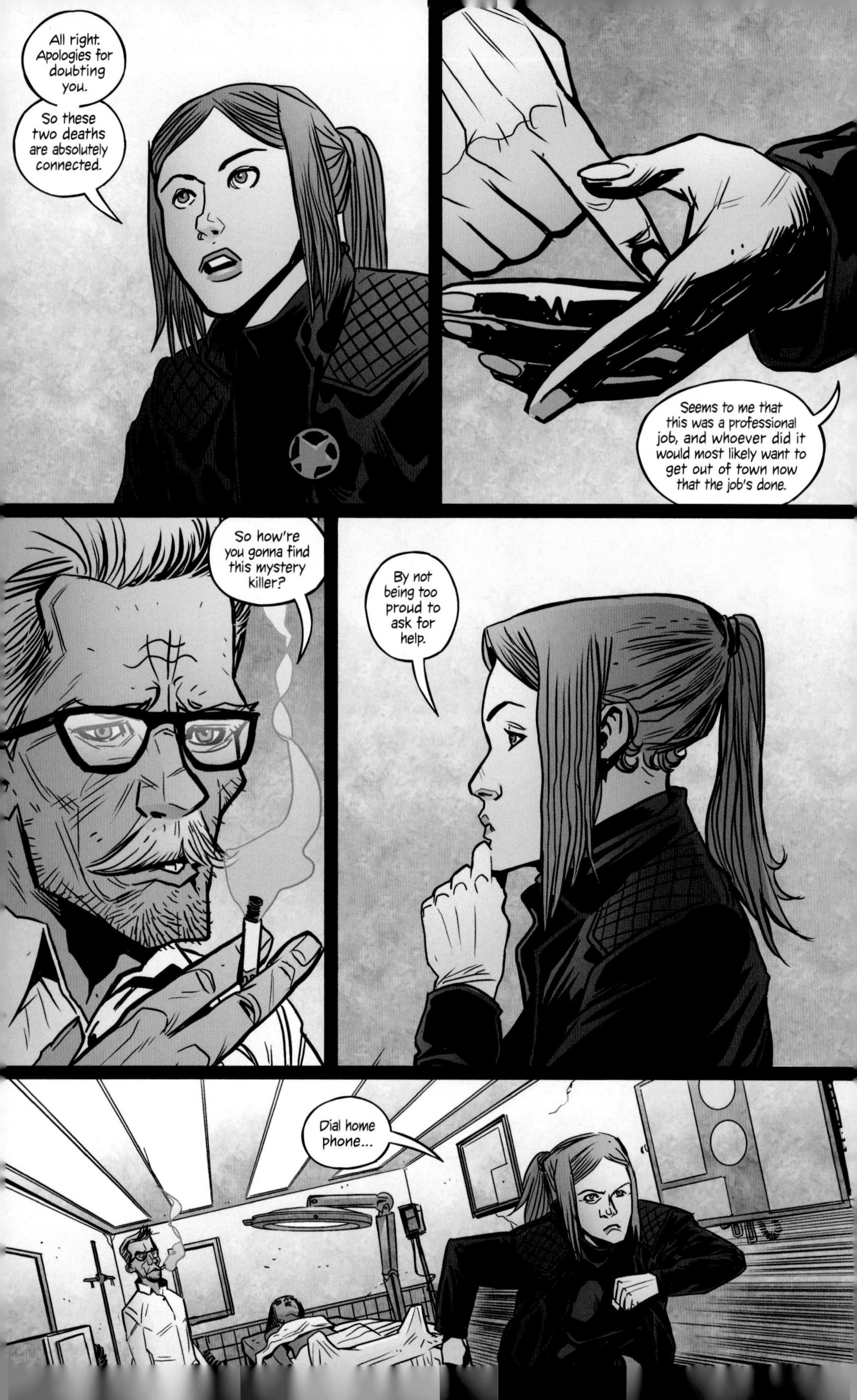
All right. Apologies for doubting you.
So these two deaths are absolutely connected.
Seems to me that this was a professional job, and whoever did it would most likely want to get out of town now that the job's done.
So how're you gonna find this mystery killer?
By not being too proud to ask for help.
Dial home phone...

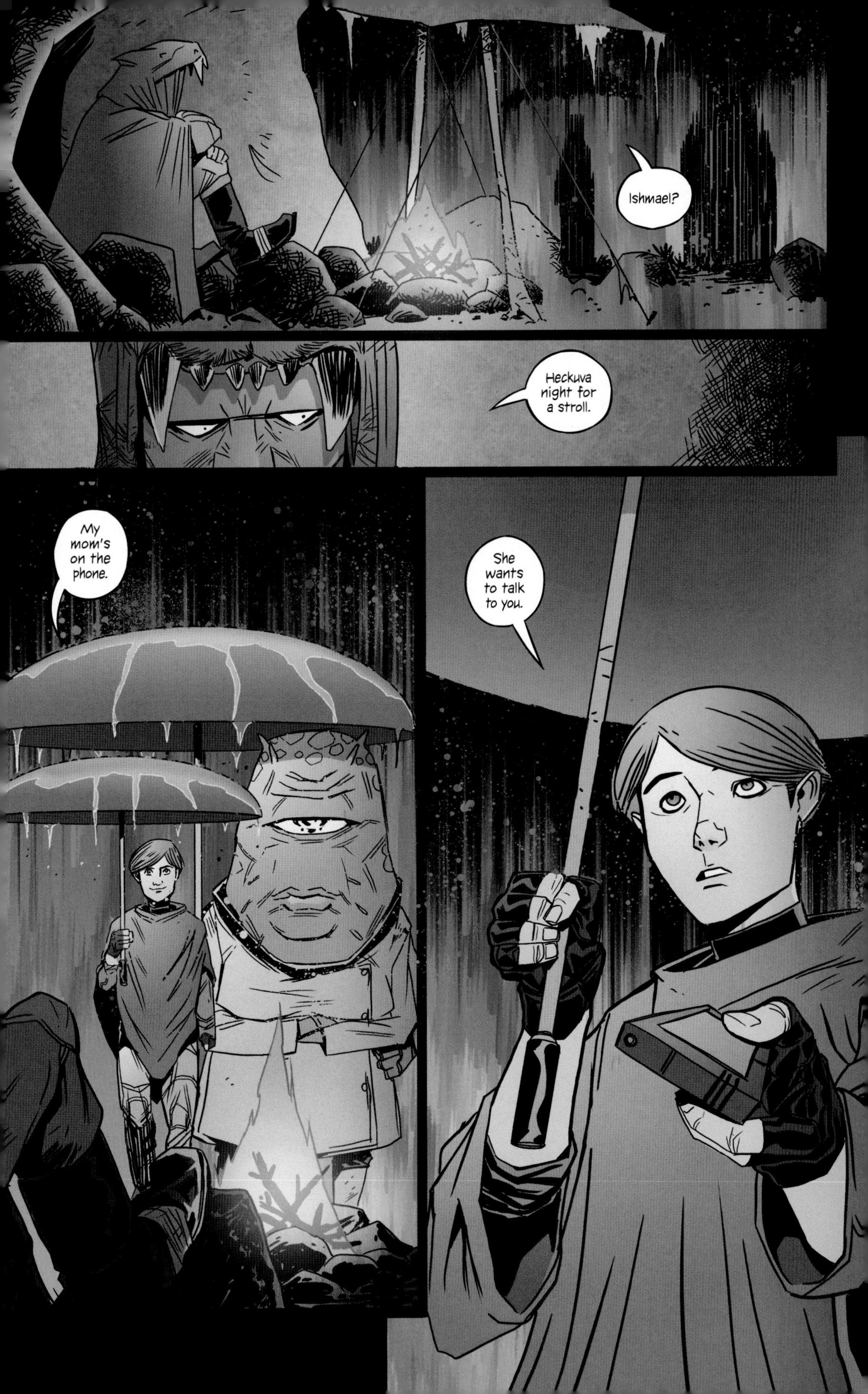
Ishmael?
Heckuva night for a stroll.
My mom's on the phone.
She wants to talk to you.

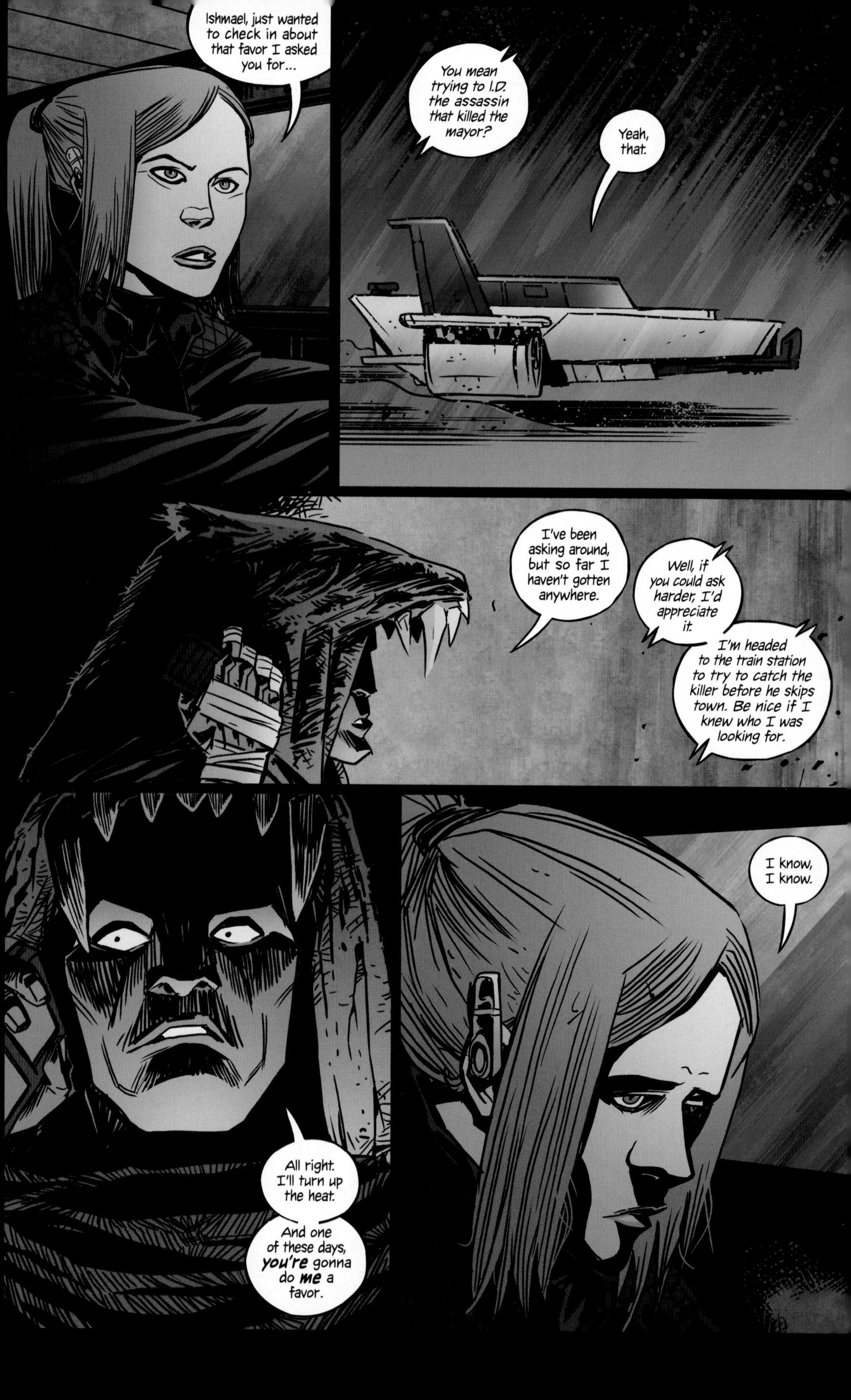
Ishmael, just wanted to check in about that favor I asked you for...
You mean trying to I.D. the assassin that killed the mayor?
Yeah, that.
I've been asking around, but so far I haven't gotten anywhere.
Well, if you could ask harder, I'd appreciate it.
I'm headed to the train station to try to catch the killer before he skips town. Be nice if I knew who I was looking for.
I know, I know.
All right. I'll turn up the heat.
And one of these days, *you're* gonna do *me* a favor.

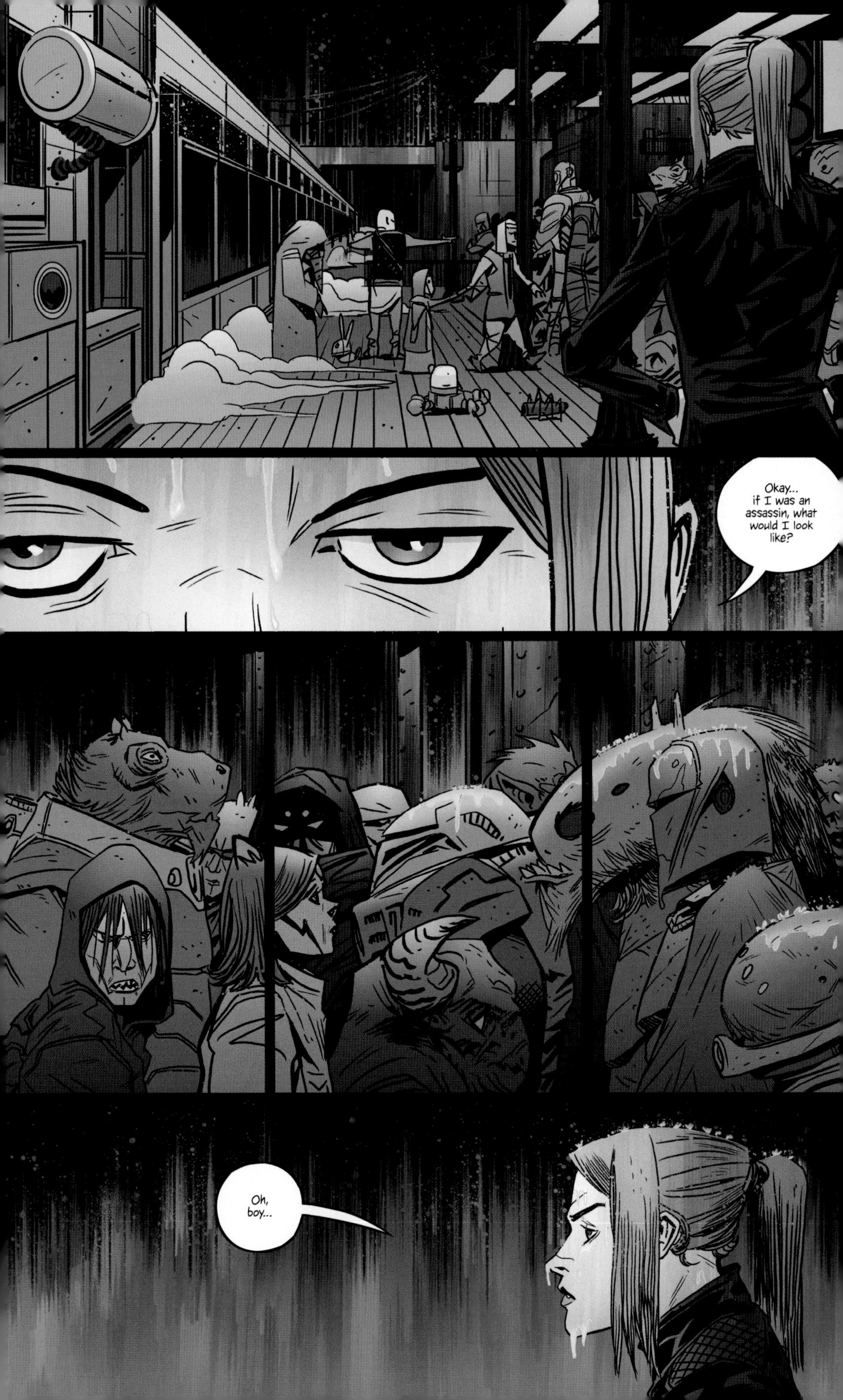
Okay... if I was an assassin, what would I look like?
Oh, boy...

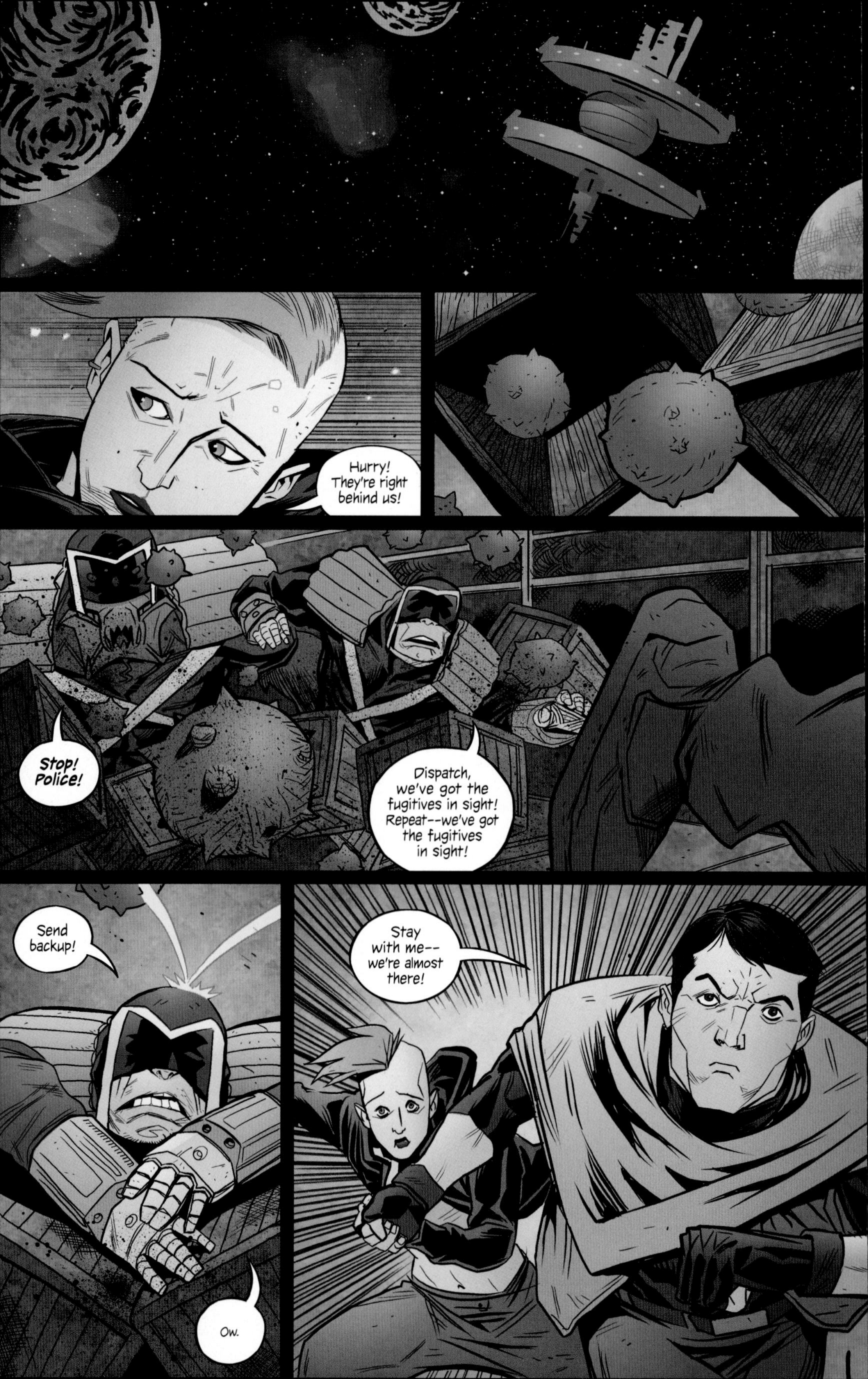
Hurry! They're right behind us!
Stop! Police!
Dispatch, we've got the fugitives in sight! Repeat--we've got the fugitives in sight!
Send backup!
Ow.
Stay with me-- we're almost there!

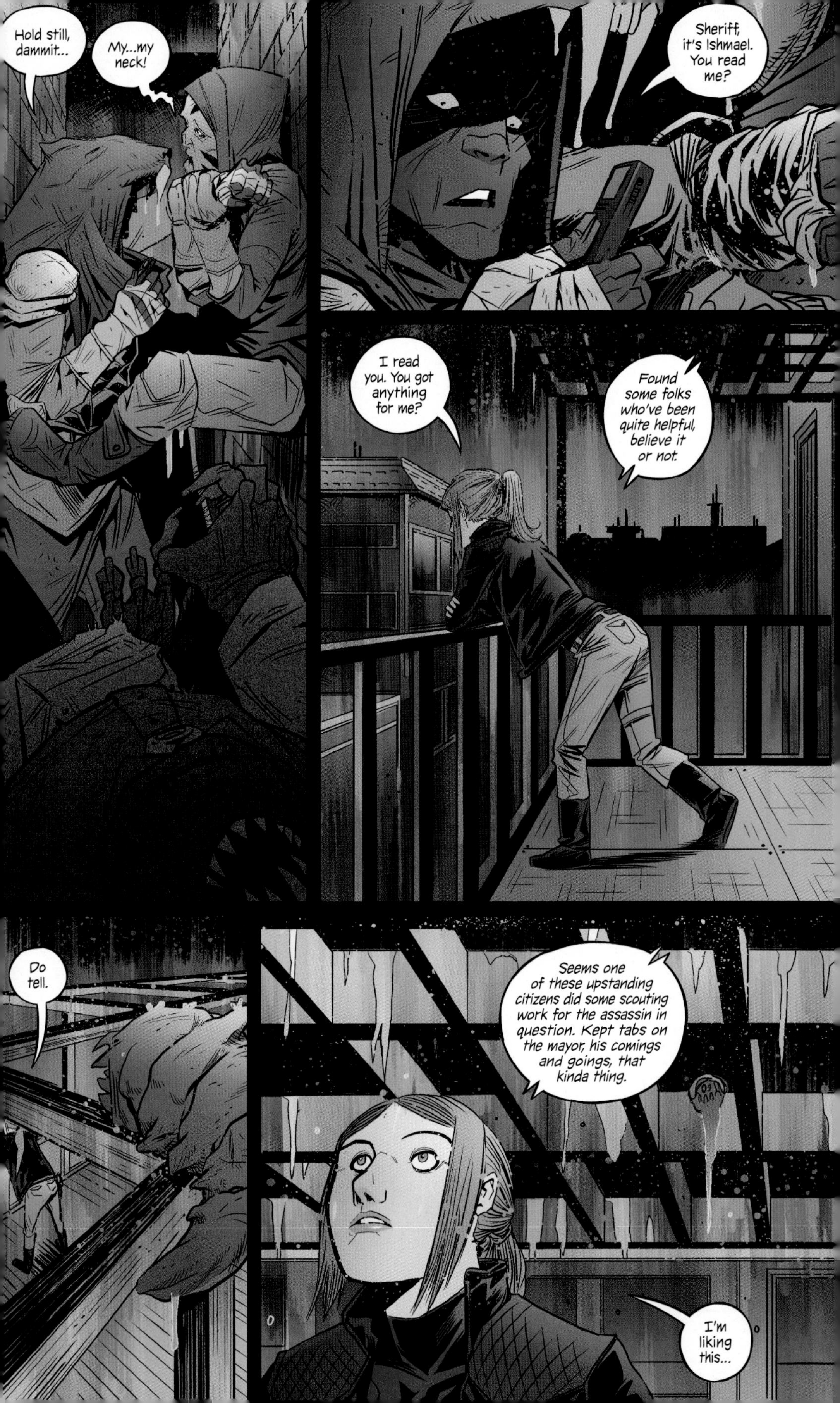
Hold still, dammit...
My...my neck!
Sheriff, it's Ishmael. You read me?
I read you. You got anything for me?
Found some folks who've been quite helpful, believe it or not.
Do tell.
Seems one of these upstanding citizens did some scouting work for the assassin in question. Kept tabs on the mayor, his comings and goings, that kinda thing.
I'm liking this...

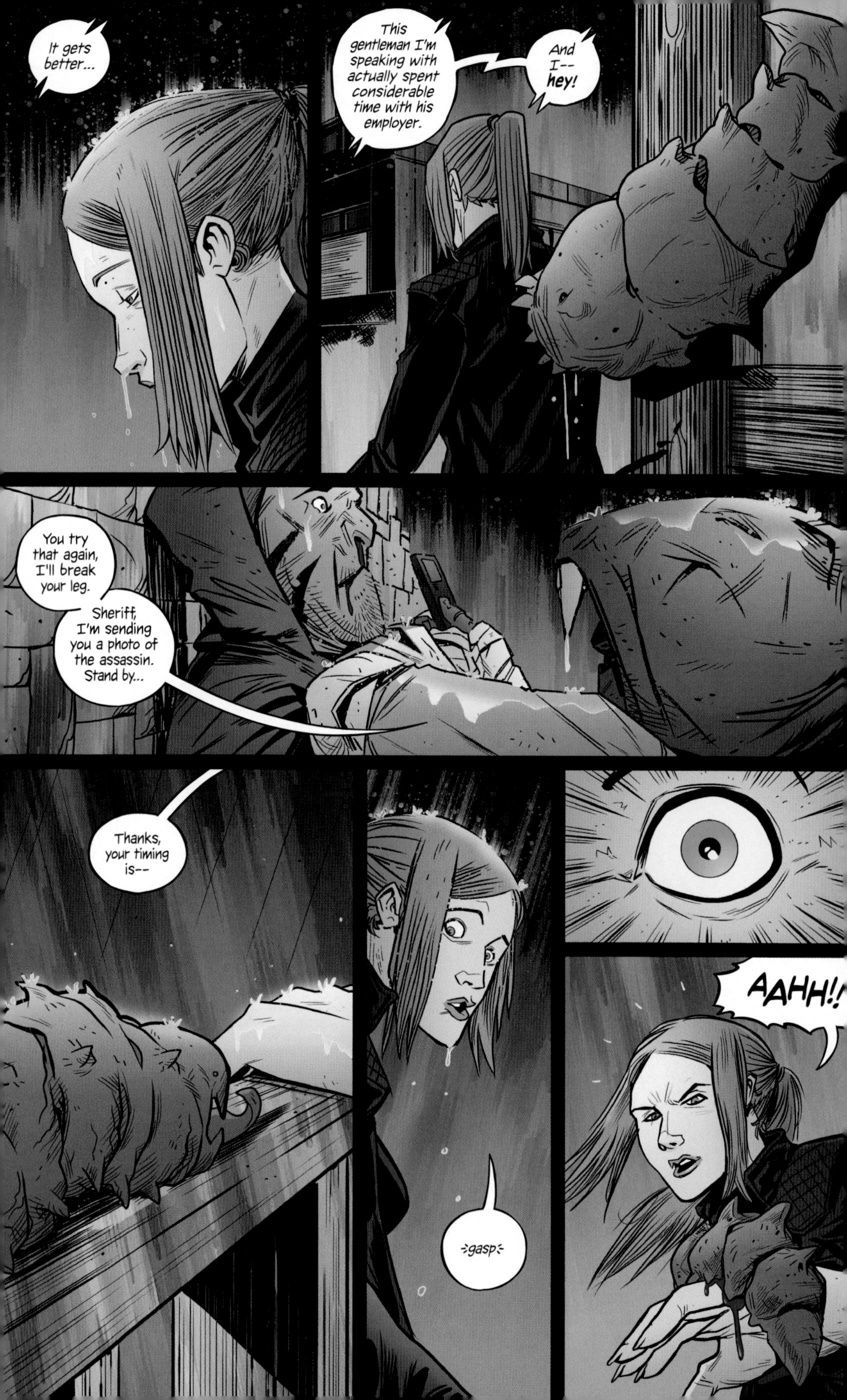
It gets better...
This gentleman I'm speaking with actually spent considerable time with his employer.
And I-- hey!
You try that again, I'll break your leg.
Sheriff, I'm sending you a photo of the assassin. Stand by...
Thanks, your timing is--
gasp
AAHH!!

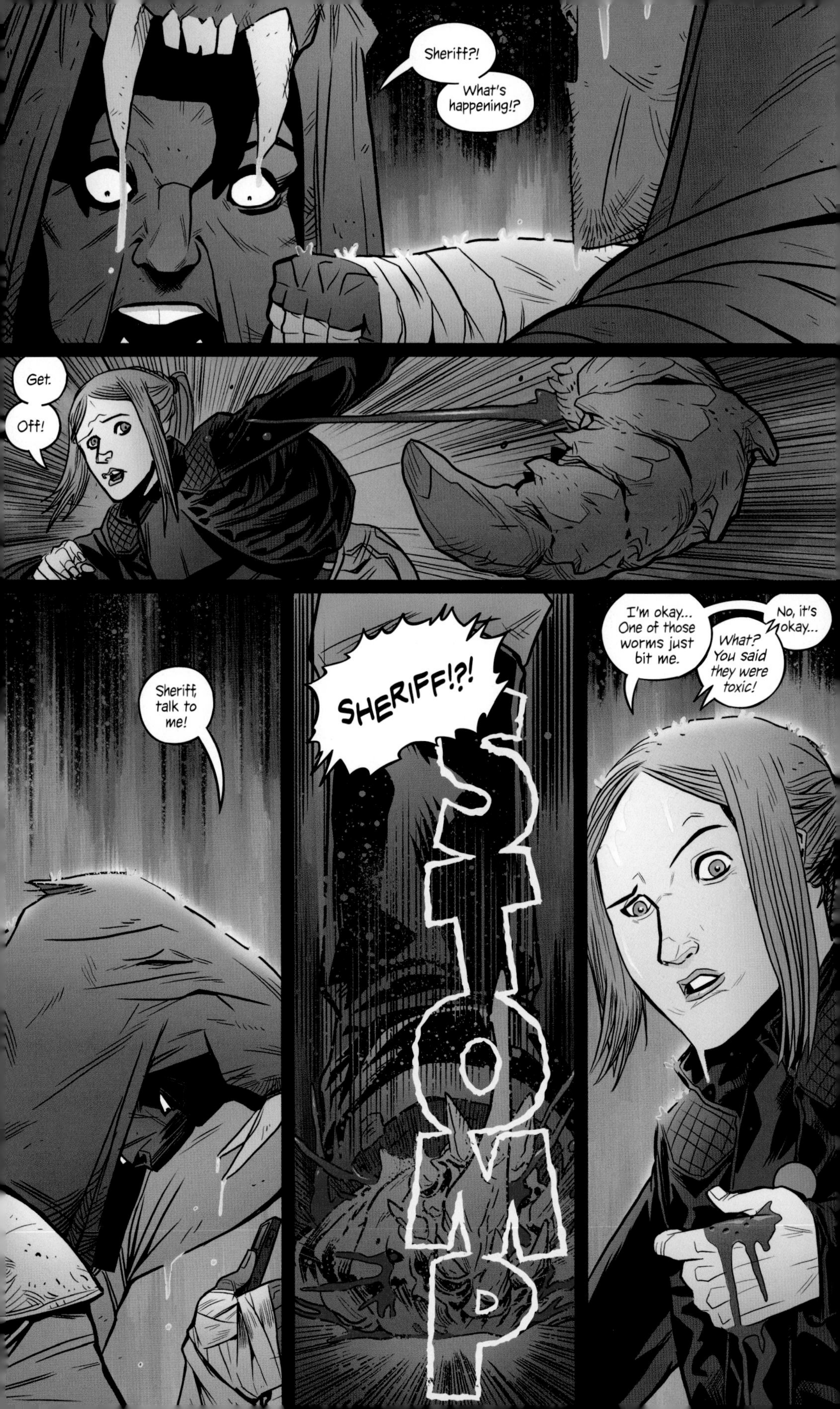

Sheriff?!
What's happening!?
Get.
Off!
Sheriff, talk to me!
SHERIFF!?!
STOMP
I'm okay... One of those worms just bit me.
What? You said they were toxic!
No, it's okay...

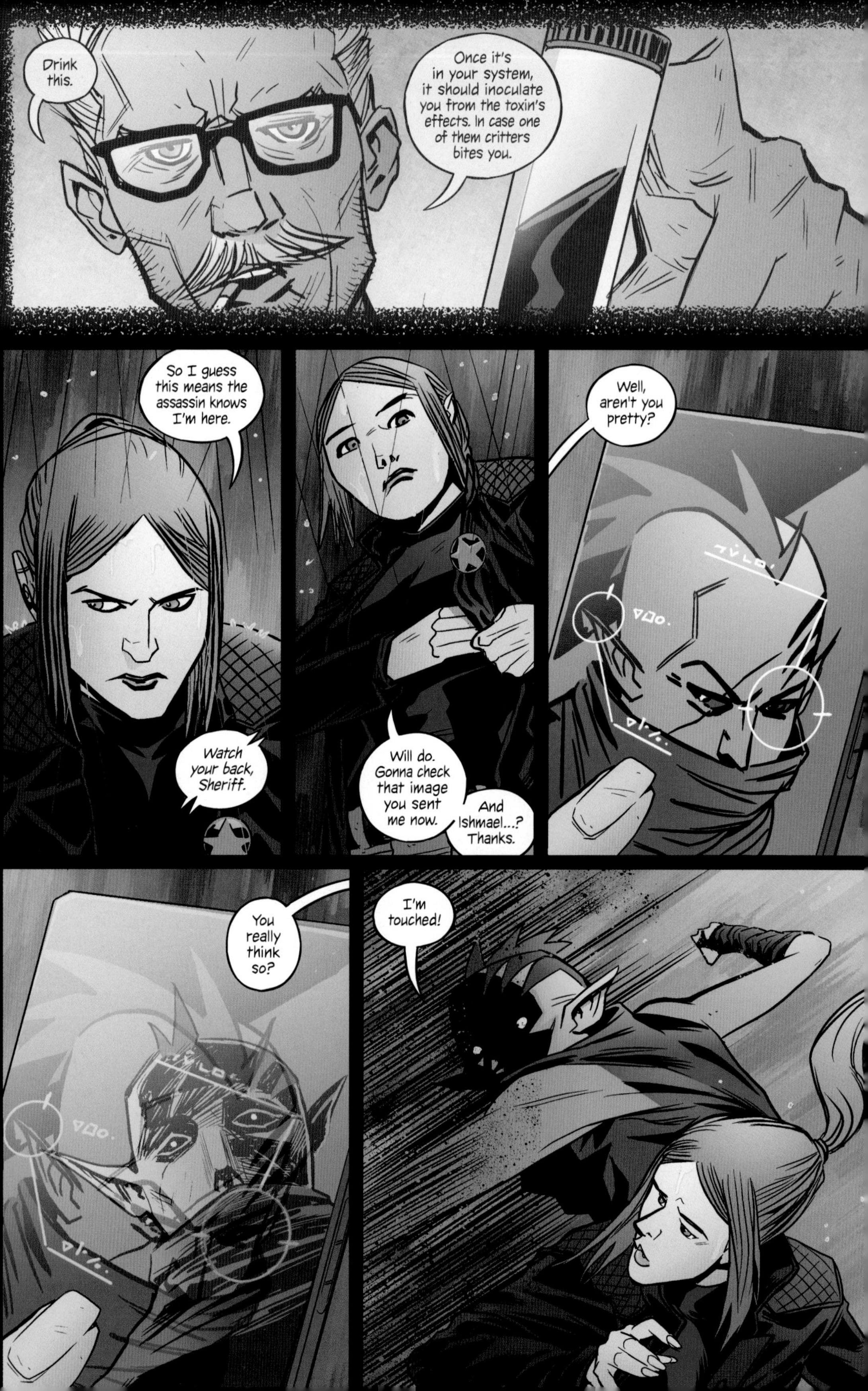
Drink this.
Once it's in your system, it should inoculate you from the toxin's effects. In case one of them critters bites you.
So I guess this means the assassin knows I'm here.
Watch your back, Sheriff.
Will do. Gonna check that image you sent me now.
And Ishmael...? Thanks.
Well, aren't you pretty?
You really think so?
I'm touched!

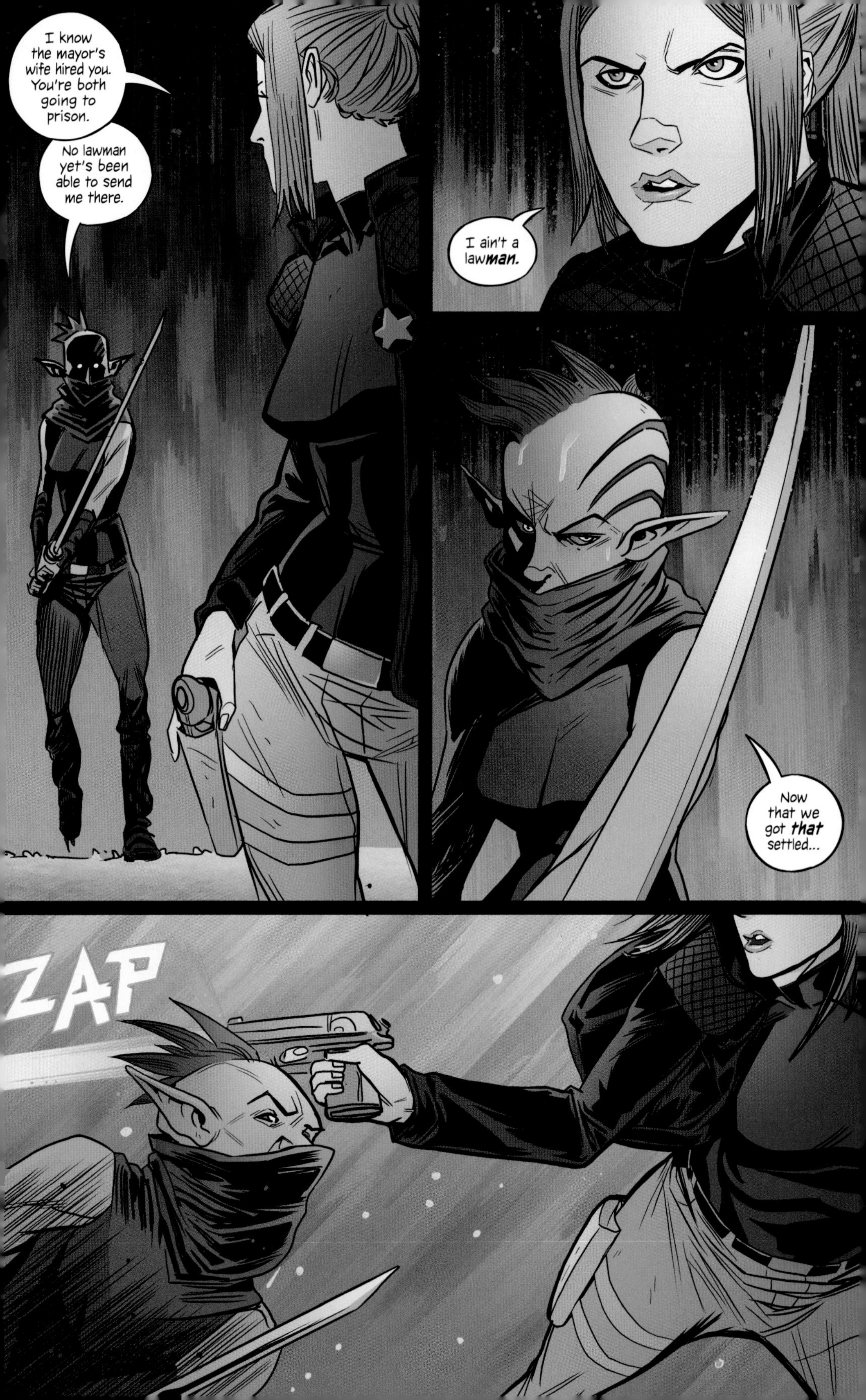
I know the mayor's wife hired you. You're both going to prison.
No lawman yet's been able to send me there.
I ain't a law*man.*
Now that we got ***that*** settled...
ZAP

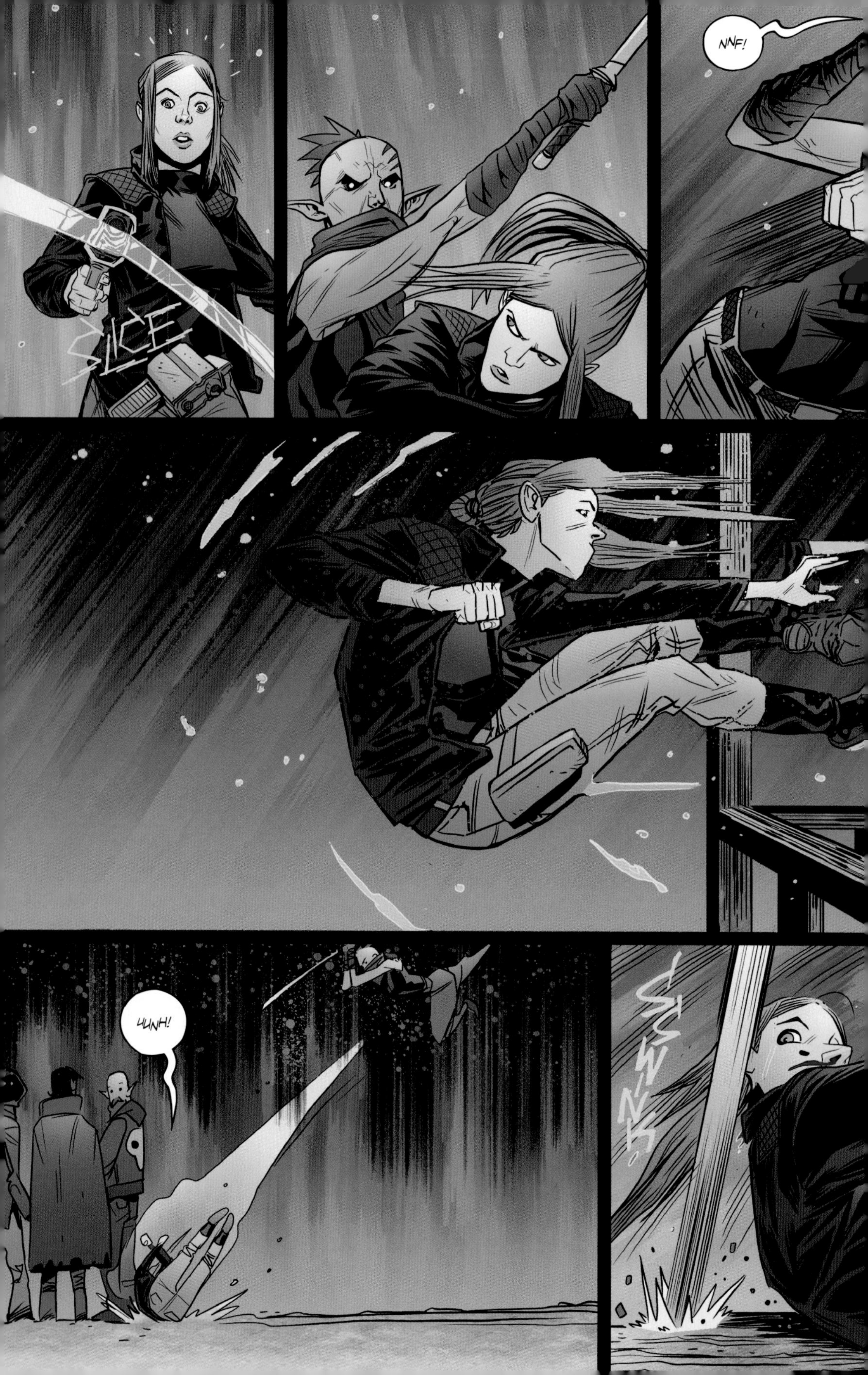
SLICE
NNF!
UUNH!
THUNK

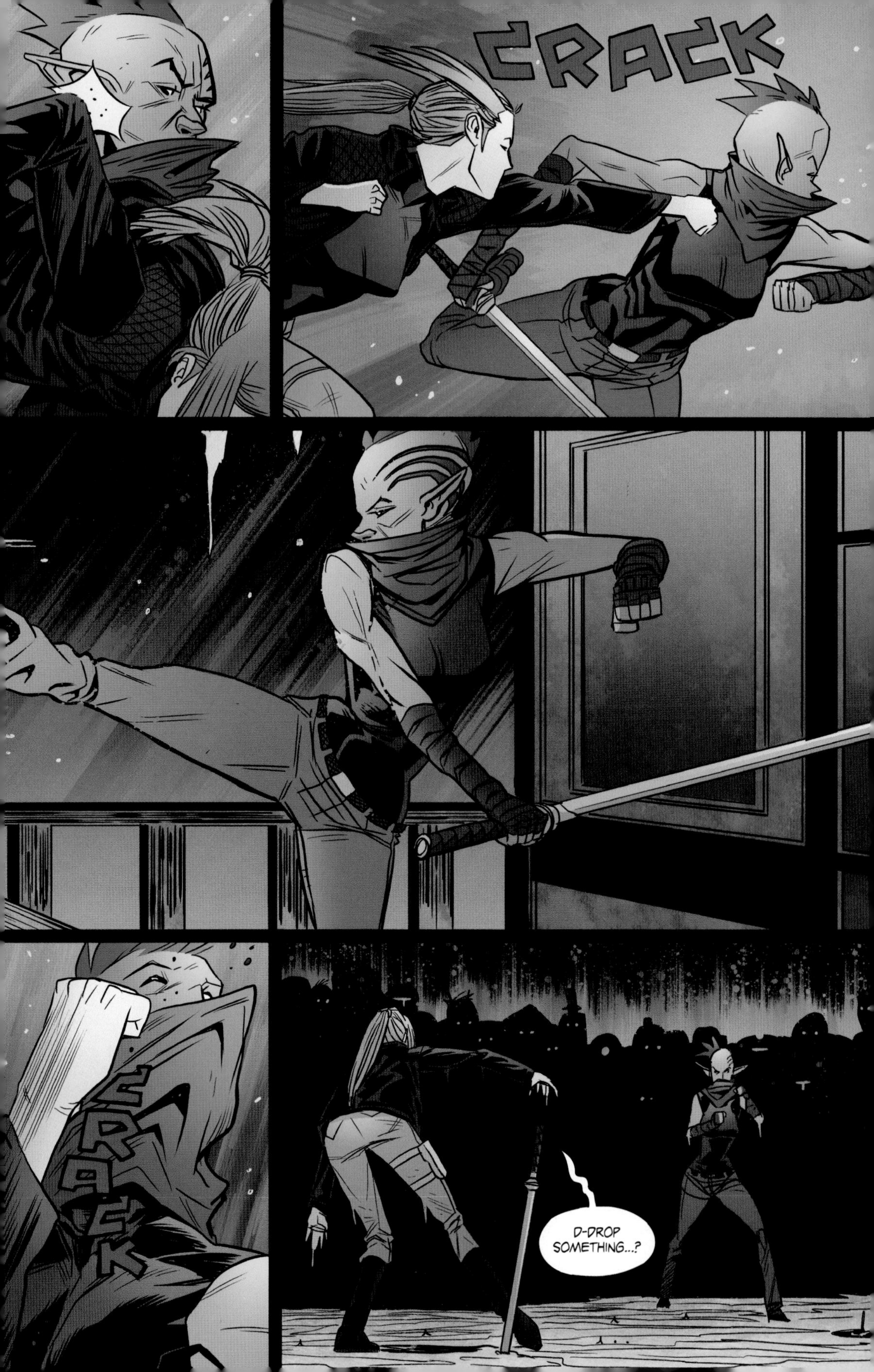
CRACK
CRACK
D-DROP SOMETHING...?

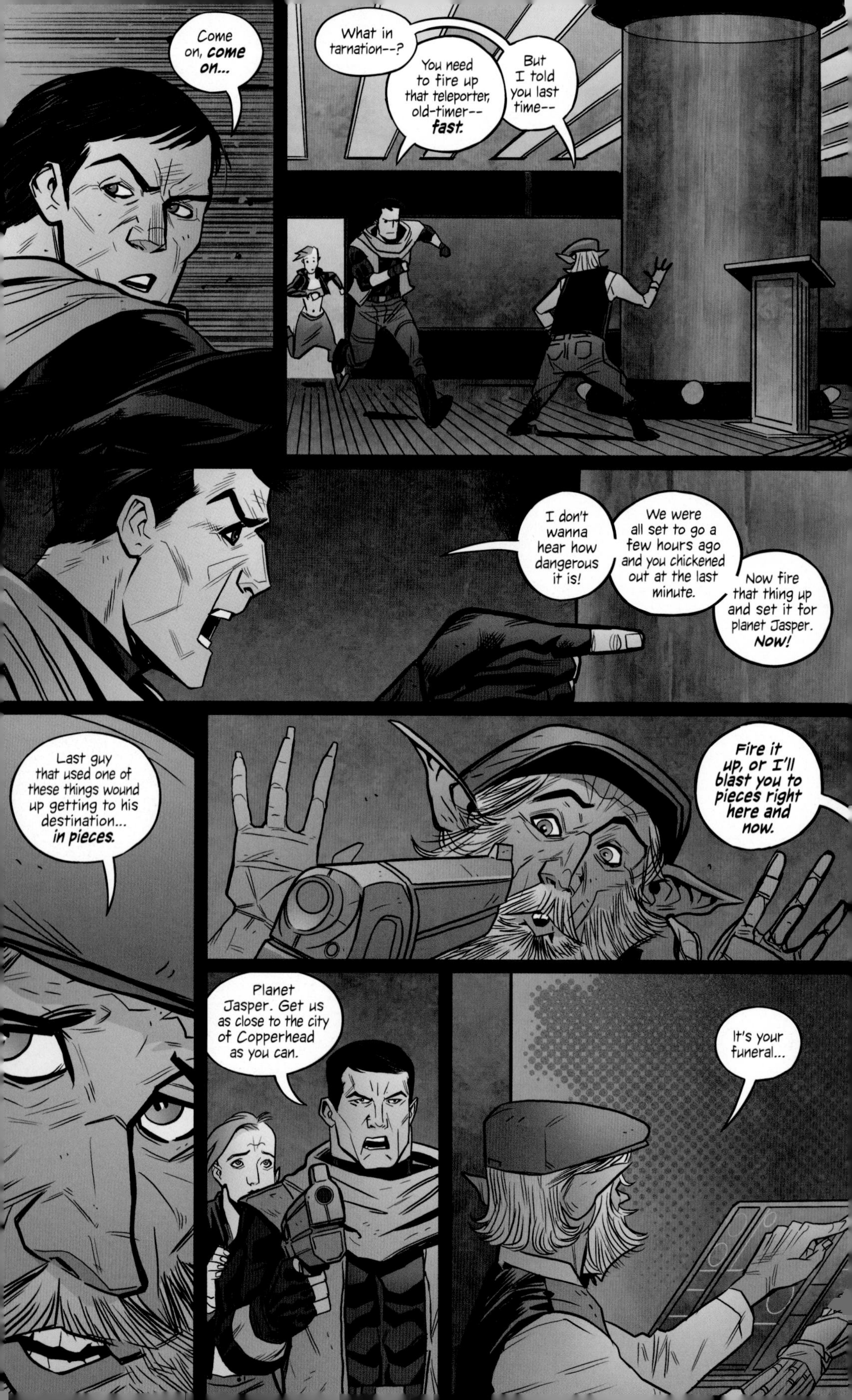
Come on, **come on...**
What in tarnation--?
You need to fire up that teleporter, old-timer-- **fast.**
But I told you last time--
I don't wanna hear how dangerous it is!
We were all set to go a few hours ago and you chickened out at the last minute.
Now fire that thing up and set it for planet Jasper. **NOW!**
Last guy that used one of these things wound up getting to his destination... **in pieces.**
Fire it up, or I'll blast you to pieces right here and now.
Planet Jasper. Get us as close to the city of Copperhead as you can.
It's your funeral...

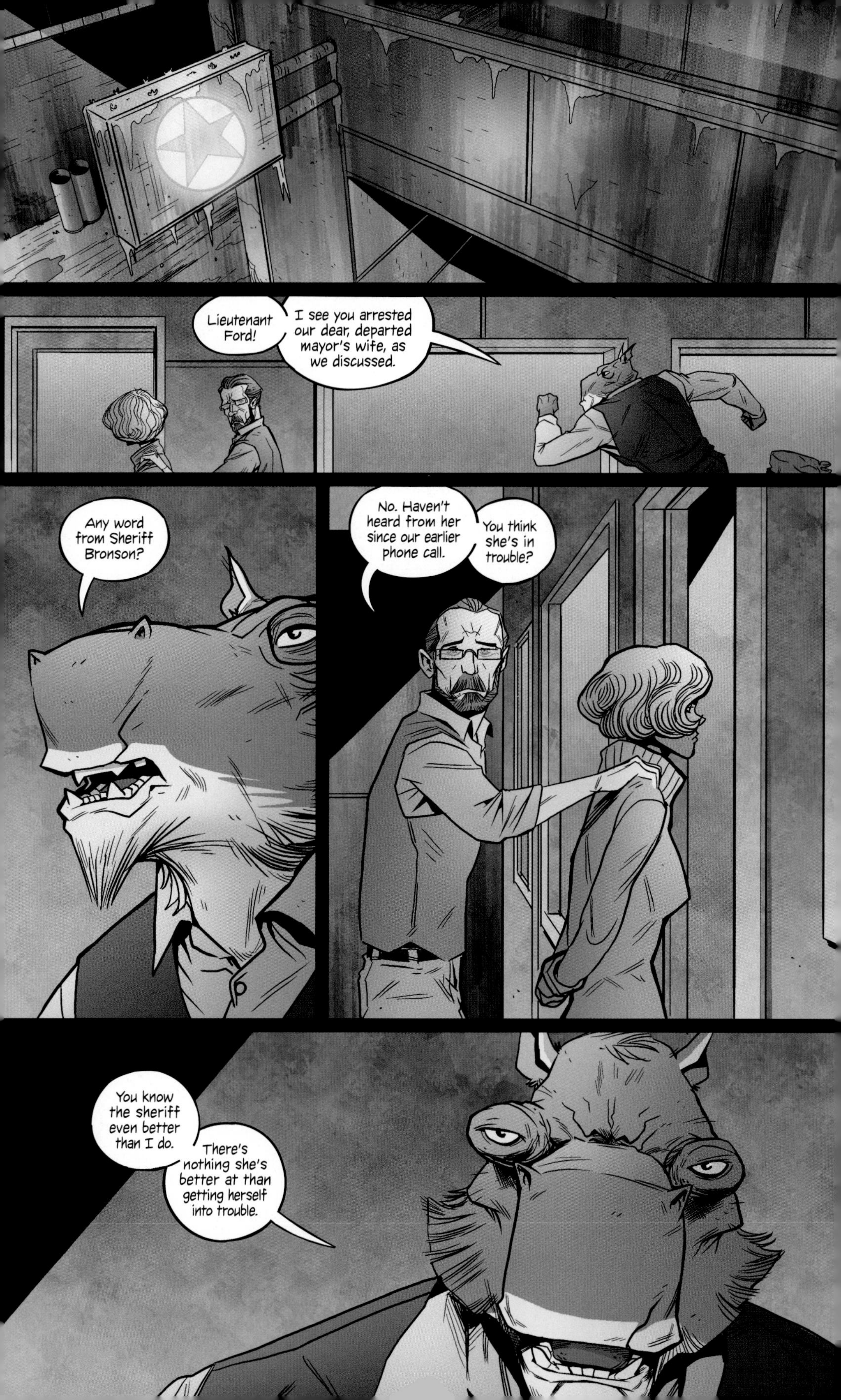
Lieutenant Ford!
I see you arrested our dear, departed mayor's wife, as we discussed.
Any word from Sheriff Bronson?
No. Haven't heard from her since our earlier phone call.
You think she's in trouble?
You know the sheriff even better than I do.
There's nothing she's better at than getting herself into trouble.

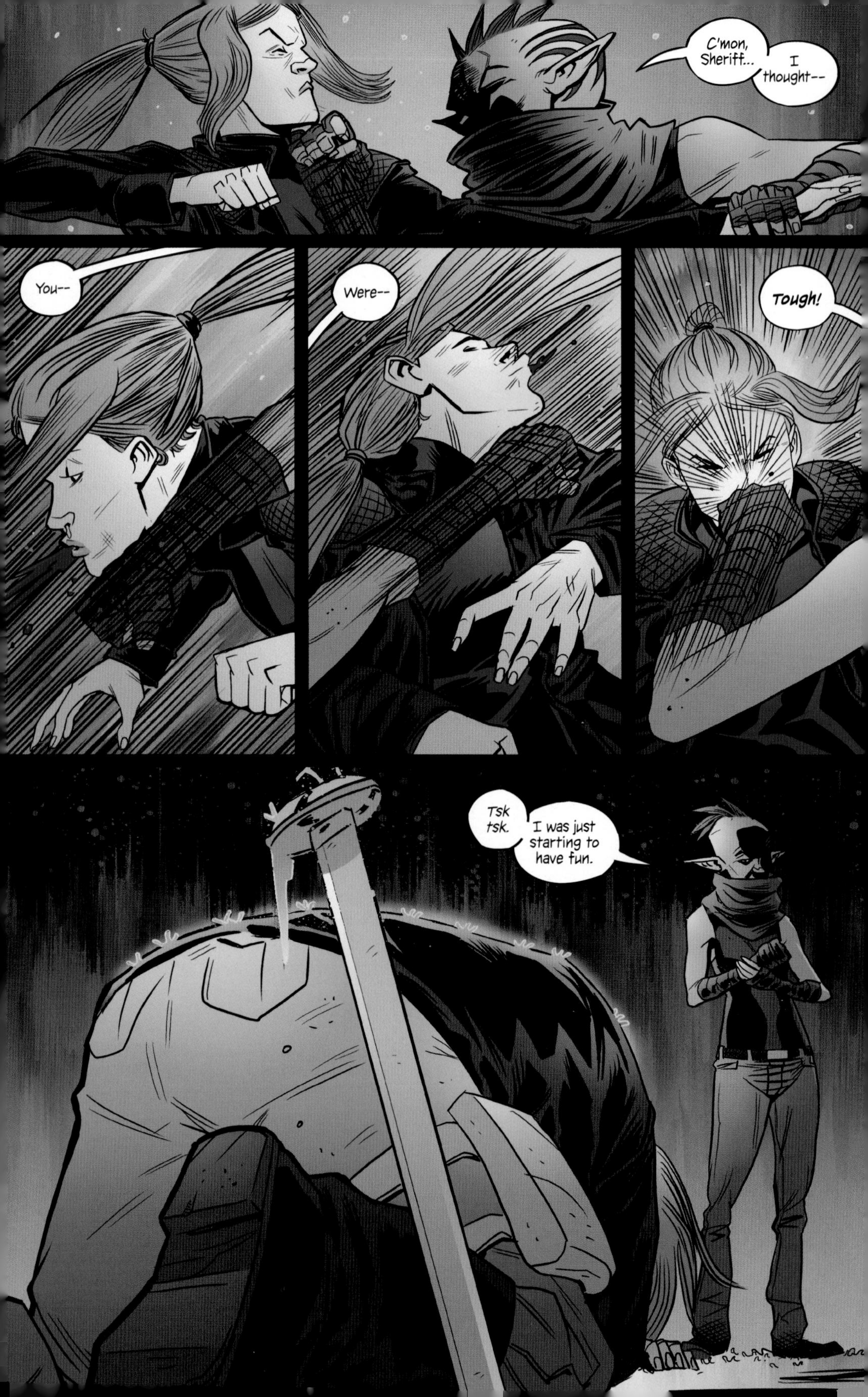
C'mon, Sheriff...
I thought--
You--
Were--
Tough!
Tsk tsk.
I was just starting to have fun.

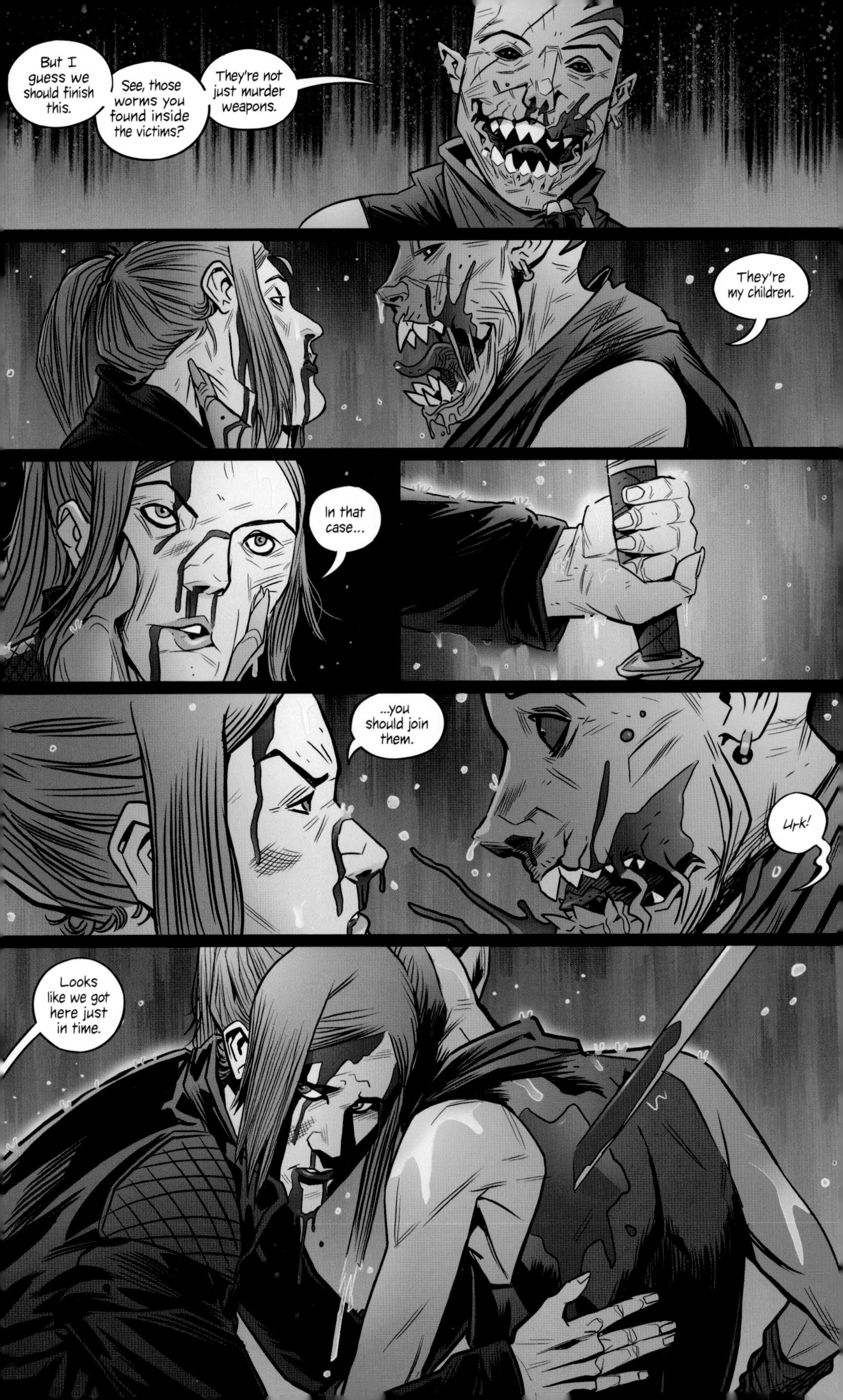
But I guess we should finish this.
See, those worms you found inside the victims?
They're not just murder weapons.
They're my children.
In that case...
...you should join them.
Urk!
Looks like we got here just in time.

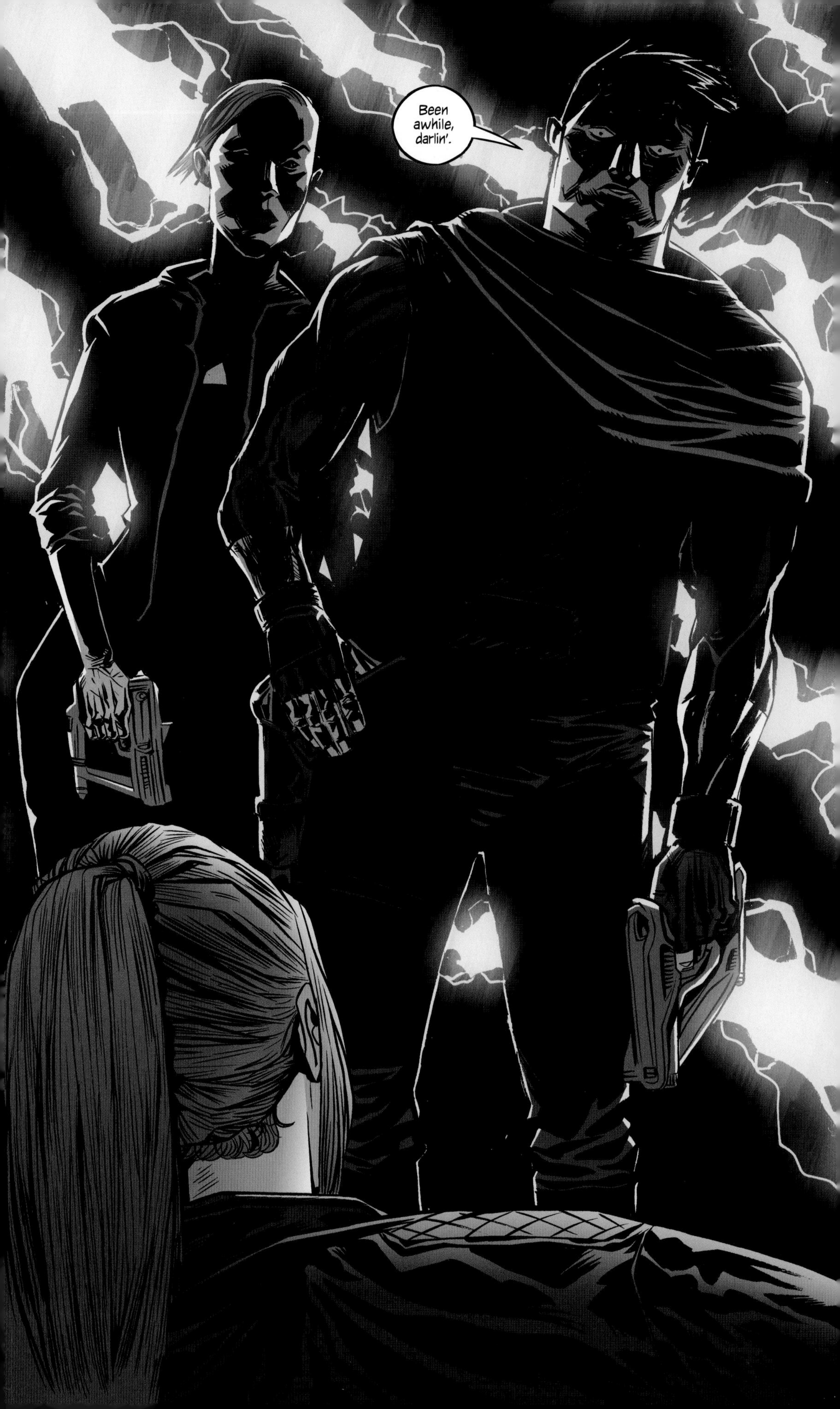
Been awhile, darlin'.

TO BE
CONTINUED

BONUS CONTENT

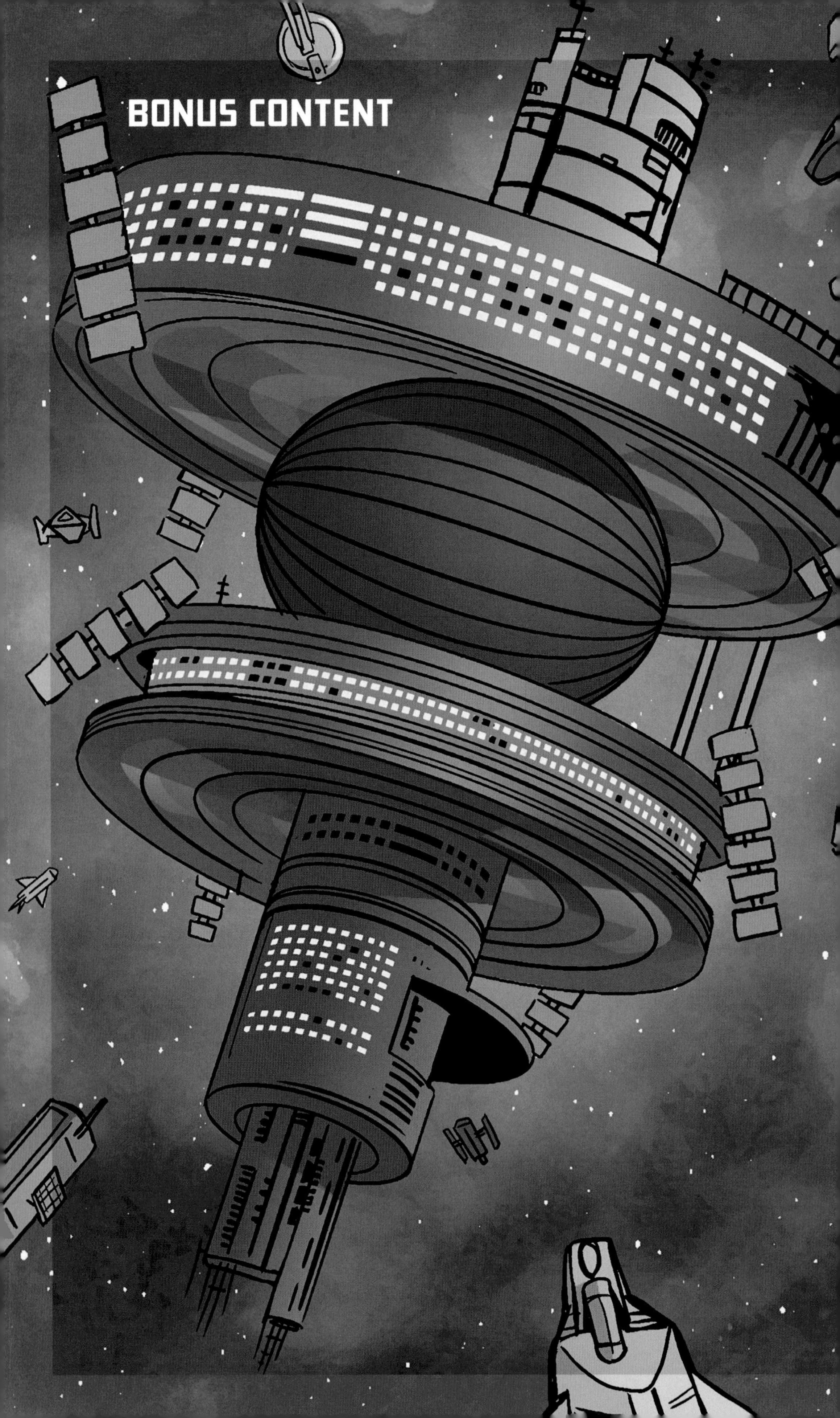

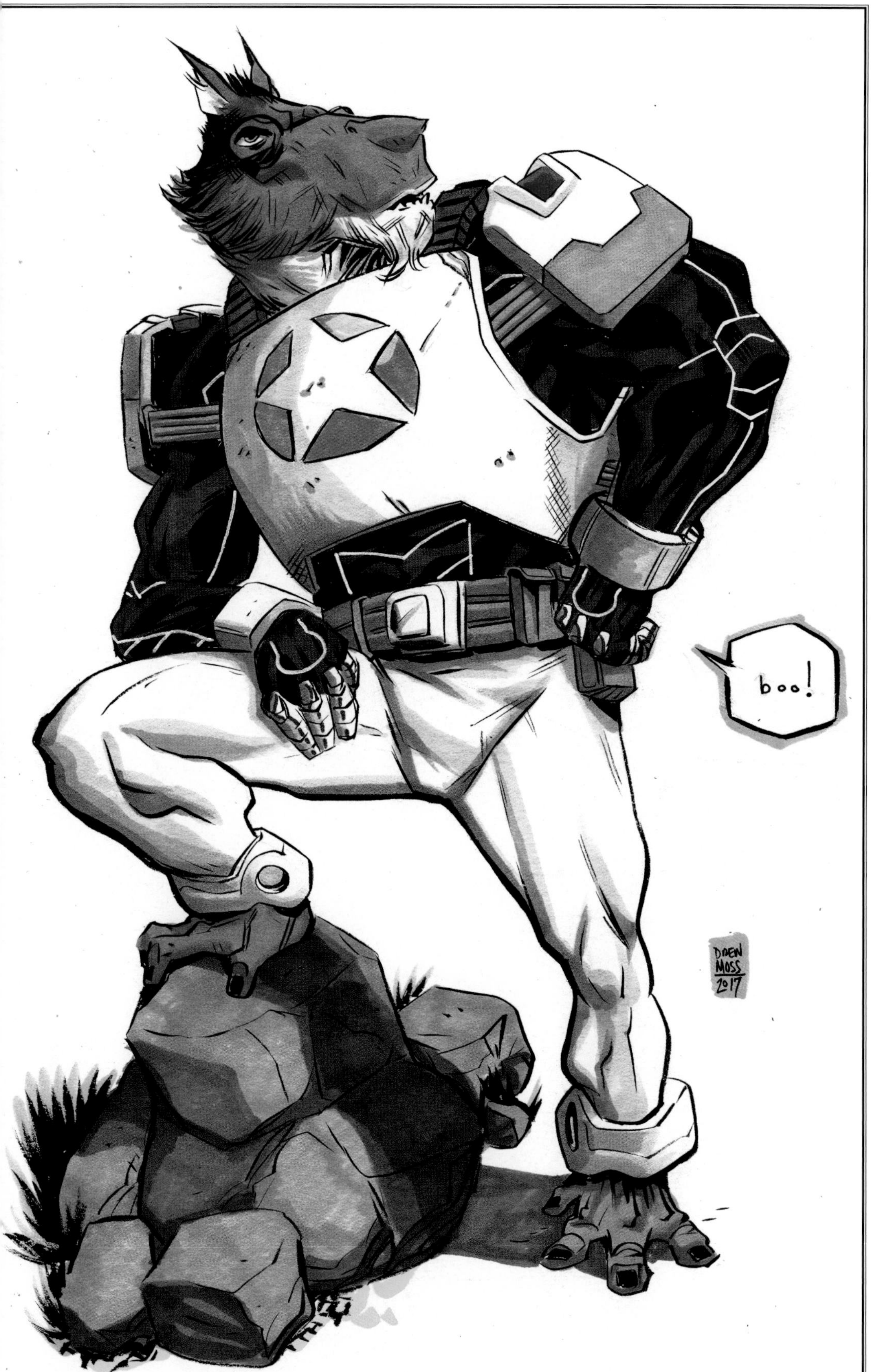
boo!
DREW MOSS 2017

Commission by Drew Moss

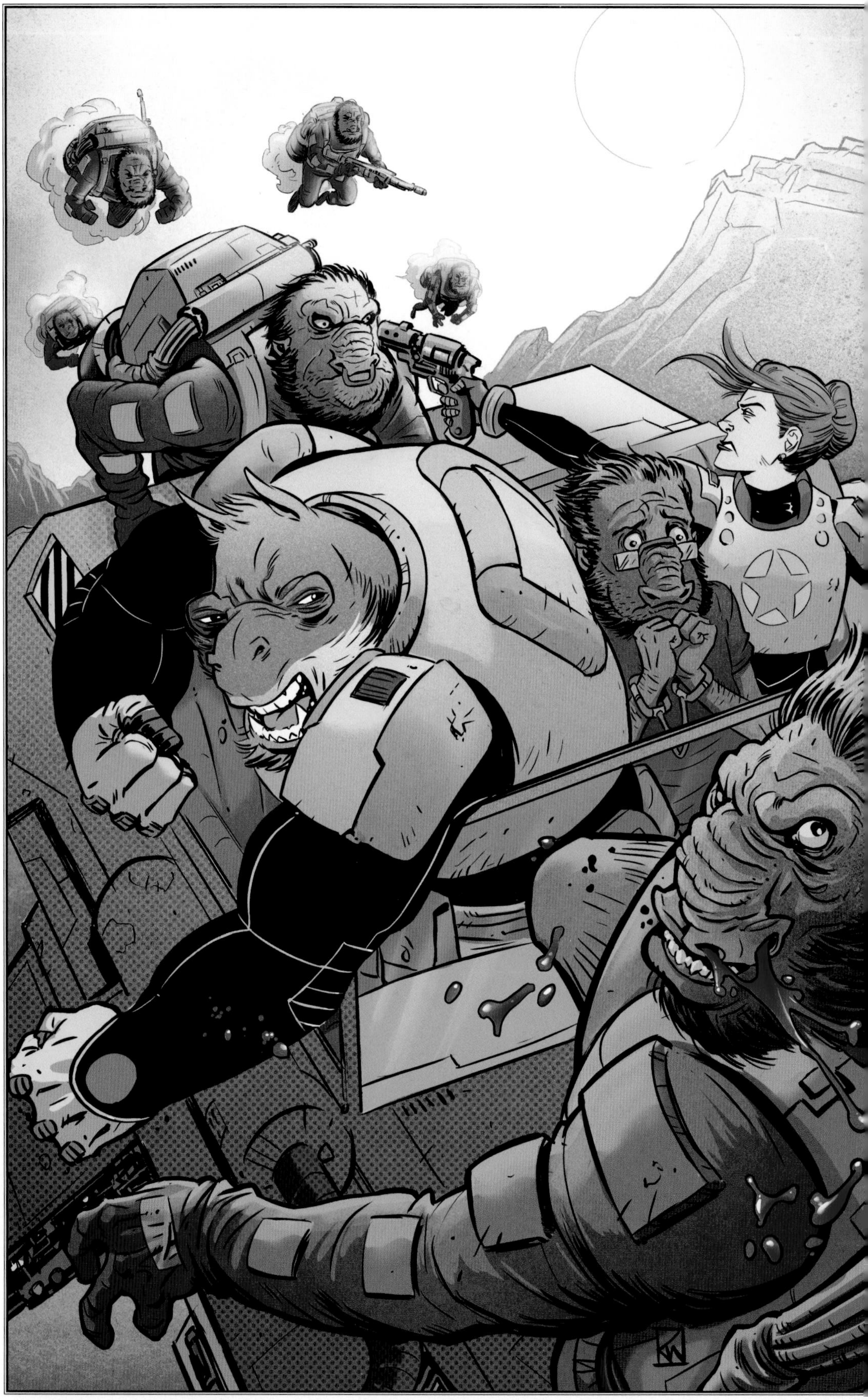

Pinup by K.R. Whalen

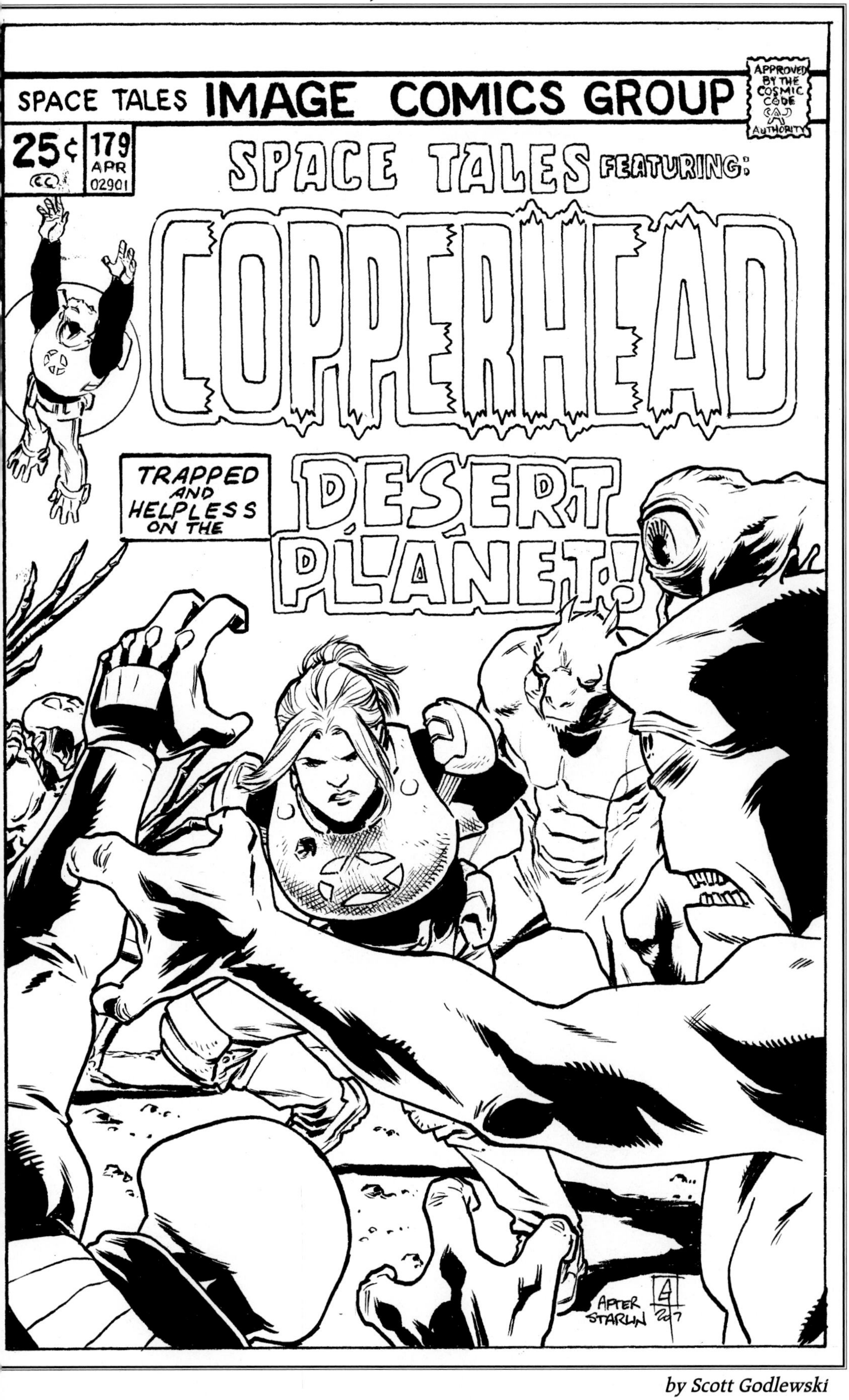
SPACE TALES
IMAGE COMICS GROUP
APPROVED BY THE COSMIC CODE AUTHORITY
25¢
179
APR
02901
SPACE TALES FEATURING:
COPPERHEAD
TRAPPED AND HELPLESS ON THE
DESERT PLANET!
AFTER STARLIN

by Scott Godlewski

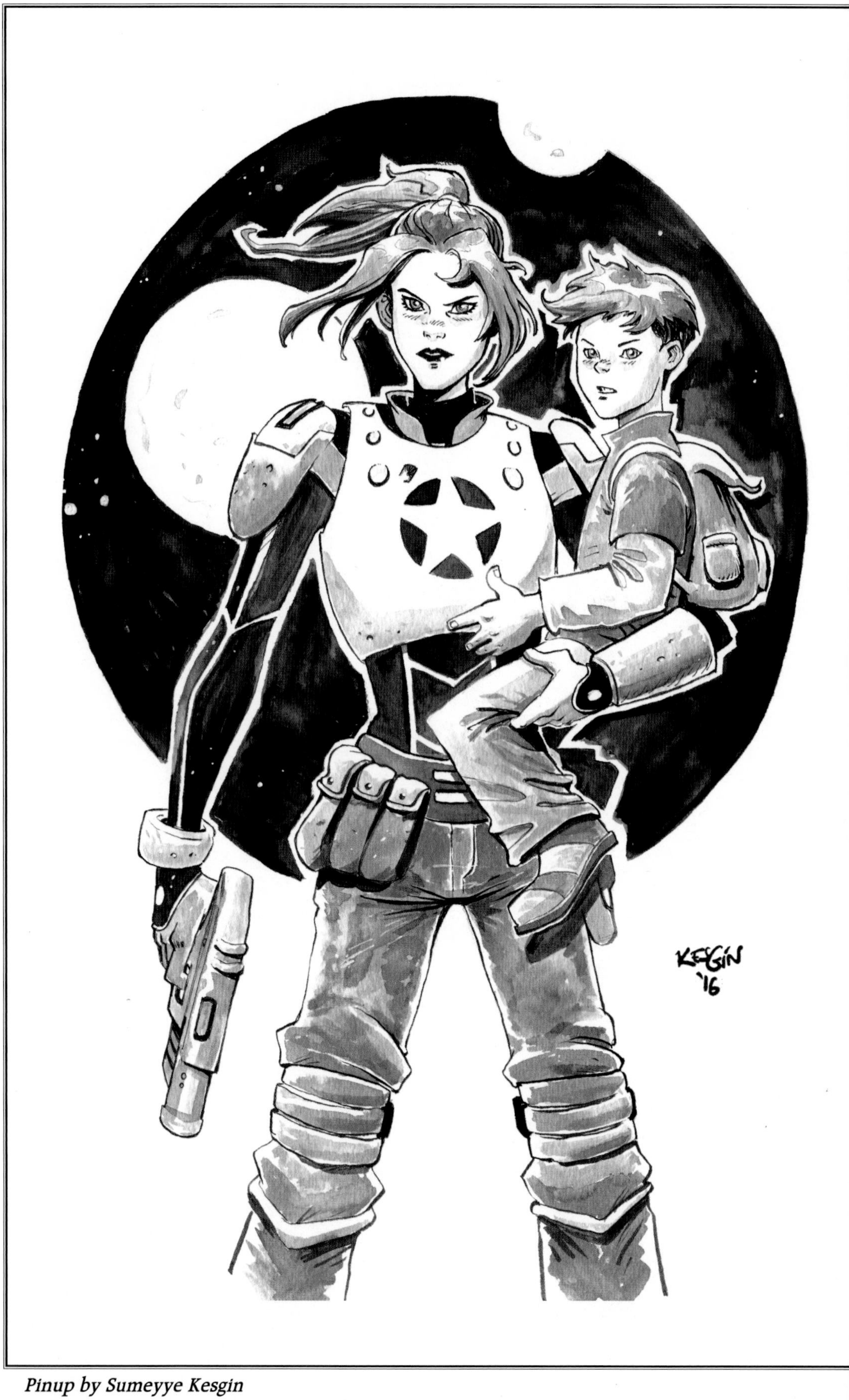
KESGIN
'16

Pinup by Sumeyye Kesgin

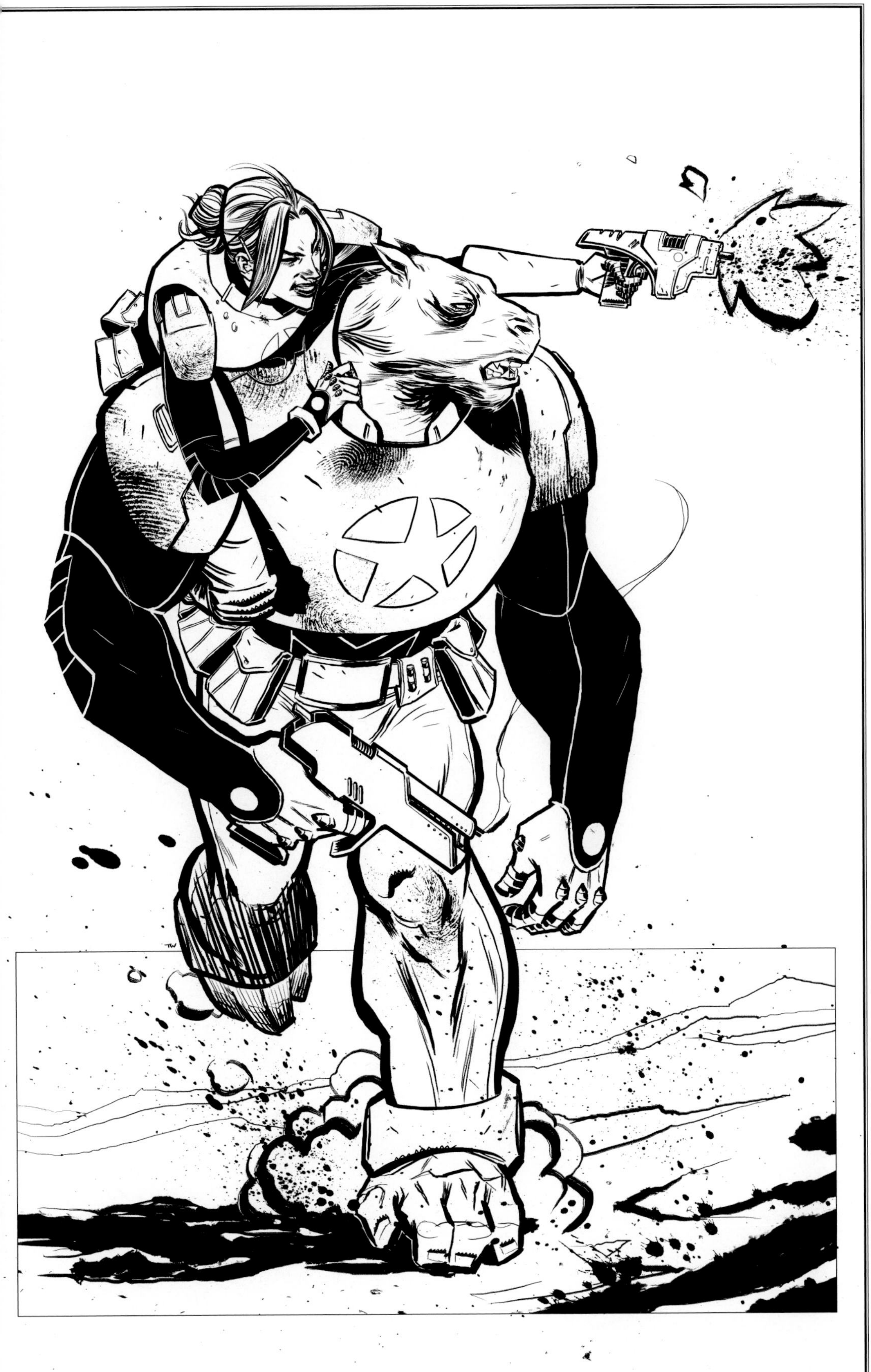

Pinup by Tigh Walker

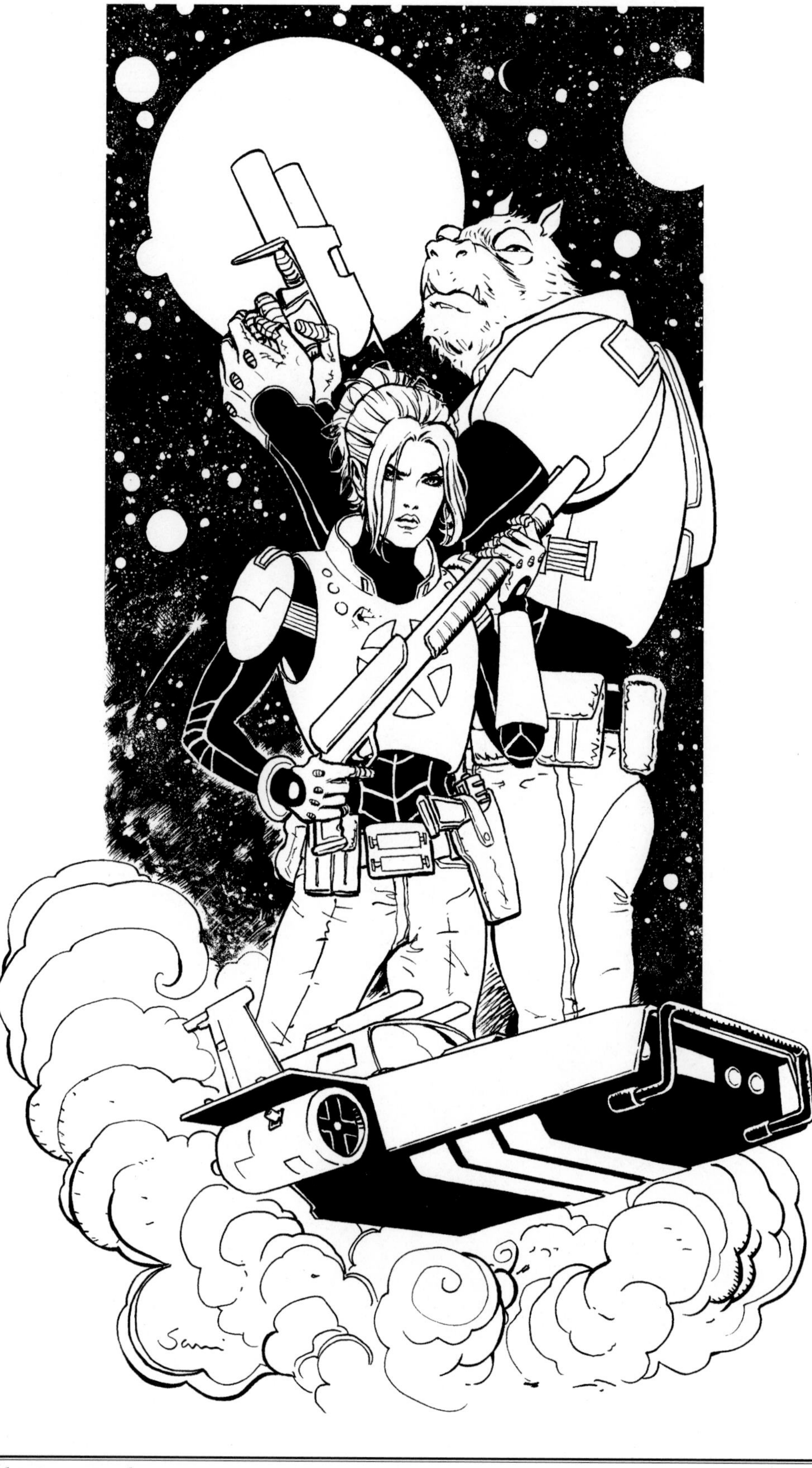

Pinup by Sami Kivela

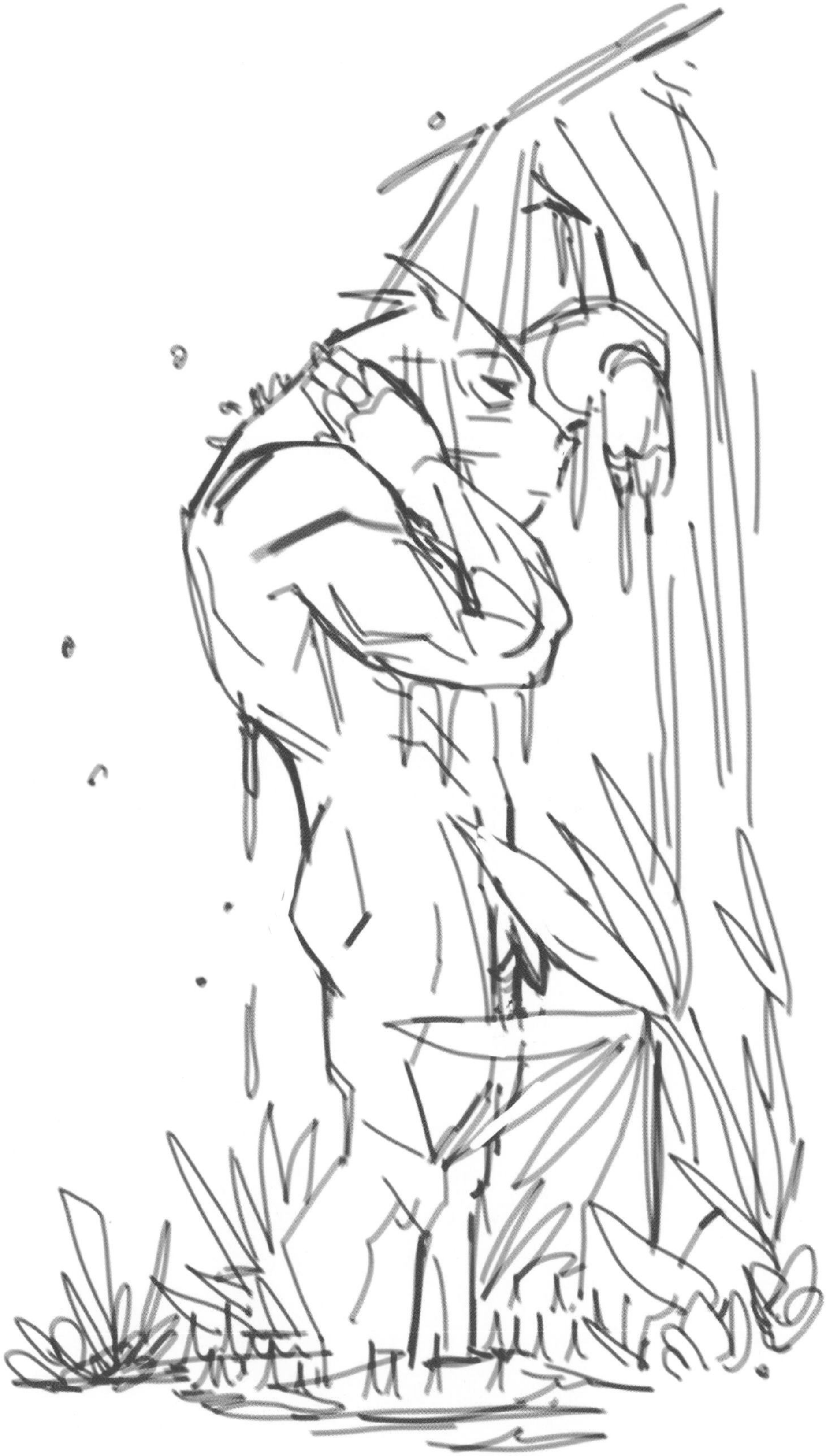

From Drew Moss' "Drawing in Cars" series

THE THREE STAGES OF PINUP CREATION

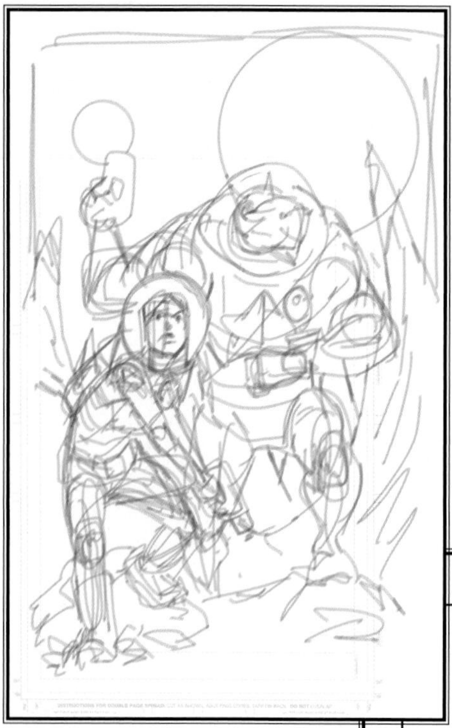

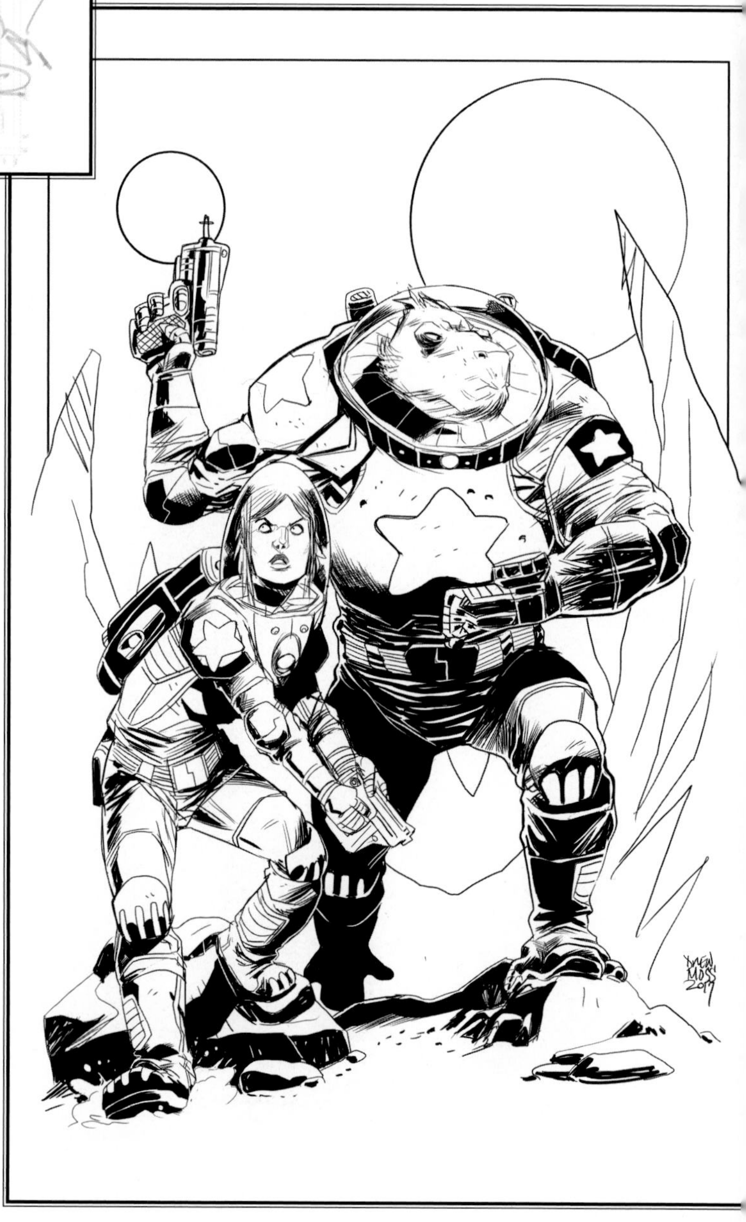

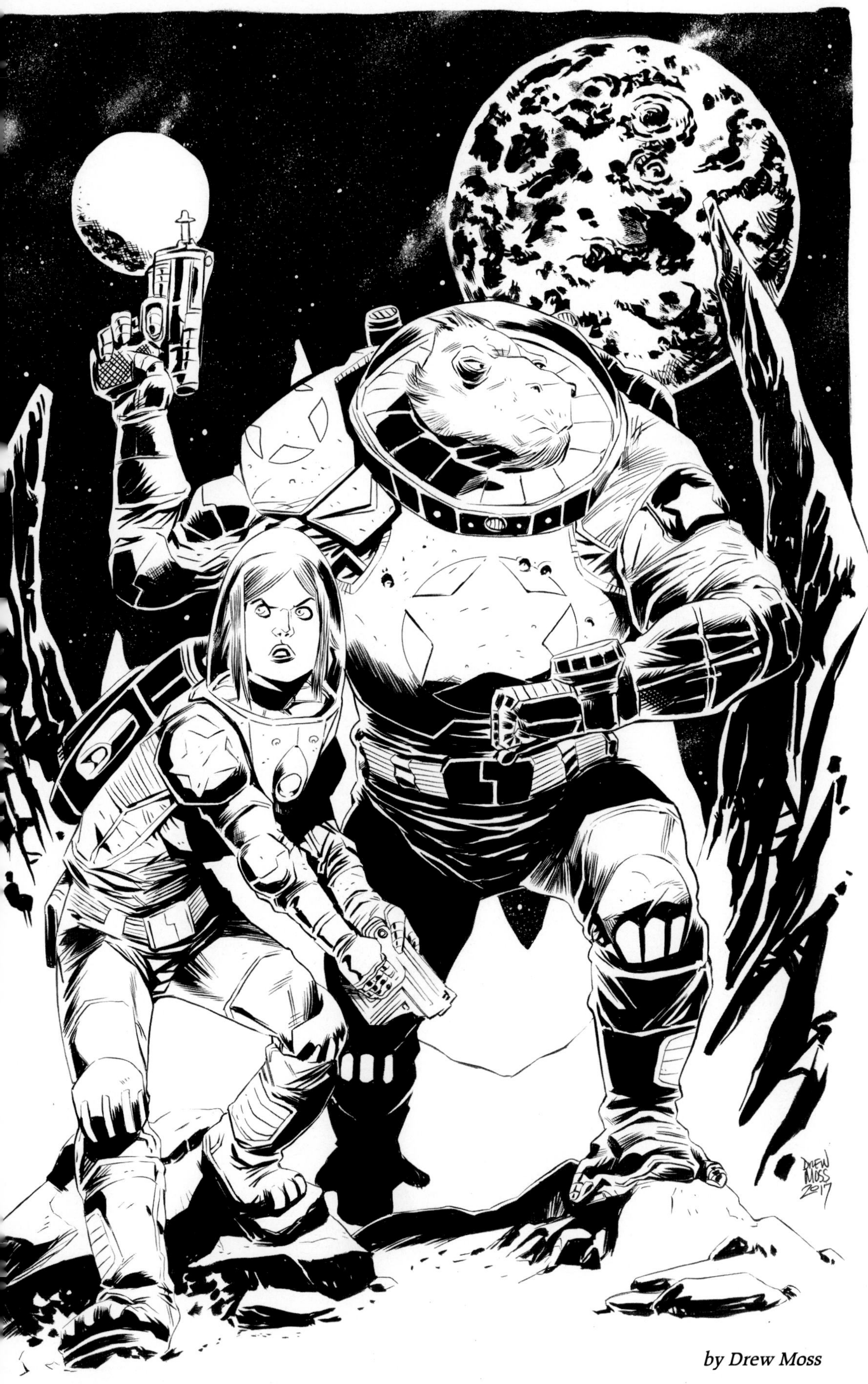

by Drew Moss

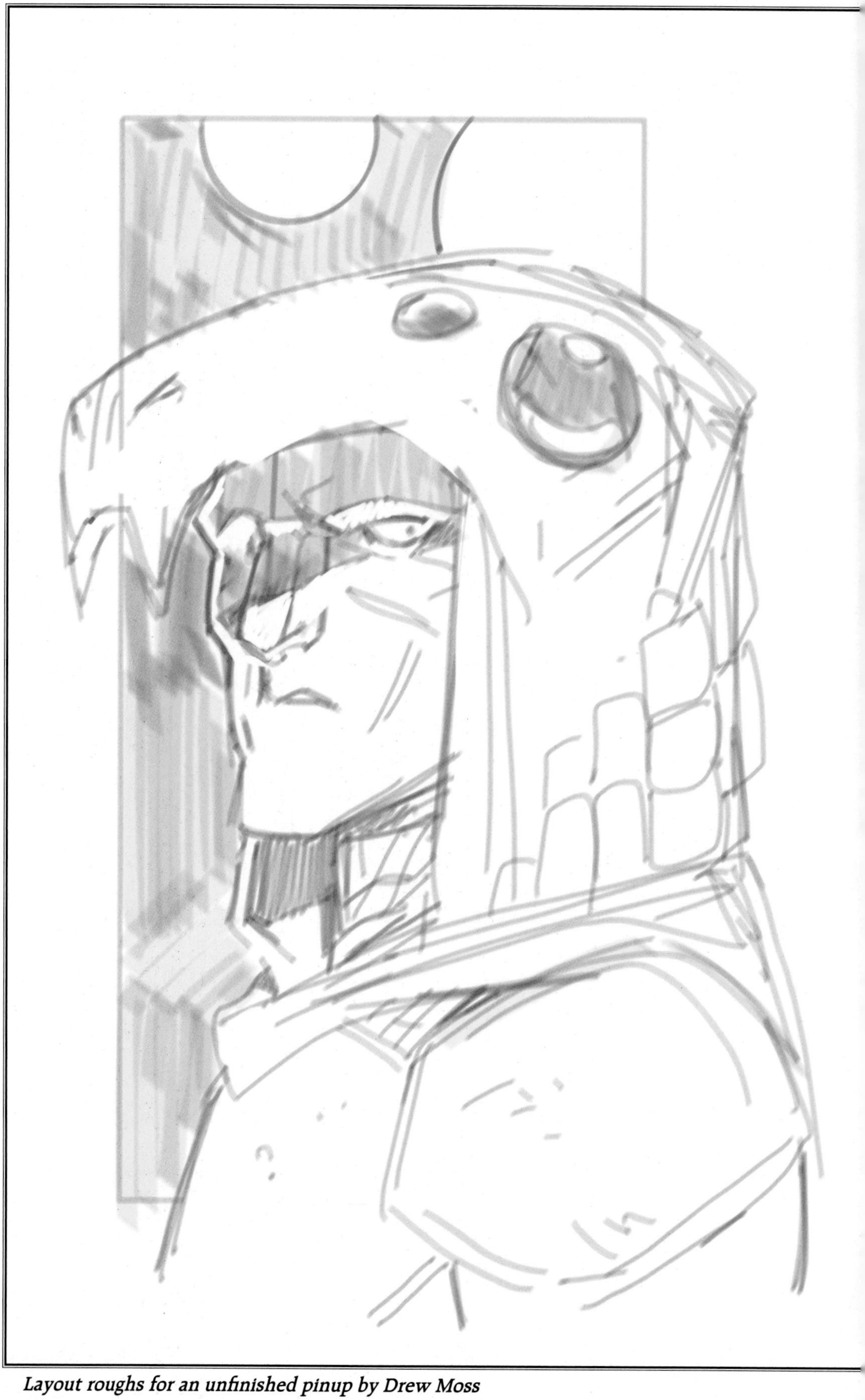

Layout roughs for an unfinished pinup by Drew Moss

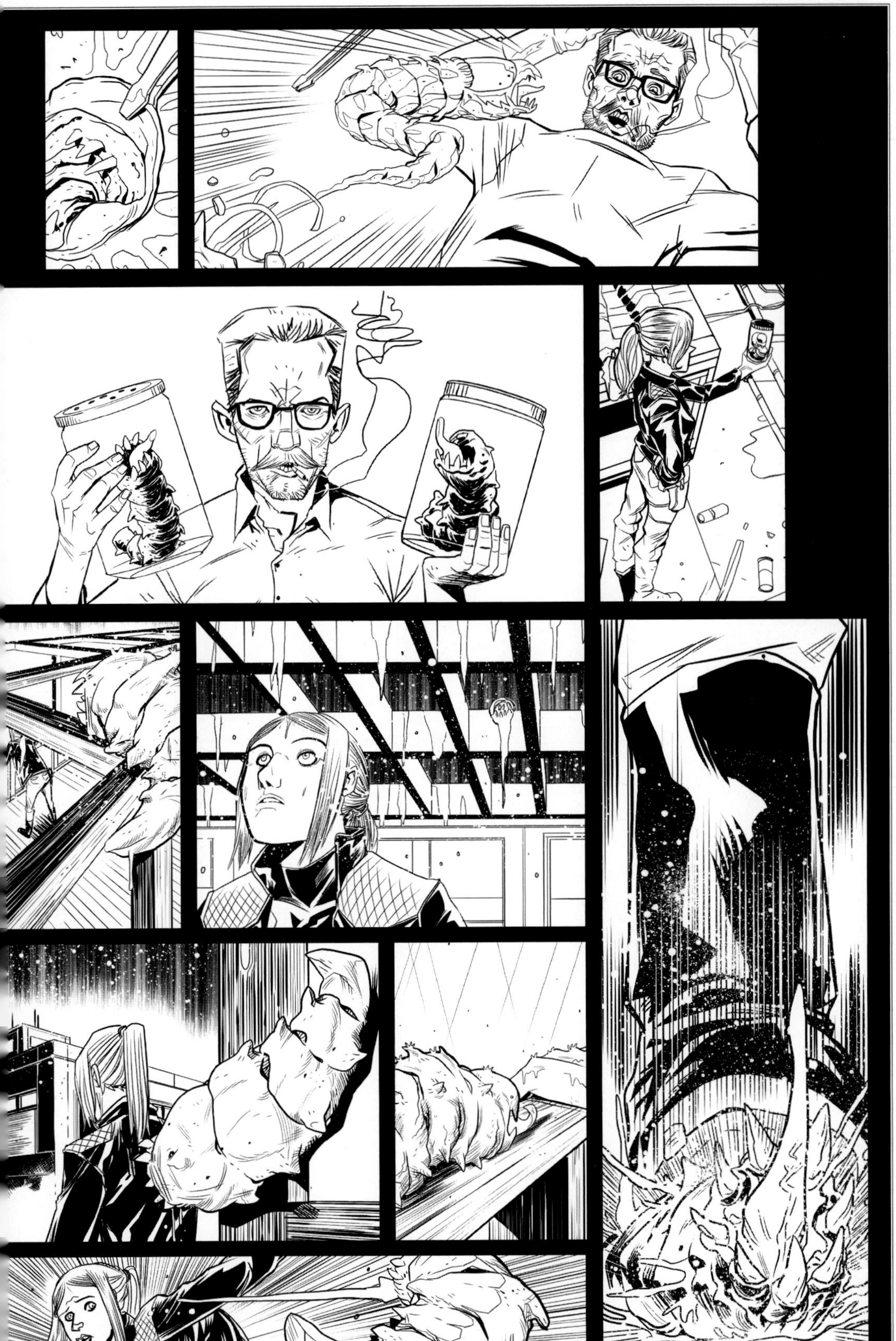

Inks from Chapters II & IV

VEHICLE STUDIES BY DREW MOSS

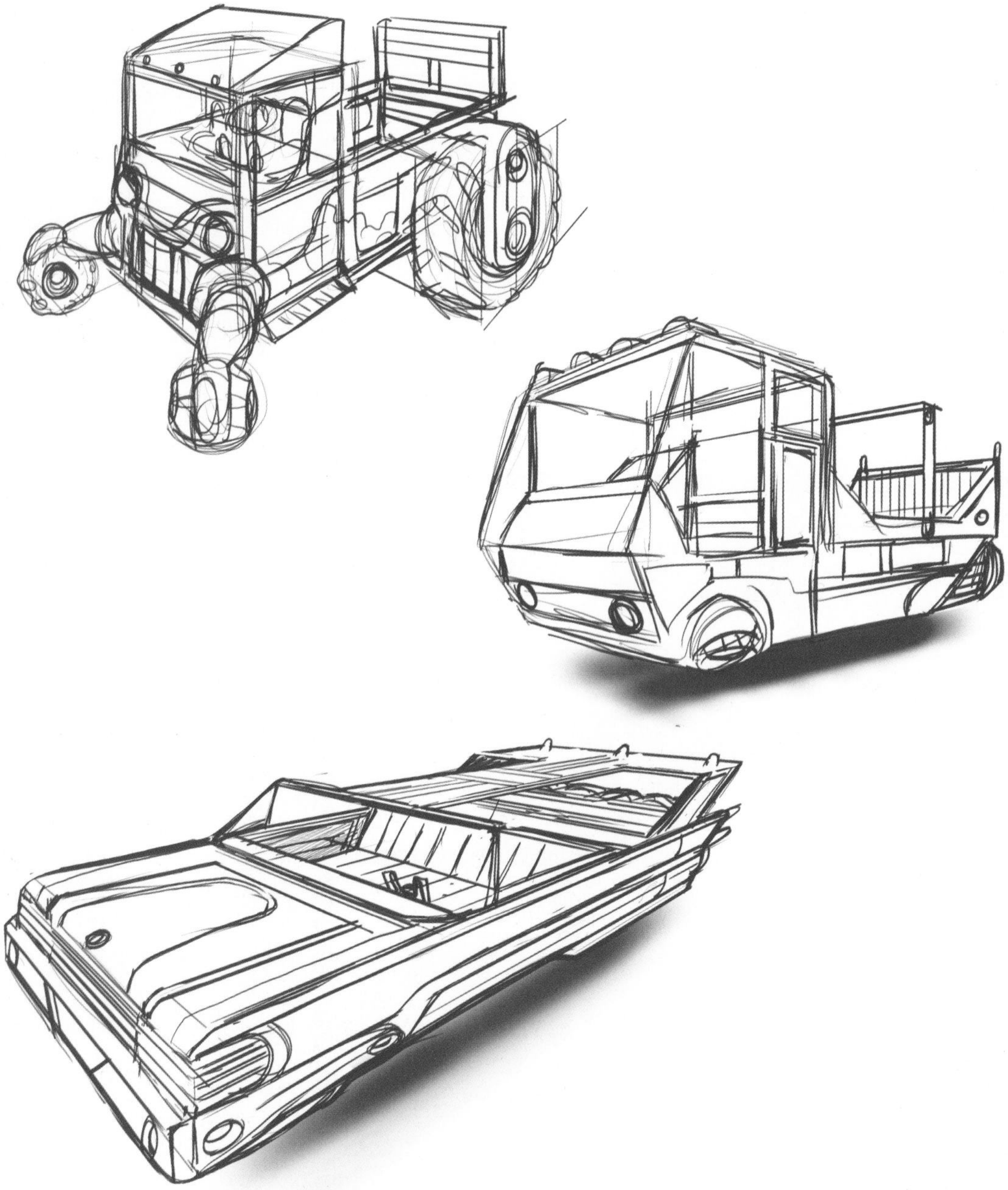

OPPOSITE: *Scott Godlewski's unused first 3 pages of Chapter*

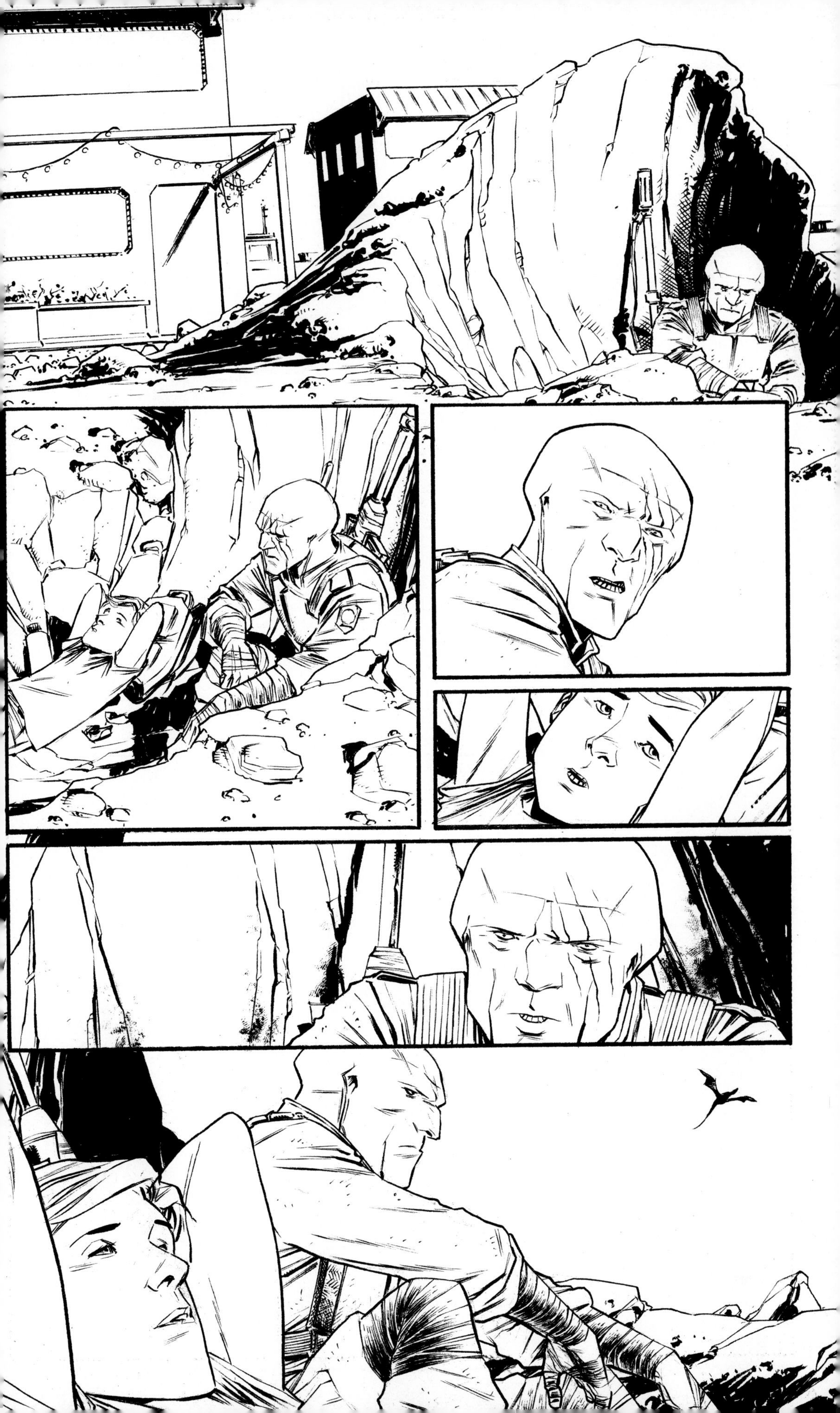

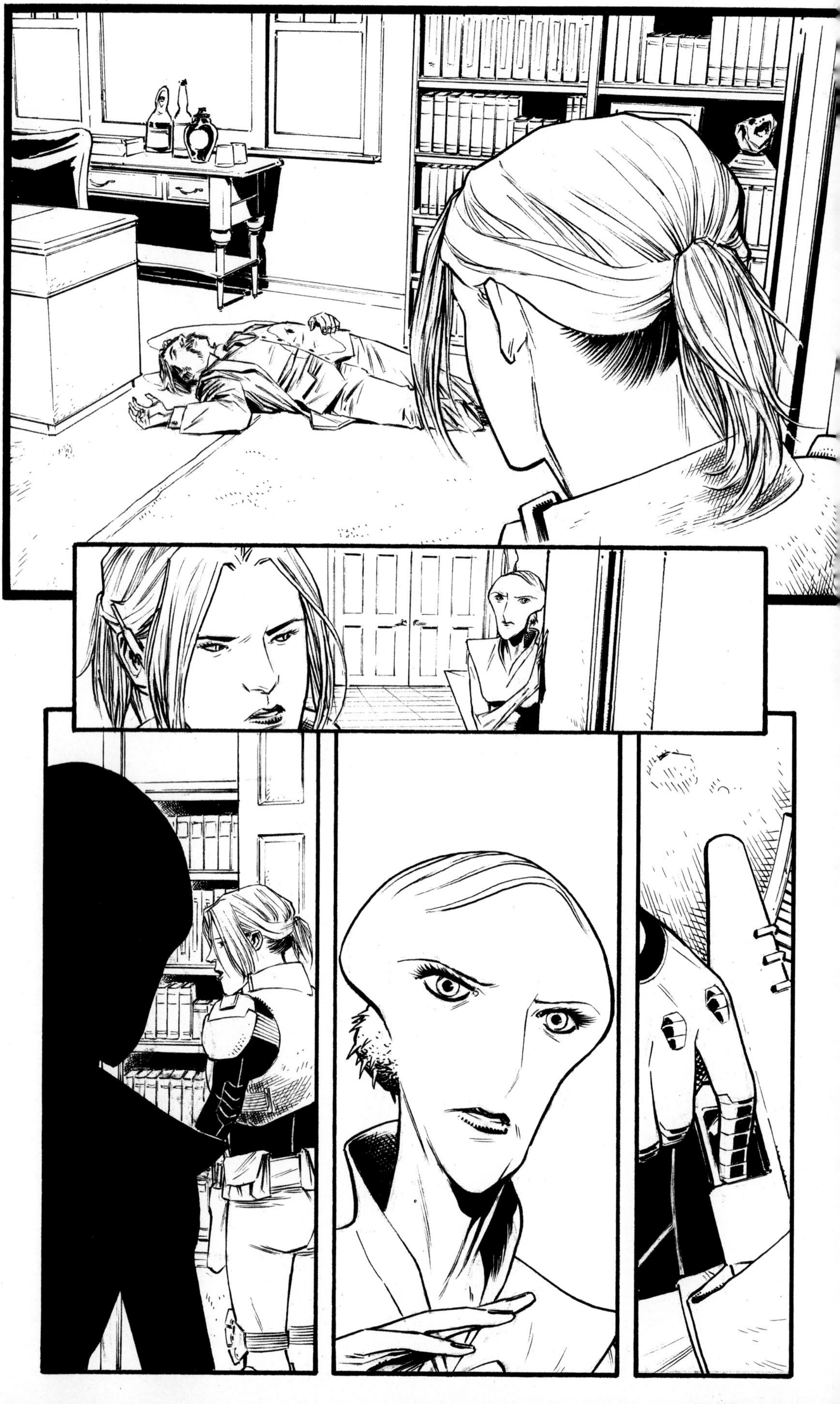

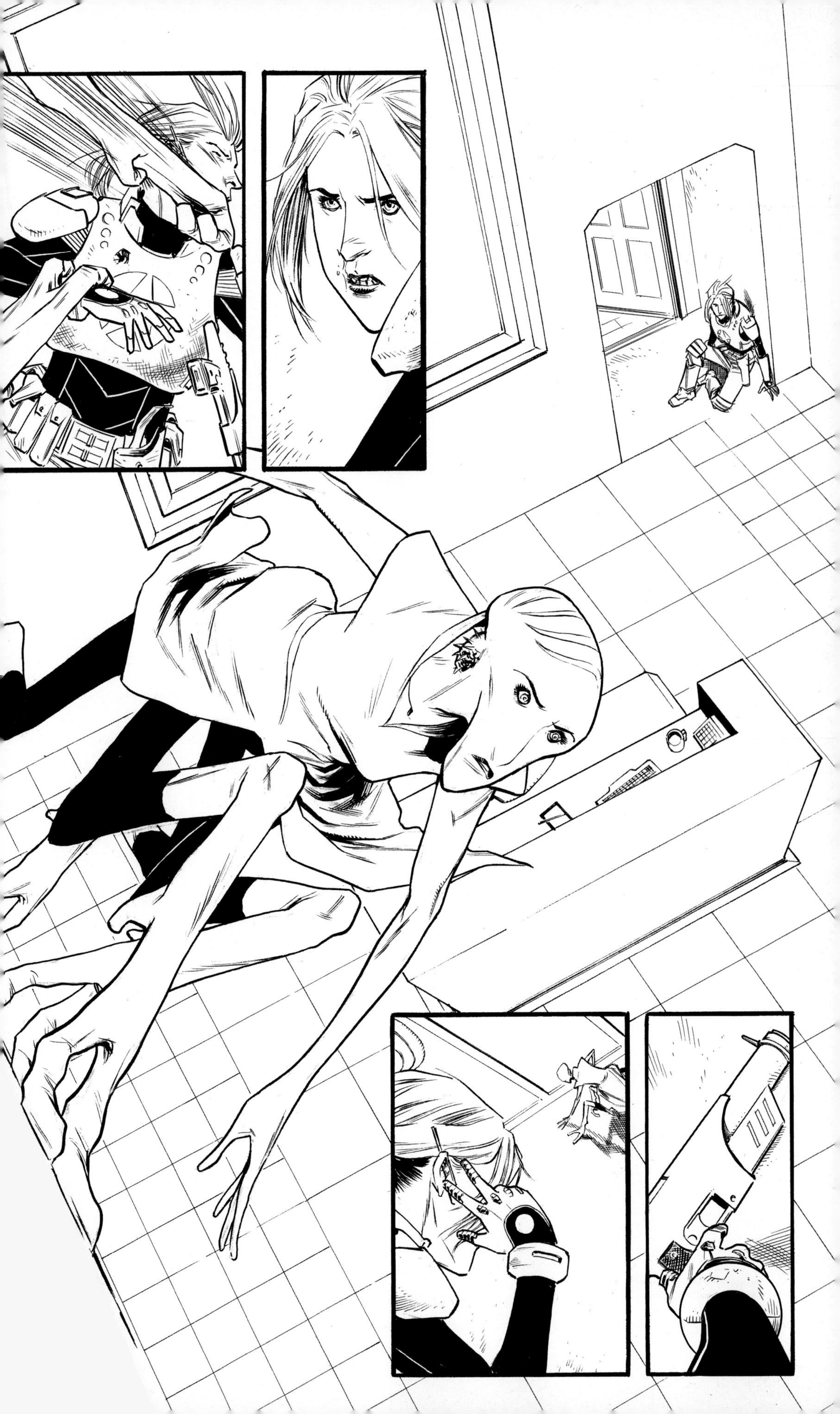

SCOTT'S VOLUME 3 COVER DEVELOPMENT PROCESS

COPPERHEAD
COPPERHEAD
COPPERHEAD
COPPERHEAD

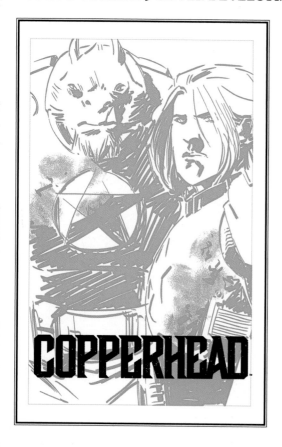

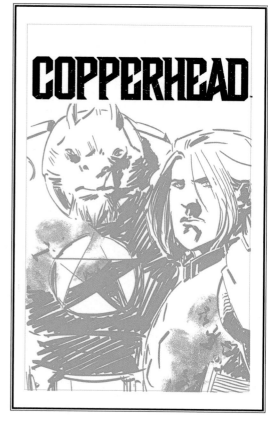

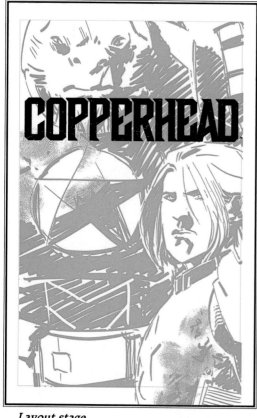

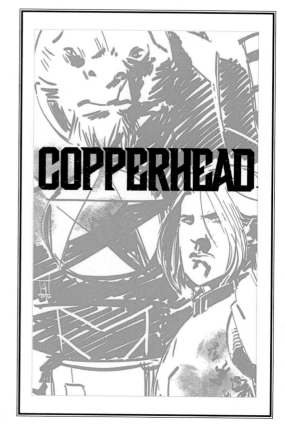

Layout stage

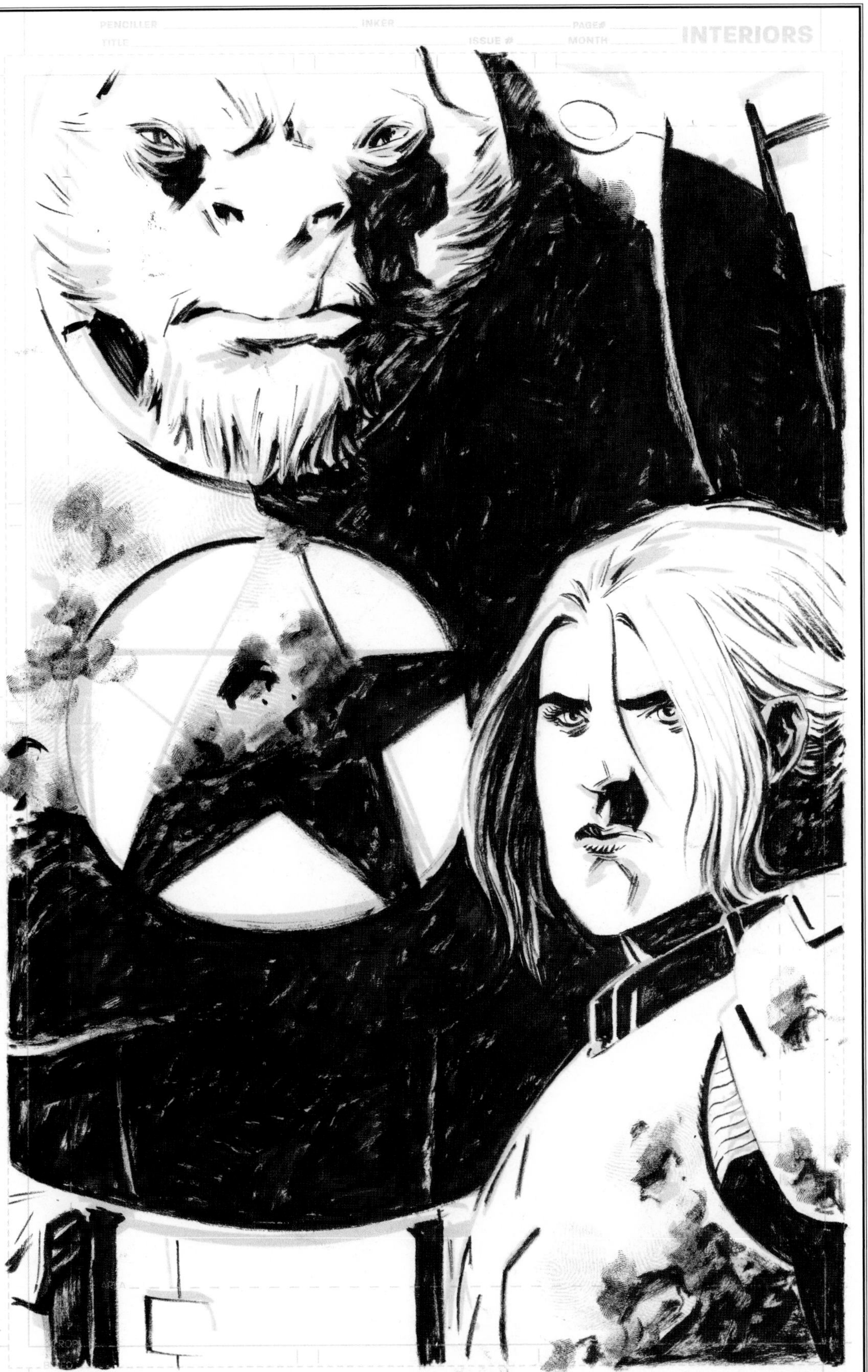
PENCILLER
INKER
PAGE#
INTERIORS
TITLE
ISSUE #
MONTH
MINIMUM BLEED 1/4" ALL AROUND

Rough inks

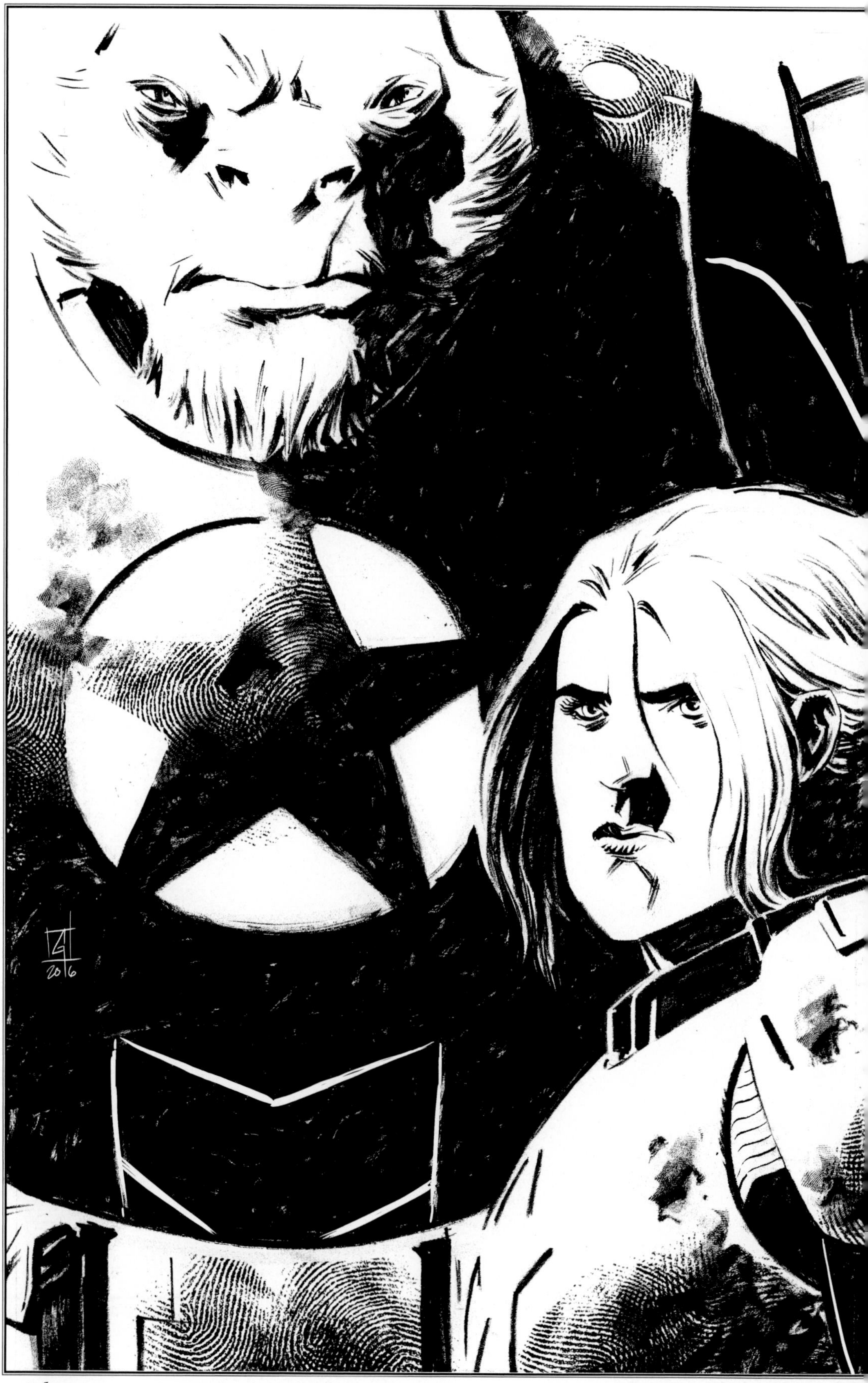

Inks

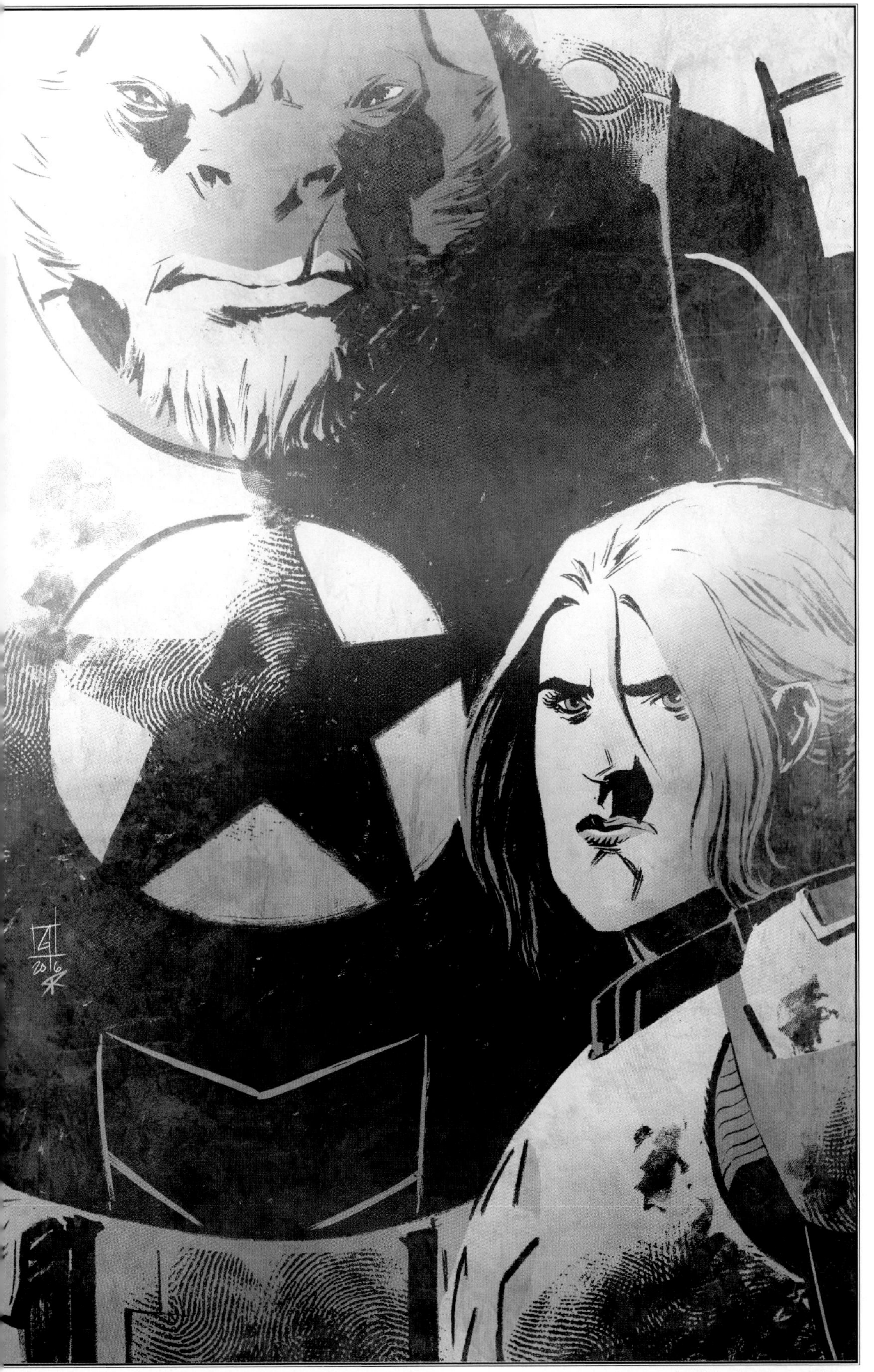

Colors by Ron Riley

ISSUE 11 COVER PENCILS

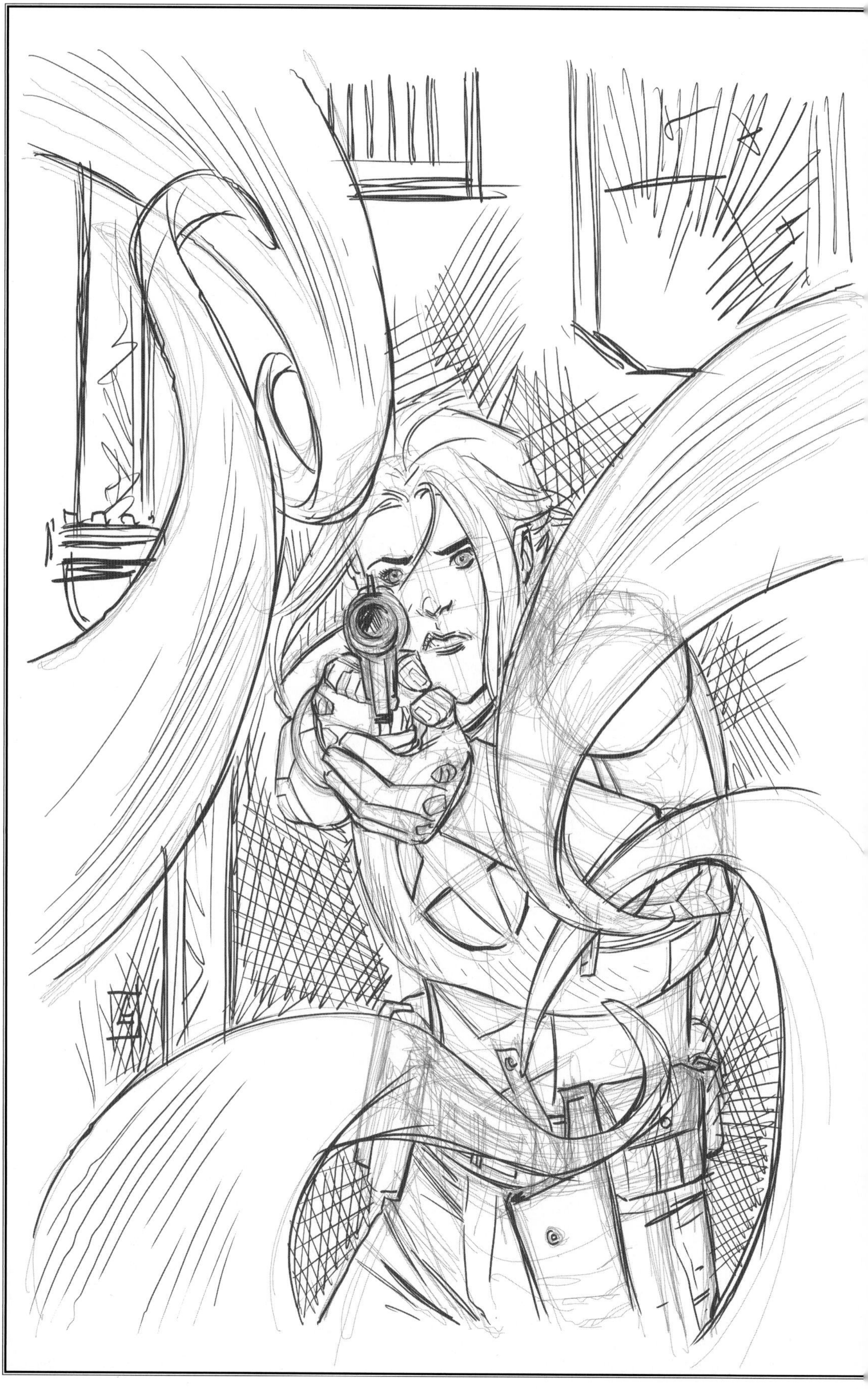

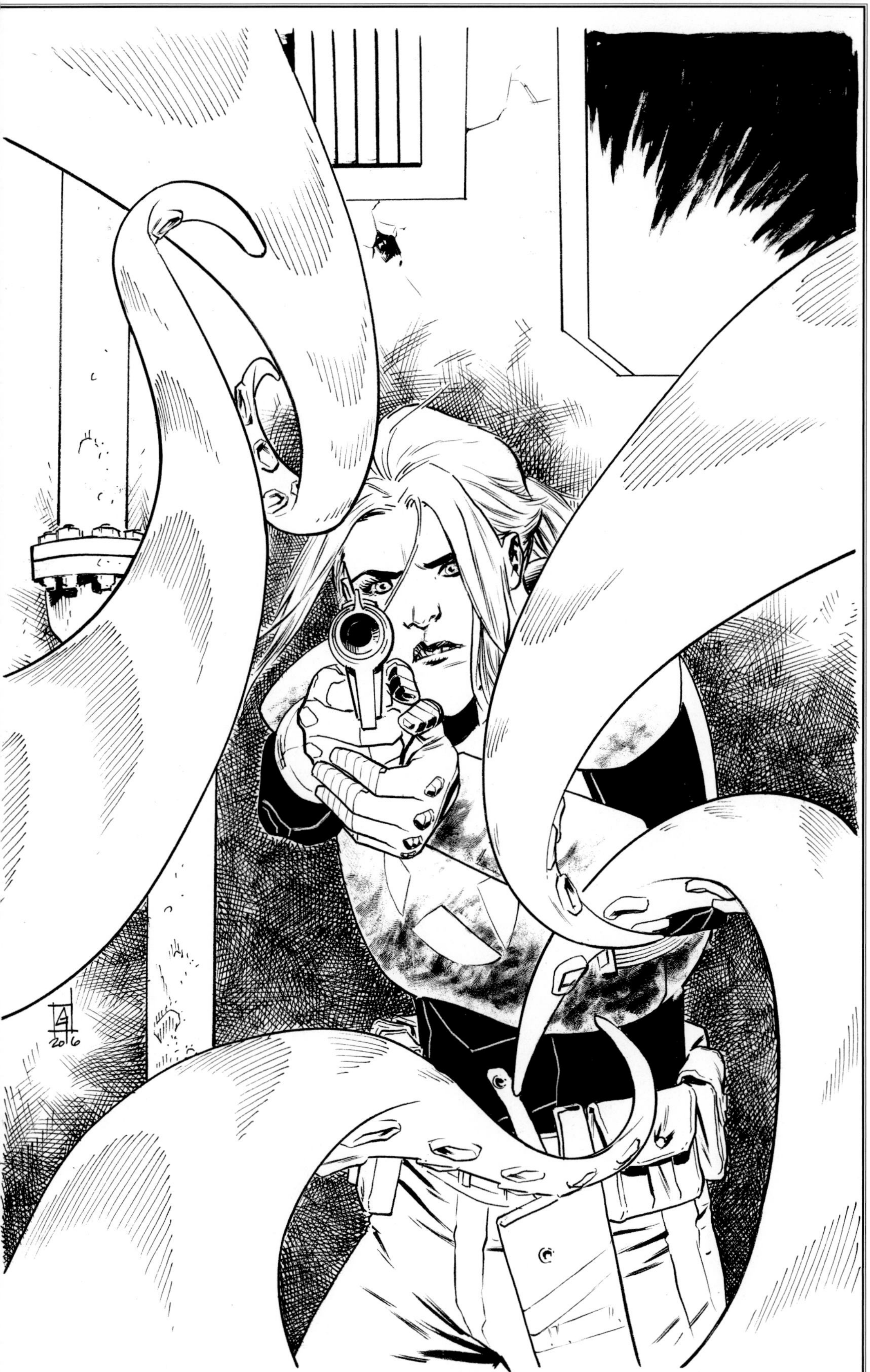

ISSUE 12 COVER PENCILS

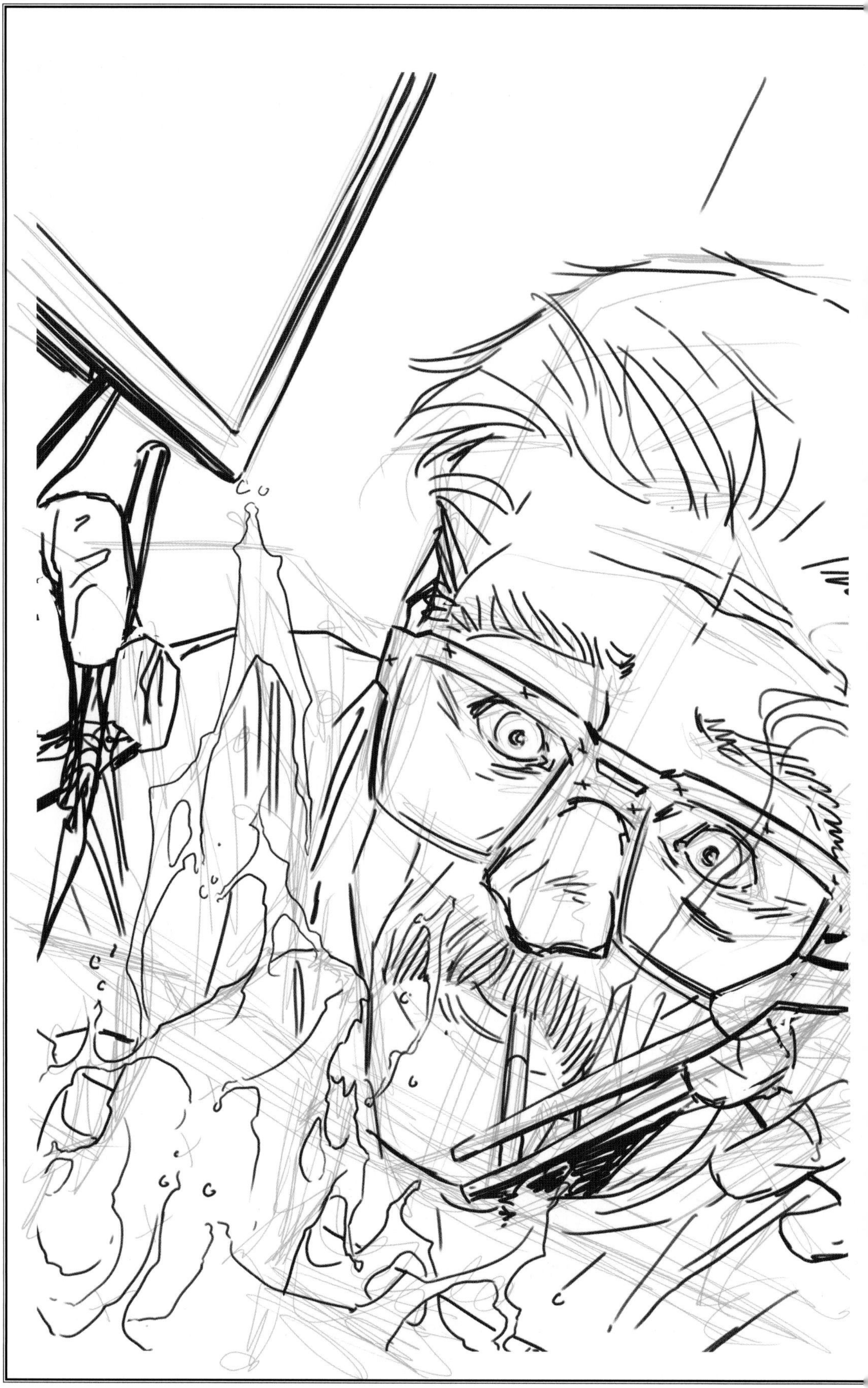

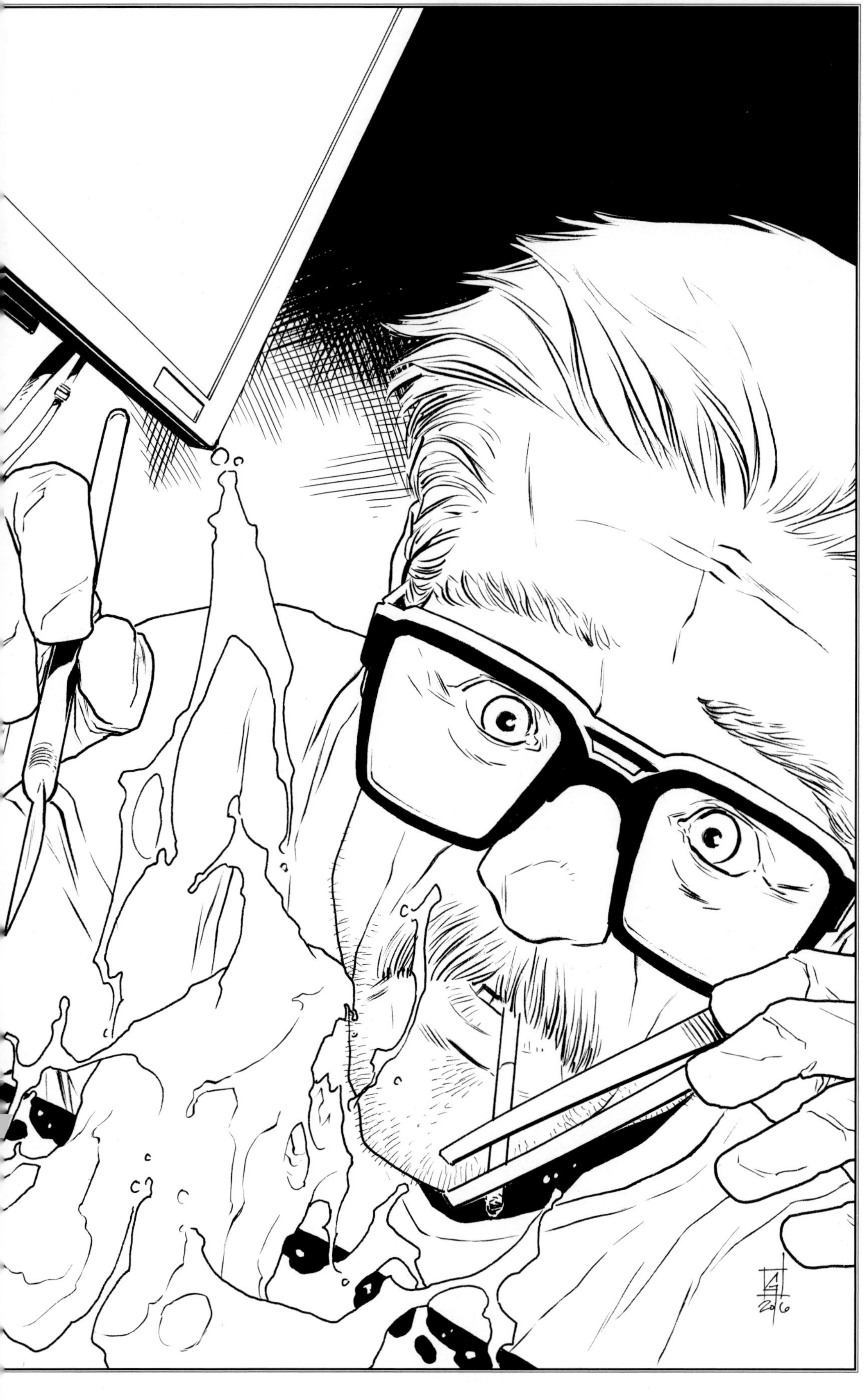

ISSUE 13 COVER LAYOUTS

A

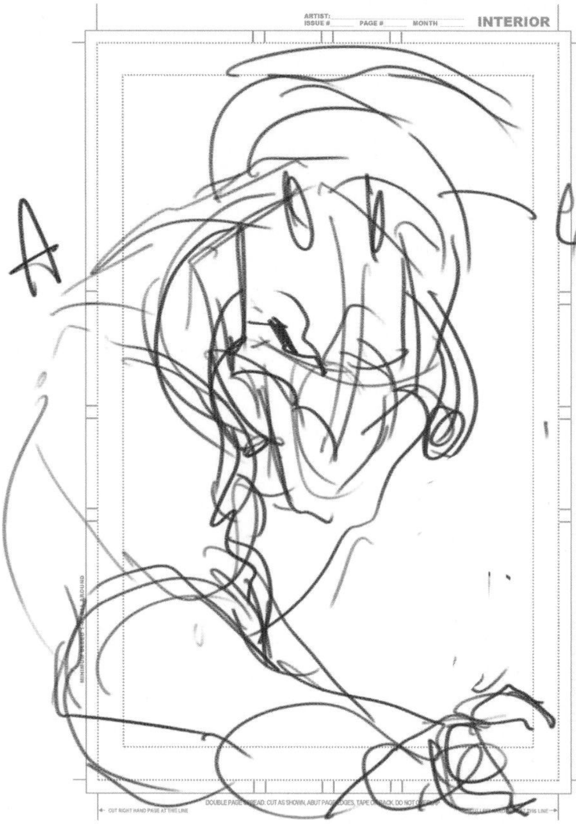
INTERIOR

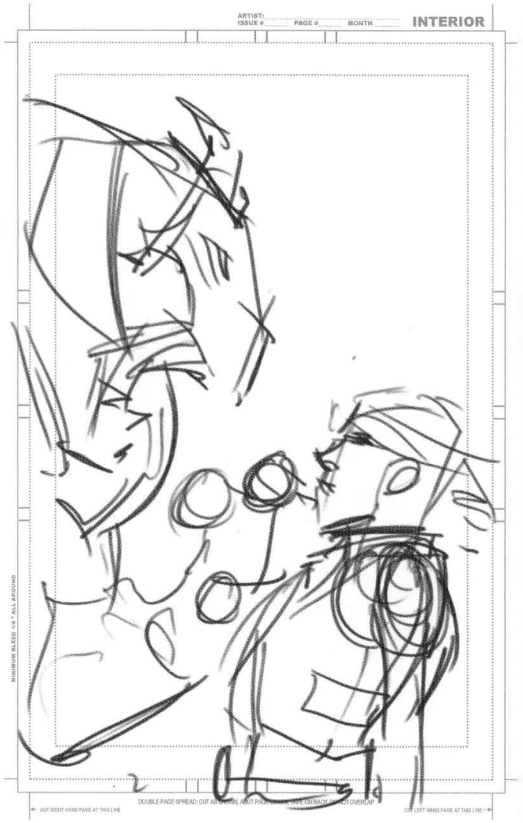
INTERIOR

C

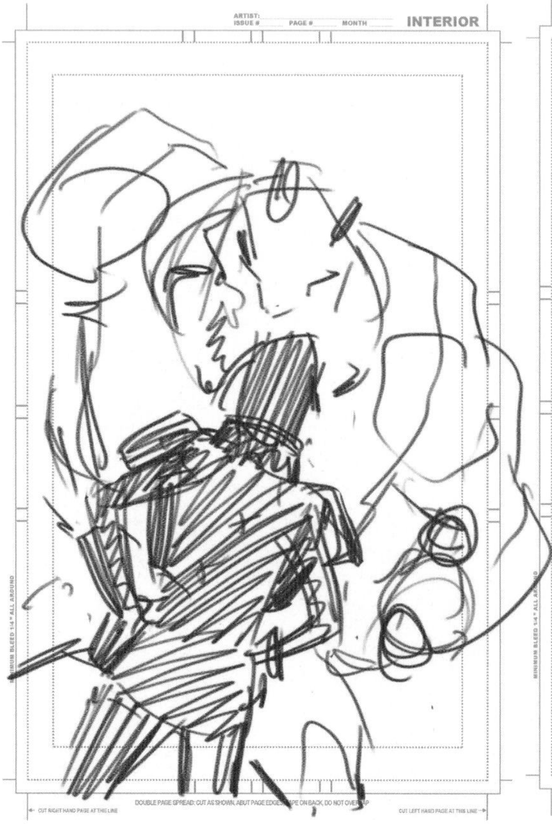
INTERIOR

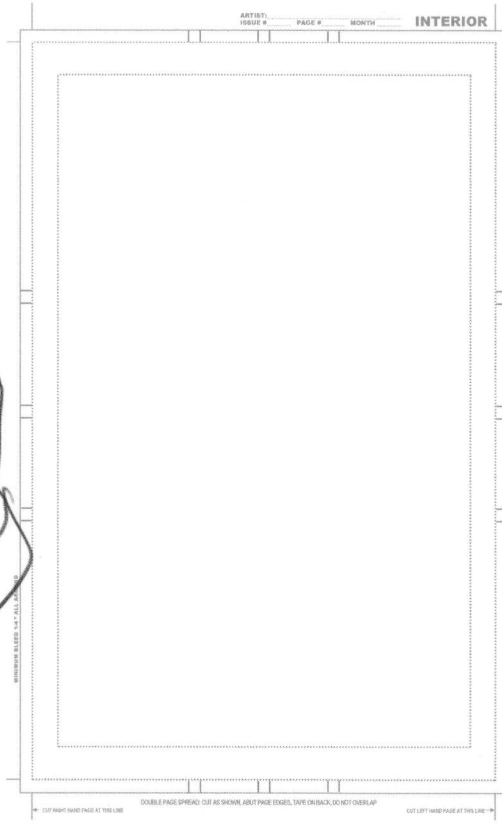
INTERIOR

ISSUE 13 COVER INKS

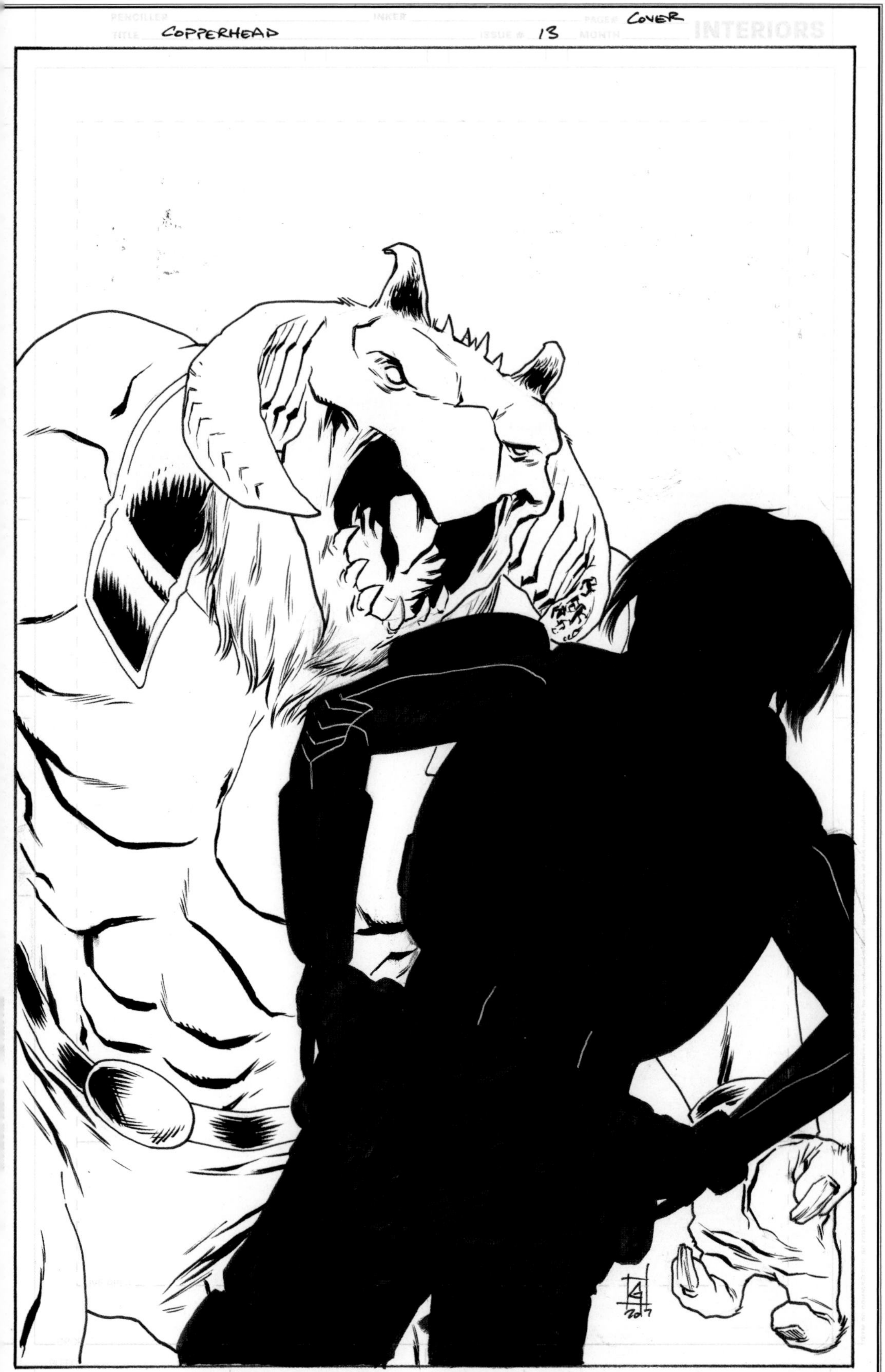
COPPERHEAD
13
COVER
INTERIORS
DOUBLE PAGE SPREAD: CUT AS SHOWN, ABUT PAGE EDGES, TAPE ON BACK, DO NOT OVERLAP

ISSUE 14 COVER LAYOUTS

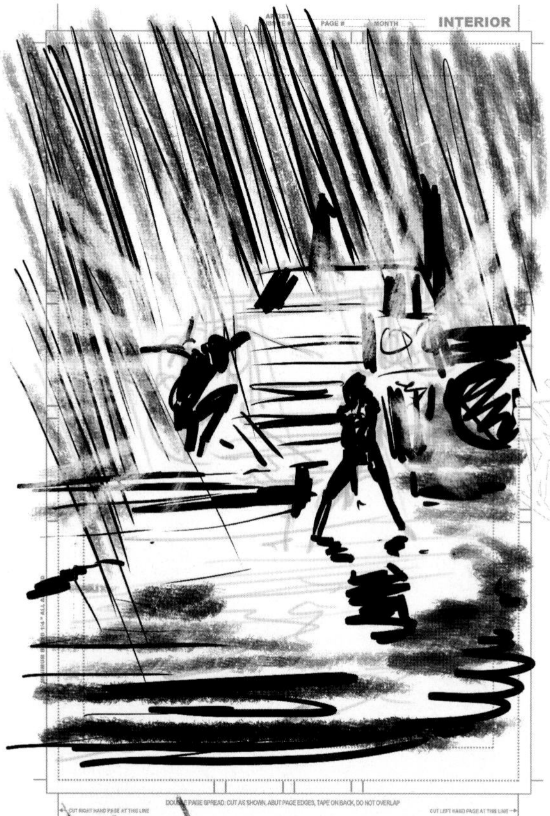
INTERIOR

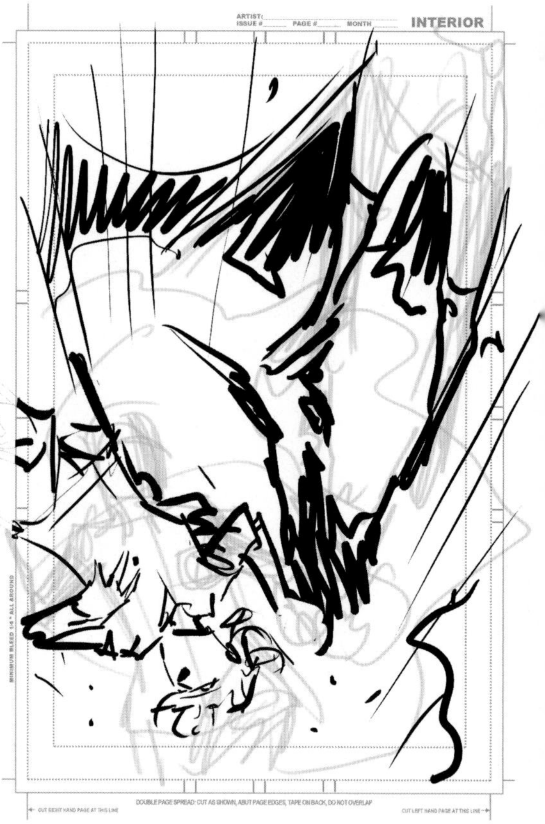
INTERIOR

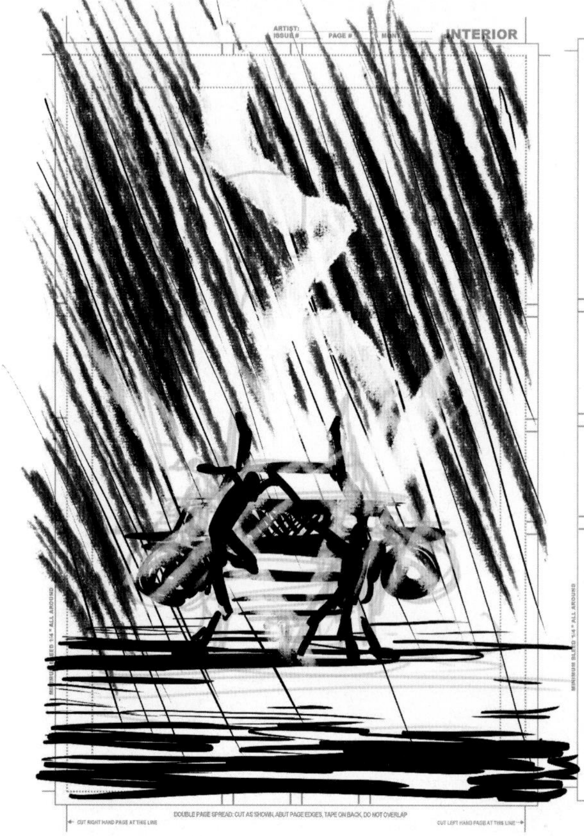
INTERIOR

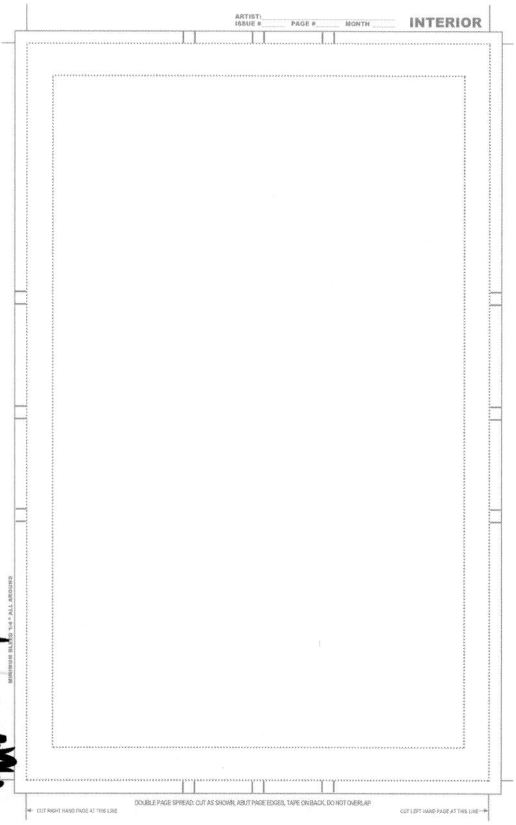
INTERIOR

ISSUE 14 COVER INKS

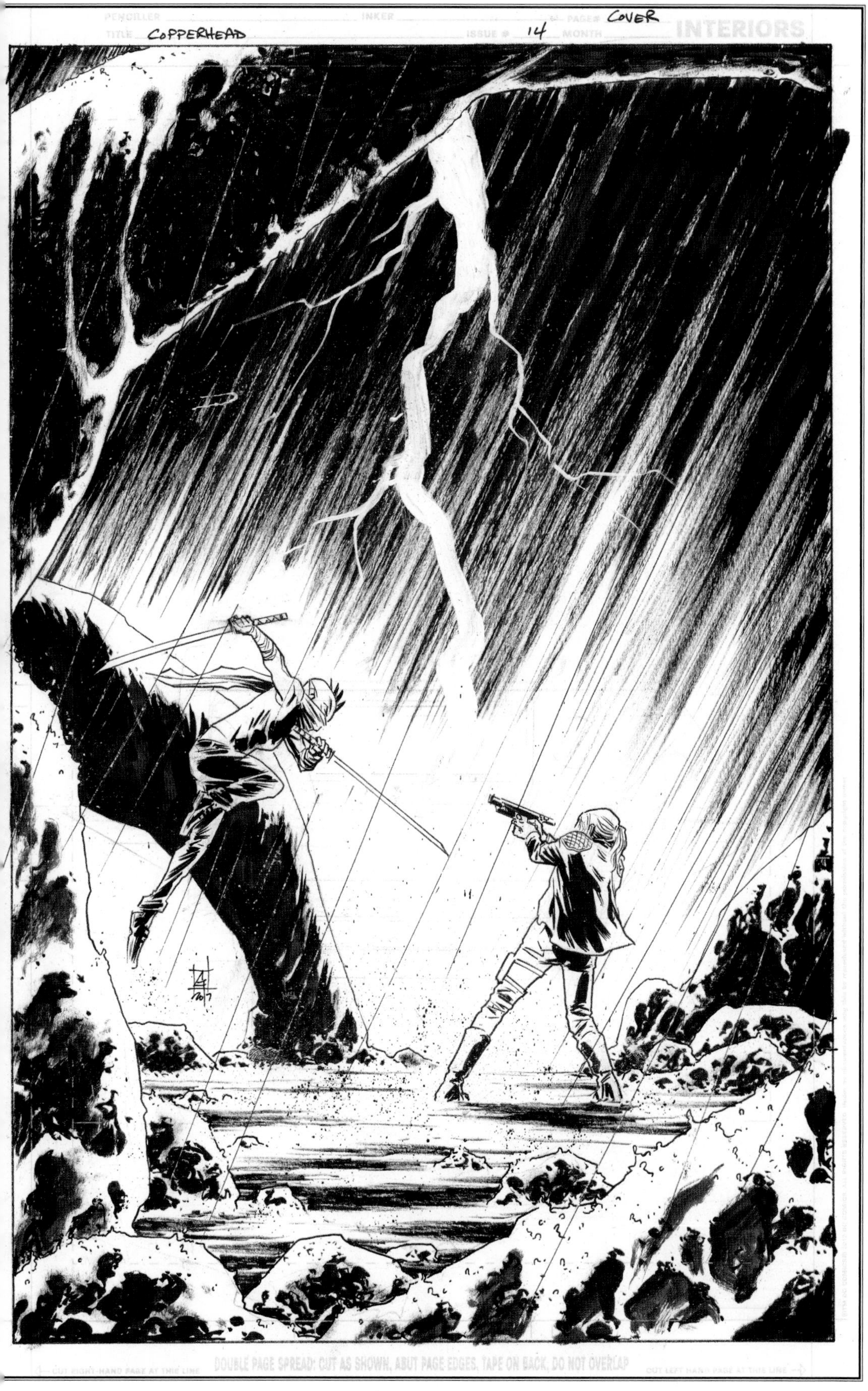
PENCILLER
INKER
PAGE# COVER
TITLE COPPERHEAD
ISSUE # 14
MONTH
INTERIORS
CUT RIGHT-HAND PAGE AT THIS LINE
DOUBLE PAGE SPREAD: CUT AS SHOWN, ABUT PAGE EDGES, TAPE ON BACK, DO NOT OVERLAP
CUT LEFT HAND PAGE AT THIS LINE

ABOUT THE CREATORS

Jay Faerber was born in Harvey's Lake, PA and got his start at Marvel and DC Comics in the late 1990s, where he worked on such series as THE TITANS, NEW WARRIORS, and GENERATION X. In 2001, he launched NOBLE CAUSES, his first creator-owned series, at Image Comics, which has gone on to garner much critical acclaim. Since then, Faerber has carved out a niche for himself, co-creating DYNAMO 5, NEAR DEATH, POINT OF IMPACT, SECRET IDENTITIES, GRAVEYARD SHIFT, ELSEWHERE, and COPPERHEAD. He also writes for television, most recently on the CBS series ZOO. He lives in Burbank, with his wife, son, dog, and cat. He really loves the Pacific Northwest and 80s television. You can follow him on Twitter @JayFaerber.

Drew Moss is an illustrator based out of southeastern Virginia and has worked for IDW (THE COLONIZED, THE CROW, MASK) Dark Horse (CREEPY), Oni press (TERRIBLE LIZARD, BLOOD FEUD) Image Comics (COPPERHEAD) and various other publishers. Drew enjoys fine cigars and whiskies and spends too much time writing bios. To see more of his work and upcoming projects you can follow him on Twitter @drew_moss or on Instagram @drewerdmoss.

Ron Riley started off colouring Robert Kirkman's TECH JACKET (which is still kicking butt at Image Comics with an all new creative team), then soon after joined the creative team of Mr. Faerber's then-relaunched NOBLE CAUSES. Ron has been Jay's frequent colouring collaborator ever since, most recently on ELSEWHERE. Ron's also been the colour artist on numerous other titles, like ROB ZOMBIE'S SPOOKSHOW INTERNATIONAL, BOOM! Studio's HERO SQUARED and TALENT, among others. Don't follow him on Twitter @thatronriley...unless you're one hip cat.

Thomas Mauer has lent his lettering and design talent to Harvey and Eisner Award nominated and winning titles including Image's POPGUN anthologies and Dark Horse Comics' THE GUNS OF SHADOW VALLEY. Among his recent work are Black Mask Studios' 4 KIDS WALK INTO A BANK, Image Comics' ELSEWHERE, THE BEAUTY, and THE REALM, as well as Amazon Studios' NIKO AND THE SWORD OF LIGHT, and the World Food Programme's LIVING LEVEL-3 series. You can follow him on Twitter @thomasmauer.

Scott Godlewski is the co-creator of COPPERHEAD and a freelance illustrator. His past credits include works with Image, BOOM! Studios, Dynamite, Dark Horse, and DC. He is also the co-host of *The Illustrious Gentlemen* podcast. You can find Scott on Twitter @scottygod.